APOKERI BAY

HOW FAR WOULD YOU GO FOR LOVE?

Jackie Watson

First published in Great Britain in 2023 by Hawthorn Wren
This paperback edition published by Hawthorn Wren

Copyright © Jackie Watson 2023

The right of Jackie Watson to be identified as the author of this work has been asserted in accordance with the Copyright, Designs and Patents Act 1988.

All right reserved. No part of this publication may be reproduced, stored in or transmitted into any retrieval system, in any form, or by any means (electronic, mechanical, photocopying, recording or otherwise) without the prior written permission of the publisher. Any person who does any unauthorised act in relation to this publication may be liable to criminal prosecution and civil claims for damages.

A CIP catalogue record for this book is available from the British Library

ISBN: 978 1 7393404 0 7

This is a work of fiction. Names, characters, businesses, places, events and incidents are either the products of the author's imagination or used in a fictitious manner. Any resemblance to actual persons, living or dead, or actual events is purely coincidental.

For my friend, Kristel

Chapter One

Anna Jenkinson sipped her dwindling water. She'd make it last the blisteringly hot mid-July afternoon. A day to be in the shade of a taverna, enjoying a cool glass of something. The easy option and not her style.

Instead, she was scrambling down a mountain with two mates on a dusty, boulder-strewn, and often indistinct eight-mile dirt track. To win a bet.

She absorbed the views, striding along with a well-worn forty-five-litre rucksack on her back and a twenty-five-litre daypack on her front. Olive, pine, and cypress trees carpeted a landscape that dramatically dropped into the Ionian Sea. Densely forested Lefkada was stunning, but the terrain that had appeared easy from a distance was much harder in reality. So often the way.

The twins stopped to bicker – again. And as ever, Anna sought the shade. This time under an ancient gnarled wild olive. She closed her eyes and smelled the tree, listening to buzzing insects and enjoying the refreshing breeze. It didn't work. She couldn't block them out.

'Are you sure it's the right way?' Charlotte shouted to the retreating figure of her brother. 'We can't afford to get lost today because of your abysmal map-reading skills.'

'Think of it as an adventure,' Anna ventured and tightened her hip belt.

'I'm sick of adventures,' snapped Charlotte. 'I'm thirsty, hungry, tired, and want a comfy bed. Whose stupid idea was it to backpack across Greece anyway?'

Simon stalked back through the scrub and stopped nose-to-nose with his twin.

'You knew what this track was like, so put a sock in it,' he hissed. 'You're only tetchy from knocking back a full bottle of ouzo last night.'

And they were at it again.

Anna sighed inwardly. They'd all shared a poky student flat for two years, which made her partly immune to their constant squabbling. Why had she thought they'd argue less Greek island-hopping than back in Newcastle?

Only a few more hours and then – alone for five blissful days. To explore and, more importantly, figure out what the hell she was going to do about sorting her life out.

A movement in the undergrowth. A pretty little blue-throated lizard scuttled out to bask on a rock. Seemingly asleep, it lunged and devoured an unsuspecting fly. Life snuffed out in an instant.

'Hey, daydreamer,' Charlotte yelled over her shoulder. 'Time to go.'

Tightening the cord of her hat, Anna tripped over a tree root and face-planted a myrtle bush.

For crying out loud, man.

They'd never win if she kept this up.

***

It had started innocently enough in Karya's picturesque village-square taverna the night before. As the wine, beer, and ouzo had flowed, all ten agreed to hike a ten-mile loop to celebrate their last day together. They would explore charming Egklouvi (reputedly the most beautiful mountain village on Lefkada) and Vafkeri, an unspoilt and semi-deserted time capsule harking back to a way of life centuries old. Everyone would then troop down to Apokeri. That was until the taverna owner understood their plan and had been horrified. The track to Apokeri was awful, poorly signposted, and baking hot. They had no chance of catching their boat, undertaking such a hair-brained scheme. He declared it impossible, and – of course – Anna, Simon, and Charlotte took the bait. Hook, line, and sinker. To win, all three must reach Apokeri fishing village in under two and a half hours, carrying all their belongings.

***

Anna felt they were making good time, but it was hard to tell. With a path that repeatedly vanished, the trio had been lost half-a-dozen times or forced to backtrack after mistakenly tramping down a goat track to nowhere. It was going to be a close-run thing. Simon kept up a breakneck pace. His stocky five-foot-eight frame scythed through the scrub and, after battling through a particularly overgrown section, he came to a sudden halt. Charlotte and Anna failed to stop on the steep slope and slid into him.

'Wow, look at that,' he exclaimed.

Fifty feet away, the ground vanished, and a spectacular view opened up. A handful of tiny fishing boats and yachts sat serenely on the shimmering water that merged with a cloudless cobalt sky. Creeping to the precipice and peering over, they were hit by a powerful stench of guano from a vertical city of nests balancing precariously on tiny ledges carved into the chalky white cliffs. The air was full of seabird cries as they circled, dived, and returned to their young with eagerly anticipated fish. Yet rising above everything was the relentless sound of waves crashing against the rocks three hundred feet below.

'Now that makes it all worthwhile, but let's get away from the edge. It doesn't look safe.' Charlotte clutched her stomach. 'The smell … I might spew.'

A wall of thick brambles blocked the way to their left. Instead, the track took a sharp right and descended into the blessed shade of trees, clinging precariously to a steep-sided ravine. Progress slowed even more as they navigated a series of tight switchbacks where crumbling ground unexpectedly gave way beneath them.

After slipping for the umpteenth time, Charlotte flung off her rucksack and gulped down the last mouthful of water. 'I hate this track.' She kicked a goat's sun-bleached skull between two pine trees. 'And don't say it, Anna.'

'Well—'

'Yes, I know. We entered into this bet freely.' She rammed the empty bottle into her rucksack. 'Why is it that no matter how stupid the challenges are, we three idiots always jump at the chance to prove everyone wrong.'

Simon soaked a neckerchief in his remaining water and tied it round his neck. 'That's better. C'mon, two of our friends are counting on us. And no matter how hard it gets we never lose.'

'I think ... this might be the first time,' admitted Charlotte. 'Leave ... me. Leave ... me. I'm done for.' She threw herself on all fours and stretched a trembling hand out to her brother. 'Go ... save yourselves ... and Simon ... send my love to our darling parents. Remember me with fondness when you plough the fields of our ancestral home. Christ, what I wouldn't give for a rain-soaked Cumbrian day on our farm right now.'

Anna burst out laughing. What a sight – caked in dust, sweat-soaked T-shirts and sticky skin from constantly re-applying suntan lotion. She itched her scalp; the wide-brimmed hat was great for sun protection but made her fine chestnut brown hair lank and greasy. 'You should be on the stage – not a farmer.'

Charlotte hauled herself upright. 'True ... I'd probably make more money.'

'Quit mucking about you two.' Simon studied the map. 'We've done the hardest bit now. It's just another two miles along the valley floor to join the village road for the final mile. Thank God, my legs can't take much more.'

'Right, let's go then.' Anna pushed prescription glasses up a greasy nose. 'And wipe the grins off the others faces.'

Forty minutes later, Simon's prediction was surprisingly accurate as the road appeared and the sound of metal grinding replaced the constant drone of insects. It was coming from a lone business ahead.

The two-storey whitewashed building was tucked between the road and cliffs - its two full-height windows open to catch any breeze. Vivid flowers tumbled over the balconies, and bougainvillaea vines with bright red flowers weaved upwards past brightly painted blue shutters and across the terracotta roof. A privacy-giving terrace was smothered in honeysuckle, jasmine, and roses, and an archway offered a sneak peek into a courtyard garden. All three took in the view. After battling through a landscape of browns and greens, the vibrant colours were overwhelming.

Anna spotted the rotating sign first. 'Get in. They sell drinks.'

'Hold your horses,' Simon declared. 'Look – something even better.' He pointed to flower-filled stone troughs sitting squat-like on the roadside.

The trio hurried around one, and sure enough – Apokeri, in black capital letters. They had made it with twenty-five minutes to spare.

'I knew we could do it!' he cried, punching the air. 'Let's get some proof.'

Group photos taken, Anna set off towards the open doorway, and with the other two close behind they entered a light and bright interior. The ample and orderly space featured neat rows of road, mountain, and hybrid bikes, including children's ones with stabilisers. Each had a helmet hanging from its handlebars and a rear pannier. Three stylish grey sofas and a chunky pine coffee table with tidy literature offered a comfy place to relax. A tall glass-fronted drinks fridge was accompanied by a large chest freezer housing an assortment of ice lollies, and a compact drinks machine promised to dispense a selection of hot beverages. At the back of the room was a long counter with a bell, till, computer, and three evenly spaced Danish pastries under a glass dome. From a doorway directly behind came the sound of grinding metal.

But what stopped them was painted on the rear wall.

A cartoon version of Apokeri spanned its entire width. Anna recognised it from her well-thumbed guidebook. It was highly detailed, vibrant, fun and featured characters going about their daily lives: young children in the school playground, a priest outside his whitewashed church welcoming parishioners, a group of older men playing dominoes in the village square, and shop owners chatting to passers-by. People waved from cars, taxis, delivery trucks, bikes, and scooters. Sunbathers basked on the horseshoe beach, fishing boats headed out from a small harbour, and the twisting village road climbed through olive groves to reach the main highway. And above it all, in a beautiful flowing script – Round the Bend Cycle and Scooter Hire.

'What a labour of love. It's brilliant,' Simon exclaimed.

Anna nodded and moved toward the inner doorway.

'You can't go through there,' he said.

'Oh yes, I can. Nobody' – she pointed to the workshop – 'is going to hear a thing above that racket. We'll be here all day, man. Plus, I'm not just after a drink, and one of those pastries has got my name on it. I'm also after a favour.'

He frowned, not wanting to ask. 'What type of favour?'

'The photos prove we made it, right.' She pulled out a notebook and pen. 'But you know what'll happen. John hates being proved wrong – especially by me. He'll say we tampered with the time display or some other claptrap. So, I'm going to ask whoever I find to sign a statement proving we reached Apokeri within the time limit. After half-killing ourselves, we are not going to lose the bet. Plus, Charlotte might die if she doesn't drink soon.'

He nodded. 'Excellent plan. We'll wait here.'

The twins collapsed onto the sofas, and Anna went off in search of some help. But a few minutes later, a scream brought her back.

The siblings had been caught napping by a young, slim, dark-haired man. He was about six-foot one, with warm-brown skin and his lovely smiling face reminded her of the rather handsome American actor, Benjamin Bratt, back in his *Miss Congeniality* days.

'I didn't mean to give you such a fright,' he said. 'There's usually someone out front, but we're short-staffed today.' He nodded to the rucksacks propped against the table. 'I take it you're not looking to hire anything?'

'No, not at the moment. We've been enjoying, or should I say enduring, the track down from Karya and could do with a drink before we get to the village,' Simon explained.

'Ah yes, we get quite a few walkers coming in here desperate for refreshments. The heat catches a lot of people out. Did you get lost by any chance?' All three nodded. 'Everyone always does. It's my favourite walk with those amazing clifftop views, but I have to admit the track isn't great. There is a plan to put in some better markers, which should help.'

'I know,' Charlotte agreed. 'The views are spectacular – but that drop! One slip … game over.'

'Yes, we've got lots of walks around here like that.' He noticed Anna's longing looks. 'Help yourself to drinks from the fridge – and for an energy boost, try a pastry.'

No one needed telling twice, and they were soon guzzling down bottles of water and sinking teeth into sugar-coated apple and raisin swirls.

'Mmmmm.' Anna brushed flaky pastry off her chin. 'I've died and gone to heaven.'

A smile lit up the nice young man's face. 'My father will be pleased. He runs the village bakery. We've usually sold out of those bestsellers by now. You're welcome to finish them inside whilst I ring them through.'

'Thanks,' she replied. 'And I hope you don't mind, but we need your help.'

She explained the bet whilst paying (pointing out his error of only ringing through two bottles of water).

'I always like a bit of friendly competition. There you go...' He winked at her. 'Any problems, send them my way.'

'Thanks. That painting's amazing!' she said, motioning to the back wall. 'The more you look ... the more you see.'

'I know. I love it. It's by our resident village artist, Kristina Nilssen. All the people featured live in Apokeri.' He pointed almost to the top. 'There I am, furiously pedalling away. It's absolute hell going up but brilliant freewheeling down.'

'I bet,' Simon agreed as he wiped his mouth.

'It isn't even her usual style.' he gestured to a series of smaller cartoon images. 'She did all those well-known Lefkada landmarks with our more well-known villagers.'

'Oh yes, I recognise Cape Ducato lighthouse, Lefkada town centre, and Nidri Waterfalls. We visited them after getting off the Kefalonia ferry yesterday. Beautiful but extremely busy.' Anna nodded at the cascades. 'I'll meet Kristina tonight ... I'm staying at Apokeri Apartments for the next few days.'

'Kristina's great and often babysat my older sister and me.' He smiled and then cryptically added, 'she's a real character, as I'm sure you'll discover! Is everyone stopping there?'

'No, only Anna. The rest of us mere mortals are heading over to Tharesseti for a rest.' Simon glanced at watch. 'Look at the time! Sorry, we need to get a move on.'

Hoisting on their rucksacks and thanking the genial young man for his help, they set off on the last leg.

As soon as they were out of earshot, Charlotte wafted herself. 'Now he was a nine out of ten. Tall, dark, and handsome. And those mischievous beautiful dark brown eyes. Just the way I like my prey ... I mean my men. What do you reckon, Anna?' She didn't bother to wait for a response. 'Of course, you wouldn't have been looking. Not with John to keep you warm at night – what it must be like to be in love.'

Yes, Anna thought. What it must be like to be in love.

***

The final section was an easy ten-minute walk along a concrete footpath. It initially ran along the roadside, hemmed in by cliffs. However, as they rounded a bend, the sandy horseshoe beach revealed itself.

'Just like the painting,' Charlotte observed.

Bookended by two tavernas, five hundred metres of golden sand gently shelved into the rippling water. Family groups, friends, couples, and individuals lazed about, built sandcastles, or strolled along the water's edge. Nobody seemed to be in a particular rush to do anything. At Dionysus, the closest and smallest, a brightly coloured awning flapped in the breeze and shaded a dozen or so customers enjoying a late afternoon tipple. Each taverna was surrounded by permanent palm parasols and wooden sun loungers. Stationed in the middle – a pedalo hire business and lifeguard station. Behind the beach, a pretty promenade with white benches, palm trees, and large planters packed with colourful flowers stretched to a picturesque and diminutive harbour. Compact Apokeri nestled around the bay, hemmed in by a natural amphitheatre of lush green hills. A predominance of traditional Greek whitewashed buildings jostled with more elaborate Venetian houses – adding architectural interest and charm. Strung out along the beachfront road was a range of two-storey structures, many with ground-floor businesses adorned with floral displays. From her guidebook, Anna knew the village was home to approximately one hundred full-time residents, and the majority still made a living from small family farms and fishing, followed by seasonal tourism.

Apokeri was famed Lefkada-wide for its flower displays, and the annual Flower and Food Festival (first Saturday in September) attracted thousands for the hotly contested Best Dressed Building trophy. With a well-deserved reputation for excellent cuisine, its three tavernas, café, and commercial bakery battled it out to win the coveted Best in Show award.

The rather dishy man from the bike shop had explained his parents - who owned the bakery and the café - went head-to-head in the competition. But only the café entered the floral competition. He'd failed to conceal his mother's obsessiveness to win and her mortification (and unbearable behaviour) last year when the café slipped to a shameful fifth. However, he was full of family pride about Makris Bakery supplying a wide variety of bread, pastries, pies, and patisserie to businesses in Apokeri and beyond. And that his mother presided over the café with a reputation that attracted locals and tourists alike. It made Anna eager to explore the village, hurry to the café, and sample a homemade gelato.

'You've got four days to eat as much ice cream as your insatiable appetite can handle,' Charlotte said to her disgruntled friend. 'We need to find the others, and I could do with a cold beer before the boat leaves.'

Unsurprisingly, they heard their friends before seeing them, happily relaxing outside, supping on beers and tucking into a late lunch at Nereus. The second beachside establishment was the grander, more cosmopolitan, and undoubtedly more expensive of the two.

Charles checked the time. 'The wanderers return to win the bet. I knew you could do it.' He cast an eye over the trio. 'You're hacky dirty. Was it complete hell?' Nodding to the range of dishes, he continued, 'Sorry we were too hungry to wait, but when I saw you heading this way, I took the liberty of getting your usual

10

lime and soda, Anna. The twins will be relieved to hear they have a pitcher of something stronger to share.'

'Thanks,' Simon responded gratefully, poured a beer, and passed it to his sister. 'I'm glad we didn't let you down.'

'Hold on,' John interrupted. 'According to my calculations, it has taken you two hours and forty-five minutes – you've lost the bet.'

Anna slapped the signed statement on the table. 'Read it and weep, bonny lad. And we've photographs proving completion in two hours and five minutes.'

After all their detractors meticulously inspected the evidence, they begrudgingly admitted defeat.

'Another one lost,' John conceded, shrugging his shoulders. 'I'd say that calls for more drinks – courtesy of me. Tuck in. It's all delicious.'

With the food demolished, no one, not even Anna, could be bothered to move.

John studied his watch and yawned. 'We've got almost an hour before heading to the pier. I reckon we stay here till then.'

'Agreed,' everyone lazily chorused.

Chapter Two

Sitting in the shade, Anna cast her eyes across the water. A mile out in the bay sat Tharesseti. The speck of land (owned by the best friend of Charles's father) was where her friends were heading.

The group was happy with the late addition (and why wouldn't they be? Only Anna and Charlotte spent hours reworking an extended five-week itinerary to benefit them all). Charles had been quick to point out that the centuries-old grand villa was a shadow of its former glory. But everyone took that with a jug of salt due to his privileged upbringing. And besides, with a ghoulish history of scandal and murder, who could resist? Anna, for one. She needed time alone with a guidebook, a scooter, and her thoughts concerning a certain Mr John Leyburn.

She'd believed he was the one during their intense two-year relationship. This time – at last – someone on the same page. Both mature-ish students seeing degrees as a way out of dead-end jobs and craving to explore the world more. They planned to do lots of activities between studying and working all hours – and sometimes did – more so if it was something he enjoyed. At least she was a highly experienced rock climber now. So, post-uni life became their focus. And it was going to be fantastic. No nine-to-five for them, but travelling the world – working as and when required. They were going to shun the rat race. They were going to be different.

It all came to nothing.

The promised shiny and exciting future was gone because her rural–Cumbrian boyfriend had big plans to climb the corporate life in the capital. "Oh, but we'll have so many more opportunities to skip over to Europe," would never happen. Her best mate thought the same, settling Stateside to explore its wide-open spaces but, in reality, working non-stop fifty weeks a year in pursuit of the American Dream. Besides, Anna hated cities; she even found her home city of Newcastle and its suburbs claustrophobic. Relocating to London left her cold.

He wanted her to go with him, but she didn't, and blazing rows ensued, with John invariably throwing up his hands and shouting at Anna to grow up and stop living in cloud cuckoo land. She needed a secure job and a successful career to get on in life. Their original plans were fantasy, a child's naïve vision. He'd realised they needed to start living in the real world, and it was high time she did as well. When John eventually understood Anna was not relocating, they agreed to a long-distance relationship. It marked an uneasy truce and the start of his campaign to wear her down. And it was driving them apart.

***

A rare silence descended as the group watched the world go by. Anna reflected how each one signed up for very different reasons, but had one thing in common – knowing what they wanted to do. All except her.

The trip was living up to and exceeding her expectations, but what direction would her life take once it ended?

'Be still my heart,' Li exclaimed. 'A Viking god is striding towards us.'

All eyes immediately turned to the promenade. And true enough, the man approaching could be a modern-day Thor. Even from where she sat, Anna reckoned he was a foot taller than her. The man was huge – at least six-foot six, with the build of an

Olympic swimmer and shoulder-length surfer-dude blond hair. He wore the same branded work attire as the young man in the bike shop – smart grey cargo shorts and a slim-fit cornflower-blue polo T-shirt that revealed tanned, muscular legs, arms, and a flat stomach. Charlotte whimpered next to her.

'That's Daniel,' Charles advised. 'And has that effect on women. He owns Round the Bend Cycle and Scooter Hire. Sensible sort of a chap. Certainly not a natural front-of-house bloke, but knows his stuff. Turned that business around once he took charge.' All eyes followed Daniel's progress along the promenade. 'And talk about competitive. I've never come close to beating him on a bike – half killed myself last year.'

Li switched to predator mode and casually leaned over to Charles. 'I don't care how you do it but get that man over here now.'

He obediently stood up and called out, 'Daniel … how the hell are you?'

'This is a bit early for your usual visit?' Daniel said with a firm handshake. 'Decided to ditch the family this time?'

'I had the chance to spend five weeks in Greece with this motley crew. You know me, never one to pass up the chance to have fun and cause chaos. And as I'm emigrating to New Zealand next month, it'll be my last chance to visit Lefkada and Tharesseti for who knows how long.'

'Wellington won't know what's hit them,' Li joked.

Daniel scribbled something on a napkin and handed it to Charles. 'My dad lives in Australia, outside Adelaide. Drop him a line with your address once you get settled. I'm hoping to visit New Zealand early next year, and it'd be good to catch up if we can.'

'Are you planning on emigrating, Daniel?' Li asked, provocatively crossing long, shapely legs and flicking back her glossy black ponytail.

The group watched with amusement as Li turned on the charm. With gorgeous Malaysian looks, an IQ off the chart, and a razor-sharp wit, it was only a matter of time before men dissolved.

'No, I'm taking some time out to see the world and spending time with my father. Since he moved back to Australia seven years ago, I haven't seen him. The business will be in very safe hands whilst I'm gone.'

Daniel was well and truly the focus of Li and Charlotte's attention with his piercing blue eyes and chiselled good looks, but Anna was more interested in his canine companion. The dog was massive, built like a St Bernard but with a short, thick, blond smooth coat, a husky-like tail, and a lovely friendly face. It immediately began nuzzling Anna's fingers with its shortish snout, then it reared up to place strong forelegs on her shoulders and set about licking her face. Taken by surprise, she laughed as the dog's weight almost caused her chair to topple backwards.

'Cassie down, now,' Daniel instructed, and the dog immediately obeyed. 'I'm so sorry about that. She's never that friendly with strangers.'

'No need to apologise, she's adorable, but I don't recognise the breed?' Anna replied as she cleaned dog saliva from her sunglasses and Cassie sneaked back to put her colossal head on Anna's lap.

'She's a Molossus of Epirus – an ancient Greek breed for guarding livestock against bears and wolves.'

'I can imagine. How old is she?' Li asked as she attempted to re-focus Daniel's attention by reaching out to stroke Cassie – resulting in a low growl.

'Cassie, no!' Daniel commanded. The dog fell silent and went back to enjoying a tickle under her sizeable jowls from Anna. 'Maybe six or seven years old. She sneaked into the shop five years ago during a thunderstorm. The poor thing was skin and bones, terrified, completely drenched through, and collarless. I put up posters in case a family somewhere was frantically searching for her, but nobody ever came forward. I reckon the owners realised a Molossus was more hard work than they thought and turfed her out.'

'And since that day, Cassie has been the love of Daniel's life,' Charles added.

'Yes, I'd have to agree—'

'We need to get going,' John butted in.

'No worries, I'll let you get away and continue my walk.'

After wishing Charles good luck, Daniel bid them farewell and set off towards the harbour.

Simon turned to Li and smirked. 'You're shameless. We all know you don't even like dogs.'

'Hmm – I must be losing my touch,' Li responded as she stood up. 'John's right. Time to make a move. We don't want to keep our host waiting.'

***

The stone pier was a short stroll away. It jutted fifty feet into the sea and overlooked a hive of early evening activity. Several boats were being cleaned and restocked after entertaining day trippers, small dinghies were being skilfully manoeuvred by well-heeled sailors from a dozen or so gleaming yachts moored in the bay, and small fishing boats returned with their daily catches. At the head of the pier stood a statue of St Peter, the patron saint of fishermen. Sitting on the plinth below, a man admired the yachts. He turned, slowly rose, and headed towards them.

'Hey guys, great to see you,' he said in a lilting Scottish accent, shaking hands with everyone.

Looking to be in his sixties, Jeremy MacNair was short and squat. A friendly frog of a man with a broad, cheerful, weather-beaten face, large ears, and very little hair.

Charles handed over a box of wine. 'Thanks for that,' said Jeremy. 'I reckon it should see us right for a day or so. I have to say I'll be glad of the company. I've been at a bit of a loose end since my sons left last week. You'll be happy to hear I've stocked up on provisions, so we certainly won't starve.' He patted an ample stomach threatening to break free from the straightjacket of a short-sleeved white shirt. 'No chance of that for me. And if the energetic ones amongst you want to burn off any excess calories, there are paddleboards, canoes, snorkelling, and fishing gear to use.'

As Anna helped store the provisions and rucksacks on Jeremy's sleek powerboat, she thanked him for organising her accommodation.

'Think nothing of it, my dear. It's the least I can do for a friend of Charles. Kristina's a good egg, and she'll take excellent care of you. Enjoy your few days exploring Lefkada. It truly is a beautiful island.' Turning to the others, he clapped his hands together. 'Right, gang, let's head on over there. We need to toast your first Tharesseti sunset with a glass of bubbly on the veranda.'

Jeremy opened out the throttle, and a whoop went up from everyone. Anna watched as they zipped over the water and into the distance. The church bell chimed six – it was time to find her accommodation.

Chapter Three

Apokeri Gallery was the last building on the beachfront street and stood proud. The Venetian-style townhouse echoed those on the Venice Grand Canal. Its golden sand hue with high-arched windows and detailed stone surrounds glowed in the early evening sun. The beautiful structure dwarfed its neighbours, and across a narrow alleyway, the two-storey whitewashed Post Office looked dumpy and plain.

Seascape watercolours and oil paintings filled the narrow ground-floor windows, from tranquil sunsets to dramatic tempests featuring the same traditional Greek fishing boat and the Apokeri coastline. The display included carved wooden bowls, beautiful aqua-marine glazed pottery, and ceramic jewellery.

A neat pocket garden hunkered below the windows with delicate grasses, dwarf roses, lavender, rosemary, thyme, and sage. The combination created an intoxicating aroma. A twisted wisteria trunk curled around one window, and its thick vines scrambled along the two protruding first-floor balconies. A second truss framed the flat roof, and cascades of lilac flowers hummed with bees.

Swapping prescription sunglasses for metal-rimmed spectacles, Anna passed through a heavy wooden double door that looked original and indicated that customers were welcome seven days a week, ten till one, then two till unspecified. What a great idea, shut up shop whenever you fancied.

The neatness continued inside a spacious and airy gallery. High whitewashed walls featured chunky wooden shelves with more seascape paintings and the same boat in each. There was a wistfulness to them, which made her sad.

A wide wooden bench displayed carefully arranged pottery – dinnerware, large serving platters, fruit bowls, vases, and coasters. Each piece was labelled with its price on a white card in the same flowing script as she'd seen at the bike shop. At the back of the store stood a glass cabinet with a well-chosen selection of ceramic and wooden jewellery. An electronic till kept company with a handmade duck-egg blue coaster and a matching mug full of steaming black coffee. Two precisely positioned wooden bar stools with matching cushions sat behind.

In the middle of the room was a generous wooden coffee table with an assortment of books on the history and landscapes of Lefkada to tempt the visitor. And, in a stroke of genius, to keep children entertained (and their parents browsing longer) were two boxes. One contained an assortment of crayons and coloured pencils, whilst the other had a pile of pre-printed colouring-in pages. A collection of tidy completed ones took pride of place on a giant corkboard, each proudly bearing the name and age of the owner. Anna smiled and remembered sitting at the dining room table with her older sister, spending many happy hours completing pictures, both focused on staying within the lines.

Beside the corkboard hung a large rack of postcards for sale, in the fun cartoon style of the bike shop mural that Anna preferred. It was difficult to think they were by the same hand. And all signed K. The Scandinavian theme with orderly displays lent a calming atmosphere with understated elegance. And there were definite similarities between the gallery and the bike shop – both spotless, both controlled. Everything had its place – no room for clutter, no room for mess.

Hearing someone merrily humming, Anna called out a cheery yassas, and a tall, slim aristocratic woman glided in. She appeared to be in her early seventies with the poise and grace of a ballerina. Anna straightened. There was a self-assured air to the stylishly dressed woman decked in billowing pink linen trousers and a long-sleeved shirt. From underneath a brightly coloured headscarf, a short, choppy mass of silver hair peeked out. Surprisingly, considering the shop sold beautiful handmade jewellery, the artist only wore a simple gold crucifix necklace.

Anna felt like a bag lady.

Kristina Nilssen had the merest hint of a Scandinavian accent and a strong handshake – not a trace of paint under the neatly trimmed nails of long, tapered fingers. Deep lines fanned out from studious blue eyes – a friendly face that smiled more than frowned.

'Welcome to Apokeri. Am I right in thinking you are Anna?' Anna nodded. 'Excellent. I've been looking forward to meeting you. Firstly, I'll show you to your home for the next few days. And afterwards, you must join me for supper. Jeremy has told me a little about your trip, and I'd love to hear more. There's plenty of time to freshen up. Food will be ready at eight.' Reaching into her deep trouser pocket, Kristina withdrew a keyring. Attached were two brass keys and a small disc engraved with the number six. 'Here are your keys. The larger one opens the front door. Please remember to take them – so you're not locked out. I've popped you on the top floor, with the best view.'

'Thank you, that's very kind.'

Kristina patted Anna's hand. 'It's the least I can do for a friend of Jeremy's.'

Unsure how Jeremy had explained the imaginary friendship, she smiled in response and followed Kristina through the open doorway, ensuring her backpack was securely in place. The Scandinavian feel continued with white walls, wooden floors, and chunky candles. At the far end, a pair of well-worn dark brown leather sofas and two leather chairs draped in knitted throws clustered around a rustic coffee table. An enormous farmhouse table with an eclectic mix of wooden chairs sat in the middle. The room should have felt snug, with two-foot-thick walls and long, thin horizontal windows. But it didn't. Instead, it was too perfect, too stylised – as if nobody spent any time there. Look, don't touch, don't live.

Passing through, they entered a well-ordered, large kitchen. This was more like it – a homely, comforting, and well-used room. Life happened here. Chats at the small wooden booth seating and table with gingham cushions tucked below the enclosed staircase. Stories exchanged leaning against the pine units running the length of the kitchen with its band of handmade tiles in shades of cream, tan, and dark brown. Secrets spilt by the impressive range cooker where a deliciously aromatic tomato-based stew simmered, the ingredients no doubt sourced from the well-stocked pantry. And sharing a joke whilst washing up at the sink and looking out over the garden.

Out through the double doors, Anna followed Kristina into a hidden oasis. A honey-coloured flagged patio housed a weathered hardwood table and chairs, a large yellow parasol, and behind – a living screen of plants. Ground-level annual and perennial flowers jostled for space, mid-tier shrubs provided structure and towering above everything were giant palms, banana plants, and a magnificent gunnera – forest planting at its best.

'Wow, this is amazing.'

'Thank you, garden design is a passion.' Kristina replied. 'Come and see the rest of my handiwork.'

Following Kristina's light footsteps along winding brick paths, Anna glimpsed an immaculate lawn; a grove of lemon, orange, olive, and nectarine trees; gooseberry and blackcurrant bushes and a very healthy-looking vegetable patch bursting with produce. Trained against the wall were branches of apples, plums, and pears. Further on, a well-stocked greenhouse, a rustic potting shed, and a beautiful parterre garden with immaculately trimmed hedges, clipped bay trees, and dozens of lavender shrubs attracting countless pollinators. In the background, hens contently clucking and the tinkling sound of water. There were intimate seating areas throughout the garden to enjoy a secluded patch of sun or much-needed shade. Her dad would kill for a place like this. With only a postage-sized yard, his second home was his allotment, and for many years, he'd doted on his vegetables far more than on his youngest daughter.

Kristina opened a simple wooden door in the ten-foot garden wall and pointed to the three-storey whitewashed Apokeri Apartments. It had beach towels hanging over every balcony except the one Anna assumed to be hers. As Kristina returned to the gallery, Anna crossed the narrow, cobbled lane that disappeared into a warren of backstreets and as she pushed open the intricately carved front door, ran her fingers over the detailed design of flowers and vines. Automatic lights revealed a small all-white entrance lobby and a door that opened into an office. A generous, white-tiled corridor ran back with two apartments on opposing walls. At the far end was a door marked Private. Being a curious sort, Anna listened to ensure no one was inside and then turned the handle to find a neatly ordered store cupboard. At least she knew where to go for an extra toilet roll. Retracing her steps, she climbed the stairs and saw that each floor had two apartments.

Dumping her rucksack and daypack, she inspected the simply furnished and immaculately clean one-bedroom apartment. The bathroom smelled of bleach and lemon-scented soap. A compact kitchen (with a welcome food pack) opened onto a small balcony to catch the morning sun whilst looking out on the crumbling chalky cliffs that stretched like a protective arm, hiding the village from prying eyes. Taking a bite of her juicy nectarine, she gazed over the flat, tiled rooftops. Directly below was the apartment block's private walled garden. Now in the shade, its lawned area was edged by drought-tolerant plants. A few wooden deckchairs littered the grass, and a children's sandpit was home to abandoned buckets and spades. A washing line provided a place for guests to hang up handwashing and a lone bright-pink sarong flapped in the breeze.

Inside, the evening sun flooded a pine-furnished bedroom. The delightful apartment was homely, with artwork on the walls and a vase of deliciously scented sweet peas.

After a much-needed shower and snooze, Anna was feeling refreshed. She donned clean clothes and, looking into the mirror, saw a tanned, five-foot-six, fairly plain-looking twenty-six-year-old with a slim, athletic build. She sighed at her slightly unpolished appearance. No matter how hard she tried, it seemed impossible to tame her shoulder-length hair. Even with a dusting of powder, her face was already taking on a slightly greasy sheen. She'd applied make-up but stuck to a self-imposed thirty-second time limit to slick on mascara, eyeliner, eyeshadow, and lipstick. She smiled, and her naturally stern expression disappeared. It was the best she could do with what nature bestowed and her patience allowed.

She wandered up the softly lit garden just before eight, brushing past roses, dahlias, and cosmos to find Kristina setting the patio table.

'How can I help?' she asked, handing over a bottle of red. 'I thought we could enjoy this with the meal?'

Kristina inspected the label. 'You've good taste. This is an excellent vintage.' She motioned Anna to follow. 'Come through to the kitchen for a drink whilst I finish up.'

Pouring two generous glasses of wine, Anna thanked Kristina for the thoughtful welcome pack and the lovely apartment.

'You're welcome. I introduced the packs a few years ago. They went down a treat and resulted in lots of positive reviews.' She tasted the stew and nodded. 'Perfect … I hope you're hungry?'

Anna laughed. 'I'm always ready for food – especially when it smells that good.'

Soon both women were enjoying gigantes plaki (beans, tomatoes, onions, garlic, herbs and spices), flatbreads, and homegrown green salad as the sky changed from dusky pink to inky black. Anna had to agree the wine was outstanding. After toasting their health, she admitted the excellent choice was courtesy of Charles and made a mental note to thank him.

To a background of crickets, the women chatted long into the night. As the candles steadily burned down, Anna discovered Kristina was quite the Lefkada wine connoisseur and had a few bottles of homemade wine from the indigenous grape varieties of Vardea and Vertzami growing in her garden. In turn, Anna entertained Kristina with her Greek exploits, including swimming in Palea Kameni hot springs on Santorini, exploring the UNESCO World Heritage site at Delos, and sampling the potent Kitron liqueur of Naxos. The group had sprinted for the ferry to Ios, and she'd clung to a runaway horse during a mountain trek on Kefalonia.

Kristina laughed. 'You've created many wonderful memories. I've seen so little of Greece, being very content here in Apokeri.'

From various snippets, Anna pieced together that Kristina's quiet life in Apokeri was in sharp contrast to what came before. Born into an extremely wealthy Stockholm family and the youngest of three sisters, Kristina had attended school in England and then an illustrious Swiss finishing school which had fostered an independent spirit and a strong sense of self-worth. There had been many childhood holidays including The Hamptons on Long Island, New York and on Tharesseti which provided ample opportunities for her ambitious father to expand an incredibly successful business empire.

After that, Kristina skilfully steered the conversation away from herself and left unanswered questions. When and how had Kristina ended up in this small Greek fishing village, and why had she chosen to stay?

Where she was more forthcoming was the turbulent history of Tharesseti. Back in the seventeenth century, an eccentric duke commissioned an opulent villa with beautiful, terraced gardens and a harbour. Over a century later, it passed to a powerful Italian dynasty after an ill-fated duel and was a fortress for decades – a place for the rich and powerful to dump their mentally unwell or troublesome relations. After a violent and allegedly unsuccessful patient breakout, the island changed hands again to become a sumptuous retreat. It was the place to be seen for half a century until the owner was suddenly declared bankrupt. A member of the British aristocracy took up ownership until a high-profile scandal saw the hotel abandoned, and it remained deserted for decades until Jeremy bought it as a holiday retreat.

'Now there's a tale and a half,' Anna said as she scooped up the remnants of her homemade blackcurrant ice cream. 'How do you know Jeremy?'

'After purchasing Tharesseti, he visited the gallery with his late wife. Over the years, they bought and commissioned several paintings and sculptures that are now on display in the villa and its gardens.'

Anna frowned. 'He doesn't come across as a hard-nosed property tycoon.'

'Don't be fooled by his jolly disposition,' Kristina said as she poured them a camomile tea. 'Jeremy is a very shrewd businessman who has built up a very successful company over the years. Since the death of his wife five years ago, he has gradually been handing control over to his two sons and planned to retire when he remarried this year. However, that didn't happen, and he has been holed up there since early May, licking his wounds. I wouldn't be surprised if he turned it back into a hotel.'

'Well, I hope he has more luck than previous owners. The place sounds totally cursed, man.'

After outlining her sightseeing plans, Anna described her bike shop stop (and found out the young man was called Filip), and her encounter with Daniel. Kristina was clearly fond of them, describing Filip as savvy and hardworking like his parents – a joker but keen to prove himself. In contrast, Daniel was reserved, tending to mull things over first. Whilst finishing her tea, Kristina pondered why Daniel planned to return to Apokeri (his heart clearly wanted to be elsewhere).

Rousing herself, she smiled. 'Ignore the musings of an old woman. I must tell you, this has been the most wonderful evening. I felt a connection when we met … kindred spirits. You know more about me after a few short hours than most of the villagers I've rubbed shoulders with for decades.'

Chapter Four

It was early. Apart from the fishing fleet putting out to sea and a few seabirds, she was alone in the cool water, losing herself to rhythmic breaststroke before marginally improving a ropey front crawl. She towelled dry on the fine sand as the sun climbed over the hills. Tharesseti stared back at her. It seemed to be whispering, 'What are you going to do about John?' She didn't have an answer – yet. And as village life stirred, she scooted back to her apartment wrapped in a beach towel and a growling stomach.

***

Anna quietly closed the apartment door and set out in search of sustenance. Based on yesterday's tasty morsel, the first stop had to be Aphrodite Café. The pretty establishment with bright blue window frames swathed in pink bougainvillaea sat on the junction of the beachfront street and the pedestrianised village square. Although still relatively early on a Saturday, the place bustled with people as she eagerly pushed the door.

Most customers ordered takeaway – grabbing much-needed caffeine and sugar fixes. A dozen or so locals stood against a counter or perched on barstools, all intent on talking over every other animated conversation. Sunburnt tourists sat on well-worn chairs, enjoying leisurely breakfasts at tables covered with blue and white checked oilcloths – absorbing the energy, sights, sounds, and aromas. In deep shade, plentiful outside seating remained empty, except for a few souls savouring a cigarette with their coffee.

Joining the queue, she studied the place in more detail. A glass-fronted counter offered tempting savoury and sweet treats, including a range of gelato with a handy external serving hatch. A huge blackboard listed the day's breakfast, lunch, and evening meals, with an impressive choice of Greek and international dishes.

The place had a welcoming vibe, and at its epicentre, a handsome woman in her early fifties was immaculately turned out in a calf-length black skirt and white shirt that flattered her hourglass figure. Her black hair softly framed a friendly face that bore a strong resemblance to Filip. It must be his mother, Sofia. Whilst serving, she gabbled away in Greek to a taller colleague whose appearance was the polar opposite.

The tall, thin woman in her late thirties was dressed in chef whites. Her narrow sour face with its hawk nose, thin lips, and faint frown lines looked like it rarely gave praise. But appearances could be deceptive. After all, Anna had what her best friend referred to as a resting bitch face. This was why, in the company of strangers, Anna always smiled – a lot. Far better to put people at ease instead of looking like you wanted to take them outside and punch their lights out.

When she reached the counter, a stern and stocky man in his late fifties came striding in from the back carrying a basket of sweet pastries. The baker's uniform and age suggested he was Vasili, Filip's father. However, Anna failed to see any family resemblance. He was the same height as the older woman, and despite his grumpy disposition, he was an attractive man with a thick head of greying hair under his baker's cap. Anna could imagine him having been a real head-turner in his youth.

She bought a divine-smelling koulouri and, along with the sesame-covered bread ring, added a triangular Kreatopita. This filo pastry meat pie would constitute lunch. In halting Greek,

Anna explained how much she'd enjoyed her sweet pastry from Round the Bend and the bread rolls in her Apokeri Apartment welcome pack. Her guesswork was right. They were Filip's parents. Sofia swelled with pride at the compliments but the other woman only appraised Anna with piercing eyes.

Anna explained her next stop was to hire a scooter and explore Lefkada. Could she pass on a message? They were short-staffed, with somebody forgetting they were due in (again), so Filip needed to pick up his pastries. To save a trip, Anna volunteered to take them.

Sofia fussed with her hair. 'Thank you, that's a huge help. To be sure, my niece is a hard worker, and the customers do love her, but often her head is in the clouds with dreams of becoming a world-famous actress.'

'That girl doesn't know the meaning of hard work,' Vasili snapped. 'How many times have I said it? Your sister needs to give her daughter a kick up the backside. When I was her age—'

Sofia winked at Anna and planted a kiss on her husband's cheek. 'Yes, everyone knows you were running the family bakery by the time you were eighteen.'

Carrying the basket over one arm, Anna bid farewell to the cheerful Sofia and her stony-faced colleague. Vasili had already turned on his heels and marched back into the bakery.

Pausing momentarily to adjust her delivery, Anna stopped at Thalia Supermarket to inspect its enticing display of fruit and vegetables. She got as far as the next shop along – Odyssey Travel – and it became too much. She took a bite of her koulouri and moaned with pleasure. The rest quickly followed as her eyes strayed to the window display with the usual tours – local boat trips, a standard Lefkada Island coach tour, a mountain-villages tour with wine tasting and day trips to Kefalonia and Meganisi. She might need to inquire about the latter, but the scooter option was best for now.

Swallowing the last bit of bread ring and checking her teeth for seeds, she entered the bike shop. Filip was immediately out from behind the counter to collect what now felt like a cumbersome basket. And he looked concerned.

'Oh no, Mama did not ask you to carry that whole basket up the street?' Anna soothed away his worries by explaining she'd offered due to staffing issues. 'That's a relief. I love my cousin, but she's becoming very lax recently. I must have a quiet word with her before Papa blows his top ... sorry, you didn't need to hear that. How can I help?'

She needed a scooter for a few days, and Filip was keen to determine her plans – to ensure the best deal. And as Anna gratefully accepted a complimentary latte, he listened to her packed four-day itinerary whilst replenishing glass plates with freshly baked pastries.

Today she intended to explore Lefkada town – particularly its archaeological museum and surrounding sea lakes with their resident flamingos. It was then to the Monastery of Panagia Faneromeni with its Ecclesiastical Museum, Agios Ioannis – the oldest church on the island – and Agia Mavra Castle. On the second day, she'd concentrate on the southwest and take in the villages of Vassiliki and Pondi with their old churches, natural springs, and traditional windmills. Day three would be spent in the southeast to see pretty Sivota and Poros. And without pausing for breath, she launched into an explanation of being unable to get the logistics to work. Instead of cycling around neighbouring Meganisi on her last full day, she'd need to take an organised trip. Having joked that Anna was likely to see more of Lefkada in the next few days than most islanders ever did, Filip asked her to call back later – there might be a solution to her cycling dilemma.

***

She was back at Round the Bend at six after a fantastic day. Initially, it took a few miles to relax on the scooter, but after that she loved zooming along with the breeze on her skin. The confidence came from wearing a helmet (a Round the Bend stipulation). In her experience, other Greek islands had a more relaxed attitude, but Filip explained Daniel had always operated a no helmet, no hire rule. If anyone disagreed, they went elsewhere.

Parking in the shade next to a battered Fiesta, Anna popped her trusty helmet in the scooter's top box and eagerly entered the shop. She patiently waited as Filip served the last customers of the day – a middle-aged German couple with precise requirements. Twenty minutes later saw them happily tackle the killer hill on their road bikes after they'd energetically pumped Filip's hand for five minutes, thanking him for all his help. Shutting the door and flipping the sign to closed, Filip massaged the blood back into his hand as he crossed to the counter.

Anna stood, bouncing on her heels. 'Well … did you have any luck?'

Her heart sank as he gave an apologetic look and sighed. 'I'm sorry to tell you it'll be an extremely early start.' He failed to keep a straight face. 'Because you need to be here at six tomorrow morning.'

She let out a massive whoop, clapping her hands like a kid at Christmas. 'Brilliant. You're an absolute star. Tell me all about it. What's the plan?'

Filip's friend was arriving from Kefalonia for a couple of days. Tomorrow they'd drive to the port at Nidri and catch the first Meganisi ferry, spend the day cycling its quiet roads and get the last one back at six. It'd give them ample time, and as the pair had biked the compact island many times before, they knew all the best routes. If Anna was happy to alter her plans, she was welcome to join them.

'Happy? I'm ecstatic. Thank you so much for inviting me. I'll warn you I'm a chirpy early-morning type.'

'So ... if you have a cup of coffee?'

'I'm hyper!'

Filip laughed. 'That might be fun. Come on, let's get you sorted with a bike.'

Although it took only ten minutes to choose her hybrid bike, it was more than two hours before she finally relaxed on her balcony and tucked into some much-needed food. Thalia Supermarket had been her undoing – an Aladdin's Cave for foodies, with delicious locally sourced produce. She'd wandered up and down the aisles salivating, then fell into her usual habit of chatting with the people behind the till – a mother-and-daughter combo who were more talkative than her. With her head full of their potted family history (including a wish to see a nomadic son settled, married and providing more grandchildren), Anna caught up with Kristina. She wore a huge straw hat and tended the gallery's flowerbed whilst happily reporting a steady flow of tourists had purchased plenty of souvenirs. Kindly refusing the offer of supper (to finish a painting and refill the gallery's depleted shelves), she wished Anna an enjoyable day on Meganisi and looked forward to hearing all about it.

Chapter Five

Anna gave a cheery kaliméra as she pulled into the car park just before six.

After a final check of the towbar and bikes, Alex Panagos warmly shook her hand. 'Lovely to meet you. It's great we get to show you beautiful Meganisi.'

'Thanks for letting me gatecrash. I'm slightly nervous as you both look ready to tackle a Tour de France stage. I'll try my best to keep up.'

In their cycling outfits, it was clear to see how ultra-fit both men were, with broad shoulders, muscular arms and legs, and flat stomachs – although Alex was shorter and stockier than Filip.

Handing over a coffee, Filip grinned. 'Let's see what that does to you. Don't worry, we'll take it easy. Today's going to be fun.'

There was easy banter during the car journey along the practically empty coastal road. Having asked Alex and Filip to speak Greek, she needed to keep asking them to explain or repeat themselves. Both showed infinite patience and she found Alex more than happy to answer her questions. By the time they wheeled their bikes onto the ferry, she knew the twenty-five-year-old met Filip during their National Service stint four years ago. He was from the port city of Piraeus, next to Athens, and they occasionally caught up when Filip visited his sister Stefania in the capital for a day cycling or rock climbing. At sixteen, Alex had begun working at one of the many Piraeus-based shipping and logistic companies and, at eighteen, he jumped at the chance to spend time in its Liverpool office. His father worked in the same company, but a promotion three years ago had seen his parents relocate to Thessaloniki. Alex had loved his job, and living in Piraeus meant he could take his bike on the myriad ferries to explore countless Greek islands – but it was now time for a change. Filip and Alex had discussed the possibility of him working in the bike shop as it was getting increasingly busy. Daniel planning to take time out to go travelling seemed perfect timing.

The trio chatted on the deck for the thirty-minute crossing, and – because she was still hyper from the coffee – the boys asked her to slow down more than once. With her Geordie accent and speed, all the words merged into one, and they kept missing what she was saying.

Disembarking with a handful of other passengers at Port Spilia (the majority of people seemed to be continuing to Vathi), Anna was delighted at her first sight of Meganisi. The hills surrounding Spilia Bay were lush with olive trees. Aside from the jetty, there were two pontoons with rows of yachts tied up, and the only building was a beachside taverna.

Anna had needlessly worried about keeping up as the boys selected a leisurely anti-clockwise route through the unspoilt, green, and tranquil island. The quiet road allowed them to ride three abreast and chat. Often a stone's throw away from the sea, the route afforded stunning views of Lefkada, and they frequently stopped at deserted pebbled beaches to dip their toes in crystal-clear water.

At the tiny chapel of Agios Ioannis and its beautiful beach, the party fell back into single file and put their heads down for the climb to Spartochori. On entering the compact hilltop village, Anna trailed behind through the labyrinth of stone-built, whitewashed houses. She absorbed the sights, sounds, and smells spilling out of courtyards filled with potted plants, shops selling local produce, and tavernas cooking fresh fish. Alex and Filip were indeed following their noses to a tiny takeaway and selected what had to be the best lunch spot in Spartochori. Perched on a wall, under the shade of an old olive tree, and with the deep blue Spilia Bay below them, they agreed this was the life.

With full bellies, they progressed eastwards on a twisting inland road to sleepy Katomeria. Its elevated position provided more stunning views across a green and undulating landscape. Armed with her camera, Anna explored the narrow, cobbled streets and captured photogenic whitewashed buildings with brightly painted shutters and courtyards bursting with colourful flowers. It was then on to the tiny Elia lighthouse.

Anna stood at the most easterly point of Meganisi and gazed out to sea. Nothing interrupted the view between her and the horizon. It stretched out, a blank slate of blue. Surely anything was possible? Coming out of her reverie, she found herself alone and set off to find the others assessing the suitability of a small pebble beach. With its lack of shade, they returned along the short track and spent a relaxing few hours swimming, snorkelling, and sunbathing on idyllic Fanari beach, with reggae and blues music drifting across from a nearby bar.

Throughout the day, Alex and Filip provided entertaining commentary on the history, mythology, and geography of Meganisi, Lefkada, and the wider Ionian islands. And both were keen to find out where Anna had visited, and her impressions. She realised they'd tailored the day around her likes and dislikes, anticipating when to slow down or stop before being asked by listening and paying close attention.

As they sat under the trees, she shared her fruit, sesame candies, and an idea. 'Thank you for a wonderful day. I've had the best time, and it struck me – why don't you set up a guided cycling tour business alongside hiring bikes? You're massively knowledgeable about the islands, you're entertaining, know the best cycling routes and how to maintain bikes. You're excellent listeners and adapted your speed to suit me. Apokeri seems to attract tourists wanting more than a bucket-and-spade holiday, and it seems to me there's a gap in the market.'

Alex and Filip glanced at each other, and she could almost hear the cogs in their brains cranking.

Filip thoughtfully chewed his nectarine. 'You know what … I think you've got something there.'

'I reckon it could work,' Alex agreed.

'It would bring in another revenue stream, extend the season and is something we could set up relatively quickly and easily.'

'If Daniel was up for it, we could start at least one tour a week in … what do you think … less than a month?' Alex added, and his eyes shone with excitement. 'Thanks. Why the hell didn't we think of it?'

The boys were buzzing, and Anna suggested while cycling to Vathi, why didn't they both discuss it?

'Absolutely not,' Filip exclaimed. 'We are your hosts for the day and will not short-change you. Come on, there's plenty more to see.'

The final stage wound around picturesque northern inlets, so close she could almost touch the water as they cycled past. The steep ground was swathed in low-lying shrubs with a canopy of pine, olive, and cypress trees. The only signs of life along the route were two tavernas, a small yacht club with a few boats, and a handful of houses. By comparison, the harbourside village of Vathi, with its maze of whitewashed houses and alleyways, appeared to be a thriving metropolis. After wandering along the promenade, they sought out a traditional waterside taverna to enjoy the laid-back atmosphere of a highly picturesque port. Indulging in towering ice-cream cones, Filip and Alex invited her to supper that night. Daniel was cooking, and it'd be great if she were there when they pitched the idea.

Initially, Anna was reluctant. She'd met Daniel only briefly, so she was unlikely to help – or, worse, might be a hindrance. And what would he think of her landing unannounced, another mouth to feed? Filip waved away her concerns as Daniel always made enough to feed a small army, people constantly popped in unexpectedly, and she would be a great help. The boys agreed to Anna's request to drop her back at Apokeri Apartments to freshen up. It was an excuse, and the real reason was to buy wine and beer – there was no way she was arriving empty-handed.

***

Bang on eight-thirty, Anna knocked on the open kitchen door. Daniel nodded her in as he continued at the kitchen bench.

'A little something to accompany the meal as a thank you for landing with little notice,' she said.

'Oh … beer. I prefer wine.'

His rudeness brought her up short. He'd been so friendly with everyone the other day outside Nereus. However, now was not the time to react so with a flourish she produced a bottle of white.

'Pity, I drink—'

'And a bottle of red. Or why not combine the two for rosé,' she replied with forced enthusiasm. Was the bloke deliberately trying to get a rise out of her?

Daniel continued mixing the Horiatiki salata. 'I see you've thought of everything.'

'It often pays to,' Anna breezily replied while gripping the bottles. She needed to remain calm but he was testing her patience with his abruptness. 'Where are we eating, and I'll take these out? Do you need any other help?'

'In the courtyard. Once you've done that, grab the plates and cutlery over there,' he said curtly. 'I'll let the guys know the food is ready.'

Anna quickly scuttled about fulfilling her duties whilst seething inside. The bloke was seriously lacking in people skills.

In five minutes, everyone was sat at the courtyard table which was groaning under the weight of so much food. Filip hadn't been joking. In addition to the giant bowl of Greek salad was a plate overflowing with spanakopita (flaky pastry spinach slices), and a substantial dish of lamb kleftiko. The smell of slow-cooked meat with herbs and potatoes was divine. Everything was homemade, apart from the Makris Bakery bread. All four quickly demolished most of the food and a good portion of the wine and beer.

Daniel was quiet and rarely spoke to Anna, preferring to address the other two chatterboxes. In their company he was polite to Anna but it was more a case of Filip and Alex filling in the blanks than Daniel talking. There was undoubtedly a close friendship, but she noticed how Daniel irritably scratched his left eyebrow, joked with Filip, and then changed the subject if he deemed the conversation was getting too personal. However, over a few hours, she managed to discover (mainly from Filip) that Kristina had been a close friend of Daniel's parents and practically raised his late mother, Lilian. His father now lived with his sister's family on their farm. The move back home had been for the best, as he had never recovered from his wife's death and, as the years passed, had found living in Apokeri increasingly painful. Daniel missed his father terribly but opted to stay, put his stamp on the family business and revive its fortunes.

As the evening progressed, Anna noticed Daniel scratched his left eyebrow the more she talked, especially about travelling. Her adventures seemed to annoy him, which seemed strange considering he was setting out himself in a few months. Fearing to jeopardise the boys' chances, she kept quieter than usual, but when Daniel hadn't scratched his eyebrow for at least ten minutes, she caught Filip's eye and took her chance.

'The business is a success from what I hear.'

'It is now … thanks to Filip. He's got a good head on his shoulders – take the business far given a chance. Of course, I could do with more help – especially as I'm going away for a few months.'

Throughout the meal, Filip jiggled his leg. The reverberations had travelled up the table legs, and he'd only stopped when he realised Daniel had paused to grip his cutlery – white knuckles against tanned skin. As Filip launched into his pitch, he started jiggling again. But this time, Anna discreetly placed her hand on his knee. It did the trick. Daniel remained relaxed as Filip explained how employing Alex to help in the workshop and run new guided cycling tours would pay dividends. They would organise the purchase of the transport and associated livery and name the business Round the Bend Cycle Tours for continuity. At first, there would be day trips (picnics provided by Aphrodite Café and Makris Bakery) and then they could extend to multi-day tours. Alex knew Kefalonia as well as Lefkada and Meganisi. The tour would extend into autumn and be promoted in Lefkada and Nidri tourism offices, Nidri's ferry building, and in Odyssey Travel. The accommodation wasn't a problem as Alex would live above the shop.

Filip leaned forward. 'You want to travel in the next few months and visit your Papa. The shop is in safe hands as Alex and I develop the tours. It is a perfect solution – what do you think?'

All three sat on tenterhooks until poker-faced Daniel nodded and shook hands with Filip and Alex.

'Okay, let's do this – I can see a great deal of thought has gone into it. And as they say – nothing ventured, nothing gained. So, Alex – when can you start?'

'Thursday.'

'Thursday? As in four days?' Daniel asked in amazement.

'A month ago, when I heard you needed an extra pair of hands, I took the chance and … I quit my job. A friend is taking my room. If all went to plan, I was returning home first thing tomorrow to pack up my few belongings and head back.'

'Bloody hell, mate – that was brave,' Daniel replied in admiration.

'You don't know the half of it,' Alex responded. 'Remember, I work in the same company as my father. Within twenty minutes of my notice going in, he was blasting me down the phone from the Thessaloniki office.' With a rueful chuckle, he went on. 'For the last month, I've had the pleasure of a daily afternoon call to tell me I was throwing my future away, wasting my life, and would end up a tramp on the street. It became comical. I put him on the office speaker phone, foolishly thinking that would stop him. Oh no, it made things worse – he loves playing to an audience. It got to the stage that my work colleagues decided to create a game called Tirade Bingo. Win prizes for the right words or sayings. Colleagues shouted out encouragement to my father so he would rant longer, and they'd score more. We had a judging panel that awarded marks out of ten at the end of each call, with points deducted for a lacklustre performance. My colleagues, and Papa, thought it was brilliant. Leave was cancelled, people from other offices took part, and by the time I left, I can honestly say I don't know what they missed more – me or my father's phone calls!'

Listening to Alex's tale of woe, Anna was reduced to tears of laughter.

'Oh, it gets worse,' he continued. 'I had no escape at home either. In the evening, a call from my mother laying on the guilt as she wailed down the receiver. "My darling only child, why are you throwing away a career in a global company? You'll go far if you stick in … and your plans … you won't tell us, your own parents! We're so worried … I've hardly eaten … Your father's more accident-prone than ever. Mark my words, son, you'll regret this until you're an old, infirm shell of your youthful self." You can imagine what I've had to deal with.'

His flatmates started to field his calls (buoyed up by his colleagues' antics). They switched between offering soothing words of comfort or agreeing with his mother that their friend was indeed an irresponsible, good-for-nothing young man. In the end, he fled and sought the sanctuary of his grandparents' house, who he knew would support his decision.

Alex grinned. 'My granny is so feisty. When Papa rang, she put her son on speaker and gave him one hell of a dressing down. How dare he behave in that manner? How dare he not support his son? Wait till she next saw him. It was great. He didn't ring back.'

'Stop … stop,' Anna pleaded. 'I'll wet myself if I laugh any more. You're a natural storyteller – it's why you're such a great guide. The tours are going to be a massive success.'

'I hope my parents think the same. I plan to tell them I'm part of a great team – building a cycling empire. Papa is a keen – if disaster-prone – cyclist. You never know, he might think it's a brilliant move.'

A toast was required. Charged with ouzo, everyone raised a glass to Round the Bend Cycle Tours. It took no time to wash up and put everything away with everyone chipping in, and with a doggy bag of leftovers, Anna made to leave and Filip insisted on accompanying her.

They strolled along the deserted moonlit street in comfortable silence. The village slept, its residents and tourists tucked up indoors. Only the gentle lapping of the sea and the whoosh of bat wings past their heads broke the stillness.

'Thank you for stopping me jiggling my leg. Half the time, I don't realise I'm doing it, and I know it infuriates Daniel,' Filip said as they walked past a lifeless Aphrodite.

Anna breathed in the heavy scent of jasmine from a flower display. 'I figured it was best not to irritate him when you needed his buy-in, like.'

'I'm amazed he agreed so readily. Usually, it takes ages … and invariably involves plenty of spreadsheets, pros and cons columns, lots of calculations, and endless discussion.'

'Maybe it's because he's got his mind on travelling and is content for you to develop the business?' Anna suggested.

The narrow alleyway between the Post Office and the gallery meant walking in single file. On reaching her apartment block, she stood lost in thought.

'Is everything okay?'

'Oh yes, everything's fine … it's so beautiful here. I wonder why Daniel would ever want to leave?' Her voice echoed along the stone walls. 'Thank you for an amazing day – I'm dead chuffed about the tour business.'

She gave him a quick peck on the cheek and called, 'Sleep tight,' before closing the door. There was a moment's silence before his footsteps retreated, and it was sometime later when she moved from the foyer.

Chapter Six

Anna sat bolt upright, called to action by some unseen force. It was early, but a gentle chugging from outside saw her pad to the balcony. The Apokeri fishing fleet was heading out past Tharesseti. She couldn't ignore the lump of rock – it demanded answers that she didn't have. She yawned and shivered. It was far too early, and climbing into bed she slipped back to sleep.

***

It was bright sunshine the next time she woke. In no rush, it was after nine when she arrived at the bike shop to find Sofia dropping off her delivery.

'I'm officially addicted to these,' Anna said as she held up a sultana swirl. 'I must have just missed you at the café. Otherwise, I'd have brought the basket up.'

'This one comes from a good family,' Sofia called out to Daniel as he restocked the drinks fridge and chose not to respond. 'You've just missed my son. He's gone to Lefkada to pick up bike parts.'

After a brief conversation about Meganisi, Sofia excused herself. The café was short-staffed as her niece had called in sick yet again, leaving Anna wondering if Filip had managed to warn his cousin.

Anna watched Daniel line up all the drinks labels. 'I take it Sofia doesn't know about Alex coming back and the tour plans?'

'No, not yet. Filip said he's going to tell them tonight,' he said as if each word pained him.

Anna stood and pursed her lips as she waited for her scooter keys, but he did not get them. From behind the workshop door came a snuffling, scratching, pining sound.

'It was … It was a good idea of yours. About the guided cycling tours. So obvious. Too obvious. I should have thought of it … Not let some—'

'Oh well, no harm done,' Anna quickly replied, not wanting to hear the end of his sentence. All she wanted was the keys so she could get the hell out of there.

And still, Daniel did not fetch them. She coughed but he refused to meet her eyes and from behind him, the sound was getting louder and more desperate. He muttered angrily under his breath and then finally had the courtesy to look up.

'You're going to have to come with me. It would appear that someone at least wants to see you.'

Begrudgingly, Daniel pushed open the door and gave a curt order. Anna followed and was almost flattened by a massive, fast-moving furball. Huge front paws reared up on Anna's shoulders, and a large tongue enthusiastically licked her face.

'You are honoured,' Daniel managed. 'She only does that to Filip and me.'

'Who's a gorgeous girl?' Anna cried, giving Cassie a good scratch behind her short floppy ears. 'You're so beautiful. Sit, sit, sit. What a clever girl. Now go get a treat from your dad for being so good.'

Cassie bounded across to Daniel and sat wagging her tail, enormously pleased with herself. On the other hand, Daniel looked furious as he fished a dog biscuit out of his pocket. Anna smiled sweetly at her small victory as he dropped the keys into her outstretched hand.

***

With a promise to return the scooter the following evening, Anna took the steep road out of Apokeri and joined the main highway, where for the next two days, she zigzagged across Lefkada's southern half.

Jeremy was right; the island was stunning.

Spectacular Porto Katsiki beach – a narrow strip of white hemmed in by towering limestone cliffs and an intense turquoise sea – took her breath away. So did the skill, speed, and agility of the windsurfers at Vassiliki. Beautiful Athani entertained with its steady stream of coaches, mini-buses, cars, and mopeds squeezing past one another with millimetres to spare and disgorging tourists to throng the small mountain village.

She even managed to shoehorn two more locations in after recommendations from Daniel, of all people. During her early morning run along the Apokeri cliffs, he'd unexpectedly appeared with Cassie, and the narrow track forced him to converse. He could have delivered his suggestions in an altruistic, enthusiastic manner. But instead, he opted to lace them with sarcasm.

'What, you mean to tell me you don't know about the snorkelling gem of Mikros Gialos beach and the views of Vlicho Bay from Katochori village? The person who prides herself on knowing everything about everything? Well, well, that is a surprise. After everything Filip has told me about you …' Anna felt she'd shown enormous self-restraint (not her strongest trait) in thanking him kindly before sprinting away. And the galling part – he'd been right.

Even with a packed itinerary, Anna failed to banish thoughts of the future and John. And with the clock ticking down, they increasingly intruded.

Pretty fishing village Sivota, with its backdrop of tree-clad hills, was set around one of the most beautiful bays in Lefkada. She'd arrived early to avoid the hordes of tourists. It was tranquil on her peaceful stroll around the deep horseshoe harbour, past unopened waterside tavernas with tables and chairs next to the clear blue water. She'd received and returned smiles, nods, and waves from those breakfasting aboard impressive private yachts lined up along the quayside. No wonder they were all happy, with those marvellous views. And as she was surrounded by all that beauty, John forced himself into her head. He'd also surfaced as she'd explored a fourth-century ruined castle at Poros and looked out to Ithaca and Kefalonia from Cape Ducato lighthouse. The man wouldn't give up, so it had been a relief to chat across the balconies with her Cornish neighbours on her penultimate evening. They'd been coming to Apokeri for years on walking holidays (and still got lost) and confided that Kristina's apartments were by far and away the best.

It was time to return the scooter, and after following narrow twisting roads (just to see where they went) on a small Vlicho Bay peninsular, she headed back. Zipping past the sparkling water, she returned to the problem at hand.

What to do next?

There seemed to be two clear choices. Go to London with John and try to make it work by doing something she didn't want to do. Or go home to Newcastle, newly single, and back to a safe office job till she saved up for her next adventure.

She had an admin job at home. It was another dead-end one, but it proved useful during university, and the people were nice. However, now she had an Ancient History degree, shouldn't she get the best career with it?

After all, wasn't that the whole point in slogging her guts out for the last three years? Was John right? Was she being unrealistic and unreasonably stubborn? It wouldn't be the first time. And London probably offered the best employment options? But it was a big, crowded, suffocating city. Or did she stick to her guns and her dreams, even if it meant going her own way and saving for the next adventure without him? It would give her the freedom to do exactly what she wanted and when. Or …

Anna's thoughts trailed off as she negotiated the mountainous interior road. At least there was a meal with Kristina to look forward to. There was no way she was going to spend her final night driving herself up the wall with circular arguments. She'd wasted too much time on them already.

***

Anna pushed open the door to find Filip plumping up the sofa cushions. He glanced at the clock. She'd made it back five minutes before closing time.

'I was beginning to think you weren't coming back.'

'So did I. There's so much to see,' Anna replied and handed across the keys and helmet.

'I wouldn't have minded if you'd brought it back first thing tomorrow. But Daniel ... well he likes all the paperwork done the night before.'

'Always best to keep the boss happy,' she said. 'Anyway, moving on to more important things, how did your parents take your news? I'm dying to find out, man.'

Filip hit a few keys and logged off the laptop. 'Amazingly, Papa was the most positive, saying it was good to see me finally making something of myself. However, Mama was full of concern. She thinks I'll be working too hard ever to meet someone.'

Anna remembered her supermarket conversation. 'I'm sensing a theme in this village with mothers wanting to marry off their sons.'

He sighed. 'You're so right. The way Mama goes on, anyone would think I was forty-three, not twenty-three. Thankfully, my sister took some of the pressure off me by getting married and then providing an adored grandchild.'

'It's a pity they live in Athens. Your parents must rarely get to see them.'

'No, not as much as they'd like, but they're here for the Flower and Food Festival. It'll be great to see them.'

***

Anna deliberately gave herself time for a snooze before showering and getting ready for dinner with Kristina. It was her last night, and she wanted to make an effort. With her flyaway hair behaving itself for once and taking more time applying make-up, she was remarkably polished – especially in a short-sleeved red paisley cotton dress and red ballerina-style shoes. Kristina as always looked effortlessly elegant in a simple linen dress and matching crocheted cardigan in peacock blue. A splash more colour came from a cerise and gold scarf, and bright-pink painted toenails peeked out of soft leather open-toed sandals.

'You look amazing,' Anna said. 'One sophisticated lady.'

Kristina laughed as she curtseyed. 'Not bad for an octogenarian.'

'What! Sorry to be rude – but how old are you?'

'I'll be eighty-three next February.'

'No way! I thought you were in your early seventies.'

'That's what you get from sun protection and a healthy diet.'

'There's hope for me. I'm good at the first … but I love chocolate too much,' Anna admitted. 'And talking of my favourite subject, if you're ready let's venture into the night and enjoy some tasty Greek food.'

***

Apollo Taverna had been a fixture in Apokeri for over a century – continuously owned by the Stipopolous family and currently managed by the youngest and most gregarious son, Max. The restaurant was a real family affair with employees related to Max or his wife. Their mothers ruled the kitchen with a rod of iron. The two matriarchs in their early sixties had no intention of handing over the reins any time soon. And would tell anyone who cared to listen that theirs was the best Greek cuisine in Lefkada. It was no empty boast as each was an accomplished cook. The women dictated the menu, which delivered an array of delicious traditional Greek cuisine and made the venue popular with Lefkada islanders and seasonal tourists. Anna had initially wondered if the beach tavernas and the café had taken any trade. However, judging by how packed it was, there was plenty of business to go around.

The taverna, set over three floors, stood in the village square. Couples and groups sat cheek by jowl at red-and-white checkerboard tablecloths. A long bar ran the full depth of the room, where four staff served customers sitting on barstools. The powerhouse was at the back and in full swing, with various chefs shouting instructions. The waiting staff bustled backwards and forwards, constantly collecting orders from the serving counter in a well-choreographed dance. A staircase disappeared upwards, and the first floor fronted an open-aired balcony packed with diners. The final floor was on the roof. Brightly coloured canopies provided overhead cover and allowed views of the village square, including its whitewashed church and primary school. The rooftop also gave views of the beach, pier, and across to tiny pinpricks of light from Tharesseti.

Apollo Taverna was an assault on the senses. The aroma of delicious food drifted across to Anna, chatter and laughter filled the air, and there was an explosion of colour from flowers and vines that climbed, draped, and smothered the frontage.

'That's … amazing.'

'You'll not be surprised to hear that Apollo has won the Best Dressed Building five years running in the annual Apokeri Flower and Food Festival,' Kristina replied. 'Come, let us find a seat.'

At the entrance was jovial Max, immaculately dressed in black trousers and a white short-sleeved shirt pulling at his belly. He reminded Anna of a portly and younger Tom Jones as he

49

welcomed in a steady stream of people, then called to his waiting team to organise their seating.

On seeing Kristina, he broke into a broad grin and embraced her. 'Kalispera. It is always a pleasure to see you … and who is your delightful young companion?'

Kristina smiled. 'This is Anna – she is currently staying in the apartments.'

'Ah, the infamous Anna of the cycle tour fame, which I have heard so much about.' He saw Anna's surprised face. 'The benefits of a small village, my dear. Filip's already visited my wonderful wife Dania to promote the tours. And Vasili told me all about his son's venture when he dropped off our bread delivery yesterday. Nothing stays secret for long in this place. But let us not stand on ceremony. Welcome to Apollo, where your tastebuds will be tantalised. Follow me as I escort you to Kristina's favourite table – you are lucky it's available.'

Max kept up a steady stream of conversation as he took them past the bar and along a narrow corridor that opened into a high-walled courtyard adorned with roses, vines, oleander, bougainvillaea, honeysuckle, and bay trees. In a corner stood an ancient olive tree with tiny lights decorating its lower branches – it was to a table below that Max guided them.

Anna's eyes shone as she looked around. 'This is beautiful.'

'Thank you, my dear,' he proudly replied. 'However, the credit must go to Kristina. It was her vision, her design and she tends it, for more years than she probably cares to remember.'

Once seated, he handed them a leatherbound menu and vanished with their drinks order. After his non-stop chatter, the quietness of the courtyard became evident. It had a very different feel from the rest of the taverna. Here, tranquillity enveloped guests at tables tucked between the planting for intimate conversations.

'I bet there have been stacks of marriage proposals here,' Anna whispered.

'Yes, it makes me happy to think I've played a small part in bringing joy to so many people,' Kristina said wistfully.

For the next hour, Anna and Kristina chatted about everything and anything. The topics of conversation flowed between Kristina's skill and love of garden design, her English boarding-school upbringing, Anna's passion for ancient history and a need to experience as much as possible, to seize life and enjoy it. But at the same time, she feared her life was rootless, directionless. She wanted freedom but for it to have meaning and not drift aimlessly, which is what most of her life sometimes felt like.

After the main course of roast monkfish, stewed fennel, and green olives, Anna relaxed into her chair. 'Even though we only met a few days ago, I open up and talk to you about things I'd only tell my closest friends.' She took a deep breath and continued. 'So … it seems fitting that you're the first person I want to tell. I'm not returning to the UK tomorrow with my friends. I'm staying in Apokeri … I love it here. It … It's hard to put my feelings into words.' Anna said and laughed. 'Okay, not that hard. Apokeri will have its irritations, and it won't all be plain sailing, but – without sounding too melodramatic – if I get on that plane tomorrow, I'll regret it forever. It's the wrong thing to do.' She sat back with her heart hammering and looked into Kristina's calm blue eyes. 'Do you think I'm being foolish?'

Reaching across the table, Kristina grasped Anna's hands and quietly but fiercely spoke. 'You have one life to live, Anna. Make it count. And no, I don't think you're being foolish – far from it. I believe everyone knows what they want … but many people are too afraid to seek it out and make it happen. I think you have the strength and courage to do what it takes to make you happy.'

Anna brushed tears away. 'I must be getting emotional with age. I rarely cry. Thank you, that means … a lot.'

Kristina gave Anna a wry smile. 'I knew you'd stay.'

'How? I only made my mind up now.'

'Instinct – I sensed we'd become good friends. It's why I told you so much about myself.'

'I think your intuition, our friendship, and my decision calls for a pudding, don't you?'

Max materialised at their table with the dessert and drinks menu as if by some sixth sense.

On seeing Anna's tear-stained face, he frowned. 'I hope you've not been crying because the meal was bad? But that cannot be true.'

'No, the food was wonderful,' Anna exclaimed. 'And I am ready to see your delicious desserts – healthy eating can wait for another day.'

Chapter Seven

Anna closed her eyes and, sitting on her third-floor balcony, let the sun and a strong coffee work their magic. The air was still cool, and she gratefully wrapped her hands around the hot mug. Nobody else was up in the apartment block, and from the warren of streets, the only sounds were a distant door closing followed by a short bark. From the hills opposite, the post-dawn chorus chirruped away. She was tired but too excited to sleep. After leaving Apollo, the two women had hunkered down in Kristina's cosy kitchen and talked long into the night, sipping on a steady supply of herbal tea to hatch a plan.

Anna stretched and yawned. 'Let's see if it works.'

Kristina had been very pragmatic when Anna ran through possibilities to support herself and was thoroughly dismayed at her cleaning job idea. "Silly child! You have a good brain – use it," she'd counselled. "Play to your strengths as I do." That was undoubtedly true. Kristina explained that she used a bartering system to acquire almost everything she needed, and the rest came from gallery sales. Anna still had no idea what had brought Kristina to Apokeri – the woman continued to avoid what must be a highly emotive subject. It was a compelling mystery, and for once in her life, Anna did not push for details. If Kristina wanted to divulge her past, she would do so in her own time.

She necked back the remaining coffee and tidied up. There was a lot to do, and it wasn't going to get done sitting daydreaming.

***

She appraised the apartment (after a final check for stray underwear) and nodded with satisfaction. The cleaners would be arriving later, but that didn't mean leaving the place a mess.

It was time for the human packhorse to head for a new home, and she didn't have far to go.

The previous night, Kristina had declared with absolute certainty that Anna must move in with her, and would brook no arguments. "My dearest child, I have plenty of space, and it will be delightful to have your wonderful company."

Letting herself in through the gate, the melodic sound of Swedish singing drifted through the garden.

'Kaliméra,' Anna said as she entered the kitchen. 'Well, I'm all set. Everything is packed. I've tidied up after myself and stripped the bed.' Depositing the keys in Kristina's outstretched palm, Anna motioned to her belongings. 'Where should I put my stuff?'

'I'll show you during the guided tour,' Kristina explained and set down her familiar mug of black coffee.

Slipping off her trusty walking boots, Anna followed Kristina up a flight of steep wooden stairs. The Scandinavian décor continued on the first floor with sanded pine floors and whitewashed walls.

Kristina motioned ahead. 'Your room is on the left. And mine is on the right.'

A snug ensuite was by the door with a generous walk-in shower, toilet, and sink. Bright cerise towels and a bathmat provided splashes of colour. Patio doors flooded the large airy bedroom with light and led onto a balcony where Anna pictured sitting at the table, sipping on something and enjoying stunning sunsets. Her room was simply furnished with a letterbox stained-glass window projecting shafts of multicoloured light onto the double bed below. On the walls hung a collection of gilt-framed intricate oil paintings of different Lefkada churches, and tapered candles reinforced a spiritual feel. However, the most noticeable feature was above Anna's head. Set into the wooden planked ceiling were six intricately carved oak beams.

'I'm inside a ship and a church at the same time,' Anna exclaimed. 'My heartbeat is slowing down as it's so restful.'

'Excellent, that's the effect I was after. The beams are from an ancient Greek sailing boat broken up years ago. I rescued them and did all the detailing myself.'

'Very impressive. How on earth did you get them up there? They must weigh an absolute ton?'

'They're hollow, which helps, but it was difficult, messy, and time-consuming as I decided – in my infinite wisdom – to do the same in my room. It took four of us with a winch. Luckily Daniel's father had the strength of two men. Daniel takes after his father there,' Kristina said and smiled at the memory. 'That was years ago – before Daniel. I cooked lots of meals to repay that favour.'

After gratefully dumping her belongings, the tour continued. The door to Kristina's bedroom was shut and they moved across the landing to a Moroccan-inspired family bathroom, painted a restful chalky pea-green. Tiny mosaic tiles and coloured glass made up the bath panel, splashback, cubicle walls shower and a counter housing two sunken copper hand basins.

'I wasn't expecting this.' Anna ran her fingers across a metal filigree lantern. 'It's beautiful.'

'Thank you, I made all the tiles myself and used recycled wine bottles for the coloured glass thirty years ago – a labour of love.'

The penultimate room spanned the back two-thirds of the building and was an opulent French Renaissance boudoir. A vast pale grey antique upholstered bed took centre stage at one end, dressed with luxurious bedding fit for a queen and behind it was a duck-egg-blue feature wall with a mural of flowers. There was a carefully positioned eclectic mix of antique French furniture and a gilded mirror and chandelier provided elegant final touches with double doors leading to a wrought-iron balcony.

'I'm seriously running out of adjectives to describe your home. You certainly missed your calling as an interior designer. Where did you source everything?'

Kristina gave a mischievous grin and winked. 'It all comes down to knowing where to look.'

Next door, a one-time decent-sized bedroom was an orderly storage-room-cum-workshop with floor-to-ceiling wardrobes, a sewing workbench, and a dressmaker's dummy swathed in scarves and beaded necklaces. A narrow glass door gave access to the wrought-iron balcony.

'Come on.' Kristina beckoned Anna upwards. 'There's plenty more to see.'

Up the final flight of stairs was a roof terrace with a three-foot perimeter wall. Sculpted steel poles reached skywards with fairy lights strung between them. Three sides provided uninterrupted views – eastwards to the hills, southwards over Apokeri village, and westwards out to sea. Seating areas and a handful of sun loungers followed the sun's passage through the sky, tucked between rows and rows of raised planting beds brimming with flowers and shrubs.

'It's a garden nursery in the sky.'

'Yes, this is where many Apokeri flowers and shrubs start their lives. In return for goods and services, I provide them to most businesses, and the village benefits by looking beautiful.'

Anna sniffed a pompom dahlia. 'A wise woman.'

'Not always,' Kristina admitted. 'That comes with age.'

On the northern side of the rooftop sat a single-storey rustic building – its lower section blended into the whitewashed wall. The upper section was a patchwork of windows with cheery blue frames supporting a slightly wonky pitched terracotta tiled roof with a small metal chimney poking up at one end.

Kristina pushed open the door and folded back the shutters. 'Come and see where I create my masterpieces.'

It was like being on the bridge of a ship with an almost three-sixty view. Inside the artist's studio, easels stood with an array of paintings in varying stages of completion. A potter's wheel stool in one corner, alongside an electric kiln. Window ledges were jam-packed with glass bottles, driftwood, shells, and pebbles. Against one wall, old wooden doors, panels, and other characterful wood were neatly stacked. It was a place for the creative spirit to run wild. Tucked next to a bench – neatly lined with paintbrushes, coloured pencils, and charcoals – was a daybed enveloped in an enormous handmade throw, colourful cushions, and a pillow. Alongside it was a small fridge, where a kettle, mug, glass, plate, and cutlery for one sat. Only a tiny cupboard (which housed a toilet and sink) interrupted the view. A diminutive potbellied woodburning stove provided the means of heating the sanctuary.

'Wow,' Anna said and pivoted on her heels. 'You must spend hours up here.'

'In the winter, I closet myself up here for days and am forced downstairs only when I run out of food,' Kristina admitted. 'So, what do you think of your new home? Can you be happy here?'

'Happy … I'm thrilled. Thank you so much for your kindness. I feel very privileged to be sharing it.'

The house was indeed beautiful, but only parts felt homely – the kitchen, the garden, and the rooftop with its studio. The rest of the rooms had a vacant feel – like entering a rarely visited museum where time stood still – and evoked the same melancholy feeling as the seascape paintings. Anna hoped moving in would inject life into the grandiose building and create happy memories.

Standing on the rooftop garden of her new home, in a new country and a world away from Newcastle, Anna pushed back her shoulders and declared with more courage than she felt, 'Well, that's stage one of the plans completed – the move. Now for stage two – breaking the news to my nearest and dearest.'

Detecting a chink in her armour, Kristina grasped Anna's hand and gave it a reassuring squeeze. 'Everything will be fine, my child.'

***

Anna didn't have long to wait before telling the first raft of people. At nine forty-five, she stood nervously on the pier. The original plan was to meet at ten and spend a final hour in Apokeri before the thirty-minute transfer to Preveza airport. The group would then split – six boarding a Manchester flight and then final journeys to Tyneside, Cumbria, and Yorkshire. Whilst the other four took a London flight to friends or parents.

She heard raucous laughter as the boat approached, and her stomach did a slow somersault. It did another one when everyone saw her and started waving energetically. After much backslapping, handshaking, and kissing of their genial host, the group was back on solid ground and bid Jeremy a safe return trip to Tharesseti for some much-deserved peace.

'You missed an awesome time,' Simon shouted above multiple conversations.

Charles checked his watch and rubbed his hands. 'Right, gang, we have time for one last drink at the handily placed beach taverna. Let's squeeze every last drop out of this holiday.'

With a unanimous cheer, everyone began to move off.

'John … Can we … catch up?' Anna asked hesitantly.

'Yes, that would be perfect,' John replied haltingly and called out to the retreating posse. 'Hey guys, we'll catch up in a bit.' He pointed towards the small fishing harbour. 'Let's go this way.'

Neither said a word, and the silence deepened. Coming to an unspoken mutual halt, John launched into what appeared to be a well-rehearsed speech.

'I've given this a great deal of thought … and it's best if we called it a day. Things aren't the same anymore. Since I accepted

58

that London job, well there's been a marked change. At first, I put it down to you being worried about a long-distance relationship and figured it'd be fine once I started. But we've moved further apart during this trip – it's clear we don't want the same things anymore.'

'Go on,' Anna prompted, sensing John needed to get more off his chest.

He took a deep breath. 'And the thing is, I-I've got feelings for someone else ... and it's mutual.' He kept his eyes firmly on the horizon and quickly ploughed on. 'At first, I dismissed it, but the attraction intensified as the trip continued. And I started to suspect that it wasn't one-sided. However, it wasn't until we got to Tharesseti that I finally confessed. And I was right – she felt the same way.' He turned, and there was no deception in his eyes. 'No one else knows. We made a pact to tell you first before we did anything – because it was the right thing to do.' His voice was wretched as he clasped her hands. 'I'm so sorry ... I-I never meant for it to happen like this. The last thing I want to do is – but I have to be honest. I do hope we can all still be friends? Li feels terrible about it.'

Anna stood for a few moments digesting the news. The breaking-up speech was not a complete surprise (although it was annoying that he'd got there first), but John and Li? No way. She'd never suspected a thing, never received the slightest hint and imagined neither had the others. So that's why Li had flirted with Daniel – to make John jealous. The woman knew how to play the game. And the more Anna thought about it, the more she could see them as a couple. John and Li had the same interests, their personalities were better suited, and they were extremely driven with a thirst to prove themselves. Both would achieve whatever they wanted. And from an entirely selfish point of view, it made things a hell of a lot easier.

Looking at an apprehensive John, she smiled. 'Thank you for being so honest. I appreciate the fact that you told me first.

You're right, our relationship has run its course. We've been drifting apart for a while and now want very different things from when we first got together. And the news about you and Li … I certainly didn't see that one coming. But it's fine – you can still count on me as a friend.'

He hugged her and looked back at Nereus. 'I guess we'd better get back to the others. Do you want to tell them about us now?'

'I suspect it'll be the first thing they'll ask after finding out what I'm about to tell you.'

And as they walked back toward the taverna, she ran through her decision.

'Bloody hell. Anna, are you sure? That's up there with your massive decisions.'

Anna laughed. 'Well, you know me. I don't do things by half. And you're right, but most of my life-changing spur-of-the-moment decisions have been the best things I ever did – so I reckon this one will turn out okay.'

'I suppose so,' John mused, sounding far from convinced. 'But what did your parents have to say? I can't imagine the news went down well with your dad.'

'The thing is … they don't know yet.' She caught sight of his stunned face and grimaced. 'Don't look at me like that. I only decided to stay last night, so it was too late to call. Can you imagine if I'd rung any later than half eight! Christ Almighty, my dad would've pitched a fit – even more than normal. I've still got that delightful conversation to come.'

John put a consoling hand on her shoulder. 'Good luck there – you're gonna need it.'

Chapter Eight

An anxious-looking Li had loitered at the taverna entrance but was now all smiles as she sat next to John and waved out the window. The others all shouted goodbyes and good luck from the departing minibus. As predicted, there'd been the expected questions about John and herself – enormous surprise being the overriding reaction – but once everyone realised the breakup was mutual and she was determined to stay, everybody wished her well. There was even time to hear that Kristina had been right, Jeremy planned to turn his villa into a hotel. The blossoming relationship between John and Li remained under wraps.

After watching her friends disappear – and wondering if she'd see any of them again – it was time for stage three to kick in. Anna had deliberately glossed over how she intended to support herself because, as it stood, things were up in the air. Hopefully, that would be rectified in the next hour, and unsurprisingly, the suggestion had come from Kristina.

The previous night, her new landlady recounted how Daniel had been badgering her to relinquish management of the apartments. He believed it was too much with Kristina up at all hours to welcome guests, run the gallery, and tend her gardens and village flower beds – in addition to creating the festival flower displays and all the time spent in the studio. As Kristina reeled off her duties (clearly enjoying them all), Anna was loathe to admit she agreed with Daniel – that workload was more than enough for one person.

Daniel owned the gallery, house, and apartments – the land having been in his mother's family for generations. When his father moved back, ownership transferred to him. Kristina lived rent-free and kept monies from gallery sales after expenses to manage the apartments and run the gallery. Both enterprises had become increasingly busy over the last few years, leading to Daniel's repeated pleas to split the role. Kristina had refused, believing acceptance would be an admission of advancing age which she had no intention of giving in to.

Every Wednesday, Daniel came to lunch and caught up on business affairs. The plan was for Kristina to finally succumb to Daniel's wish, which would cleverly create a ready-made role for Anna. Unsure at first, she pointed out that welcoming guests at all hours would prevent her from getting a much-needed second job. However, there was a ready-made answer. Guests would let themselves in using the external multi-key safe. If it was such a good idea, why not do that already? It was simple. Kristina admitted to being a nosy so-and-so who wanted to meet guests on arrival to give them the once-over. With her mind put to rest on that front, Anna agreed to the plan.

A little after one, the shop bell tinkled as Daniel arrived and Anna heard his arrival from the kitchen, where she'd been banished to. Despite Kristina's reassurances, she had spent the last twenty minutes pacing backwards and forwards like a caged animal. This needed to work, but she didn't hold out much hope – judging on past encounters Daniel hated her guts. Why on earth would he give her a job? Thank heavens she'd remained civil to him, otherwise there'd be no hope. Anna grabbed the tray of food Kristina had prepared and dashed into the garden. Moments later, the pair appeared and Daniel barely acknowledged Anna before enthusiastically tucking into the food.

'As always, this is amazing, Kristina. You're so good to me … and know now how much … I love briam,' he managed between mouthfuls before quizzing her about the latest apartment guests, the number of recent bookings, and gallery takings.

Kristina provided a rundown of the guests. A lovely Greek family from Lamia was in both apartments on the middle floor for the next fortnight with the grandparents in one, and the parents with their six-year-old triplets in the other. The grandmother, intended to give her son and daughter-in-law some much-needed rest so the children would probably spend most nights, if not every night, sleeping with them. Subsequently, Kristina had factored in more cleaning time. A delightful couple from southwest England was on the top floor all week. It was their fifth visit, and they had already booked in for next July. An extremely quiet young French couple from Marseilles was on the ground floor.

Daniel nodded. 'Yes, I've met them – came in yesterday and hired a scooter for the week. Extremely polite – I can't see a problem there.'

Then there was a Greek family from Louros for ten nights. Parents in their early thirties, with a toddler and a beautiful six-month-old baby girl. And tonight, a couple from Rome was arriving for three days as a surprise fortieth wedding anniversary. They'd visited Apokeri thirty years ago, and the wife had always wanted to return. As a nice touch, the usual welcome pack would include flowers, homemade chocolates, and a bottle of homemade elderflower champagne.

Daniel chased the last piece of courgette around his plate before loading on seconds. 'Excellent. How you remember so much about the guests … is beyond me.'

Kristina smiled indulgently. 'Because it's good for business, my dear. And it's why I believe so many guests return and recommend us. I could say much more about our guests, but I know it wouldn't interest you.'

'You're right – a typical bloke in that respect. But I'm interrupting. Carry on.'

Kristina paused as if debating whether to address his typical bloke comment before explaining the apartments were fully booked till the end of September. She'd turned people away and recommended other Apokeri accommodation, but most accepted the alternative dates. The season was extending. At one time, it was rare to have bookings outside late May to early Oct, but now people wanted to book year-round.

'Yes, I've noticed, and that's why I reckon the cycle tours will be successful. Dania was excited about advertising them, and she knows her stuff – they've already got trips booked up next week. I think they were both surprised by the take-up.'

'The apartment business is thriving, and the gallery. I've sold several larger canvases, as well as plenty of prints. The pottery always does well, along with the jewellery. It's non-stop, and I must get back into the studio to replenish the stock ... and with the gardens, I hate to say it ... but I'm exhausted.'

Daniel frowned. 'I keep telling you to slow down – but will you listen?'

Anna smiled to herself. The trap was sprung.

'It's funny you should say that, because ... well ... I've been giving the matter some thought and finally concede managing the apartments, running the gallery, and working the gardens – it's too much for me. And as you rightly point out' – Kristina sighed – 'I'm not getting any younger, am I?'

Daniel pushed his plate away and raised his hands skywards. 'At last – it's taken you long enough. But it does present us with a problem. It'll be nigh on impossible to find the right person in peak season. And whoever it is, they've got big shoes to fill.'

'As I see it.' Kristina began ticking off each attribute on her fingers. 'We need someone who lives in the village, has excellent customer service, is proactive and full of ideas, friendly but at the same time a no-nonsense type, needs attention to detail, and with excellent English.'

'Sounds perfect,' Daniel replied longingly. 'If we found that person, I'd bite their hand off.'

Kristina beamed. 'Well, this is your lucky day as I've got an exact match. And even better, they can start immediately.'

Daniel gripped the table. 'Who?'

'Me!' Anna piped up.

'You?' He disdainfully looked her up and down. 'I need someone who is going to stick around and not leave when the shine of the holiday adventure wears off. Living here all year is very different from spending a few sun-filled days sightseeing, you know.'

Anna held herself in check. He was appraising her like something unpleasant found on the sole of a shoe! Who the hell did he think he was?

She clenched her fists under the table and swallowed her first expletive retort. 'Yes, Daniel. I am well aware that a Greek holiday resort is very different in the middle of winter. And I would counter... What makes you any more certain someone from Apokeri will stay any longer? Do you not agree they can just as easily leave for a new life somewhere else? Like Filip's sister Stefania? And haven't you just hired Alex from Piraeus because he has the right skill set?

Daniel sat across the table staring at her.

Warming to the theme, she jabbed her finger at him. 'You said it would be a tall order to find someone with the required qualities. I have them all. I live in Apokeri, and I have excellent customer service skills with glowing references. I'm full of ideas – like the cycle tours – and already have ones for the apartments. I'm friendly and approachable but not a pushover. I'm thorough and English. I'm not yet fluent in Greek, but I know enough to hold a conversation. I've been reading Greek newspapers on my trip, and whilst I certainly don't understand everything, I get the gist – and living here, my Greek will improve. I don't give up easily or disappear at the first sign of things getting tough. I'm independent and have lived away from home since I was eighteen. I studied modern-day Greece as part of my Ancient History degree, which means I know something about the country's political, social, and cultural makeup, so I don't have a rose-tinted tourist perspective. To sum up, I've travelled extensively and worked in different places across the globe. I've spent the last five weeks exploring five Ionian and nine Cyclades islands. And in all that time, Apokeri is the only place I've ever fallen in love with – the only place I want to settle in.'

After delivering her impassioned speech, she fell silent and waited. Daniel's face was devoid of emotion. He finally turned towards Kristina, who raised her eyebrows.

'In my opinion, you thoroughly deserved that. And remember, dearest boy, I too was an outsider over sixty years ago. So—'

'Okay!' He held his hands up. 'I might have been a bit harsh. And Anna, you're right. Someone from Apokeri could quit or probably do half a job because they're a distant relative or an old schoolmate. You answered eloquently, and I cannot argue with a single point. I, therefore, agree with Kristina – you're an ideal candidate, and I am pleased to offer you the job. Do you accept?'

'Yes, please.' Anna shook the outstretched hand. 'I promise you won't regret it.'

'Excellent.' Kristina clapped her hands. 'Anna, would you make us some coffee?'

'Certainly. And thanks again, Daniel.'

***

Daniel watched Anna walk back into the kitchen, carrying the dirty dishes. Kristina waited until she'd disappeared and then asked, 'Well, what do you think?'

He irritably scratched his left eyebrow. 'Listening to her prattle on the other night and just now – she's clearly never had any real responsibilities in her entire life. All she's done is travel here, there, and everywhere, saving up enough from boring office jobs. Granted, she did have the gumption to knuckle down and finish a degree her darling parents undoubtedly financed. Heaven forbid she had to work while studying. And Ancient History? I mean, how useful is that going to be? It's hardly a trade.'

'Don't be nasty, Daniel. It doesn't suit you.'

'And she's always smiling, happy, and so goddamn helpful. How can anybody be that cheerful and nice all the time?'

Kristina collected together a few loose crumbs to place on the bird table. 'Anyone would think you had sour grapes. Is it because she just wiped the floor with you? I did find that highly amusing. Or is there another reason—'

Daniel fiddled with his placemat. 'I gave her the job, didn't I?'

'Yes, you did. And thank you. Look, she'll be perfect, and that's the most important thing – regardless of whether you like her or not.'

'Mama always said you were an excellent judge of character, and … I've never known you to be wrong about anyone.' Daniel placed his forearms on the table. 'Your intuition is spookily accurate … are you always right?'

Kristina's calm blue eyes gazed across the pristine garden.

'Kristina?'

She was clutching her crucifix and had retreated into a distant past. Daniel recognised the signs. He'd witnessed it countless times before, as had his mother. His friend – no, she was much more than that, she was the closest thing to family. He had blood ties in Apokeri but found his uncles and cousins boisterous, loud, and in your face. He was more like Kristina – quiet, orderly, and an observer rather than a participant. But then again, different. Kristina sought the solace of the past, whereas he looked toward the future. After all these years, this wise woman before him remained a mystery. Where did she disappear to? What scenes played through that shrewd mind? The clucking of laying hens drifted across the garden.

'Sorry … I-I got distracted. Thinking about …' she trailed off and adjusted her scarf. 'Make the effort and get to know her. What harm will it do?'

Daniel crossed his arms. 'No thanks. My traitorous dog is friendly enough for both of us. The rest I'll leave to Filip, Alex, and your good self. Christ, here she comes – Little Miss Bloody Sunshine – with the drinks.'

Anna smiled as she passed Daniel his coffee, but he abruptly stood up.

'I must get back to work – can't afford to sit in the sun all day. Some of us have businesses to run.' Kissing Kristina on the cheeks, he gave a slight nod to Anna. 'Welcome aboard.'

'Thanks – boss.'

But he'd already turned and was striding away up the garden.

***

Anna held the coffee cup in mid-air, feeling a total prat. What an absolute dick! Fine, if that's the way he wanted to be. She'd argued well to secure her job – and that was the main thing. Pity the sense of satisfaction had lasted less than sixty seconds before being doused in cold water. She slowly started to smirk. Okay, Sonny Jim, two can play at that game. From now on, every time they met, she was going out of her way to be super-sickly-sweetly nice. Ha! He'd hate it – that'd teach him.

Kristina scrutinised her as the gate slammed shut with enough force for all of Apokeri to hear. 'He can sometimes come across as a bit offish, but he's got a heart of gold – just like his late mother. He took Filip under his wing as a kid – despite strong objections from some quarters – and nurtured a lifelong passion for bikes. A mentor, you might say. Filip's always been grateful to Daniel for that. Those two boys make a great team. As you heard, the business is flying high.'

'Yes, it is, isn't.' Anna glanced back down the garden. 'And you know him much better than me. Right, I suggest you show me the ways of the Apokeri Apartments Manager. I'm your willing disciple.' She smirked again. 'Let's not give his royal highness an excuse to pull me up on anything. After all, Round the Bend isn't the only success story.'

***

For the rest of the day, Anna learned from a true expert and discovered that her role would take far less time than anticipated by being half as organised as Kristina. Soon, she was familiar with the booking system, cleaning rota, and other managerial responsibilities. In response, Anna started to put her ideas into practice, including guest information folders with helpful hints on eating establishments and things to see and do, a feedback form to capture testimonials, and personalising the email address from info@ to Anna@.

It was time to video call her parents, and she deliberately chose a time when her father would be at his allotment. The bloke spent more time there than he did with Anna's mother and his two kids back in the day. But to her amazement, he answered.

'Decided to call us, have you? Is there not much happening? Thought you'd better get in contact with the people who brought you into the world? Compared to your sister, you really are poles apart.'

And in less than ten seconds, Anna felt all the usual frustrations start to simmer and couldn't help biting. 'Oh yes, when was it you last spoke to Julia?'

Anna knew fine well it was last month. The siblings were close and messaged nearly every other day.

'Well, not as frequently as she'd like. With that successful marketing career of hers – she's always away and often in different time zones. It makes it difficult to call. And when she rings … you know … I'm often down the allotment.'

'Hmm, so you hear from Julia as frequently as you do from me then?' Anna shifted positions on the bed.

Her father quickly moved to his second favourite subject – his allotment. Anna listened patiently as he predictably cycled to the weather before coming full circle and back to listing her many failures compared to Julia.

'Your mother and I are amazed you finished that degree of yours. What was it in again?'

'Ancient History, Dad.'

'Oh yes, I keep forgetting. That's why you decided to go traipsing around Greece for weeks instead of knuckling down and getting a proper job after uni like your sister did. I mean, she beat how many other candidates to get that graduate job? It was in the hundreds if not thousands.'

'Yes, Dad, I know.' She rolled her eyes. 'You've told me before.'

At least she'd paid her way through uni and held down countless jobs rather than accepting any parental handouts like her older sister had.

'And what about you? Likely to get a decent job with this qualification of yours?'

'I hope so.' Anna anxiously tucked strands of hair behind her left ear. She just needed to come out and tell them. But her father wasn't finished.

'I don't like the sound of that wishy-washy response, young lady. Wasn't the whole point of getting this degree to better yourself?'

'Yes, Dad. And that's why I'm ringing.'

'Well, it's been nice talking to you, Anna, but I must go. With a free night, I want to finish my library book and get it back a week early. I'd like to say we'll hear from you soon, but—'

'Dad, that's what I wanted to—'

'Let your mother know. I'll go get her.'

'But Dad—'

'Bye.'

Anna fought an overwhelming compulsion to scream at the vacated sofa but smiled as her mother's face appeared.

'Hi pet, how's it going?'

'Hi Mam. I've got some news.'

The conversation with her mother – as expected – went well. As a supremely risk-averse type, Anna's mother was relieved to hear she had secured gainful employment and somewhere to live. And once her sun-worshipping father understood she was living somewhere far warmer than Northumberland, he'd barged back into the conversation for Anna to endure another barrage of criticism.

'Oh, so you've split up with John, have you? Another failed relationship. How many is that now? Julia's been happily married for years, and those grandkids are a delight.'

The call ended with a philosophical outlook from her mother. 'You do revel in spur-of-the-minute decisions, don't you? We shouldn't be surprised at the direction your life takes – but somehow, we always are.'

***

Anna washed her breakfast dishes as Kristina bustled about the kitchen with her first mug of coffee and they recapped on the final stage of the plan. Both women agreed Anna's Greek history obsession, a sponge-like ability to soak up information, entertaining storytelling, and a love of the natural world were her strengths. Perfect attributes for a community that welcomed increasing numbers of visitors. And it was to a pivotal member of the community Anna was heading for next.

The church bells chimed nine as she entered neat and welcoming Odyssey Travel for the first time. Previously, a look at the window display had sufficed. Today, Anna happily saw Round the Bend Cycle Tours was there. As an apartment manager, she checked out the competition and was surprised at the range. In addition to five apartment blocks, there were rooms to rent, bed and breakfasts, farm stays, and villas.

Like the gallery, there was an upmarket feel to the shop. Two desks housed computer terminals, keyboards, and phones. Framed images of Lefkada landmarks hung on the walls and there was a seating area around a table for customers to peruse leaflets and brochures.

The only other person inside was a young woman, who looked up from her computer and, in an Eastern European accent, asked how could she be of assistance? Anna found Dania was available after ten and to call back then. The dark-haired young woman was keen to find out if Anna enjoyed Apokeri. Always intrigued by people's lives, Anna soon extracted a potted history from Max's cousin. Her father flew the Apokeri nest as a young man, met his Bulgarian wife, and settled in Plovdiv. His daughter was currently studying a Geology master's degree in Sofia and spent the summer holidays working for Dania and catching up with her expansive Apokeri family.

Along with Bulgarian and Greek, the young woman was fluent in English and Russian, spoke conversational German, and was learning Swedish from Kristina. The conversation ended when a customer entered. After establishing they were German, she immediately switched languages. Promising to call back later, Anna left feeling very inadequate. She'd met so many multilingual people – it made her determined to become fluent in Greek.

***

With time on her side, Anna strolled up to the bike shop to discover more about the fledgling enterprise. Before she even had a chance to ask, Filip was out from behind the counter to offer his congratulations. He picked her up in a massive hug, thrilled to hear she was staying and managing the apartments. Anna, in turn, was delighted to hear how well everything was going. The first tour started next week, and the next three weeks were already fully booked. With a range of routes in place, the realisation had hit that they required extra staff for next season. And feelers were out with friends and acquaintances who were qualified guides. A thrilled Anna offered her Lefkada and Meganisi photos to help with planned marketing materials. She'd provide a testimonial, share posts, and include affiliate links on the apartment website. It resulted in him extending a dinner invitation to go through his plans the following evening. Filip unashamedly admitted he intended to mine her brain for ideas.

***

A little after ten, Anna returned to Odyssey, welcomed by the voluptuous, bubbly, and diminutive Dania. Over coffee, Anna explained she was stopping by to introduce herself as the new manager of Apokeri Apartments. Unsurprisingly, Dania already knew that and happily passed over leaflets for the new guest information packs and listened to Anna's idea. It was a tailored guided tour proposal. Anna knew Dania wanted to sell bespoke tours and strengthen ties with local businesses. The current options were very similar to those available across Lefkada. Anna's idea was a selection of small-group tours that got off the beaten track to highlight the beautiful fauna of the region and lesser-known cultural sights, incorporating high-quality artisans. The trips benefitted from being fully escorted by a passionate and highly knowledgeable guide (Anna) and a driver. The emphasis would be on providing a uniquely inclusive experience where guests felt special. On existing tours, people were often a number, discharged off coaches to aimlessly wander about a place or subjected to a formulaic commentary ending with a visit to an appointed shop to be sold lots of things they didn't want.

Over an hour, Dania thoroughly questioned Anna, probing to determine the amount of research done and her potential tour guide's level of knowledge. It was clear that Dania was a woman who recognised an opportunity. Yes, she liked the idea and needed to talk to her husband and make some calls. They agreed to reconvene in Apollo at eleven on Sunday morning.

***

Buoyed up by her chat, Anna felt a treat for Kristina and herself seemed only proper. And what better place to go than Aphrodite with its upbeat and happy vibe. Sofia chatted to Anna as she ordered and handed back her change.

Anna looked down. 'Sofia, you've given me way too much.' She handed the extra back as her tall female colleague slammed down a divine-looking chocolate cake.

'Is it true what Filip has told me? That you will be staying?'

Anna beamed as she picked up her bag of cinnamon swirls. 'Yes, it's true – I've fallen in love with the place.'

'This is good news indeed. Come, I want to ask you something.' Sofia guided Anna to a corner table whilst calling over her shoulder to a very sour-faced chef. 'Agnes, bring over two coffees and a koulouri.'

The sesame ring and latte were practically thrown across the table. Anna winced as the hot liquid slopped onto her hand. Sofia failed to notice Agnes's smirk.

'Eat, eat, my child. You look half-starved.' Sofia spooned sugar into her drink and leaned forward. 'You're probably wondering why I want to talk to you? Well, it's like this. It would seem that my niece has not had her head in the clouds after all. She's just landed a part in a new television drama series that'll start filming in a few weeks.'

74

'That sounds exciting.'

Anna saw Agnes hovering out the corner of her eye – like a malevolent vulture.

'As you can imagine, we are over the moon for her and found out yesterday when she came in with my sister. I don't know who was more excited. My niece has so much to sort out before she goes, and we've agreed her last day will be Tuesday. When I heard you were staying, my immediate thought was to see if you'd like to work here for a few days a week?'

Anna was genuinely taken aback. It was so unexpected, and she quickly ran through everything in her head – the time spent managing the apartments, helping with Kristina's flowers, and her potential tour guide role. Working in the café was ideal for meeting lots of locals; it would help her Greek, and Sofia was lovely. But before she could answer, Agnes burst in.

'I must protest. Does the girl even have the experience and capabilities to work in a café? She could be absolutely useless for all we know.'

Don't hold back there, pet.

Sofia waved away the outburst. 'There's no need to worry. I have it on good authority from Filip that Anna has plenty of hospitality experience. Why she's worked all over the place – haven't you?'

'Yes, I have,' Anna directed her answer at Agnes. 'In the UK, Australia, New Zealand, to name a few.'

'See, there's nothing to worry about.'

'She might have worked in many places,' Agnes retorted and scowled. 'But it doesn't mean she was any good.'

'I can provide references, if required.'

Sofia waved away the ridiculous notion. 'Oh, there won't be any need for that, my dear.'

'Thank you for thinking of me; what a lovely thing to do,' Anna said and smiled sweetly at Agnes. 'I would love to work here – the only thing is … I'm meeting Dania and Max on Sunday to chat about a potential job. Can I let you know how many days I can work here on Monday?'

'You are a good girl.' Sofia patted Anna's hand. 'Yes, pop in on Monday morning and let me know. We best get back to work.' She drained her coffee and added. 'With Agnes having worked on cruise ships for all those years, the two of you will have plenty to chat about.'

As soon as Sofia turned, Agnes sneered, suggesting she'd rather die than voluntarily converse with the interloper. With the lunchtime rush beginning, Anna savoured her food and reflected that Agnes didn't only have a resting bitch face – she was a bitch. It was going to make for an interesting working dynamic.

Chapter Nine

'Let's recap, shall we.' Filip handed her a plate of rabbit stifado. 'You arrived in Apokeri seven days ago and in that time gave us the idea for a new business venture, relocated your life to another country, settled into a new home, and could potentially have three jobs. That's good going.'

'Okay, it sounds a lot when you put it like that,' Anna acknowledged and fleetingly wondered if she might be taking on too much.

'And let's not forget you've given us some invaluable insights and saved us money with your brilliant photos,' Alex added as he raised a glass.

'What are friends for,' Anna replied and raised hers. 'It helps with an older sister in marketing. I wouldn't know half that stuff otherwise.'

The trio enjoyed a relaxing evening in the courtyard, and again an easy banter flowed. Anna shared her recent intel about Jeremy transforming Tharesseti into a luxury hotel. They hadn't heard a thing – the Apokeri grapevine didn't always know everything.

'Kristina reckons it's why he's coming to next week's village committee, being keen to involve local suppliers.'

The committee was an Apokeri institution that had convened once a month for decades. It had an open-door policy, with everyone welcome, and regular attendees were from village businesses, local farms, the fishing fleet, the church, and the school. The main topic this time would be the upcoming Flower and Food Festival, and Anna had jumped at the chance to accompany Kristina. Filip often went in Daniel's stead.

'The meetings can get quite heated,' Filip said. 'There are some strong personalities – Papa is one. He loves Apokeri and gets fired up if he sees its way of life threatened. When properly managed, development is a good thing and results in a thriving economy – but not if monies are hived off to foreign investors. There's general agreement on this … but people disagree on how to do it.' He nodded towards Alex. 'We've seen it happen in other places with dubious developments, or with profit put first.'

'Tourism brings in huge amounts of money and jobs, but small accommodation providers sometimes find it challenging. And huge all-inclusive complexes can see holidaymakers spend little money in local villages,' Alex conceded. 'It's a balancing act.'

'I believe Apokeri can retain its charm and welcome more visitors sustainably,' Filip added confidently, but cautioned Anna. 'Ideas are always welcome at the meetings, but make sure they're well thought out if you put any forward. I guarantee my father will be the first to pounce on any weaknesses – the man thrives on a good argument.'

Anna appreciated the warning.

***

It was another beautiful day when Anna arrived at Aphrodite Café a little after seven and found Sofia and Adriani chatting with their regulars who were busy collecting early morning caffeine hits. The place was already three-quarters full.

Sofia caught sight of her and laughed. 'I know I said to start on Monday morning, but I wasn't expecting you this early. Have you had time for breakfast? You must not be eating enough – far too thin.'

Sofia clucked over Anna like a concerned mother hen while replenishing the coffee machine.

'I couldn't sleep; I was too excited,' Anna replied and refused an iced bun. 'I've already been for a run this morning and had a filling breakfast – your son will testify to my healthy appetite.'

Anna had hardly slept a wink after meeting Dania and Max. Her tour guide suggestion had lit a fire in their bellies, resulting in two full-day itineraries with suppliers lined up – and Anna was thrilled Max had agreed to be the driver. He thought it was good to get away from the restaurant and do some networking.

The first tour started a week on Saturday, the second on the following Wednesday, and they would run all the way until the end of October. Anna had spent the rest of Sunday studying the routes, swotting up on Lefkada facts and writing up tour notes. It was going to be brilliant.

In the café, Sofia agreed with Anna's request to work three days a week and was delighted that Anna wanted to start immediately. With Adriani's departure, regular customers were popping in to wish her good luck (and remember them when she was rich and famous), so Anna delivered Filip's pastries before being introduced to the Makris Bakery team. She was already acquainted with Vasili, and the other two members were Viktor and Nikki.

It would have been impossible to miss Agnes' husband in a crowd, with his imposing broad and muscular six-foot-seven build. His rugged face told a fascinating history – a nose broken more than once and a long thin white scar across the left cheek. Deep-set almost black eyes, slightly dishevelled short dark hair, cropped beard, and a trimmed moustache lent a brooding look. However, the man had an aura of calm, with measured movements and a soothing voice. Anna relaxed in his presence, relieved he didn't share his wife's hatred of her.

Nikki was another kettle of fish entirely. At sixteen, the bakery apprentice kept up an ongoing dialogue concerning the latest Apokeri gossip as she buzzed around completing her duties. Anna quickly surmised she was not someone to keep a secret and that, with a rotund figure, she enjoyed munching on bakery products. The family resemblance to her aunt Dania was unmistakable – the same short stature, emerald-green eyes, and flame-red hair threatening to burst out of its hairnet.

She returned to the café and found a highly animated and distressed Dania. A full coachload of holidaymakers was booked on an island coach tour tomorrow, but the guide had come off his scooter that morning. There was no replacement at such short notice, which would mean cancelling the full-day excursion and refunding the money.

It was an English-speaking trip, dropping tourists off at appointed places before counting them back on, with no requirement to accompany them. Dania had the itinerary and would take Anna to the collection point and pick her up. Anna would get the guide's fee and refreshments – including lunch. It would gain Dania massive brownie points from the tour company and get Anna into the swing of being a tour guide.

'What do you think? Will you step in?' Dania begged.

Anna scanned the running order. 'I'd be delighted. I've been to all these places, so no surprises. And I can never turn down free food.'

Relief flooded Dania's face, and she hugged Anna before rushing off to tell the tour company the good news.

'That was an excellent thing you did, my dear.' Sofia squeezed Anna's hand and then left to help Agnes.

***

For the rest of the day, Anna shadowed Sofia's niece. The young woman was an excellent tutor with infinite patience, an easy charm, and a quick wit. Anna could easily see why she was a favourite with customers. Adriani possessed the same striking good looks and hourglass figure as her aunt and the eighteen-year-old had the indefinable X factor. Although, the teenager seemed genuinely oblivious to the attention she generated and failed to notice the admiring looks from customers.

Anna soon discovered Adriani was both an excellent observer of human behaviour and an accomplished actress. Her way of explaining the regular customers' likes and dislikes, along with their quirks and pet names, was by good-humouredly impersonating them. It was hilarious – especially as it was done with the full consent of those involved as Adriani responded to each customer's request to imitate them. She became highly animated when someone with an unusual accent entered, and tried to master it. She relished the challenge of Anna's distinctive Geordie accent and pulled off a half-decent one with accompanying mannerisms by lunchtime. There was also valuable advice on handling Agnes (just ignore her) and the ill-tempered Vasili.

'He's a pussycat. All you need to do is stand your ground,' she explained as Vasili appeared and restocked the breadbasket. 'Is that not right, uncle?'

'You're far too cheeky,' he retorted as Adriani kissed his cheek.

'You'll miss me when I'm gone.'

'Unlikely,' Vasili grunted.

However, Anna saw a smile tug at his mouth as he disappeared.

***

A shadow fell across the table as Anna tucked into a late lunch in the employee courtyard. It was Agnes – and she looked none too happy at being in such close proximity.

'Is everything okay?' Anna put down her spoon. 'Am I needed out front?'

'Sofia has everything under control.'

'Alright then.' Anna went back to eating. 'Compliments to the chef. Your Swedish soup is delicious.'

Agnes didn't respond.

'I understand from Kristina it's so popular in Sweden that the armed forces eat it once a week at lunchtime.'

'Yes. I heard that too,' Agnes replied, haughtily staring down her nose.

Anna continued to eat, and the silence lengthened.

'Is there something I can help you with?' Anna said without looking up.

'Sofia sent me out here.'

It was like pulling teeth. Attempting to be civil, Anna motioned to the other seat. 'Why don't you sit down?' The woman didn't move. 'Or stand – whatever you prefer.'

Agnes dragged the metal chair across the concrete and perched like a hawk. The screeching sound cut right through Anna's head, but she refused to show it.

'I have been told – it's such a ridiculous notion – that you may know of some regional delicacies from…' She swept her eyes over Anna as if coming across a dead fly in a batch of crème caramel. 'Where do you come from exactly?'

Anna was sorely tempted to say 'under a rock' but resisted and politely replied, 'Northeast England.'

'Oh yes. What do they call the people from there? Georges?'

'Geordies. If you're from Tyneside or nearby, or born along the River Tyne. You can be from northeast England and not necessarily be a Geordie.' Anna knew she was rambling but kept going. 'For instance, if you are from Sunderland, a city only twelve miles south of Newcastle, you'd be referred to as a Mackem.'

'Yes, quite,' Agnes replied and yawned. 'As I was saying, you might – but I suspect not – know of something suitable to grace the menu.'

The woman looked utterly appalled at the very idea, but Anna brightened. It was the chance she'd been waiting for. Aphrodite Café had a well-deserved reputation for its ever-changing selection of delicious international cuisines – a reputation that could be traced back three years to when Agnes started. She was an exceptional chef and, along with her husband Viktor, had brought praise and a loyal following to the café and bakery. Agnes thrived on creating cuisines from around the globe, and the more unusual or unknown, the better. Anna was willing to bet that nobody had heard of ham and pease pudding stotties, the griddle-cooked fruit scones known as singin' hinnies, Tyneside floddies potato cakes, or the potato, onion, and cheese layered pan haggerty. Yes, yes, yes, Anna wanted to rub her hands together. She was on the verge of scoring big.

'Oh yes. I've printed some recipes out.'

Anna frantically rummaged in her rucksack and handed them across but, in her haste, knocked over her water, forcing Agnes to jump backwards.

'Watch it!'

'Sorry, sorry. It was an accident,' Anna said as she quickly grabbed her napkin and mopped up. 'Lucky for me, you've got lightning reflexes. Not a single drop hit you.'

More's the pity. Anna thought as Agnes stood and cast her eyes over the recipes.

'Right. Some of these … seem adequate, I suppose. I might, and it's only a might, add one to the menu. At some stage.'

Don't knock yourself out, pet. Anna thought and cocked her head. 'You're not related to Daniel Eckvardsson by any chance?'

'No. I'm originally from northern Greece. Why do you ask?'

'Oh, you remind me of him, that's all.'

As in, you're both thoroughly unpleasant and hate my guts.

'He's a good guy – gives up his time to teach cycling proficiency at the village school. My twins have so much confidence, thanks to him.' Agnes shoved the recipes in her tunic pocket and stood motionless for a few seconds before muttering, 'I'm … I'm glad you liked my ärtsoppaa soup.'

Anna sat in a sliver of sun. At least it was a start – even if Agnes almost choked on those departing words. And her sly dig about Daniel being taken as a compliment. How funny.

Chapter Ten

Anna leaned back in her office chair and stretched. It was early August, and she was settling into village life – even if Daniel and Agnes persisted in being pains in the backside. A great deal had happened in the last fortnight, including an illuminating village committee.

As expected, the focus had been on the Flower and Food Festival. There was a real buzz about the upcoming event and a healthy competitive spirit concerning who would win the Best Dressed Building Award. Each entrant was confident that this year they would topple Apollo. However, Max had utter faith his business would triumph for the sixth year running.

Under the competition rules, each entrant grew ninety per cent of the flowers themselves. Most businesses did this already to decorate their establishments from early spring to late autumn. However, for the flower competition, most turned to the expertise of Kristina. Each competitor could erect their display from seven the night before and it had to be completed by seven the following morning when judging would commence.

When the competition first started, Apokeri Gallery won easily. Kristina's horticultural and flower-arranging expertise put her head and shoulders above anyone else. However, after a few years of winning, Kristina decided to withdraw herself from future competitions as she had seen a business opportunity. Instead of entering, she would offer her services to any competitor. It was a clever strategy. Each year Kristina made available the flora she would grow that year. It was then up to each business to provide a brief of which species, the design, and the budget.

Max knew Kristina was good from her design and upkeep of Apollo's secret garden. He therefore asked for the maximum ten per cent of allotted flowers and for Kristina to design the entire display – there was nothing in the rules to prevent that. By doing so, Apollo won easily, and the savvier business owners quickly cottoned on and – not wanting to be outdone – asked Kristina to design their displays. Although the ever-competitive Max gloated about retaining the crown for five years, and it was a foregone conclusion, the winning margin was dwindling.

Everything was on track for this year to be bigger and better. It would see the village square and school hall transformed with food and craft stalls, a cultural and historical display, and live music. The suggestion, by a cautious Anna, that non-food businesses could have a booth had been well received.

Representatives from all the local businesses and organisations were there, and Anna met many pillars of the community. The rather formidable-looking priest had shepherded his Apokeri flock for the past thirty years. When introduced, Anna was seized by a sudden fear that he would sense a non-churchgoer and demand her immediate attendance. This notion was, of course, absurd. He gave her a hearty handshake, welcomed her to Apokeri, and said he was always available to chat if she needed it. Then there were members of the Andino family including the undisputed head (Stelios) and his wife. This couple in their early forties seemed to be a case of opposites attract. She was the serious, systematic, and organised village pharmacist which was reflected in her appearance. Dark hair scraped back into a severe bun, and black eyeliner, mascara, and dark red lipstick only exaggerated a harried expression. It looked like the woman was bearing the world's weight on her slim shoulders.

Her laid-back husband (Daniel's third cousin), was completely different. He was slightly shorter and a few years younger than his wife – a solidly built man and a natural charmer with a flirtatious and confident manner. The Andinos were another Apokeri family with multiple businesses – Epione Pharmacy, Atlas Laundry, and Nereus Restaurant. With his three fishermen brothers, Stelios also owned an apartment block that was significantly larger but cheaper and less sophisticated than Anna's. The entrepreneurial spirit was alive and kicking in the youngest brother. He was keen to tell Anna how he planned to switch from fishing to scuba diving and snorkelling trips during the tourist season. Accompanying him was his wife, who taught at the village primary school. Anna could see how the kids must adore their teacher. The slightly plump woman with a short pixie haircut and twinkling brown eyes radiated positive energy and excitedly talked about the school's involvement in the festival. Anna struggled to keep up with her rapid-fire Greek and felt quite drained afterwards.

There had been plenty of other business to discuss as everyone tucked into various plates of food they'd brought along – a fantastic and somewhat competitive idea. Dania introduced the new tours and was looking for interested parties to develop a culinary cruise – Agnes, Viktor, and the youngest Andino brother agreed to meet separately.

Jeremy had submitted planning approval for his luxury hotel and, if successful, expected to open it in eight months and partner with local suppliers wherever possible. He intended to offer guests bespoke services such as diving and fishing trips and art classes. Any other suggestions were welcome. There was a flurry of queries and interest from many quarters. Welcoming Anna, it was then over to Filip and Alex to officially announce their new cycle tour venture. And Daniel revealed he was permanently relocating to Adelaide after travelling and would leave at the end of October. Filip and Alex had bought his business, but he retained ownership of the adjoining house, Apokeri Gallery, and Apokeri Apartments. A few people at the meeting had been privy to the decision but sworn to secrecy. For the rest, it was a complete shock mixed with genuine sadness. On the other hand, Anna was secretly relieved. She was tired of his ongoing sniping.

On the whole, Anna enjoyed managing Apokeri Apartments and ran it well. The visitor information packs were a success; her social media and website amends, including affiliated links, resulted in more traffic, enquiries, and bookings. Kristina, Daniel, and herself continued their weekly lunch meetings, and their boss was pleased with her progress. Anna made sure of it by triple-checking everything, so he found nothing wrong – no matter how hard he tried. Therefore, he could leave it to them when he moved to the other side of the world and keep out of her hair for good.

The inaugural bespoke tour had been a hit with the small group gelling and loving the intimate approach. Getting off the beaten track, meeting local artisans, tasting high-quality produce, and enjoying a relaxing lunch in an olive grove appeared to be a winning combination. What surprised Anna was the guests – drawn from Lefkada or returning visitors. And the reason for booking? It offered something different. Anna was already looking forward to the next tour, and Dania reported that future trips were filling up fast.

There was also an unexpected turn of events.

On the day that Anna had stood in for the injured tour guide, Dania spent a few minutes chatting to the much older coach driver; they had known each other for years. However, as soon as Dania left, the shutters came down. Her Greek colleague clammed up and wholly ignored Anna as they drove to each pick-up point and she welcomed guests aboard.

Anna initially thought it was going to be a very long day, but the Jenkinson Stubborn Gene kicked in. She slowly but surely began to chip away at the driver's stony façade to drag information out of him with open-ended questions. Anna cheerily thanked him at each sightseeing stop as she exited the coach, and he disappeared off for a quick cigarette. Chatting to the guests as they waited patiently for his return, Anna would again kindly thank him as he opened the doors precisely on time, and they all trooped up the stairs. Anna was not required to provide any commentary but naturally found herself highlighting various places to the passengers as they drove by; she provided an overview of each location before arrival, with recommendations of must-see sights. As the morning progressed, Anna's efforts eventually brought rewards. He decided to introduce himself and willingly began conversing as he drove. At the lunchtime stop, she was pleasantly surprised when he invited her to join him and all the other coach drivers. It was a turning point.

The group knew each other well and soon swapped stories about various trips, trying to outdo each other. Anna found herself egging them on to recount the funniest, scariest, or strangest ever encounter. It became a pantomime with people oohing, aahing, or laughing at the tall tales and only needed the audience to shout out "he's behind you" to be authentic. Anna switched between English commentary and Greek with Cosimo, and after bidding her guests farewell, he sidled over to apologise for having underestimated her. She'd made an effort. All the other foreign guides expected the drivers to speak English or only talked to the tourists and ignored them – as if they were second-class citizens. Hadn't she noticed the guides sitting together at lunch – away from the drivers? Having driven since probably before her parents were born, it'd been years since he'd enjoyed himself that much at work. Inundated with glowing reviews, the tour operator offered Anna a full-day Lefkada coach tour role. Cosimo made sure he drove.

Another turn of events saw Anna splitting her time between working in the café and the bike shop. Daniel, Alex, and Filip were flat out, and Sofia suggested it would be more beneficial for Anna to help manage the increasing bookings, run the website, and generally keep the shop running smoothly. It was an arrangement that suited Anna, with Agnes stepping up her unpleasantness. And besides Kristina, Filip was Anna's closest friend in Apokeri. When time allowed, they chatted for hours.

Sofia had convinced herself Anna was not looking after herself properly – working seven days a week. The fact Anna worked the same number of days as most people in the village made no difference. It didn't help that Filip agreed with his mother. The upshot was Anna sat down at Sofia and Vasili's table at least twice a week with Filip, joined by an ever-changing line-up of the Latsis and Makris extended family. These were animated affairs as everyone talked over the top of each other. Anna thought all the energy and noise were brilliant. Her childhood mealtimes saw four around the table, but the minimum was ten at Sofia and Vasili's house.

Anna constantly disagreed with Vasili on marriage, religion, and history – to name a few – and soon realised she was the only one to argue back. Filip confided his wider family eagerly anticipated the highly entertaining debates, and his father thought her feisty and loved to do battle. The result – even more dinner invitations and larger gatherings. A homecooked meal prepared by someone else was great, but constantly having to be on top form, be entertaining, and put your best foot forward was exhausting. She longed to slob out and simply be, but she was her own worst enemy.

***

Anna, Filip, Alex, and Kristina rarely had a free night together but tonight was one. The sixth of August – never noteworthy to Anna – marked the annual Feast of Lentils at charming Egklouvi (touted as the most beautiful mountainous village on Lefkada and famed for the best green lentils in the world). She had mentioned her interest in the festival to Cosimo on their second coach tour.

90

He knew it well, having lived there all his life, and with her keen interest in island history and customs, he invited Anna and her friends to join his family. Part of her wanted nothing more than to crawl into bed, but the dominant side didn't want to miss out. And even better, Daniel wouldn't be there. He was off visiting some police friend or other. Filip had told her the details, but she'd only feigned interest.

They wound their way up to the small and ancient church of Agios Donatos, set a few kilometres above the village. After giving thanks, everyone gathered outside to enjoy wine, sardines, and bowls of lentil soup from enormous vats.

Hundreds of people sat together at long trestle tables. Anna and her friends were with Cosimo and his wife, along with their two daughters and their husbands. The family party was complete with four children under ten. It was lovely getting to know the family, and the lentil soup tasted even better than on her first visit. She was informed it was because this time, the village women had made it.

After food and drink, the party continued lower down in Egklouvi. Anna danced with Filip or Cosimo's wife and her two daughters. At one point, his wife commented on Anna's close friendship with Filip and how he clearly liked her. Anna glanced across to him. Above all the noise and distractions, he was aware of her gaze and, after grinning and waving, turned back to his conversation.

And then it hit her.

How could she be so dense? It was obvious and made complete sense. All those invitations to family meals, all the times Filip walked her home and readily agreed to her working in the bike shop. Why had it taken her so long to see it? There was no time to act on her suspicions tonight, but she only needed to wait until the next evening.

***

Before arriving at Filip's parents for supper, Anna seized the opportunity to question him and was proved right. He had been too fearful of losing her friendship to say anything. Losing track of time, they arrived over an hour late. The ever-punctual Vasili lost no time criticising them, but that vanished on hearing the reason.

Anna had never seen someone as happy as Sofia finding out her child was part of a couple. She sprang forward, grabbing both of them in a hug – it was what she'd hoped for, how happy it made her, how well-suited they were, and how Anna already felt part of the family. As if some telepathy was at work, more and more relations happened to drop by, and it was early morning before Anna crawled into bed.

*****

The alarm sounded, and Anna thought she'd been hit over the head with a frying pan. She dragged herself into the shower and still felt like death warmed up. Kristina did not help matters either by laughing at the pathetic figure gingerly entering the kitchen.

'Someone had a heavy session,' Kristina said as she passed Anna a mug of strong black coffee. 'I heard you come in after one.'

'I'm so sorry if I woke you up … I think I'm going to die,' Anna sobbed as she laid her head on the counter. 'I was having such a good time, and my glass kept getting topped up, so I lost track of how much I was drinking. When will I ever learn?'

Anna could have done with longer in bed but wanted to tell Kristina the news about her and Filip and not have her hear via the Apokeri grapevine. Handing her some much-needed toast, Kristina declared she wasn't in the least bit surprised.

*****

The early morning walk to the café did Anna a world of good with the fresh breeze and deep breaths of cool air. Even so, Sofia took one look and chuckled whilst Agnes smirked – which didn't bode well.

'It's not funny,' Anna mumbled. 'How come you're fine, Sofia?'

It was true; Sofia looked immaculate as always. You would never know the woman had been downing shots of ouzo hours earlier.

'I only had a few,' Sofia claimed while filling salt cellars. 'Hopefully, I've got something that will cheer you up.'

Anna prayed it was a miracle hangover cure but no such luck. Instead, it was an invitation to join Sofia and her sisters that Thursday evening.

'I know how you love history, and there's a festival in Karya which has revived old customs and features traditional music and dancing. Would you like to come?'

Anna immediately perked up. It sounded wonderful. Yes, she would love to. However, the rest of the day was torturous as Agnes scraped, scratched, whistled, and generally made as much ear-shattering noise as possible. Anna fought to keep calm – a tall order – being forced to down rocket-fuel-strength coffee to stay awake, interspersed with litres of rehydrating water. It was a sign of how bad things were when lunch comprised of a solitary slice of toast and a cup of tea. When her shift ended at four, she almost wept with joy and, taking off her apron, promised to be human for her next shift and went straight home to bed.

***

With the next two days comprising tour duties and shaking off the last traces of a hangover, it was Thursday morning before Anna caught up with Filip. Dropping off the pastries, she excitedly told him about the trip to Karya – it was as if she'd slapped him in the face with a wet fish.

'What's the matter, Pip? I thought it was lovely of Sofia to ask me, and I was looking forward to spending time with your mam and aunties. They're a scream.'

'What … do you know … about the festival?'

'Only what your mam told me – my guidebook doesn't mention it.'

She was missing something; Pip was holding out on her.

The frown disappeared, and he kissed her. 'Sorry, I was being silly. You'll love the festival with the coven of witches. Let me know what you think of it.'

***

It started at six, and Vasili insisted on being their taxi service. He skilfully negotiated the traffic with one hand blasting the horn if he felt any driver required an ounce of encouragement. In this way, the three sisters and Anna barely needed to walk. The sisters took the lead, and their commanding presence saw the crowd part easily, and their party snagged the best spot. More and more people poured into the village square, and there was a real buzz of anticipation.

The church bell struck six, and as Sofia explained the re-enactment was part of a three-day celebration, a man in a traditional outfit walked onto the stage. He thanked everyone for coming, how wonderful it was to see so many people and asked them to show their appreciation for … the Lefkada Traditional Wedding Representation. The crowd clapped and cheered. Anna turned to Sofia and began to laugh.

'I thought you might like it.' she replied with a grin.

94

Chapter Eleven

Anna closed the garden gate, ran along the cobbled lane to the boundary of Kristina's property, across the small car park and the bit of scrubland littered with weathered fishing dinghies, lobster creels, crab pots, and buoys before a right turn, and started up the steady incline. The birds tweeted, the insects droned, and the sun radiated off her black leggings. A few people were out early, toiling up the track. She pushed on and was soon to the top of the cliff and past Kristina's beautiful carved oak bench. Anna's watch beeped – the halfway mark, time to turn back.

The track dipped steeply into a tunnel between thick tangles of scrub, and she automatically sidestepped to avoid the mass of bramble thorns, not wanting to get caught a second time. Her legs and arms pumped hard, helping her to come up and out into the sunshine. The crosswind caught her but only for a moment before she dropped again. The dense vegetation blocked all other sounds except her breathing and her feet rhythmically hitting the dusty, uneven track. Downward momentum caused her to pick up speed with eyes fixed on the ground to prevent tripping. The snap of a twig. She glanced up. Too fast to stop. She slammed into the person blocking the way ahead.

'Be careful there,' Daniel said gently as he instinctively reached out to prevent her from toppling into a hawthorn bush. 'Are you okay?'

Anna mumbled a quick thank you as he quickly dropped his hands and stepped back, which gave Cassie the space to bound forward with an enthusiastic welcome, much to Anna's relief.

His face was etched with concern. 'You really shouldn't run alone. Not along here. You can't see who's coming. And if you sprained an ankle, or worse – there's no phone signal.'

'I-I don't carry a mobile when I'm running.'

He was being so lovely and it not only caught her off guard but made her unable to switch on her sickly-sweet persona.

'Do you think that's wise?' he asked kindly.

She couldn't believe he was being so nice when they were alone together and she actually looked behind her to check. It made for a pleasant change and she eyed up the head-height vegetation. It was difficult to see anyone ahead … and … something did happen, maybe?

'You are not to run along here anymore,' he snapped. 'Do you hear?'

And the old Daniel was back. It hadn't taken long, and similarly, she fell into her sickly-sweet character.

'Thank you so much for the concern, Daniel, but there really is nothing to worry about. I've run alone for years in perfect safety. Now, if you don't mind, I really must be going. There simply is so much to do, and as you know, businesses don't run themselves.'

Pushing past him, she ran a little bit faster than usual to get back home.

***

Sitting on the patio enjoying breakfast, Kristina asked how the health drive was going – had it been an enjoyable run? Anna mentioned Daniel's unusual behaviour – nice one minute then rude the next. She couldn't understand why he was worried. There were always plenty of people on the track, and she'd bumped into quite a few guests that morning. Firstly, love's young dream from Arta in northwest Greece – Anna was surprised they'd made it outside. And then the two young men who'd been island-hopping for the last few weeks.

'They quizzed me about the best routes to take and said it was time for them to get back in shape after too much good food and drink. I told them to drop by the office to pick up a map, and said I'd mark my favourite tracks.' Anna glanced at her watch. 'Flipping heck, is that the time? I need to get a shifty on. I'll catch you later. Enjoy your day.'

After quickly tidying up, Anna strode down the garden to her office and was so engrossed in work that she failed to hear a polite knock on the open door. It was not until a gentle cough that she looked up from the computer to see one of the lads from room six patiently waiting.

'I'm very sorry. I didn't mean to break your concentration.'

Anna smiled and motioned him in. 'That's perfectly fine. I often get lost in my own world.'

After discovering a shared passion for Greek history, he perched on the desk and fell into an easy conversation, comparing places they had visited. He preferred the tenth-century Minoan settlement on Amorgos to the iconic Portaro, or Great Gate, of Naxos. Still, both had been fascinated by the ancient town of Akrotiri on Santorini. Like Pompeii, it had been covered in ash and lava from a devastating volcanic eruption. Anna was outlining running routes when Kristina popped her head around the door to say Filip had rung, and it sounded urgent.

'Thanks,' Anna replied. 'I'm sorry to cut short our chat, but I'd better ring straight back.'

'Not a problem. You've been extremely helpful, and I now know where to go. We'll probably go for a run tomorrow morning and might even bump into you? I better let you get on. Thanks again, Anna. I appreciate your time.'

Waving goodbye, she picked up the receiver. 'Hi Pip, is everything okay?'

'I need your help. Can you get here now? I know you're not due to start yet … b-but … Christ … I've wiped all the tour bookings. Nobody knows what to do.'

'Don't worry, don't touch anything – I'm on my way.'

***

It was an easy fix; he apologised for being stupid and asked about her morning. She was bemused to find that he agreed with Daniel. 'Don't worry about me,' Anna replied and stretched out her calves. 'Anyway, you'll be pleased to hear I'm not running tomorrow. I won't have time with coach tour duties, and I promised to help Kristina with the festival flowers.'

'Watch you don't overdo it – I know what you're like,' he warned and kissed her. 'And there's no need to cook later as we're at my parents tonight.'

The day passed off without incident until Agnes sauntered in at closing time to purchase cycling shorts for the twins and, as usual, found subtle ways to infuriate Anna.

Once her nemesis was out of sight, she let rip. 'Did you see that? The way she looked me up and down?'

'No.'

'Of course, you didn't. Mrs Benrubi is far too clever for that. If there's one thing that boils my blood—'

'Are you sure it's that bad?'

'Yes, it bloody well is. I'm not joking, Pip – I don't know how much more I can take. I'm that close' – she held her thumb and forefinger millimetres apart – 'to losing it … have you any idea how much self-restraint it's taking—'

'I can imagine. You don't do self-restraint well.'

'The woman hates me for no reason … no reason at all. She goes out of her way to be a nasty, sly, and spiteful cow.' Anna slammed the lid down on the tea box. 'She deliberately turned up right before closing, spilt her coffee all over the bench and went through all her cards, getting the PIN wrong just the once. And then, after all that, decided to pay cash but accidentally moved her hand away, making all her change scatter across the floor and forcing me to scramble around like a servant kneeling before her mistress.'

'Don't hold it against her,' Filip said as if pacifying an enraged bull.

She snapped off the coffee machine. 'Are you kidding me? Every bloody time I'm in the café, I've got her sneaky digs to contend with. I thought I'd scored some brownie points when the singin' hinnies went down a storm – your mam was dead chuffed – but it made her worse. I just don't get it … what have I ever done to her, like?'

Filip hugged her. 'It's not you. It's because, well … it's because of me – and Mama.'

'How's that?'

'Because Mama cannot help pairing me off with any suitable female who has "Filip potential", and once they appear on the radar, her little tests start. Some never make it past the first one. But when they do, heaven help them. Her formidable matchmaking goes into overdrive.' Filip sighed as he straightened up the brochures on the table. 'Agnes has endured it countless times. She'll be watching, waiting, and knows from experience that the fallout will be greater every time the intended female delights my mother.'

He walked along the rows of handlebars and straightened the bike helmets. 'Of course, it always ends up a dismal failure, and when the poor thing works in the café – that's the end of her. Agnes is left to pick up the pieces whilst my mother rants about her unbelievably picky son. "Oh Agnes, why do I bother? Is nobody ever good enough? There's always something wrong. That's it – the last time. I give up." And then the cycle starts again with the next one. So, Agnes is steeling herself and has grown to loathe whoever Mama picks. I feel sorry for her and guilty for my part. But you know what Mama's like. It's easier to go along with it.'

'Brilliant,' Anna retorted as Filip locked up.

'Yep. Life's a bitch.'

'Well, I'm going to have to figure out a way to make her like me and hope you don't chuck me – so I don't get sacked!'

She clicked her seatbelt in place and stared at Filip until he did the same.

'Yes, you'll have to watch your step, my girl. Do what I say when I say.'

'Right – like that's ever going to happen.'

'Tell me about it.' Filip looked both ways before pulling out. 'How have I managed to be going out with one of the most stubborn females on the planet?'

'Because my many other talents make up for it.'

'Very true. Well, enough of me stroking your ego. It's time for dinner with my parents. You never know – there might be another test.'

'No way. I've passed them all now. Out of interest, what form do these tests take?'

'I'm not sure, but her first one is giving too much change and seeing if it's handed back – which you did.'

'Honesty is always the best policy, wouldn't you say?' Anna said as she waved to Nikki, who was walking up the street and eating a vanilla slice.

'Well … maybe not always.'

***

Anna stood looking at the northern cliffs, dressed in her running gear – despite saying she wasn't going for a run. She'd woken up even earlier than usual and felt sluggish, having overindulged the night before. Exercise always did the trick. She paused and glanced towards the pier. Maybe she should go a different way?

But then she angrily remembered Daniel's orders and it was enough to change her mind. Turning right, she struck out on the familiar uphill route.

With plenty of time to spare, she ran further than usual and clambered down to her favourite secret swimming cove. It was incredibly peaceful, a hidden slice of heaven where nobody disturbed her. At a wide-open section on the way back, she met her new running guests from room six who were amazed at how early she must have set off and, laughing, they admitted to almost sacking theirs off for a longer lie-in. Daniel's concerns were silly. The views were gorgeous, and people could always be found milling along the route if she ever did take a spill. There really was nothing to worry about.

Anna was flying. In the zone when everything flows. Mind and body in sync. This was why she ran. No need for drugs. The track levelled out and continued right along the cliff edge, and she looked down on the gliding seabirds. It was tempting to gaze out to sea, but with so many ruts underfoot, it wasn't wise. A mass of brambles acted as a hedge on her left before the ground steadily rose. It was a mass of green. Thousands of olive trees marched up the hillside as far as the eye could see.

Straight ahead, two figures approached, and one deliberately blocked the way. Behind him, an excited canine strained to get by.

'Sit,' Daniel barked. The dog refused and tried to push past her master's legs. 'Cassie, I'm warning you. Sit down now.'

Ever so slowly, she complied. Anna suppressed a giggle when Cassie refused to meet Daniel's glare. By clever design, he'd placed himself on higher ground, forcing Anna to look upwards like a naughty child.

'What the hell do you think you're doing?'

'I would have thought that was obvious,' Anna calmly replied, refusing to be intimidated.

'Even when I said not to?'

'No, you ordered me not to. Like me, I cannot imagine you taking kindly to being bossed around.'

Daniel just stared at her.

'I thought not. Do you know something? I did listen at first because – for once – you were being lovely. But you soon switched back to being an arse again.'

'I don't believe it!' He jabbed a finger at her. 'You admit I was right but still ignored me.'

'What did you expect?'

'That you'd listen. Goddammit.'

She gained a perverse delight in watching Daniel become more and more irate.

He held himself ramrod straight, arms pinned by his sides, fists balled. 'It-it's for your own good. Anything could happen out here.'

'You don't have the faintest idea what's good for me – never having made the slightest effort to converse with me like a decent human being. Always being so bloody snide and trying to score points.'

He shook his head. 'I should've known it was a complete waste of time talking to you.'

'I've been nothing but nice to you, Daniel – it's made sod all difference. Why on earth would I listen?'

His eyes narrowed, but there was something besides disdain – triumph.

'If I'd been nice,' he mused. 'Like Filip is?'

'Yes, like Pip.'

'So pray tell, Miss Righteous – why did you fail to listen when he asked you not to go running alone? I do believe you said you weren't going for a run this morning?' He smiled sarcastically. 'But surprise, surprise, here you are.'

'Pardon me?'

'You heard. I thought you'd actually pay attention to Filip, but alas, no. It's all about doing what you want, isn't it, Anna?

Clinging to that stubborn pride. Refusing to hear anyone but yourself.'

Anna was at a loss for words.

Daniel drew himself up to full height, scornfully eyed her up and down, and gave a grim laugh. 'Christ, it must be exhausting, going out with you. How does Filip stand it?'

Anna shook with rage. 'How dare you look at me like that! Nobody tells me what to do. You know what, I'm going to keep running along this route, and you can't stop me. Go to hell, Daniel.'

With all her might, she savagely pushed him into the brambles, vaulted Cassie, and sprinted away.

***

A shower did nothing to calm her, and, still livid, she crashed and banged about the kitchen, making breakfast and ranting at Kristina, who adopted a neutral position sipping coffee next to the sink. The phone rang. Anna snatched it up, expecting it to be Daniel ringing to apologise, but it was Filip. She barely got into her stride when he cut in.

'What the hell do you think you're playing at? Daniel's just told me what you did.'

There was a hard edge to his voice that he'd never used with her.

She adopted a conciliatory tone. 'Don't you want to hear my side?'

'No, Anna, I don't. I don't want to hear how you ignored Daniel's advice yet again. I don't want to hear how you think you're always right. The guy is cut to ribbons thanks to you.'

'Well … it serves him right. He shouldn't have wound me up. I don't like people looking me up and down. It's rude.'

'Anna, you will apologise to Daniel. And then, you're to stop running alone. Do I make myself clear?'

It was too much to ask. Say sorry to Daniel! Fat chance. Plus, another bloke was attempting to exert control. Forget it. Her rage ramped up to a rolling boil.

'I don't believe it. I'm going out with my father!' she snapped. 'What is it with men? Always trying to put me in my place, telling me what I should do, what I should think – my father, your father, Daniel, and now you. I thought you were better than that, Pip – I really did.'

There was silence on the other end of the phone.

'Stay away from me for the next few days – if you know what's good for you,' she roared down the phone before disconnecting. Grabbing her toast and giving Kristina a cursory goodbye, she stormed out.

***

Kristina waited till the gallery door banged shut, picked up a miraculously undamaged receiver and hit speed dial.

'She's gone.'

An agitated voice spoke rapidly.

'Yes … I agree. We have no choice but to' – Kristina grasped her crucifix and sent up a silent prayer – 'continue as planned.'

***

The coach tours were a welcome escape, and Anna threw herself into the role with more gusto than usual. Cosimo quickly lifted her mood, and all the passengers went away happy. However, arriving back at Apokeri, the red mist descended. For everybody's sake, she locked herself in the office to furiously hammer away at the keyboard, ignoring repeated and insistent knocks on the door, even when someone pushed down the handle. They were brave. Making sure the coast was clear, she speedily retreated to her room and spent the remainder of the night stewing in her own juices.

The following day, she was still fuming and deliberately ran the same route. Pounding along the clifftop, she was spoiling for a fight, but the track was empty. On her return, Kristina was nowhere to be found, and after bolting down a quick breakfast, she sped along to meet Max and pick up their twelve guests. The tour was another resounding success, and Max was especially thrilled as most guests intended to eat out at Apollo that evening. Buoyed up by such a great day, Anna decided to stop by the café and purchase coffees and cakes. They would be an apology for the tirade Kristina had endured. However, she still felt wholly justified in her behaviour and anger towards Daniel and Pip.

As she entered the café, Agnes, Sofia, and her brother-in-law were talking behind the counter – it was handover time between the two chefs. He was another individual who fell for the charms of Apokeri – or, more accurately, fell in love with Sofia's older sister at first sight. He immediately dumped his fiancée (they were on their holiday) and returned after packing up his life in Napoli. Within a fortnight, the pair married. Ten years later, Sofia's sister still called him her Italian Stallion and professed every woman should marry a man eighteen years their junior.

On seeing Anna, he blew a kiss before retreating into the kitchen to bond with his beloved pizza oven. Sofia greeted Anna with her usual enthusiastic welcome. Pip had clearly, wisely, kept quiet about their argument – and Sofia was determined to tell her something.

'Come now, I haven't seen you for two days. Sit down for a chat before hurrying away. You are always rushing about. I will have a word with my son. We cannot have you wearing yourself out.' Sofia fussed around her and then dropped her voice to a whisper, forcing Anna to lean forward. 'You've missed all the drama. You'll never guess what's happened.'

She began talking so rapidly that Anna threw up her hands. 'Whoa! Slow down. My Greek is not as good as that, man. You're talking way too fast – there's no way I can keep up.'

More slowly this time, Sofia began again. 'We heard this afternoon from one of our regular customers, who heard it from his brother in the police. The two young men who were staying at your apartments – they've gone. Put on the first flight back to wherever they came from … by the police.'

'What?' Anna exclaimed. 'There must be some mistake, surely? I chatted to them both, and they were lovely lads. Dead friendly and really polite.'

'Yes, we said as much.' Agnes joined them and failed to conceal her delight. 'Imagine them staying at your apartments and you being none the wiser. I mean, we've never had any bother with visitors before. Is this what we have to look forward to? Now that you're in charge?'

Sofia missed the dig. 'He was adamant. There had been a tip-off about a pair of young men staying in Apokeri, strongly suspected of planning to commit a serious crime against someone. He knew that the pair had been backpacking around the Greek islands for several weeks and had committed a raft of identical crimes across other resorts.'

'But with not enough evidence to bring charges,' Agnes continued. 'The police escorted them to the airport, where they flew out.' Agnes smirked. 'Oh dear, I cannot imagine getting a good review from that booking.'

'He wouldn't say what the crimes were – but they must be extremely serious. Is this what happens when a place becomes more popular? Evil creeps in?' Sofia cried as she wrung her hands.

Nausea washed over Anna as cold sweat trickled down her back regarding the intended victim's identity.

She shot up so fast her chair clattered over and, without a backwards glance, abruptly excused herself. 'Sorry, Sofia. Sorry, Agnes. I-I need to be somewhere, so we'll catch up … another time.'

106

Chapter Twelve

Anna waited till she was clear of the café before sprinting along the street. The gallery was closed, which did not bode well. Turning, she tore along the alleyway and took the apartment stairs two at a time. The door to room six stood open, and all signs of the guests were gone. That was wrong – the booking was until tomorrow morning. Flying back down the stairs, she wrenched open the garden gate and ran into the house, where she frantically searched the rooms, calling out for Kristina. Anna knew her friend had to be somewhere, and there was only one place left. Anna saw her sitting in the rooftop studio, staring at the horizon. She turned when Anna burst through the door.

'It was me, wasn't it? They were targeting me, weren't they?'

'Yes. We've been so worried. I-I've been so scared for you,' Kristina whispered.

In two strides, Anna was across the room. She flung herself into outstretched arms, dissolving into guilt-ridden sobs that shook her whole body. Kristina rocked her back and forth till she finally cried herself out.

Standing up slowly, Anna pulled over a chair and slumped into it. 'I'm so very, very sorry … for everything I put you through. I wouldn't listen, would I? I wouldn't listen to the warnings. Three times – three times I ignored them.'

'This is not your fault,' Kristina fiercely replied.

Anna dropped her head. 'It doesn't feel that way,' she mumbled.

'We hoped you wouldn't find out. Nobody from the police should have said anything, but we failed to account for human nature and the need to gossip. Filip rang a couple of minutes ago after Sofia telephoned him, saying you went white as a sheet and left in a hurry.' Anna sat bolt upright, but Kristina shook her head. 'Filip made up an excuse for your behaviour, and Sofia didn't put two and two together.'

'That's a relief.' Anna crumpled backwards but, after a few minutes, said adamantly, 'I need to know what happened. How did you all figure it out? I didn't have a clue. I never picked up the slightest hint that anything was wrong. Some judge of character I am.'

Kristina slowly explained how it had started when the pair first entered the gallery. As soon as they walked in, her skin began to crawl. It was like watching predators on the hunt, like sharks circling a victim. Oh, they were very polite young men, with their smiles and genial conversation. And keen to tell her all about the other Greek islands they'd visited, how her gallery was the best, how fortunate it was that they'd waited to buy gifts for their girlfriends, etc. She didn't care about a sale and wanted them gone – as far away as possible. There was absolute loathing in her voice as she described getting her wish. But on leaving, they smiled – sharp white teeth behind frightful grimaces – and wanted her to know how happy they were with the apartments. They proudly explained how Anna was so accommodating, going out of her way to help, and had certainly made an impression.

A siren exploded, her heart froze, and Kristina was scared. No, terrified because she knew they meant to hurt her young friend.

Anna reached for Kristina's hands and held them tight. Kristina had immediately rung Daniel – he would trust her instincts and not dismiss them as the imaginings of the crazy Swedish lady. She went to Daniel first, being unsure if Filip would believe her. Anna stirred, but a head shake stopped her. Kristina was wrong – Daniel immediately told him, and he wanted to get hold of the pair and beat them to a pulp. However, Daniel believed the predators were too clever, too cold-hearted and it would only result in an assault charge. He was adamant anything they did needed to be inside the law. It took the combined efforts of Daniel and Alex to persuade Filip, but finally, he agreed and conceded that violence rarely solved anything. All four kept an eye on Anna from that point on. Daniel took it upon himself to tail the pair and used walking Cassie as a cover. He chatted to them on the track and casually enquired about their plans, whether he could help, and established they were tracking Anna's movements; they knew she ran but didn't know where.

Another wave of guilt hit, and Anna squirmed in her chair. 'Oh, God. Daniel warned me, and then literally ten minutes later, I was merrily chatting away to one of them and tracing my bloody route on a map. I showed them where I ran. I told them the exact paths and even the time I usually went out.'

Filip had rung Anna, pretending to have wiped all the tour bookings – the idea was that he would interrupt her, and stop her talking to the two lads. But he was too late, and Kristina had overheard Anna giving up the required information. Things needed to step up, and luckily Daniel had a childhood friend in the police. Inspector Marinos was fantastic, took the concerns and suspicions seriously and started to investigate. He uncovered incidents of women attending hospitals on various islands the pair had visited, and all displayed identical injuries consistent with violent sexual assault. The medical staff Inspector Marinos spoke to remembered the women were non-Greek – either backpackers or seasonal workers. They were highly traumatised but refused to press charges, claiming they had consented. One nurse was so appalled by the injuries that she took it upon herself to go to the police and raise her concerns. Unfortunately, investigations quickly hit a dead end as the woman had provided hospital staff with a false name and address. However, Inspector Marinos saw similarities that made him take the threat seriously. He said there was a clear link between the assaults, and worryingly the intensity and frequency were escalating – they were gaining in confidence. The knowledge was terrifying.

'With the first two warnings going unheeded, Daniel agreed to bump into you again and persuade you to listen. Afterwards, he was mortified about losing his temper, but you must understand, Anna, we were so worried. And we completely underestimated your reaction. You were so angry that it made your behaviour more unpredictable.'

'Did any of you knock on the office door last night?' Anna shamefully asked.

'No. We knew how angry you were and agreed to keep out of your way. Plus, we had our plan in place by then and didn't want to risk anything going wrong.'

The women looked at each other, and there was a shared understanding that all the careful planning would have been in vain if Anna had opened her office door. They would never know for sure, but it seemed obvious who had been repeatedly rapping on the door. Anna sent up a silent prayer. Stubbornness had probably saved her.

'I'm sorry, I keep interrupting you. Please go on. What was the plan?'

'The pair were due to leave in the next few days, and we expected them to strike on your running route.' Kristina gestured to the hills behind the village.

Early morning, the police and Daniel had taken a position above the track, and Kristina stationed herself with a pair of binoculars in the back bedroom to watch room six. As soon as there was movement, she rang Filip, and Alex ran along the track behind the cycle shop to let the stakeout team know the pair were heading their way. As soon as they were sighted, the police trailed them, listening to their conversation. It went along the lines of 'she'll be coming along there', 'this is the best place to wait', and 'nobody else will see us from here'. The police held off until the pair took up their ambush position before moving in and then led them back along the track and took them away for questioning.

'What happened then?' Anna whispered. 'And where are their belongings?'

When the predators left, Kristina went up to their room. Everything was packed, ready to disappear today. Filip came to collect their stuff and took it to the bike shop, where the police loaded everything into a van. The pair stuck to a well-rehearsed story even when questioned separately for over an hour. Both stated they were simply waiting to surprise Anna and knew she'd find it funny. When confronted by the allegations on the other islands, they denied all knowledge. Inspector Marinos said that the pair never once lost their composure, from the moment they were apprehended. It was clear that they knew their rights and knew the police did not have anything on them – so did the police. They even thanked Inspector Marinos for taking them to the airport, saying it had saved them a taxi fare.

Anna sat back in her chair. 'I cannot stop thinking about all those women who weren't as lucky as me, what they must have suffered and must still be suffering. The bastards got away with it, didn't they? Free to do it again. I'm so angry I could scream.'

Inspector Marinos would be contacting the relevant police force where each suspect lived. It was little more than a goodwill gesture, as technically, no crime had been committed, and there was no hard evidence. The only crumb of comfort was that the men must know how close they'd come to being caught, or they wouldn't have willingly gone to the airport – and that might stop them from carrying out future attacks. Inspector Marinos believed they'd continue but hoped the pair would slip up.

'I'm so sorry, Anna. I hope it hasn't changed your mind about living here?'

She gave a tight smile. 'It's better knowing. I've had a very lucky escape, and it will make me more cautious in the future, especially what I reveal about myself to strangers. Thank you for everything you have done, and I am very sorry for having put you through so much. You'll be happy to hear I've no intention of leaving. It could have happened anywhere, and I still love the place and its people. One thing, why didn't you tell me your suspicions?'

Kristina looked decidedly uncomfortable. 'I knew you wouldn't believe me.'

Anna started to protest, stopped, and sadly conceded. 'You're right. I might as well be honest. I would've listened, made all the right noises and then brushed them aside like I did with Daniel and Pip.'

'It's because you see the good in people,' Kristina pointed out. 'It makes you who you are – and why we love you.'

Anna hugged her friend again and wiped away the last tears. After weeks of non-stop work, being nice to everyone no matter how rude they were, trying to fit in, constantly being perky or interesting, and keeping up her exercise campaign, she suddenly felt utterly exhausted.

'I think … I want to go and see Pip now.'

'You've suffered a massive shock. Take some time out. I'll handle the apartments until you're ready. It would be good for you to spend some time with Filip.'

'Thank you. And there are some others I need to thank.'

***

Anna thought she'd exhausted all her tears, but seeing Pip working behind the counter, they coursed down her cheeks. She felt small and vulnerable standing in the doorway. The space between herself and Pip stretched out forever, and her leaden feet were incapable of moving.

Glancing up, he rushed out from behind the counter. 'Anna, please don't tell me you walked up here by yourself? Why didn't you ring me? I'd have driven down to pick you up, sweetheart.'

There was no anger in his voice, only concern, making her feel more wretched.

'I'm … so, so sorry, Pip. I'm such a terrible person,' Anna sobbed into his chest. 'Kristina told me … the whole story. She told me what you all d-did. How can I ever th-thank you enough?'

He kissed her head, and she sank into his protective arms. 'You're not a terrible person at all. And thank me? Anna, what I've done doesn't begin to make up for everything you continue to do for me. Do you know how eternally grateful I am to have you in my life?' He brushed tears away from her face and looked straight into her dark brown eyes. 'I don't know what I'd do if anything ever happened to you.'

Hearing a sound, they both turned.

'Thank goodness you're safe,' Alex cried. 'I've never seen Filip so worried or angry.'

She kissed both boys and motioned toward the back. 'There's someone else I need to thank.'

'Are you sure you want to do that now? You're shattered. I'm sure Daniel would understand,' Filip protested.

'No, I need to do it now … before my courage fails me.'

***

She entered the tidy workshop to make the hardest apology ever. Daniel's broad back was bent over an assortment of bike parts, and he was utterly absorbed in the task. What the hell must he think of her? A stroppy, spoilt, and self-indulgent brat – at best. She cleared her throat, and he turned. Again, there was that expressionless face. Unable to determine his thoughts, she launched straight in. Words tumbled out over one another. She apologised for being a bitch, apologised for refusing to listen to him, apologised for screaming at him like a banshee, apologised for being unbelievably stubborn, apologised for pushing him into the bushes. She winced at the angry red scratches still crisscrossing his arms and thanked him again and again for everything, saying she would forever be in his debt. And finally, she asked him to thank Inspector Marinos and his team for going above and beyond. Throughout, he remained stony-faced, and it seemed an eternity before he spoke without the slightest trace of emotion.

'It was nothing – the least I could do. I will pass on your thanks. I'm sorry I lost my temper with you. It was wrong of me.'

And with that, he turned back to his task. It was an obvious dismissal, and Anna walked away with one overriding thought – how was she ever going to repay him?

Chapter Thirteen

Where were the carved beams? Then everything flooded back.
She was in Pip's studio flat above the shop, it took considerable
effort to swing her legs onto the floor. She groggily padded across
the room and smiled at the vase of flowers and the covered
breakfast tray. Guilty tears welled up as she read his message of
love inside a pretty card.

The private courtyard was her sanctuary. Sitting in the sun,
stroking Cassie, and watching the bees buzz between the flowers
brought a feeling of peace that soothed her soul. On hearing a car
pull away, Anna realised she must have nodded off. Working the
crick out of her neck, she peeked into the shop to find Pip
rearranging the central coffee table.

'They look fantastic.' Anna nodded as she watched him lay out
copies of the new Round the Bend Cycle Tours brochure.

'Thank you – it's good to see you awake and refreshed – I've
been keeping an eye on you.'

Hugging and thanking him for her gifts, she asked if he'd like
lunch making? Filip laughed. It was almost five, and he'd eaten
hours ago.

'I'm about to close for the day. We could take Cassie up to my
favourite viewpoint? I'll then make us something to eat. Daniel
and Alex won't be back till late and said they'd grab something
on their way home.'

The walk worked wonders as Cassie bounded about whilst
keeping Anna in sight. As they absorbed the clifftop view, she
was transported back to when she first stood on the exact spot

with Charlotte and Simon all those weeks ago – how her life had changed. And as the three of them watched the sun slowly sink, Anna knew with a certainty that surprised her that she'd never move back to Newcastle. It was over an hour later when their head torches picked out the shop.

***

After three nights staying with Pip, she was her old self again, and she tracked Daniel down in the workshop. Could he spare Cassie for an hour? She wanted to go for a run and would feel more comfortable with the dog by her side. It was the first time since apologising that she'd seen him laugh. But of course – as if Cassie would allow Anna out of sight. It would be interesting when Anna left that afternoon.

It took considerable effort to persuade Pip that she couldn't remain wrapped up in cotton wool forever. Everyday life beckoned. Reluctantly he'd agreed, but he wasn't the only one unwilling to see her go. Cassie sent up howls of protest and refused to stop. In the end, Pip and Cassie accompanied her home, and only after being satisfied that Anna was safe would Cassie consent to being led away.

***

Life did indeed go back to normal, and Anna threw herself back into work. With the Apokeri Flower and Food Festival fast approaching, preparations were cranking up, but things weren't all rosy.

A week later, Anna stood behind the counter with Pip and finished running through last-minute preparations for the next cycle tour. It was almost closing time when the door opened. In walked a very professional businesswoman who looked to be in her thirties. Moving with utter confidence, she was tall – Anna reckoned five-foot-ten – and wore four-inch stiletto heels that would have Anna flat on her face. Impeccably dressed in an expensive black trouser suit and cerise silk top that flattered an hourglass figure, her glossy, jet-black hair was swept away from a flawlessly stunning face. Perched on her hip was a pretty child of no more than two years old – fast asleep and clinging tightly to a fluffy blue bunny. Anna took in the scene – a fraction of a second – before Pip spoke.

'What a wonderful surprise, sis. I wasn't expecting you for another ten days,' Filip whispered, not wanting to wake his sleeping niece.

Of course, the family resemblance was unmistakable. Here was the infamous Stefania that Vasili constantly raved about. He adored his extremely successful, clever, and beautiful eldest child and waxed lyrical about her meteoric rise up the corporate ladder as a highly talented lawyer. It strongly reminded Anna of the fatherly praise heaped on her own sister.

After being introduced and receiving a firm handshake, Anna stood rooted to the spot, holding a still-sleeping child after Stefania requested a private chat with her brother. Okay, she could do this. She'd babysat Julia's kids a few times, although not as often as she'd have liked as they'd lived two hundred miles away. But how different was one toddler from another? Please be a quick discussion. Thirty minutes on, Anna was still cradling a stirring toddler but wisely sat on a sofa to relieve her aching arms.

The conflab ended, but Stefania immediately left to visit her parents. With Pip so agitated and preoccupied, Anna sought the courtyard and successfully distracted the little girl with flowers, creepy crawlies, and stroking a placid Cassie.

Time ticked by and, desperately running out of ideas, she gratefully heard a car door slam and headed for the shop. Standing in front of her brother, Stefania was incredibly distressed and angry. Without her sunglasses on, it was clear the woman had been crying. Anna's arrival elicited an awkward silence, and she quickly took the child back outside. Five minutes later, Pip came to find her. He enveloped his niece in a hug and, to squeals of laughter, began throwing her high up into the air. He calmly advised Anna that everything was fine, and he'd agreed with the request for Anna to work in the café tomorrow instead of the bike shop. He was spending the rest of the evening with his sister and niece and would see her tomorrow. Anna had been dismissed.

***

Anna spent the evening catching up with Kristina and took the opportunity to find out about Stefania. Kristina barely knew her now, as she'd left for university at eighteen. Stefania rarely returned, and then only for fleeting visits. However, Kristina remembered her as a child – the intellectual sibling, academically brilliant, and multi-talented. A rare individual who appeared to master anything they put their mind to. As a child and into her teenage years, Stefania spent countless hours in the studio with Kristina, chatting away whilst painting and transforming lumps of clay on the potter's wheel into things of beauty. The girl had considerable talent and could have become a successful artist. Kristina described her as very obedient, respectful to her elders, and she'd never given her parents any cause for concern. She'd been a daddy's girl and adored her brother. The siblings were close, and Kristina remembered Stefania spending hours tutoring Filip to improve his grades. The conversation provided Anna with a picture of Stefania as a child and teenager but not as a woman and she was certainly no closer to working out what had happened a few hours earlier.

***

The next day, Anna arrived bright and early at the café to discover a marked change. The place felt flat – operating on low battery mode – as if it drew its power from a markedly changed Sofia.

Even the brusque Agnes shrugged her shoulders. A subdued Sofia asked Anna to deliver the pastries, still sitting in the bakery, and casually asked if she'd met Stefania yesterday. Anna watched for a reaction when describing how upset her daughter had been – there was none.

She expected to find Vasili in the bakery, but only Viktor and Nikki were hard at work when she collected the basket. Again, the difference was palpable. She'd never noticed what a larger-than-life presence Vasili was. It felt as if three people were missing. Nikki launched into a detailed explanation of how terrible Vasili had looked that morning, how he was unusually quiet and uncharacteristically kept making mistakes. The girl adored Vasili – even though they constantly argued – and had told him to see a doctor. Instead, he'd gone to church.

***

Up the road, Anna found an equally subdued Pip managing the shop, whilst Daniel worked out the back and Alex was off on a cycle tour. Again, Anna enquired what was wrong, describing his parents' altered state, but he stressed she needn't be concerned.

'Steffi's not well, so I'm looking after Leyla tonight. I know you're tied up for the next two days, so let's catch up Saturday night?'

'I'd love to, but remember we were babysitting for Dania and Max. Why don't you spend the time with your sister and niece instead? You rarely see them. I'm fine looking after the kids myself, and they're always well-behaved.'

After agreeing to catch up on Sunday night instead, Anna returned to the café for a strange day. Sofia chatted as usual to the customers, but any lull would see her immediately retreat to the small courtyard out the back. It was here Anna found her sitting in the afternoon sun.

'Sofia, are you okay? Is there anything I can do to help?' she tentatively asked.

'Thank you, but everything is fine.'

'Why don't you go home and rest? I'm sorry to say this, but you don't look very well.'

'No, I need to keep busy,' Sofia dully responded in a lacklustre attempt to explain herself. 'I've so much on my mind with the upcoming Flower and Food Festival. Thank you for your concern. You're a good girl.'

Anna was being shut out and felt utterly helpless as she returned indoors.

***

Two days later, Anna popped into the café after confirming babysitting arrangements with Dania and was shocked at the change in Sofia. It was as if the woman had aged ten years in forty-eight hours, and she noticed that Sofia scuttled out the back as soon as she walked in.

Once she disappeared, Agnes actually confided that Sofia was very distressed about something but refused to tell her what. The café was to close early that night and open for reduced hours on Sunday. Something was seriously wrong. The high season brought in most of the café's money and stayed open late every night. Anna was troubled and, in her quest to find answers, found Sofia slumped in a courtyard chair. Her twinkling eyes were flat, clothes wrinkled, hair untidy, face devoid of make-up. The glum figure was a stark contrast to the woman who always prided herself on being well turned out.

'Sofia, please tell me what's going on. I'm really worried now. You've reduced the café hours and won't tell either Agnes or me what's wrong. You're like family; I want to help.'

'You wouldn't want to be part of this family if you knew,' Sofia mumbled and hung her head.

'What does that mean?' Anna cried.

'Nothing, ignore me. I'm rambling.' And then rousing herself, she said, 'We have decided to reduce the hours tonight and tomorrow, as everyone will soon be flat out with the Flower and Food Festival. There is nothing for you to worry about. Now go and get ready for the onslaught of the terrible twosome. You will need all your strength.'

'I know you're not telling me the whole truth. I'm going to figure a way to sort this out,' Anna obstinately responded as she kissed Sofia on the cheek and left the woman to brood.

**

On the dot of seven, Anna entered the Stipopolous household.

'Somebody looks very smart,' Anna remarked.

Max wore a tailored two-piece charcoal grey suit with a crisp white dress shirt, a silk magenta paisley tie, and highly polished, Oxford-style shoes.

'Thank you. We rarely go out for a posh meal, so I thought I'd dig out my best suit, shirt, and tie. Unsurprisingly, Dania's still running around.'

A voice from beyond shouted, 'I heard that, and I am ready.'

Max shook his head at the lie. 'Come through. Your waiter and waitress are expecting you.'

A puzzled look turned to utter delight when Anna entered the kitchen. Standing to attention was his five-year-old son dressed in a black suit, white shirt, red tie, and black polished shoes. He bowed deeply. His four-year-old sister delivered a perfect curtsey, smartly dressed in a frilly white blouse, a knee-length polka-dot skirt, tights, and shiny red shoes. The children took a hand each and steered Anna to the table. After being seated, she received a typed menu.

Stipopolous Family Restaurant
Main Course
Vegetable pasty accompanied by the finest
baked beans and creamy mashed potatoes.
Pudding
Blackberry and apple crumble with delicious
Lefkada single cream.
NB. Portion sizes per Miss Jenkinson's healthy appetite.

With a practised flourish, her waiter placed a napkin across Anna's lap, and her waitress carefully walked across the kitchen to proudly place the main course in front of her.

'Why, this is the best restaurant I have ever eaten in,' Anna declared after taking a bite of her pasty. 'What service and what attention to detail. Compliments to the chef.'

They giggled and, remembering their essential duties, took another bow and curtsey. 'Thank you. It is our pleasure.'

'What do you think?' Dania declared as she tottered into the kitchen in towering heels and gave a twirl.

'Mama, Mama. You're so pretty,' her children chorused as they ran up and carefully stroked her elaborately patterned red and gold Chinese-style dress.

'Come, my gorgeous queen, it is time for us to depart,' Max said and stuck out his arm.

Sofia's earlier comment about the terrible twosome was groundless. The siblings behaved impeccably every time Anna babysat, and tonight was no exception. After finishing her main course, it was bath time, and after checking their teeth had been brushed, it was time for a bedtime story that followed a set routine. On selecting a book, Anna would begin reading in Greek, to cries of, "No, no. In Geordie English." Anna would then restart, and after each sentence, they tried to copy her distinctive accent. Within a few minutes, all three would be laughing, and twenty minutes on, the two would drift into the land of nod.

Tonight, they kept to the script, and Anna bent over each sleeping child to kiss them goodnight. After ensuring each had their favourite cuddly toy, she tiptoed out to leave the room bathed in the warm glow of a night light.

She had just settled down on the sofa with a generous portion of crumble (even by Jenkinson standards) when there was a knock. She opened the door half expecting to find Pip but instead found Sofia.

'Come in; what a lovely surprise. Would you like to join me in some blackberry and apple crumble with cream?'

'No, thank you. I cannot stay long,' Sofia politely replied.

Anna tucked her feet up under her on the sofa and waited. Sofia sat quietly, twisting a handkerchief in her fingers whilst asking a series of questions. Did Anna think she was a good mother? What would her definition of a good mother be? Did Anna believe that Sofia worried too much about other people's opinions? Had Anna ever fallen out with her parents, and finally, were there conversations that could never be unsaid? Anna answered as best as she could.

'Vasili is working through the night in the bakery, and with Peter working in the kitchen tomorrow, Lucinda has asked to work in the café – I think my sister gets a bit bored being retired and only doing the odd bit of accountancy. So, I popped by to say take tomorrow off. Go and spend it with my son, daughter, and granddaughter. I was joking with my terrible twosome comment. Dania and Max have two wonderful children,' Sofia explained as she headed for the door.

'So do you,' Anna replied.

'I know,' Sofia sadly responded and left.

***

Babysitting duties complete, and now wide awake from the conversation with Sofia, Anna decided to walk home via the bakery. When she saw the light on and the door slightly ajar, she went inside. Vasili was hard at work and, on hearing a sound, looked up.

'Why am I not surprised,' he said, shaking his head. But there was kindness in his voice.

'May I join you?'

'Please do. Although I fear I'm poor company tonight.'

Anna watched his quick and precise dough kneading and recounted the earlier cryptic conversation with Sofia.

'If you don't want to tell me what's going on, I completely respect your decision. However, I'd like to help in any way I can. I'm worried about Sofia and you. The spark and swagger have gone from both of you. What can I do?' Anna pleaded.

'Have you ever been in a situation when you were certain you were right? You believed in what you were doing, only to discover that your actions had led to untold damage to your nearest and dearest?'

'Yes. I ignored repeated warnings from those who care deeply about me. I refused to listen and – what's worse – deliberately went out of my way ... to do what I was told not to. I put those I love through p-pain and distress. I'm so ... so ashamed of what I did,' her voice shook at the admission, and seeing Vasili process the information she ploughed on. 'However, I apologised – and everything worked out.'

'I don't think an apology will work in this instance. I've caused too much lasting pain.'

'Have you tried?' Anna calmly pressed.

Tears streamed down his cheeks. 'No. I'm too scared ... I'm too ashamed.'

She kissed him on each cheek and took his floury hands in hers. 'People have a great capacity for forgiveness. I know this from first-hand experience – remember that. Can things get any worse than they already are?'

'I don't know ... I really don't know.'

Chapter Fourteen

With a day off, Anna headed up to the cycle shop early, determined to make some headway with Pip and Stefania and found the siblings sitting together in the courtyard. As they watched Leyla on her playmat, she repeated her wish to help.

'All I can see is pain, fear, and regret on all sides, highly destructive emotions. But I can also see that you all love each other. I spoke to both of your parents separately last night. They're ashamed of whatever it is and worried that what's been said and done can't be forgiven. Is that right? Is there some way to work this out?' Anna gently probed.

Filip reached for his sister's hand and took a deep breath. 'We've agreed to tell you what's been going on. It'll enable you to understand the past, present, and our decisions.'

As her daughter played with building blocks, Stefania quietly began. When she arrived in Apokeri and spoke to Filip, she had headed to her parents and told them she'd left her husband – walked away from a beautiful home, expensive clothes, holidays, and a lavish lifestyle to come home and start again. As expected, the news didn't go down well, and Steffi received a lecture on the sanctity of marriage and how much it would shame the family, being a divorced, single parent. What would everyone think? How did she intend to support Leyla? Did she expect them to provide a roof over their heads? She should be keeping them as they got older – not the other way around.

She'd asked them if they wanted to know why she'd left her husband, and was asked what possible reason could there be? Her marriage vows must be valued, and couples resolve problems. It must be something headstrong Steffi had done – putting herself ahead of their grandchild and a successful and well-respected husband. Yes, they'd had initial concerns with him already having been divorced. But what choice did he have with such a wanton first wife – a wife who broke the sacred bonds of marriage and had an affair? An unfaithful husband was not necessarily an acceptable reason to seek a divorce. Stefania shouldn't be too hasty. Men sometimes strayed – especially when their wives had recently had a child. Forgive and forget, yes, that was what she must do. But she'd asked, what if there was another reason? They'd repeated, what other reason could there be? Did she want to be judged by God for falling short of her solemn vows? Steffi asked her parents to please believe there was a good reason; wasn't her happiness and their only grandchild's well-being the most important thing? She'd pointed out that she'd never let them down before. No, she was told, so she shouldn't start now. They had instructed her to return home to beg forgiveness.

Stefania paused to pour herself a drink before continuing. Her usual composure had disappeared, and she was furious and upset at their failure to listen. Once she'd started, she didn't hold back. All the pent-up emotions since childhood broke free. She called them hypocrites. It was fine for a man to stray but not a woman. How could they be happy if she went back to someone who cheated and didn't respect her? Her husband was having an affair, he had proudly announced, his parting shot was that he was off to the mistress, who knew how to satisfy a man – his bit on the side, the talented lawyer who'd replaced her. Stefania stared into her wine as she swivelled the glass backwards and forwards before taking a gulp. Her parents had heard the marriage was a sham, and how Steffi had stayed because she stupidly valued her marriage vows and wanted to make it work, enduring years of mental and physical abuse.

Anna cried out, and Stefania gave a grim laugh. 'You wouldn't think it to look at me, would you? I give the appearance of a woman in complete control.'

Of course, things didn't start that way. She was excited to work at his Athens law firm and met him as part of a small team a year later. It was for a complicated merger, worth a great deal of money and prestige to the firm, and involved working long hours, late nights, and weekends. Throughout, he was so charming. The merger went ahead, the success brought more high-profile cases, and she gained another well-deserved promotion. He started to pursue her, showered her with gifts, and said she drove him crazy with desire. It was flattering. He was, after all, an extremely successful, attractive, and influential man at the top of his professional field. He mixed in social circles she could only dream about. But he was married with young children, so she told him in no uncertain terms that she would have nothing to do with him. Even if his wife was an adulteress who no longer loved him, it made no difference. Marriage vows were sacred, and she would not be his mistress. For months he kept up his campaign, said he was serious in his intentions and wanted to spend the rest of his life with her, but she still did not relent. He filed for divorce to prove how deeply he cared. And finally, she yielded.

It was a whirlwind romance as he continued to shower her with gifts and saw her second bedroom transformed into a walk-in wardrobe to house all the new designer clothes, shoes, and accessories she wore to lavish events. They were sleeping together by then, but Stefania refused to live in sin, as her mother was fond of saying. He respected the decision – it was a credit to her beliefs.

She could not believe her luck. Professionally, she gained recognition from peers and rapidly rose through the ranks. In her personal life, she had captured the heart of a handsome, rich, and powerful man and mixed with elite Athenian society. How far the quiet and studious girl from Apokeri had come.

Stefania looked at her brother and smiled at far-off happier days. 'Do you remember my wedding?' He nodded. 'It was amazing – a private estate on the Athenian Riviera, with two hundred guests, overlooking the sea. My whole family flew in to celebrate – no expense spared – everyone I loved was there. I wore the most beautiful dress. No bride was as happy. And my wedding present – a beautiful clifftop villa overlooking the Argolic Gulf. A fitting gift to his bride to escape work pressures. I was living the dream.'

But then things started to change. It was very subtle at first and began with comments. Would Stefania not prefer to spend time with him instead of her friends? Why did she not wear this dress? It was so much more flattering than her choice. Should she be eating that piece of cake? Surely, she didn't want to spoil her gorgeous figure. He insidiously chipped away at her independence and confidence, but she didn't realise because she was blissfully happy. Her friends drifted away, and as they did so, she sought his reassurance on more and more everyday decisions. And then, just after their first anniversary, he hit her. The memory was crystal clear. They'd been to a gala dinner – a wonderful evening, or so she'd thought. But back home, he said she'd disrespected him by making a joke at his expense. She laughed and told him not to be so stuffy as everyone found the comment funny. And out of nowhere, he slapped her hard across the face, knocking her to the floor. He towered above her and demanded to know if she found that amusing? Steffi was completely stunned, but that quickly turned to anger. She jumped up and told him that nobody hit her, and she left. Luckily, she had kept her apartment. He came to see her, begged her to come back, explained he had been drunk and was appalled at his behaviour. He would never forgive himself. He had never raised his hand to a woman before; it was a terrible mistake, and he faithfully promised it would never happen again. She refused. For the next month, he continued his campaign to win her back.

Eventually, it worked and sealed her fate. It started slowly. Every few months, she received a beating for some alleged slight against him, some inappropriate behaviour. She would walk out, and his campaign to win her round began.

As time went on, the length of time it took to forgive him diminished – till she stopped walking out, and he stopped apologising. Stefania then became the reason for his violent behaviour. She brought the beatings on herself, and slowly but surely, she believed him. And he was clever, only hitting her the first time across her face. After that, he struck her where it wouldn't show, and she went to work covered in bruises beneath expensive business suits. The villa had a pool, but she hadn't used it in years. Instead, she'd sit on the side, hiding bruises from others and herself.

Pain-filled eyes held Anna's. 'Oh yes, I could see the irony. Ever since I went to university, I've given my free time to a charity helping victims of domestic abuse. Once I became a lawyer, I took on cases in my spare time. I fought battles in court and provided whatever support I could. However, I was unable to fight my own battles. I made myself sick at my hypocrisy.'

She stopped taking on cases and fundraised instead. She reasoned that, with her social connections, she could raise the charity's profile and a great deal of money. Oh, how full of praise her husband was in public for her philanthropic work, and of course he gained plenty of media coverage from being such a generous benefactor. Her life was fake. She hated herself and was ashamed of what she'd become. And things were about to get worse. Stefania was horrified to find out she was expecting after being so careful – she didn't want to bring a child into a violent home. But to her amazement, the beatings ceased. Her husband was ecstatic that his beautiful and faithful wife was making him a father again. Life became idyllic as she sailed through pregnancy – the picture of health. The man she fell in love with had returned. He was attentive, and nothing was too much trouble. She agreed to leave work. They had plenty of money, and she could dedicate all her time to their child. She had been right to stick with the marriage.

When Leyla was born, Steffi was overjoyed but soon discovered her husband did not feel the same way. He was bitterly disappointed. She had given him a daughter, not a son. At first, Stefania put it down to being unduly emotional after the birth. Surely, he was delighted with their beautiful and healthy baby daughter? No, she had let him down yet again. Even his whore of a first wife had managed to bear him two sons. Stefania was clearly at fault, and the beatings started again.

She contacted his first wife, Isobel, to establish if she had suffered the same fate. When they met, Isobel came straight out and told her about the years of physical and mental abuse. Had he ever lifted a finger against his sons? No, she was adamant on that. He had doted on them and said it was her only crumb of comfort that she was the only one to receive his punishment. Producing the much-anticipated sons had not spared her either. He had railed against her, constantly berated Isobel for letting herself go and was disgusted to look at her. Isobel admitted to being unfaithful. She had been amazed that any man still found her attractive and, when divorce proceedings started, she'd been terrified she would lose custody for being unfaithful. Luckily for Isobel, her husband was so infatuated that it overcame any paternal instincts. She was so grateful for this and immediately agreed that the boys would spend every other weekend with their father – that rarely happened. So desperate to get out of the marriage, she submitted to everything he said and financially walked away with nothing. Because who would ever believe that a man of her husband's standing was a wife-beater? Isobel admitted that she would never have left her husband, being utterly dependent, and her family – being in complete awe – would never believe him capable of such a thing. She shamefully admitted to being thankful that Stefania highly valued marriage vows. Continuing to refuse her husband's advances made him more determined to secure his mistress, ultimately leading to the divorce.

Stefania lowered her voice, requiring Anna to lean forward. 'Do you know how many times after that conversation I thought if I hadn't been so bloody righteous about marriage and slept with him straightaway, he probably would've got bored of me and moved on? Of course, I'll never know, and it's pointless to dwell on such matters. At the end of the day, I have a beautiful daughter who brings me so much joy. It's impossible to describe how much I love her, and I'm a far better person for having Leyla in my life.' Stefania's eyes shone as she looked at her daughter, happily playing with toy farm animals.

Her husband was a serial wife-beater. He hadn't touched his sons, but would he be the same with his daughter? Her husband was never left alone with Leyla, and he showed no interest in wanting to spend time with her. He'd thankfully started spending more time at the office. Stefania's happiness centred around Leyla and when Filip came to stay at the villa. She was very proud of him – he had become his own man. National Service was the making of him. Her little brother brimmed with confidence, and she'd listen to him regaling her with his plans as they sat by the pool and he entertained Leyla.

Anna glanced at Filip, whose face betrayed a turmoil of emotions. He grabbed the wine bottle, tipped the remainder into a glass and knocked it back.

Stefania thought she'd been so clever, carving out a semblance of a life. But no, things were never that easy. Her husband started to talk about a second child, a son. Stefania felt physically sick and was living in a nightmare, enduring the unwelcome attentions of someone she despised. She was disgusted to admit she regularly put in an Oscar-winning performance as the grateful wife. She submitted to his advances, knowing what would happen if she refused. This time, she took steps to ensure there would be no repeated accidents – but fate had other ideas. An acquaintance spotted her picking up the prescription, and with a stupid throwaway comment, her husband's suspicions were aroused.

Stefania tightened the grip on her brother's hand – a lifeline to save her from drowning in an ocean of misery.

Last week, she'd put Leyla down for a nap and was busy with the daily task of ensuring the house met his exacting cleanliness standards when he appeared in the bedroom. Home early – unusual behaviour, and never a good sign. She was immediately on alert, flashed a dazzling smile and quickly apologised for not having quite finished. What a lovely surprise to see him sooner than expected. Why didn't they go for a family walk before she prepared the evening meal?

Anna shivered as her skin started to crawl. She wanted to block it out – didn't want to know anymore. It was going to be bad. Very bad.

'Stefania, if-if you don't want to tell me … it's okay.'

In her own ears, the words sounded feeble. Stefania and Pip must think her pathetically weak.

'No, Anna. You have to know. You need to understand.'

Anna pushed down her cowardice and nodded. After everything Stefania had survived, the least she could do was listen.

The husband slowly turned and closed the door. Stefania was to play the dutiful wife role again between the sheets. He tenderly laid her on the bed with a smile. Carefully pushing her arms above her head, he straddled her and whispered, 'My beautiful wife, I know you never intend to bear another child. I know about your secret visits to the chemist to take precautions. Did you think I wouldn't find out?' And then the onslaught began.

The blows rained down again and again as she twisted and desperately crawled away. He grabbed her hair, dragged her onto the floor, and started savagely kicking Stefania in the stomach. All the time shouting, "We know there's nothing in there." She curled into a foetal position and prayed for it to stop but kept quiet, terrified Leyla would wake up. Her silence seemed to make him worse.

When the blows stopped, she cautiously raised her head and watched, horror-stricken, as he slowly unbuckled his leather belt and leisurely removed it. He kept his eyes on her as she cowered on the carpet – a mouse cornered by a snake – and then he struck, viciously bringing the strap down over and over. She was beyond terrified. This was it. He was going to kill her right there on the carpet in their home, and she'd leave Leyla motherless. She needed to make him stop. The pain was unbearable, so she grovelled, begged, and pleaded for forgiveness. He was right – he was always right – there'd be a son. She frantically fumbled to find the right words to make him stop. And then her heart stopped at a tiny, terrified voice calling out for her. Leyla stood framed in the doorway, half asleep and holding her fluffy blue bunny. In two strides, he was across the room. She screamed at him to stop. He turned with disgust and hit Leyla across the face. The force knocked her to the ground. She didn't make a sound, but instead stared at her father and then her mother with enormous saucer-like eyes.

Stefania had scrambled up, grabbed hold of Leyla, and backed away. With a look of utter contempt at them both, he informed her not to expect him back till the weekend, at which point she'd demonstrate what a loving wife she was. And she would continue to do so until she was expecting his son. Once he stormed out, she was overwhelmed by guilt. What kind of mother was she? How could she have ever tried to justify staying and putting Leyla in danger? As soon as the car screeched out of the driveway, it was her final chance. He might come back any minute. Mustering every ounce of self-control, she calmly told Leyla they were going on a trip to see Nana Sofia, Granda Vas-vas and Uncle Filip earlier than planned, and it would be so much fun to surprise them. Bless her, Leyla jumped up excitedly, and after being told to choose a book for the journey, she scampered away, grasping her beloved bunny. Stefania tore into the bathroom, scooped up some essentials, and quickly redid her make-up – she needed to look presentable for her next destination. After a hastily scribbled note to say she had taken Leyla away for a few days and would be in touch, she was at the bank thirty minutes later emptying her safe deposit box, and then on the road.

'Bloody hell,' Anna whispered. 'Did you tell your parents all that?' Stefania nodded. 'And what did they say?'

'Nothing. They sat stonelike and stared at me like I was an alien.' Stefania dragged her hands over her face. 'I waited for them to say something. To say anything, but they remained silent – so I kept going.'

She asked her father did he ever wonder why she'd been so keen to leave at eighteen? Did he wonder why she was so passionate about helping victims of abuse? Did he think it might have something to do with her witnessing him repeatedly hitting Filip since he was little? It was hard to forget all the times she'd desperately clung to his arm and begged him to stop, trying to explain how Filip was clever – in a different way. And how she'd spent hours tutoring Filip, so his grades slowly improved, and he was spared the slipper or belt. She left home hoping it would stop the comparisons and beatings and downplayed her university and professional successes for fear of them being used against Filip. And she knew about the night at the bakery with Filip, and wished Viktor had never arrived.

Anna turned to a red-eyed Filip.

'Everything Steffi has said is true. Never book-clever, I acted up in class to make people laugh and became the archetypal joker – a constant irritation to a hardworking father, who took it as evidence of laziness.'

He started to hang around the bike shop to escape. Instead of being shooed away, Daniel's father took him in – despite what Filip's father said to Arthur. And encouraged by this, he began to spend more and more time there. He became Arthur and Daniel's little helper and discovered a talent for fixing bikes. His papa disagreed and repeatedly said he was wasting his time in a place that would never amount to anything. It was Filip's duty to take over the family business, and it was high time he knuckled down instead of daydreaming his life away. Every time Filip opened his mouth, it fuelled the fire of disapproval. Maybe if he completed National Service, it would prove he was a real man.

Going away was the making of him, and he met so many different people from so many walks of life with varied backgrounds and life experiences. The people who made the biggest impression were returning home to dutifully follow their parents' wishes (utterly miserable at the prospect) or intended to follow their dreams. Filip made a pact with himself to stand his ground when he returned home.

It started innocently enough when he called in to see his father on one of his long nightshifts at the bakery and tell him he was starting full-time at the bike shop. With Arthur emigrating, Daniel had total control, and Filip could see how successful the place would be and wanted to be part of it. He excitedly explained his ambitions to become a future partner, but it only resulted in another lecture about wasting his time there and his duty to the family business. His father relished throwing cold water over Filip's plans. But this time, Filip stood his ground and explained Viktor was an excellent baker with worldwide experience. In a few months, he had revolutionised the product line with so many highly successful and profitable ideas. Viktor was the perfect successor – not Filip. It was far better to have someone with passion running the business and whose quiet determination would ensure future expansion.

Filip thought he'd argued his case well, but his father got angry and said he'd made a lifetime of sacrifices and would not stand by to see the business pass out of the family. Filip still refused to back down and was called a disrespectful son. Why could he not be like his sister? She was always obedient and highly successful.

Filip also lost his temper and matched his father's shouting. Why could he not love his son for who he was instead of forever comparing him to someone he didn't want to be? Why was nothing ever good enough? Filip was his own man and would do what he wanted with or without his father's blessing. At that point, he was slapped hard across the face and told he was a disgrace. If Filip had ever done anything worthwhile, he would have earned his father's respect, but he would forever be second best until then.

Something snapped inside, and Filip hurled his father against the wall and pinned him up against it by his throat. And then Filip was borne up and placed gently on the bakery floor. The broad six-foot-seven-figure of Viktor stood between him and his father. In a calm voice, Viktor instructed him to return home and said what had happened that night would stay within the bakery walls, and it was time for Vasili and himself to talk.

Filip stumbled home, scared at how close he had come to doing something unspeakable. He slipped into his room, not wanting Daniel to see how upset he was. The phone rang, and Filip answered, worried something might have happened between Viktor and Papa. It was Stefania, and she immediately knew something was wrong. Filip broke down and confessed everything, but it must remain a secret.

Although his father never apologised for his actions, he never raised his hand again. He never mentioned Filip taking over the business and never compared him to Steffi. The next day, Filip thanked Viktor profusely for stepping in and saving more than one life that night. He had shaken Filip's hand and said, "Thank you for your gratitude. It is greatly appreciated. You have a good heart and a good soul. Always remember violence is never the way."

Anna realised she was sitting with her hands around her throat and quickly dropped them. 'And your father changed.' Filip nodded, and she brightened. 'That's a good thing then ... isn't it?'

It was brilliant for Filip but did not change Stefania's circumstances, and she had turned on her mother next.

What kind of woman stood by and let their husband hit their son? Oh yes, on the occasions she witnessed it, she told him that was enough, and he would stop – but there had always been another time. How hard had she tried to change his behaviour? Didn't she care that he showered praise on one child and delivered such harsh treatment to the other? Not waiting for an answer, Stefania reached her crowning glory and called her mother a true hypocrite who was always so quick to pass judgement on the behaviour of others when her own fell far short of the high standards she preached.

With great delight, Stefania told them she knew why they always joked about forgetting their wedding date, why they never celebrated their anniversary and why there were no wedding photos. As a studious teenager, she'd loved learning about the history of Apokeri and spent hours in the church sifting through old parish records. Imagine the surprise at discovering her own parents' wedding entry only six months before her birth. Sex before marriage and a baby conceived outside wedlock. Was that the only reason they married? Because her mother had been so eager to spread her legs? Not such a good girl, after all. How much love was in the marriage? Had they stayed together to merely save face? How dare they pass judgement on their daughter's decisions? After that, her father stood up and said, with a sombre finality, "Now we know what you think. Do you have anything further to add?" She did not, and the last thing he said to her was, "I believe it's time for you to leave." So, she did.

Anna sat shell-shocked. It was far beyond anything she'd ever encountered in her safe and stable childhood and fairly everyday adulthood. In light of everything – it seemed ridiculously insignificant – but the only thing she could think to do was hug them and say how truly sorry she was.

Stefania looked utterly wretched. 'I was full of hell when I stormed back here after that conversation with my parents. But it didn't take long for the dawning realisation to hit me. I didn't give my parents the chance to respond. No wonder they sat stonelike ... they were in complete shock, and I passed judgement. Do I believe they'd want me to remain married? It'd never enter their heads that my marriage had a dark side ... and I had betrayed Filip's confidence – for what? My father isn't perfect – who is? But he's changed. And any fool can see my parents love each other, so why bring up the revelation about their wedding? And ... worst of all ... I questioned my mother's behaviour towards her children – me, the mother who'd knowingly stayed with a violent man after her own child was born. Jesus Christ, who the hell am I?'

Anna gripped the chair's arms. 'For crying out loud, Stefania, you've suffered years of sustained physical and psychological abuse – no wonder you lost it. I don't know how you coped all those years and aren't a complete basket case.'

'No, there's no excuse for what I said to my parents. I'm ... horrified ... and ... utterly ashamed of my behaviour towards them.' She slumped back in her chair. 'Now you know our sorrowful tale. We appreciate your love and perseverance shown to our family – but too much has happened. The matter is closed. Time to move on.'

Anna knew she'd gain nothing by arguing the point and hung her head in sadness. The three sat lost in thought as Leyla chuntered away and constructed a toy farmyard.

'On a more positive note,' Filip said. 'Do you want to hear our plans?'

Chapter Fifteen

The polished appearance was back, and Sofia had revved up to seventy per cent power, but there was automation in her conversations and behaviour. The same with Vasili. It forced Anna to take up the slack – Lucinda was more entertaining than any real help. Rushing around, Anna completed her tasks whilst thinking about the resilient human spirit.

Yesterday, she'd discovered the vision for Round the Bend Cycle Tours had stepped up several gears. Steffi, as Anna now called her, was financing and project managing the building's transformation to incorporate guest and staff accommodation. And the plans didn't stop there. She was in advanced talks with Daniel to purchase his house with its courtyard, garden, and associated land. Once complete, Filip and Alex would vacate the studios over the shop and move into the house, thus surrounding Leyla with a stable home environment. Daniel was keen to push through the transaction as it would provide financial independence and the funds to establish a new life in Australia.

And Steffi pointed out there'd be plenty of space when her brother decided to marry and have children – the lack of subtlety brought some much-needed laughter. Anna and Filip exchanged meaningful glances, which Steffi accepted as proof.

It was lovely to see an animated Steffi explain the renovations. Still, at the same time, Anna found herself unexpectedly saddened at Daniel giving up his family home. Ever since Cassie became her running partner, his attitude had thawed and in turn she no longer needed to adopt her sickly-sweet persona. His personality was guarded, not open or as quick-witted as Pip, nor did he have the easy humour of Alex, but Anna enjoyed their in-depth conversations and lively debates about politics, Greek culture, history, and travel. Like everyone else, she'd known he was settling close to his father after travelling but realised a part of her had expected him to return. Selling his home indicated a further severing of his Greek roots. Anna loved Apokeri so much, she couldn't understand why anyone would want to leave.

To raise funds, Steffi sold her Athenian apartment and contents to Isobel as a holiday let. And the clifftop villa was on the market, contents an optional extra. Over the years, Steffi had marketed the sophisticated property well, renting it out as an exclusive holiday getaway, a location for films and television, a backdrop for lifestyle and wedding publications, and a romantic setting for marriage proposals and intimate weddings. There'd already been some serious interest, and Steffi was confident that the whole package would complete quickly.

Anna had been delighted to hear Steffi's soon-to-be ex-husband was quickly re-discovering what a talented, determined, and ruthless lawyer his beautiful wife was. As it turned out, he'd rather unwisely admitted to enjoying dishing out every beating. And if she filed for divorce, he would see to it that she walked away with nothing, shred all her belongings, paint her as an unfit mother and destroy her reputation as a lawyer so that she could never practice anywhere again. With the recorded call, evidence of her injuries over the years, and Isobel's testimony, Steffi was confident he'd agree to her two requests – sole custody of a daughter he did not care for and her belongings shipped across.

Anna stood behind the counter and studied the customer faces before her. How much did we know anyone? She was brought out of her reverie by Agnes, who, since Sofia's altered state, had transitioned from a spiky, poisonous sea urchin to an unpredictable neighbourhood cat who'd scratch your arm one minute and then weave around your legs the next. It was an improvement.

'Penny for them, is that what you say?'

'I was miles away.'

'Be warned, have your wits about you today. Sofia is on a mission – determined not to be outdone at this year's festival. The woman's obsessed.'

Every year, Sofia entered the café into the Best Dressed Building category and was consistently awarded first or second runner-up. Except for last year, when the café only managed a paltry fifth place. Sofia had been an absolute nightmare for weeks afterwards. Even now, she was still smarting, repeatedly telling Anna how mortifying it had been when the supermarket and pharmacy placed higher. The latter previously had only ever achieved eighth place. Sofia was only thankful for having beaten the laundry. It would've been beyond humiliating if she'd lost to that.

Anna knew how well attended the festival was, and year on year it had grown and developed till the flower competition was only a tiny part. The event now drew visitors from right across Lefkada and the mainland. At first, Anna naively saw the competition as light-hearted fun between the various Apokeri businesses. She quickly came to realise that was not the case. Each sought to outdo their opponents, delightfully broadcasting their successes and rivals' failures.

Sofia had ramped up her family's chances to move back up the rankings by employing Kristina to design the whole display and provide the full ten per cent of flowers. And for the first time, Makris Bakery had entered. Sofia reasoned it would create more visual impact if both took part. Vasili had tried to point out that as the bakery was a commercial enterprise, what possible benefit was there in taking part? Entering was a complete waste of time and money. However, Sofia ignored his opinion and went ahead regardless.

A month before the festival, Anna had noticed that various people in the village were casually quizzing her. How much did she know about the competitors' designs? Did she know how much each was spending? It was fine to tell them – they could keep a secret. She politely advised each enquirer that only Kristina knew and, under competition rules, Anna only helped with growing and weeding. She would assist with the final floral arrangements but didn't know whose they were until the drop-off. Anna found the enquiries amusing and had told Agnes as much. 'I guarantee you will not be saying that with a week to go,' had been the sober response.

Agnes was right. As the date got closer, Anna found herself unable to go into any Apokeri business without being interrogated – purchasing groceries in the supermarket, suntan lotion in the pharmacy, or stamps in the Post Office. Constantly ambushed walking up the main street, she moved about by the back lanes. Of course, it made no difference when she arrived at work. Sofia, Vasili, Dania, Max, Pip, Alex, and Daniel kept on at her – she must know something. There was no escape even in her apartment office. Stelios had taken to collecting the laundry and would sidle in to find out what she knew. He would turn on the Andino charm to try and winkle out information. Eventually, Anna's long fuse ran out and, in no uncertain terms, she told anyone who asked that she knew nothing and to kindly leave her in peace.

After the warning to be on her guard, Anna muttered in exasperation, 'Howay man, I know the festival is good for the village, but this competitive spirit is getting out of hand – I can't wait till it's over.'

'Yes, but only if we come in the top three,' Agnes wisely responded.

***

142

The morning rush was over, and Anna was updating the blackboard when she heard the café door open.

'What a lovely surprise. Can you not keep away from the place?' Sofia, standing next to her, exclaimed.

It was her brother-in-law Peter and Lucinda.

'I decided to treat my fair lady to a late breakfast,' he explained. 'Luc couldn't wait to try one of the new strawberry tarts when I told her how delicious they were.'

Sofia took their order, and as she began to make their coffees, Lucinda appraised Anna's handiwork. 'I see the latest Geordie phrase is updated.'

The Geordie Phrase Phenomenon began shortly after Anna started. One afternoon while battling to open a jar of olives, in mounting frustration, she cried out 'howay man' before the lid popped off. Agnes snapped in her usual bitchy way, 'Pick a language – Greek or English – instead of wittering on in Georges.' More diplomatically, Sofia advised Anna that she peppered her conversations with mysterious words and phrases. Until then, everyone had been too polite to say anything.

It had never occurred to Anna that the confusion and blank expressions were due to Geordie slang – not her fast speech or accent. Whilst working in Australia, her accent was an issue for many locals. How embarrassing to find out that your pronunciation of coke sounded like you were asking for a cock! She'd instantly switched to soda water with lime and adopted a drawling voice.

Adriani's impersonations would be a hard act to follow and would be massively missed. The Geordie Phrase Phenomenon had been Anna's attempt to introduce humour and at the same time help people understand her. Astonishingly, it was an instant hit. Sofia loved it and could often be heard exclaiming 'wey, aye man' and 'canny' whilst Agnes became more obnoxious – although Anna sometimes heard 'howay man' coming from the kitchen. When Nikki and Vasili bickered, 'pack it in, man', 'just dee as ya telt', 'how man', and 'divvn dee that man!' drifted out of the bakery. Regular customers now greeted Anna with 'Kaliméra, pet' and 'Kalispera hinny.' There were also lots of 'right', 'like', and 'man' tacked onto orders. Anna was making her mark and hoped the latest phrase would be as successful.

'I got wrong – to be told off, to be disciplined. For example, I got wrong for not doing my homework,' Peter read aloud.

'Is that from personal experience?' Lucinda asked.

'No. I was a total swot, always did my homework as soon as I got it.' She saw the couple's disbelieving faces. 'You're looking at a complete square whose school reports always stated, "Anna is a very conscientious student." I'm sure that was more to do with the fact I was quiet, so the teachers probably didn't know who I was. How about you two – were you both good students?'

'Hell no,' Lucinda scoffed. 'I left everything to the last minute – scribbling off essays at the kitchen table whilst everyone else enjoyed breakfast.'

'I can confirm that's true.' Sofia handed over two espressos, a strawberry tart, and a cinnamon bagel with lashings of butter. 'Not that it did you any harm, Luci. You always scored far higher marks than me.'

'I was even worse,' Peter recalled. 'I was convinced it was my destiny to be a world-famous goalkeeper, playing for Italy and Napoli. So, I did the bare minimum, but I significantly overrated my footballing skills. Luckily my father recognised his son's delusions and encouraged me to work in a pizza place whilst I was still at school, much to my mother's relief. I loved it and worked my way up to Head Pizzaiolo. Thank goodness I found where my real talent lay.'

'That's an understatement,' Anna exclaimed. 'I keep saying it – enter yourself in the World Pizza Championships.'

'I'm far too content in Apokeri. I've no desire to trundle off to Parma. Instead, I'll stick to competing in our annual festival instead.'

144

It was the wrong thing to say and immediately set Sofia off about the fantastic café and bakery flower displays that would guarantee a place higher than last year. Sofia was thankfully interrupted mid-flow by the phone. After a few minutes, she reappeared with Vasili. Both looked uneasy – it had not been a good conversation.

Sofia signalled for her sister and Anna to join them and whispered, 'That was Kristina. There's something wrong with our flowers. She didn't want to say any more on the phone, just told me it'd be best for us to come along as soon as possible to see what's happened.'

'The judging is this Saturday,' Vasili groaned. 'There's so little time left. I refuse to finish behind Stelios and his laundry. Kristina will have to fix whatever the problem is.'

'Luci, I know this is not ideal, but would you mind jumping behind the counter and helping Anna if things get too busy before we get back?' Sofia implored.

'So much for our relaxing morning,' Lucinda exclaimed to her husband but quickly added. 'It was a joke, Sofi. Of course, I'll give Anna a hand. Now go and see Kristina. I know how much the competition means to you both.'

And with that, the couple departed but took the backstreets as Vasili refused to walk down the main road. He was paranoid that his rivals would suspect something if they saw them entering the gallery.

'I didn't think it was possible for anyone to be more obsessed with this competition than my sister, but I was wrong. Vasili is far worse.' Lucinda sighed before joining her husband to hopefully enjoy their late breakfast.

Initially, Vasili had wanted nothing to do with the competition, reluctantly agreeing to take part only when he had no choice in the matter anyway. However, the man had undergone a radical transformation. He was a peacock, strutting about the place, telling his customers that Makris Bakery and Aphrodite Café would wipe the floor this year. His deliveries now took considerably longer, especially when he called into Apollo. Over coffee, Max and Vasili would taunt each other about who would win. When Vasili would eventually return from his rounds, Nikki was quick to say it was nice he'd finally decided to do some actual work. Her comments had the reverse effect, and as the festival drew ever closer, his round took longer as he bragged about his amazing flower displays. Vasili had also been the one to badger Anna long after she instructed everyone to leave her alone.

There was no denying a large part of the couple's obsession was an attempt to distract them from the ongoing family fracture, which showed no sign of healing. Neither party displayed any animosity, but the topic of reconciliation was taboo. Sofia and Vasili always asked after their children, and in turn, Anna answered Pip's and Steffi's enquiries. Leyla still visited her grandparents but was dropped off and collected by Anna. The festival was going to be a night of flitting between both parties. She didn't want to think about it. The entire affair was utterly depressing.

Chapter Sixteen

Kristina replaced the receiver and sat motionless in her kitchen. She felt heartily sorry for Sofia and Vasili after delivering the bad news. The couple so clearly wanted to do well with their flower displays this year, and Kristina had been excited about the arrangements. After a few minutes, she roused herself to make them all a coffee and grabbed some homemade biscuits in an attempt to soothe their inevitable distress. The gallery would not open that morning. It was the least she could do.

It seemed only seconds later that the anxious figures of Sofia and Vasili were standing in her kitchen. After handing them both a drink and reaching for the plate of cookies, Kristina slowly led the way upstairs. She had deliberately given very little away, stating it was better to wait until they were on the rooftop garden. After hurrying over and climbing two flights of steep stairs, the couple was out of breath. However, they were keen to see the damage and chivvied Kristina forward. Although they were behind her, Kristina could imagine them eagerly eyeing up all the flowerbeds as they wound their way across the roof. Directly behind the last raised flowerbed was a table and chairs where Anna and Kristina had taken to watching dramatic sunsets. She could feel the breath of Sofia and Vasili on her neck, and being so close, they couldn't see anything ahead and were utterly unprepared when Kristina stepped aside to provide a clear view of two people sitting at a table. And those two people were poring over an artist's rendering of a reimagined home and cycle business.

Time stood still as two generations of the Makris family eyeballed each other before they turned to face Kristina. The silence broke when a figure stepped forward.

'If you're going to be angry, be angry at me. I'm the one behind this.'

As soon as Sofia and Vasili had bustled out of the café, Peter had given Anna the thumbs-up. It worked; they'd taken the bait. After a few minutes – and a much-needed hug and encouragement – she'd set out. Pulling this off required a massive amount of luck.

Flitting along the backstreets, she'd caught sight of the walled garden door closing and, like a stone sentinel, stood outside and waited. Gauging time as best she could, Anna quietly turned the handle, stole along the brick path and crept up the stairs. Luck was indeed on her side, and with impeccable timing, she stepped forward and made herself known. Now came the hard part. The thunderous faces of her boyfriend, his sister, and their parents glowered at her.

Okay, Jenkinson, it's time for you to step up to the mark.

'I took things into my own hands when it became increasingly apparent that none of you intended to make amends with each other.'

Vasili stirred until a withering look of her own stopped him.

'I'm not finished,' she notified her audience. 'It has taken a considerable amount of guile and planning to bring you together this morning. Kristina, Daniel, Alex, Lucinda, and Peter have all been instrumental in this, and I will not have their invaluable help go to waste.'

As one, the family group straightened.

'It was not an impromptu visit to the café this morning by your sister and brother-in-law, Sofia, but a carefully orchestrated one,' she said with tenderness. She turned towards her boyfriend and his sister. 'The same goes for your visit. It was no coincidence that Daniel and Alex just happened to be free for you to view the new plans.'

Looking across the faces of the Makris family she loved, Anna was filled with a renewed determination to kick-start reconciliations.

'The four of you will remain on this rooftop until you have worked things out. I do not want to see a single one of you until then,' she commanded and could have sworn the corners of Vasili's mouth twitched upwards into a wry smile. 'Now, Kristina and I are going to leave you to it. We will be downstairs in the garden.'

Anna turned on her heels and marched off the roof. The cloak of confidence disintegrated the moment the door closed. Gripping on to the banister, she made her way down the stairs on shaky legs and collapsed into a patio chair. Kristina vanished and soon returned with a cafetiere of strong coffee and a large bar of chocolate. Not usually one to sit in the sun, Anna closed her eyes and basked lizard-like in the therapeutic heat, and gradually her heartbeat slowed. She sought the shade after a few minutes, but her hands still shook as she poured the coffee. Kristina had already broken into the chocolate bar and devoured two rows.

'What a turn up for the books,' Anna observed. 'Someone getting to the chocolate first who isn't related to me.'

'I needed that.' Kristina licked melted chocolate off her fingers and sipped her coffee. 'That was some performance you gave – I almost laughed when you ordered them to remain there and sort things out. All four looked like naughty schoolchildren.'

Anna winced at the memory. 'You don't think it was too much, do you?'

'No, I do not. It needed saying. They needed a shove in the right direction, which will hopefully work.'

Anna sat back and sent up a silent prayer that her friend was right. She felt indebted to her co-conspirators – all of whom had immediately signed up without needing the full facts. Anna had kept the confessional conversation with Pip and Steffi confidential. It was not her place to disclose such information. She felt sure Daniel, Alex, Lucinda, and Peter knew some family history but not about Steffi's abusive marriage.

The chocolate and coffee were long gone, with still no sign of life from the Makris family. Due to her increasing anxiety levels, Anna had a bad case of verbal diarrhoea, and Kristina showed infinite patience in listening to her nonsensical ramblings. Had she done the right thing? Should she have kept her nose out and enormous mouth shut? Were they up there killing each other? Was this another instance of the Jenkinson Stubborn Gene making matters worse? Would they all stop speaking to her? That would be dreadful but it would be far worse if she caused a wider family rift with Lucinda and Peter and a fallout with Kristina, Daniel, and Alex. How could she hope to fix that monumental mess? After twenty minutes of berating herself, Anna finally ran out of steam, but before falling silent, she beseeched Kristina to go and open the gallery. The woman had already given up so much precious time, and valuable revenue ebbed away the longer they sat in the garden. Anna was fine to wait alone, fortified by caffeine and one of her greatest loves – chocolate.

'Absolutely not. I have not come this far to miss out on the concluding stages,' Kristina exclaimed. 'My child, you have done everything possible. I'll bang their heads together myself if this fails.'

Time dragged, so the women went over the flower display schedule, what needed doing, and when. There was still a Herculean amount left to do. Finally, the kitchen door opened and out strode a grim-looking Vasili with a red-eyed Sofia following closely behind. There was no hint of a smile on his face now, and Anna steeled herself for the inevitable repercussions.

'I want to have a word, young lady,' he sternly announced. 'And do me the courtesy of coming over here.'

Anna thought she saw Sofia flinch at her husband's instruction and gingerly approached, taking a deep breath.

'I have only one thing to say to you,' he growled, and she braced herself.

The next thing, she found herself hugged and profusely thanked. Tears of gratitude streamed down the married couple's cheeks, and tears of relief rolled down hers. A minute later, Pip and Steffi embraced her. Everyone was crying – including Kristina – who received heartfelt thanks and embraces.

'On behalf of our family, I want to thank you, Anna. Through your sheer determination—'

Filip winked. 'And bloody-mindedness.'

'Yes, and a lot of that,' Vasili continued. 'Beyond all hope, you've made our family whole again. Something none of us thought possible, and we all agree that nobody else could be brave or foolish enough to try.'

'Thank you. Oh no, you've set me off again.' Anna sniffed, wiping away more tears. 'It wasn't all down to me. I could never have done it without the help of Kristina, Lucinda, Peter, Daniel, and Alex. I owe them a great deal.'

'We owe them a great deal, you mean, and we will thank them,' Vasili explained.

Relief flooded through her, and a realisation hit. 'What has come out of this is acknowledging my stubbornness is a good thing. Wouldn't you all agree?'

Filip laughed. 'Oh no, you don't. On this occasion, yes, but it's not a green light to unleash your bullheadedness on us all.'

'It was worth a shot,' she replied with an impish grin and turned to Vasili. 'I think it was very cruel, pretending to be angry with me.'

Sofia chuckled. 'Well, we had to have some fun to get you back for luring us here on false pretences.'

'I would like to add – it was all Filip's idea,' Steffi broke in with complete innocence.

'Is that right?' Anna cried as she gave her boyfriend a playful shove to be rewarded with a kiss.

'That's enough, young lovebirds,' Steffi joked. 'Come on, Filip, it's high time we headed back to relieve Daniel and Alex from shop and babysitting duties. Perhaps we could play the same trick on them and pretend we're outraged?'

'Hmmm … maybe.' Filip stroked his chin. 'Anyway, despite your deviousness, Kristina, thanks for the plans. Is it okay if we get back to you after the festival? I think you've enough on your plate till then.'

'Of course, my dear. Take all the time you need.'

As everyone made ready to leave, Sofia piped up. 'There is one thing I need to straighten out, and it's of utmost importance.'

The formal tone stopped everybody, and with a collective intake of breath, they waited, unsure of what to expect.

'Our flowers for the competition? They are okay after all this?'

'Yes, Sofia, you have my word on that. All your flowers are in perfect condition,' Kristina resolutely replied.

'Thank heavens,' everyone responded.

Chapter Seventeen

The day of the annual Apokeri Flower and Food Festival had finally dawned. Unknown muscles were protesting from Anna's recent gardening exertions. Listening to the waves gently lapping, she was more relieved than excited and, with considerable effort, craned herself upright. Herbal tea wasn't going to work today. She required turbocharged coffee for what promised to be another busy one. The last few days had been frenetic. There were nine flower arrangements to complete, and every business wanted theirs delivered at precisely seven in the evening to give them the maximum twelve hours before judging opened at seven the next morning.

Nine arrangements shouldn't be too onerous. But what Anna had failed to consider – before enthusiastically agreeing to help Kristina – was the size of each building. A ten per cent flower display for the small shopfronts of Epione Pharmacy, Odyssey Travel, and Atlas Laundry was easy enough. However, Apollo was huge with its three floors. Nereus and Dionysus had four visible sides, and the combined wall space of Aphrodite and Makris soon totted up. Anna was eternally grateful to Helena, who arranged for her son and his new girlfriend to pick up the displays for Thalia and Dionysus. Helena confessed to taking full advantage of her son's recent loved-up status. Being so ridiculously happy, he did anything she asked.

Daniel had also been an enormous help by picking up the displays for Round the Bend. Although no longer the owner, he was desperate for his former business to do well. His swansong was to achieve fourth as fifth was the previous best. There was a good chance. For the first time, Kristina had free rein to design the whole display and incorporate the total ten per cent allocation of flowers. During the penultimate evening, both women toiled away on the rooftop garden, and Anna discovered Kristina usually had a crew of volunteers. For various reasons, it was only the two of them this year. With the Best Dressed Building being ridiculously competitive, Anna had felt it was worth reassessing things, and surprisingly Kristina immediately agreed. This festival was her curtain call on flower arranging, and she conceded it must be advancing age. Even without the apartment business, she still craved more time to paint, read, potter in the garden, or go for a plodge in the sea (a Geordie phrase, meaning to paddle). Anna had pointed out that – having done more than her fair share for the village – Kristina deserved to relax. Next year's festival flower-arranging needed addressing at the upcoming village committee. And with that, they continued working long into the night to make sure the flower displays were the best ever.

***

The festival started at seven in the evening – two hours to go. Anna finished her tour guide duties and beheld a wondrous sight. Apokeri was resplendent. The pretty village always looked beautiful with its flowers, shrubs, and trees, but everyone pulled out all the stops for the festival.

Anna and Kristina might have completed nine arrangements, but every business and household had created their own masterpieces. Every window featured elaborate flower boxes with cascades of frothy foliage and vibrant colour. A cheerful festival banner adorned each lamp post, strung between pretty handmade bunting that had been lovingly crafted by local school children and stretched right along the street and promenade.

154

The place itself buzzed with people, many clutching the official festival booklet. Designed by Kristina, it included a detailed map indicating the location of each competition entrant. A tear-out page enabled people to vote for their favourite, and as an incentive, a lucky individual would be drawn at random that evening to win a meal for two at Apollo. It was a clever strategy to entice people into walking around the whole village, visiting each business, and hopefully spending their money. Even if not today, they might do so in the future and spread the news of what a brilliant place Apokeri was.

Festival HQ – the village square – was a hive of activity as an army of volunteers erected stalls on three sides. And once up, they would be commandeered by various Apokeri businesses selling their wares. In its centre, additional tables and chairs had been sandwiched between the two lines of plane trees and well-used benches.

All Apokeri eateries had jointly agreed on the food selection to entice visitors with the broadest range of delicious dishes. Anna was excited about all the fantastic cuisines and attempted a modicum of restraint at lunch but, as usual, spectacularly failed. It wasn't her fault when it looked, smelled, and tasted so good. This evening, her strategy was to encourage everyone she knew to purchase a different dish for her to taste. She knew the options from the committee meetings. Dionysus Taverna would be serving up chicken souvlaki and loukaniko spicy sausages. Apollo would also be serving from one stall (the feisty matriarchs preferred to combine their talents) to offer stifado and kleftiko this year. Nereus Restaurant elected to take a couple of booths and let their two chefs battle it out for the Best in Show trophy. The Head Chef was offering a menu consisting of pastitsio (a Greek baked pasta dish with ground meat and béchamel sauce), deep-fried meatballs called keftedes, and a courgette-based option, both served with a tzatziki dip. The second Nereus chef (a close friend of Agnes and Viktor since their cruise-ship days) had opted to go back to his roots for the festival and offer mouth-watering Indian street food with Railway lamb curry, Bengali chicken curry, and vegetarian kadhai paneer. Another establishment where the chefs pitted themselves against one another was Aphrodite. Peter was embracing his first love, and pride of place on his stall was a wood-fired pizza oven where he would entertain and dish up margherita, puttanesca, funghi, and Capri options. Agnes was shying away from a Greek offering with a multi-cultural selection of chilli con carne, Thai green chicken curry, and vegan falafel wraps with salad. And finally, Makris Bakery was getting in on the act with Viktor and Nikki serving up a range of sumptuous pastries and cakes to tempt the crowds into fitting in a few sweet-based calories. And with so many spicy main meals, a selection of indulgent ice creams would also be on hand to cool palates.

Amongst the organised chaos, the whitewashed parish church stood proud at the head of the square and looked magnificent with dozens of new hanging baskets and flower boxes. Anna knew from the committee meetings that the church, Post Office, and primary school did not believe it was appropriate to spend funds on flower displays. As a well-loved priest with a large congregation, Father Katechis was never short of diligent members who took it upon themselves, or dutifully instructed others, to lovingly create homegrown arrangements.

The official opening and the award ceremonies would take place on a stage to the left of the stone church steps. Afterwards, live music and dancing would entertain the masses until late. The Festival Committee had booked traditional Greek singers, dancers, and musicians. And coming only a week after the Lefkada International Folklore Festival, an eclectic mix of groups from Mexico, Paraguay, and (to Anna's amusement) a troupe of Dorset Morris Dancers, had agreed to stay and perform.

The village school impressed – railings and open gates interwoven with vines, flowers, bunting, and banners welcomed visitors inside. On entering, Anna found last-minute preparations underway. Conducting these in rapid-fire Greek was the ever-cheerful school teacher, Sarah Andino, closely watched by her boss – the imperious headteacher Miss Irene Stipopolous. At fifty, the five-foot-five wiry-framed woman had a commanding air and piercing stare that kept unruly children and many villagers in check – her serious personality a complete contrast to her exuberant nephew Max. Anna quietly slipped out of the school hall to find Pip setting up stall eight with Alex and his family clan.

Alex's parents and grandparents had made a surprise visit to help out with Round the Bend flower displays and discover more about the business. Walking into the shop yesterday afternoon, his pint-sized grandmother, Madalena, asked a bemused Daniel to fetch Alex. At eighty-four, she wished to hire a tricycle in her size as she fancied cycling up to Karya. Given half a chance, Anna suspected this eccentric granny would have given it a go.

How much help Alex's relations provided last night was questionable. Most of the time, Alex spent the evening repeatedly arguing with his grandmother to get down from the top rung of a twenty-foot ladder. He'd keep finding her precariously balanced, peering through thick jam-jar glasses to attach hanging baskets from a series of hooks way off the ground. She, of course, paid no attention and retorted he should stop being so bossy and instead be more grateful for her assistance – given the fact she'd backed his decision to come and work in Apokeri. In addition, Alex's father, Seb, kept wheeling out all the men's bikes to race them up and down the road in the dark and, on his return, enthusiastically asked Alex to explain the pros and cons of each model. Eventually, after much gnashing of teeth, the displays were complete. At the moment, Alex's family were behaving themselves, standing laden down with Round the Bend merchandise. On espying Anna, Filip excused himself and made his way over to her.

'Thank heavens,' he cried, clinging desperately to her. 'Please save me. I always thought Alex was joking when he said his father's side of the family was slightly crazy, but he wasn't. And his grandmother is by far the worst.'

Anna was shaking with laughter by the time Pip finished recounting the day's exploits. He kept finding Madalena out the back trying on all the branded Lycra cycling gear. Discovering a tiny octogenarian in various stages of undress had been extremely unsettling. Madalena, on the other hand, hadn't batted an eyelid. At least the fashion show entertained Leyla, and the pair were now best friends. Alex's father kept trying to help service the bikes, but Alex pre-warned Filip and Daniel that Seb didn't have a clue and wasn't to be let anywhere near them under any circumstance – that'd been fun. Grandfather Pello kindly volunteered to make everyone lunch but fell asleep in the sun and only woke up to a dozen eggs exploding across the kitchen when the pan boiled dry. Steffi spent the next hour tidying up the mess. It was clear Alex got his common sense from the maternal side. His mother, Arali, wisely made herself scarce by taking Cassie for a very, very long clifftop hike early that morning and luckily returned with lunch just as the kitchen became habitable again.

'When did you say they were going home?' Anna asked, trying and failing to keep a straight face.

'Thank heavens they're leaving tomorrow afternoon. At the behest of Seb, Alex, Daniel, and I will take him on an early morning bike ride before opening up. I know it'll be a disaster,' he predicted and looked traumatised at the unavoidable prospect. 'And don't you look too smug, missy. They're descending on Aphrodite for lunch during your shift. I'm telling you they'll have the place in an uproar. Agnes is going to have a meltdown. And remember, they're also stopping at your apartments tonight. Surely, they can't cause too much damage in one night.'

Anna felt sure Pip was exaggerating for dramatic effect and pulled her reluctant boyfriend back to the stall before the Panagos family destroyed it.

***

The church bells finished chiming seven as Father Katechis climbed onto the stage to a rapturous reception. The square was packed with people impatient to get proceedings underway, and they listened to the priest thank everyone for coming and remind them there was only one hour left to win a meal for two at delightful Apollo. The Festival Committee had worked their magic, and donations from Apokeri businesses and their suppliers meant a fantastic range of raffle prizes to raise funds for the new church roof appeal. Tickets could be purchased in the school hall. Father Katechis thought the case of wine would be a perfect addition to his collection. It elicited a chuckle from residents – everyone knew how partial the priest was to an evening tipple.

In the school hall, visitors were encouraged to read about the fascinating history of Apokeri, including first-hand accounts. There were plenty of colourful drawings and stories by the talented primary school children, and prizes awarded to each year group. At nine, all the gifted chefs would discover who had won the Best in Show trophy, and Anna was glad she was not in the judges' shoes. And the crowning glory of the night would be the coveted Best Dressed Building trophy. As soon as Father Katechis announced this, Anna could see the anxiety on Sofia's face surface, and she sent up a silent prayer for a satisfactory result.

After the blessing and an instruction for everyone to enjoy themselves, the annual Apokeri Flower and Food Festival was officially declared open. A brightly dressed Peruvian band and its dancers then took to the stage to perform their Valicha dance

159

and, out of nowhere, multiple queues sprung up at all the food stalls. Anna waited in the long line to order her kadhai paneer and a Railway curry for Pip. She was transported back to being a twenty-one-year-old, standing in the Andes foothills as panpipes, drums, flutes, and the unique stringed charango filled a fiery red sky.

***

'I'm going to explode,' Steffi groaned and massaged a full stomach. 'Why did I eat that last falafel?'

'Because you're a piglet,' Filip responded with a snort. 'And also, because everything tastes amazing. Like Anna, I find it impossible to say no. I feel like I should fast for a week.'

'How, man!' Anna swiped her boyfriend. 'I've been amazingly restrained – so far.'

'Yes, that's true,' he conceded. 'I should have adopted your tactic to try a little from everybody's plate instead of wolfing down four large portions. The puttanesca did it – I cannot resist olives, capers, and anchovies on a pizza.'

The reunited Makris family sat by stall eight, along with Alex and his family, Daniel, Kristina and, much to Anna's delight, Cosimo and his family. Her friend was working that night – a perfect opportunity to enjoy the festivities and earn some money.

After a rousing cheer for the Dorset Morris Dancers, it was the prizegiving ceremony. Most of the raffle prizes went to people unknown to Anna. However, she was thrilled when Cosimo won the meal for two at Apollo. He joked it was always wise to vote for 'him upstairs.' All the well-behaved children trooped up to receive their prizes, and Agnes's daughter was especially cute. On being awarded the first runner-up, she politely curtseyed before waving to her very proud parents – her mother looked fit to burst with pride.

It was then time for the Best in Show trophy, with chefs invited to the stage as Father Katechis explained the combined dishes scoring method. This year had been the closest run competition, with an exceptionally high standard. It had been tough, but the judges eventually reached a unanimous decision. A hush fell over the crowd as the envelope slowly opened, and the winners were announced in reverse order. In third place: Agnes Benrubi, Head Chef of Aphrodite Café, with her international range of dishes. A massive cheer went up as a scarlet-faced Agnes mumbled a quick thank you and scuttled back in line with her bouquet. Peter Antonis, Chef at Aphrodite Café, was the first runner-up with his pizza selection and an even bigger cheer went up. Being no shrinking violet, Peter blew kisses to the crowd and bowed deeply to Father Katechis as he received his bouquet and thanked the judges. And then, it was time to announce the winner. Father Katechis smiled as he described that this chef continued to elevate dishes to another level. It was an enormous pleasure to reveal the Best in Show trophy winner to be Ahmad Yadhav of Nereus Restaurant.

The square exploded with cheers, whistles, and applause as the crowd agreed. A very humble Ahmad thanked Father Katechis and all the judges. His emotional speech praised Stelios for his ongoing support and the freedom to push culinary boundaries, and his colleagues, who were a joy to work with. And finally, he was grateful to everyone in Apokeri. The village was a special place with its close-knit community, and he felt fortunate to call it home.

After the applause died down, everyone eagerly anticipated the Best Dressed Building category. However, Anna and a select few knew what was happening next. Father Katechis invited the Deputy Chair of the Festival Committee, Miss Irene Stipopolous, to join him. In a typically strident voice, she explained there would be a break with tradition. Two further accolades needed bestowing. A murmur ran through the puzzled people seated closest to Anna. The first tribute was for an Apokeri individual who consistently delivered exceptional service with an ongoing commitment to the welfare and development of others. This person would be greatly missed by the community and was wished all the luck for their exciting future. The crowd was then asked to show their appreciation and welcome Daniel Eckvardsson to the stage.

The village residents and many other islanders who knew him sent up a rousing cheer. Anna glanced across at Daniel, who sat in his seat dumbfounded. So much so that even with encouragement from Filip, Steffi, and Kristina, it was only when Alex's grandfather lent over and gently whispered that he needed to make a move that Daniel was spurred into action. He cast a quizzical look towards Anna before weaving his way forwards.

There was a tear in his former teacher's eye as she handed Daniel his bouquet and a small envelope containing something useful for his trip. And grasping his hand, the gruff teacher displayed a softer side.

'Your mother would be so proud of you.'

She was rewarded with a rare hug from Daniel and a round of applause from the audience. Anna could hear sniffles around her, especially from one person, and it suddenly struck her how much Kristina was going to miss Daniel, and how much she must still miss his mother. Taking the microphone, Daniel gave thanks to those who had been a formative part of his childhood and helped develop him into the sensible chap he had become. He would miss everyone but felt sure they understood a longing to see his father in Australia. With a grin, Daniel declared it was now his turn to surprise a member of the audience.

'This honour has been accorded to someone who has been a pivotal member of the Apokeri community for many years. This person has helped raise the profile of Apokeri and been instrumental in its ongoing transformation into the beautiful and vibrant place we love and enjoy today. And finally – on a personal

162

note – this individual has always been there for me. Providing wise words and a kick up the bum when I needed it.'

Laughter rippled through the crowd, especially when a male voice shouted that Daniel had definitely needed the latter over the years.

Shrugging his shoulders, Daniel smiled. 'It is my great pleasure on behalf of the Village Committee to award the Freedom of Apokeri to Kristina Nilssen. Kristina, can you please join me.'

The applause rang out across the square and continued as an overwhelmed Kristina stood up and made her way to the stage, but stopped to hug Anna.

'Thank you, my child. I know this was down to you.'

Daniel presented a beautiful bouquet and a framed Freedom of Apokeri honour. On taking the microphone, a choked Kristina thanked Daniel and the Village Committee for the great tribute. It meant the world to her. After being welcomed by the people of Apokeri so many years ago, she had wanted to pay back their generosity in a small way. To be recognised for that was humbling.

Kristina coughed before continuing. 'Anyway, enough about me. It is now my immense pleasure to announce the winners of the Best Dressed Building. This year's standard is exceptional, and every entrant should be rightly proud of their achievements. There were twelve commercial businesses in the running, and without further ado, I can announce the winners in reverse order are …'

Anna looked over to where Sofia and Vasili sat holding hands. It was an adorable family picture. Leyla perched on her mother's knee, rested a small hand on her grandfather's arm, and balanced her faithful blue bunny on his shoulder. Steffi was holding fast to her father's hand, and on the other side, Filip had linked arms with his mother. Collectively, the Makris family was holding its breath.

'In third place,' Kristina's clear voice rang out. 'It is Round the Bend Cycle and Scooter Hire.'

Anna worried her eardrums had perforated with the deafening noise. Alex and Filip were like synchronised swimmers shooting upwards and punching the air in perfect unison. Leyla squealed with excitement at then being spun around by her uncle. On the stage, sensible Daniel vanished as he jumped up and down whilst frantically motioning for Alex and Filip to join him. The trio soon hugged each other and enthusiastically thanked everyone for their support.

'Thank you, boys.' Kristina took back the microphone and motioned the exuberant second runners-up to clear the stage. 'In second place with an exceptional display providing real impact is Aphrodite Café with Makris Bakery.'

Again, a massive cheer went up. Filip, who had only just taken his seat, jumped back up again. Sofia burst out crying as Vasili enveloped her in a hug. Steffi and Anna beamed at each other, silently telegraphing the same thought – thank heavens for that. It was a very emotional Sofia and Vasili who climbed onto the stage to accept their bouquet and a congratulatory hug from Kristina. After giving thanks, the couple quickly departed.

'It is now the moment we have all been waiting for. I am delighted to announce that the Apokeri Flower and Food Festival Best Dressed Building Award goes to Apollo Taverna.'

It was well-deserved and, looking at the splendid façade, Anna acknowledged that the winner had never been in doubt. The restaurant looked fantastic with its tapestry of colours, from rich magenta to delicate lemon, and flower forms including singles, doubles, spikes, umbels, trumpets, and pompoms. The explosion of colour was tied together with a supporting cast of grasses, vines, palms, and towering tropical-looking plants with huge leaves. On being lit at night, the effect was magical as entwined fairy lights and cleverly positioned spotlights cast dramatic shadows. The cheers and applause continued as a surprisingly modest Max accepted the trophy, and then the animated character was back.

'Is everyone having a good time?'

Everybody responded enthusiastically, but Max shook his head.

'Is that it? The best you can do? I thought I was in Apokeri on Lefkada, not sleepy Port Spilia on Meganisi. I said are you having a good time?'

This time the response was deafening.

'Well, that's more like it. Let's have some fun and party like there's no tomorrow.' Waving the trophy above his head, he left the stage.

Chapter Eighteen

'Are you okay in there?' Kristina enquired through the closed bedroom door.

'No,' Anna wailed and slowly pushed herself off the cool porcelain toilet she had been clinging to for the last hour. Opening the bedroom door, Anna met with a bright and breezy Kristina, who looked the picture of health. 'I am holding you completely responsible for my current state.'

'I'm not the one who decided to drink the bar dry, young lady.'

'That's true, but you were the one who invited half the village back here after the festival ended. Whenever I tried to sneak off to bed, my way was barred – mainly by you.'

'What do you expect? It was a celebration. I think I need to capture this moment. It'll make a great photo for the mantlepiece.' Kristina sniggered.

'Don't you dare,' Anna screeched as she rushed back to the bathroom but had nothing left to retch up.

Last night, everyone had taken Max at his word and partied hard. After his winning speech, Anna enthusiastically tucked into a double-scoop strawberry and mango ice cream, followed by a wedge of chocolate cake. After helping to clear away the little left on the stall, she danced with an ever-changing rotation of people who tried but failed to keep up. The festival finished at midnight, and with half an hour to go, everyone embraced traditional Greek music, and with over-exuberance, those worse for wear collided and fell over. When Filip apparently overbalanced, Anna went to help him up but realised he was on bent knee and holding a ring.

Gently taking her hand, he asked if she would do him the great honour of agreeing to be his wife. Standing amid the melee, Anna felt completely floored; it was utterly unexpected. At that stage in their relationship, marriage was a casual remark, not a serious topic of conversation. He'd often joked about what she'd do if he ever proposed? Her answers varied between a flippant 'What to me?' and 'That'll never happen' or a more truthful 'I don't know.' On being asked, everything stopped, and Anna clearly remembered the expectant faces of everyone watching and waiting. Looking past Daniel, Alex stood grinning and gave a thumbs-up. Turning to her handsome boyfriend, this amazing man who she loved so much, Anna replied she would, and he slipped a slim gold band with a single diamond onto her finger. That's when things went awry with a never-ending series of toasts that Anna knocked back. After midnight, all the musicians and dancers had finally left the stage after umpteen requests for one more, and as it was far too early to end the celebrations, they had simply moved along the street.

Hunched over on the bed, she recalled snapshots – doing the conga around the garden holding tight to Vasili's waist, spitting out her drink when Alex explained his grandparents were skinny-dipping, and dancing to a dodgy Europop CD under rooftop fairy lights with Adriani and, amazingly, Agnes. Anna had been very drunk. And then, of course, telling everyone repeatedly how much she loved them and how happy she was in Apokeri before trying to sneak off to bed.

In the end, completely exhausted, she'd crept into the beautiful parterre garden and, amongst the immaculately trimmed hedges, clipped bay trees, and lavender shrubs she'd curled up under a blanket on a bench and passed out. Filip had found her and, despite half-hearted protestations to be left in the foliage, wisely piggy-backed his shattered fiancée to bed. And after leaving a bottle of water on her bedside table he'd re-joined the celebrations.

167

'What time did everyone go home?' Anna whispered, fearful speaking any louder would crack her skull wide open.

'I think it was four,' Kristina replied brightly.

'How are you perfectly fine?' Anna whimpered. 'I know you were drinking; I remember all the toasts you kept giving.'

'Dear unobservant one, I took small sips. I was not chucking alcohol down my throat as if it was going out of fashion.'

'When will I ever learn? I'm twenty-six, not sixteen. Okay, tell me the worst. What time is it? How many hours to pull myself together? In the vain attempt to appear semi-human for my shift at the café? I can hardly ring in sick to my future mother-in-law,' she said pitifully and collapsed back onto the bed, thankful the room had ceased spinning.

'It's seven now. And I think you said you start at ten?' Kristina said and laughed at the pathetic sight of her friend sprawled out on the duvet. 'Here, drink this.'

Anna hesitantly reached for the cup of steaming yellow liquid and took a sniff. She almost spewed at the smell. It was absolutely vile.

'Do you use this to clean the kitchen floor?' Anna managed in disgust.

'That, I will have you know, is my sure-proof hangover cure. It is a closely guarded secret, so do not ask me for the recipe because I will not give it to you. Drink it down in one go – you'll be as right as rain in no time. And then ring your parents.'

Holding her nose, Anna downed the revolting tonic and set to work making herself look halfway decent for the day ahead.

***

Here goes. Anna pressed the icon and waited.

'Hello? Hello? Anna, is that you? There's something wrong with your screen. We can't see you.'

'Yes, it's me, Mam. It's the same at this end. I thought I'd give you a quick ring before heading off to work.'

'It's Sunday morning.'

'I know that, Dad. I work Sundays … remember?'

'You work too much. All hours. It's not good for you.'

Maybe her dad had a point. She felt wrecked and not just from the mother of all hangovers.

'Alkobery slave labour … that's what I call it.'

'Hardly. They do pay me, Dad. And it's Apokeri.'

She'd told him a zillion times.

'Not enough, I expect … now take Julia …'

Ahhhhhhhhhhhhhhhhhhh! Anna silently screamed, shaking her mobile. Yes, the lack of a video screen was infinitely better. Why was it so difficult to have even the most straightforward conversation with her father? And breathe.

'I need to tell you something … I-I-I'm engaged.'

She waited for a response.

'Hello? Hello? Is anyone there?'

'I'm sorry – Mam … Dad – I can't hear you.'

Her father's curt response cut through the extended silence. 'That's because we haven't said anything, young lady.'

'Oh … right. Okay then.'

'The first question is an obvious one – who exactly are you engaged to?'

Ah yes. In her excitement, Anna had forgotten – they didn't know she was dating anyone. Why set yourself up for another fall? Oops.

'He's called Pip – well, that's what I call him. To everyone else, he's Filip. You're going to love him.'

Anna waited for the invariable paternal criticism. Instead, it was her mother's steady voice.

'Of course, we will. But Anna, I thought you never wanted to get married – again? You always said once was more than enough.'

Lack of sleep and feeling like death had dulled her senses. Of course, the conversation was going to be awkward.

'I assume you've told Julia?'

'No, Dad, I rang you both first.'

'What, even before your best mate, Annalise? I must say we are honoured. That Annalise is lucky, I've never told her parents about what went on with you two in the States after your good-for-nothing first husband up and—'

'Dad ... we've been through this before.'

Anna tucked hair behind her left ear – again. The nervous habit always surfaced when talking to or about her father. She was surprised there wasn't a permanent groove.

'Well, I'm sorry, but I expected better from her. She was brought up proper. Like you, I might add. But when's that ever stopped you?'

'Dad ... can you just ... let it go? Annalise was acting in my best interests. I told her not to say anything. She was being loyal to me. Haven't you always drummed it into us – loyalty? Anyway, let's not focus on the past. Let's celebrate the future.'

'You're right, pet.' The calming influence of her mother silenced any further negativity. 'Regardless of what it sounds like from your father, we are happy for you. Aren't we, Robert?'

There was silence.

'Robert!'

'Yes. Yes – of course. How could you think otherwise?'

'Anna? Are you still there? We need to know about Pip and his proposal – it was him who proposed, wasn't it? And the wedding plans.'

'Yes, Dad. Sorry ... I've just realised the time. I'm going to be late for work. I'll tell you everything later.'

***

Striding along the street, Anna laughed, and it released the tension. In hindsight, it would have been better to tell her parents she was dating Pip first and then break the engagement news a few weeks later. Oh well, since when had she ever done anything the easy way? She'd ring back with a lengthy explanation of how they had met and what he was like. To be fair, a speedy engagement was the one area her parents couldn't disagree about – they married within ten months, over thirty-five years ago. The news would also give her father a further excuse to book their fortnight holiday for the following year, to come and inspect her choice of husband – that'd be interesting. And she'd better sit down with Pip to discuss their wedding plans.

As she passed along the street, the breakdown crew had done a fantastic job with stripped lamp posts and a village square devoid of stalls, stage, and any other festival paraphernalia. Everything was spotless, as if nothing had happened. The resident group of older Apokeri gents was already set up under the plane trees, doing battle over dominoes and putting the world to rights.

The café was heaving – these people should be nursing hangovers on the beach or in bed. Apokeri residents and tourists were hardy souls. Perhaps Kristina was secretly selling her remedy out the back of the gallery? She'd make a fortune. Anna had been transformed from a member of the living dead to bright-eyed and bushy-tailed in a matter of hours. Okay, she felt a little ropey and a bit tired – but an early night would sort that out.

'Sorry I'm late,' Anna announced as she stored her bag under the counter and hurriedly tied an apron around her waist. 'I got caught up on the phone with my mam and dad.'

'Late?' Sofia queried. 'You're a day early.'

'What?'

'Oh, hello. What are you doing here?' Agnes commented as she set down a spinach, feta, and pine nut filo pie. 'You look much better than the last time I saw you. It's a miracle you're upright.'

'Congratulations,' Adriani remarked, kissing Anna on the cheek whilst retrieving her banana smoothie. 'My cousin is a lucky guy. I thought you'd be enjoying a lie-in. I didn't expect to see you till tonight's family gathering.'

'Have I stepped into a parallel universe?' Anna said as she glanced at everyone – especially a nice Agnes. 'What's going on and what family gathering?'

'I gave you today off. I didn't think you'd be in any fit state,' Sofia patiently explained. 'Don't you remember repeatedly thanking and hugging me after I told you? And declaring to everyone what a fantastic mother-in-law I'd be?'

'You also kept rubbing it in that I had to work today when you didn't,' Agnes added with undisguised glee.

'Don't you remember the lengthy conversation with my friends last night?' Adriani smirked and nodded to a group of five people smiling and waving. 'They kept getting you to talk – not that it took much encouragement – as they love your Geordie accent.'

Anna hesitantly returned the greeting. She did remember a brief introduction to the drama series production crew earlier in the evening. On hearing Adriani's wonderful description of the highly competitive festival with its colourful characters, they'd made it their mission to attend.

'How much do you remember about last night?' Agnes asked and was shaking with laughter.

'Not much, it seems,' Anna admitted. 'This is extremely embarrassing. I'm sorry if I was a complete prat last night.'

'No, but very entertaining,' Peter added as he came in from the kitchen. 'And why are you here? Kristina said she would remind you this morning that your services were not required.'

Everyone burst out laughing at the short-sighted and short-tempered rhinoceros flaring her nostrils.

'I'm going to kill her. She deliberately didn't tell me, gave me her vile but highly effective hangover cure to drink and then tutted at me for being late when I rushed through the gallery. You wait. I'll get her back for this. You see if I don't.'

Instead of storming back along the street to rampage around the gallery, spraying saliva and snot over the paintings, Anna declared she would complete her shift.

'Would this be the infamous Jenkinson Stubborn Gene in action?' Peter noted. 'Well, that's enough talk. I need to get back into the kitchen. I promised Seb a masterclass in pizza making, and he'll be here soon.'

'So that explains why you're here. I did wonder,' Anna commented.

'You know me. Always happy to spread the pizza gospel.'

***

The shift proved highly entertaining due to Alex's relations. Filip's prophecy of complete carnage was right. All four descended on the café at midday, led by Seb, who now had a noticeable limp. In an attempt to recapture his youth, he'd tried a wheelie and promptly fallen into a ditch. Luckily, there was only minor damage inflicted due to his snail-like speed. Hobbling inside the café, Seb declared at least he had managed to go on the bike ride. Unlike Daniel, who was firmly ensconced in his room and so horrifically hungover, no one expected to see him soon. The pizza-making masterclass began well but, lulled into a false sense of his abilities, Seb dramatically began throwing pizza dough above his head. Being hit in the face and back by out-of-control pizza bases had been a sore trial for Agnes. However, when one sailed across the kitchen and dropped into an enormous bowl of cake batter, sending a tidal wave of sticky chocolate mixture over her, the Head Chef beat a hasty retreat outside to the sanctuary of the courtyard with a restorative camomile tea.

Even Viktor, with his zen-like calm, was challenged. Keen to see the inner workings of a commercial bakery, Pello helped by accidentally switching off all the ovens, throwing the container of precious sourdough starter in the bin, and he somehow managed to unbalance the huge floor-mounted mixing bowl and unlock its dough hook. Luckily, the eagle-eyed Viktor averted disaster by discreetly resetting everything. Not to be outdone, Madalena decided to lend a hand behind the counter and, to her credit, was an excellent listener but then took it upon herself to state what her customers would have. Sofia was powerless and adopted the tactic of standing behind Madalena to mouth silent apologies. Unbelievably, no one took offence, and most embraced the new suggestions. Whilst all this was going on, Arali took the opportunity to natter with Lucinda and Nancy. Sofia's sisters had popped in to find out the evening's arrangements and, on seeing Anna, dragged her over for a congratulatory chat. It was then Anna discovered her early night would not be happening. Sofia and Vasili had initially planned a small affair to thank immediate family and colleagues for putting up with their obsessive festival behaviour. Their first-runner-up position (mentioned to every customer), their son's surprise engagement, and their daughter's divorce terms agreement called for a far bigger celebration. The intimate gathering had morphed into a get-together encompassing all their Lefkada relations. Totting it up, Anna reckoned there would be at least forty adults and fifteen children. Once her shift finished, she hoped to get in a much-needed snooze. Staring at the tablecloth, she realised the conversation had moved on. Arali was busy explaining that although her husband and in-laws were a walking disaster area, they did it in such an amusing way it was impossible to stay angry for long. It was always entertaining, but a downside was finding her own family unbelievably dull by comparison.

174

On cue, an incredibly proud Seb trooped out from the kitchen and bore a tray aloft with four misshapen pizzas. Lovingly placing the rustic creations down, he announced that buying a pizza oven was a priority when he got home. The Panagos family soon assembled, accompanied by a period of calm, as they enthusiastically tucked in. Agnes took the opportunity to sidle back into the kitchen and assess the damage done to her cherished domain.

***

The miracle hangover cure had lost its potency. Anna half-heartedly nudged a slice of toast around the plate whilst her cup of tea cooled.

'May I sit down?'

'Please do.'

Agnes fidgeted in her chair before looking up.

'Okay, this has been a long time coming … but … I'm very sorry – for being off with you these past few weeks.'

'Are you apologising because I look so pathetic?'

Agnes grinned and handed over a bottle of water. 'Perhaps.'

'Thank you. I've drunk so much this morning and still haven't been to the loo – I mean toilet.'

'I know what you meant,' Agnes replied. 'You know … I massively misjudged you. I've known Sofia and Vasili for over three years, and they're good people – if slightly obsessive and outspoken.'

'Just a bit.'

'But it wasn't me who worked to resolve whatever was eating them up. I stood by and watched them become more and more miserable. No, it was the newcomer.' Agnes fiddled with her cuffs. 'The person I've gone out of my way to hate by being an absolute bitch.'

'You're very good at it.'

'Viktor pulled me up on it countless times, but I refused to listen to him.' Agnes looked at her carefully. 'I've got to hand it to you, Anna – you will not be beaten.'

'Yes,' Anna replied. 'I've been told it's one of my best ... and worst qualities.'

Agnes tentatively held out her hand. 'Friends?'

'Friends,' she replied and felt an overwhelming sense of relief, and – in her fragile state – there was a distinct possibility she might blub.

Don't you dare cry, Jenkinson.

As the women shook hands, Viktor appeared in the doorway. Anna suspected he'd been eavesdropping in the bakery – the timing was too perfect.

'Get in, man. Our lass, I'm owa the moon. And you didn't even get wrong for being a propa workie ticket.' He beamed at Agnes and then asked a bemused Anna. 'Right, pet. What do you reckon then?'

'I think you're well on the way to becoming an honorary Geordie.'

'Nee way!' Agnes cried. 'One's more than enough,' she said, and with a cackle disappeared into the kitchen.

Chapter Nineteen

Life post-festival was supposed to be less chaotic – a chance to recharge and catch up on a week's worth of sleep – but no. There were no signs of any part of her life slowing down.

The villa sold, and Steffi bought the house, so Anna helped to move Steffi, Filip, Alex, and Leyla in – and Daniel out into one of the cycle shop studios. Refurbishment of the business and house was to start in November – after he'd left. Anna had scrubbed, swept, mopped, painted, polished, lugged boxes around, disassembled and then re-assembled furniture for days whilst entertaining a toddler who had now decided that sleep was for wimps.

At the post-festival village meeting, everyone agreed all the hard work had paid off – all businesses recorded an increase in enquiries, footfall, and turnover. The village's profile received a massive boost from local media – including fantastic photographs of the celebrations and awards ceremony – and graced many an Apokeri business website and social media platform. Everyone met Kristina's retirement from flower arranging with sadness – or distress if you were called Max – and tabled a new approach. Fresh ideas to extend the festival were minuted, including cultural talks and cooking demonstrations to profile the fishing fleet and farming life. After all, the two elements were still the lifeblood of Apokeri. And then a ripple of excitement when Jeremy confirmed hotel planning approval, and they all inspected the impressive virtual reality model and artistic impressions. Work was to start immediately and open for the new summer season.

Then a final surprise – from Daniel – a chance to visit Japan now meant he'd be gone in less than a month. The meeting was his last, and even though nobody had known, Stelios conjured a cake and drinks out of nowhere. Only Daniel and Anna opted for a soft drink – their hangover memories still too recent.

The apartments, café, bike shop, and guided tours continued to thrive, so Anna had spent little time with her friend. Kristina looked sad across the patio table, nursing her coffee – lost in thought and clutching her crucifix.

'Let's go out for a meal tonight,' Anna said, tapping the table with both hands. 'My treat.'

'Oh yes.' Kristina carefully tucked the small gold cross away. 'How lovely. We should go to Nereus – I never got to try Ahmad's food last week, and it sounds like I missed out.'

'That sounds a plan,' Anna replied as she stacked the breakfast dishes. 'By the way, some of the rooftop lights aren't working. We'll replace them before going out.'

'Let's do that.' Kristina checked her watch. 'Time to open up. See you later.'

***

Kristina pushed the last pile of wood sideways and arched her back out. Perfect – now the studio had plenty of space. She wiped dusty hands on her apron and wandered into the sunshine. The rooftop garden looked forlorn with its rows of empty raised beds. With cut flowers no longer required, she needed a plan. Anna might have some ideas? Something to discuss tonight.

Anna was a treasure but needed to slow down – she was taking on too much, too willing to help. And Kristina had mentioned it, on more than one occasion, but Anna always laughed away any concerns, even if the laughter sounded forced at times. Overall, Anna appeared fine – more than fine. Her friend was living the dream, and her engagement was the icing on the cake. It might have come as a surprise to some but not Kristina – she had an inkling for such things. The pair were a good fit with their strong work ethic and desire to do well. Filip's laid-back and cheeky attitude complemented Anna's more serious personality, and the couple deeply loved one another.

One engagement brought up memories of another – Kristina's own, so many years ago. Not a day passed without her thinking about Adrian and what might have been. She sat down and quenched her thirst with a glass of cold water and cast her mind back over seventy years ago to an idyllic childhood playing with Adrian during her annual family Tharesseti holidays. The youngest Andino brother always accompanied his father on the daily delivery of fresh seafood. As young children, Kristina and Adrian explored rockpools whilst his father took great pains explaining to the chef what he'd brought, what was fishing well, and what he expected to return with the next day.

As a keen fisherman, Kristina's father always chartered the fishing boat each time they visited. As the men traded stories and cast out their lines, Kristina swam and sunbathed with him and her two older sisters, Birgitta and Pernilla. However, on her penultimate holiday, friendship blossomed into something more. At sixteen, Kristina was clever, confident, and stunning. Adrian was a full-time fisherman two years older, working with his father, uncles, and three older brothers. The time at sea transformed his body into tanned muscle. She could still remember the feel of his smooth body once they became secret lovers – snatching any moment they could. While she was attending finishing school, a steady stream of letters flowed between them, and they spoke of their undying love and future. They'd marry and emigrate to Australia. For Kristina, that meant a life free from stifling upper-class constraints, free from parental pressures and expectations. Their love was all that mattered and would see them through. But – as she had found out – life was never that simple.

She slid the gold crucifix against its chain.

It was still difficult to contain the pent-up rage – undiminished after decades.

The crucifix sawed backwards and forwards against its thin chain.

Her obsessive father, with his insatiable need to succeed at any cost.

The chain chafed her neck.

His interference, his unshakeable obsession for the never-ending expansion of his precious family business.

She hated him, despised him, loathed him.

Backwards and forwards went the gold cross. Faster and faster.

It was his fault – triggering an irreversible chain of events that had brought death and destruction to all she held dear. She was engaged a mere twelve hours before her world collapsed.

Let him be rotting in hell for what he'd done.

'No,' Kristina cried in anguish.

The delicate metal rope had snapped. Tears welled up as she scrambled to collect the tiny pieces. It was the only thing left from happier times. Thrusting them into her deep trouser pocket and blinking back saltwater, she jammed the stepladders against the perimeter wall.

The past remained unchanged, but she could do something about the present – surprise Anna by fixing the lights so they could get to Nereus quicker. They'd have more time to relax and have a proper natter, as Anna was fond of saying.

Perched on the stepladder on a perfect September afternoon, Kristina gazed out over Apokeri. She loved her Greek-village life – so far removed from a privileged but dysfunctional upbringing. She fought to regain her usual calm composure and saw Daniel's car bringing the promised supply of wood and a surprise – something she'd be delighted to have.

Kristina watched the car manoeuvre its way between delivery trucks with their hazards flashing, confused tourists walking into the road whilst looking the wrong way, and stray cats that sped out from parked cars. His going would leave a void, but she took solace that he was finally following his heart. And perhaps would fall in love Down Under – like his mother. He'd be here any minute. There was enough time to change the lights, if she hurried.

Kristina took stock of her handiwork. The lights were all done – except for one fractionally out of reach. There was no need to move the ladders – far easier to lean sideways. She grabbed the tiny bulb, but her outstretched fingers nudged it away. Frustrating but no big deal. It was coming back – the second time would do it. She stretched an extra centimetre, almost there … The distance was too great. Gravity took over …

In hideous slow motion, the ladders teetered towards the gaping chasm, and with a terrible realisation, she saw the immense drop and the sliver of alleyway pavement far below.

How unbelievably stupid. What a way to go.

They were the very last thoughts to run through the mind of a usually wise woman before everything went black.

***

It was going to happen sooner or later, Anna supposed. The first disgruntled guest – understatement of the year – was the nastiest, rudest, and most opinionated man in existence. Even prior warning failed to prepare Anna and Max.

The gentleman in question booked against Dania's advice. She'd patiently run through the itinerary and explained its unsuitability in her professional opinion. The fifty-two-seater coach option was ideal based on his budget and fitness. But he had been adamant, after reading so many glowing reviews, and was always fine on similar tours. Reluctantly Dania sold the seat after he signed a disclaimer.

The complaining started immediately as he railed about the kerbside pick-up. Anna kindly explained that whilst booking and on the printed itinerary, it stipulated a hotel reception meet-and-greet. At each stop, he was unhappy. They spent too long here, spent too little time there, the place was too commercial, or not commercial enough. The list went on and on.

Professional throughout, Anna answered each criticism in her bubbly manner. Unusually, all the guests were British, but that didn't prevent them from giving him an ever-wider berth. While guests enjoyed a dramatic clifftop mid-morning refreshment stop (and more complaints), Max and Anna agreed if things failed to improve by lunchtime, Mr Unbearable would be offered a full refund and transported back to his hotel. Far better to lose money and have the rest of the group happy – but he'd refused and kept spewing out spite. Until an uprising saw a fellow Yorkshireman take out his wallet, slam down the tour cost and tell the unwanted guest he was an embarrassment to God's Own Country, take the money and leave. With the other guests applauding (and the money remaining on the table), Mr Unbearable was led away.

Max and Anna were still standing outside Odyssey, reliving the day's extraordinary events, when Dania rushed out giddy from excitement.

'You're not going to believe this! That man—'

'Mr Unbearable,' Max and Anna grunted in unison.

'He was only a mystery shopper.'

'What—?'

Instead of a torrent of abuse on his arrival, Dania received a smile, a handshake, and an admission – their guest was an award-winning freelance travel writer with a career spanning thirty years. It was easier to say who he hadn't written for, and whilst many an establishment had fallen victim to scathing attacks, his assessments were honest and well-respected. Armed with his real name, Dania did some internet snooping and found everything to be true. He'd booked the tour being highly sceptical of too many glowing reviews but found it to be one of the best. The knowledge, enthusiasm, itinerary, attention to detail, refreshments, rapport with guests, professionalism, and handling of criticism were remarkable, and he was frankly amazed the tour was in its infancy. He'd volunteered to forward his published articles, had provided a testimonial, and apologised for taking things too far. It was the first time a tour group had turned on him – high praise indeed.

Declining a lift to his hotel, he'd gone to explore Apokeri after reading about the recent festival. Dania had left messages at the other tour guests' accommodation to explain and let them know they might feature in an article and future Apokeri reviews.

Anna practically skipped along the street with excitement. Maybe Kristina had received a visit from the mystery shopper? She became aware of a car beeping behind and, turning, saw Pip at the wheel of Alex's car.

He slammed on the brakes and flung open the passenger door. 'Get in … we're going to the hospital. There's been an accident.'

Chapter Twenty

She jumped in, the car spun around and sped out of Apokeri.

'What accident? Is it your mam ... dad ... Leyla ... Steffi?'

Filip floored the accelerator up the steep road. 'No – it's Kristina.'

She was Anna's oldest friend, but the most unexpected answer. The woman spent her day sitting in a gallery, for crying out loud.

'Daniel rang ten minutes ago, and I drove straight down to get you,' Filip explained whilst haring past a woman on a scooter laden down with two crates of agitated chickens – what the hell? 'The guy was in shock and made little sense, but I figured out he'd found Kristina unconscious on the rooftop this afternoon ... something about an upended step ladder – and then he lost it. I got him to calm down. The paramedics were fantastic ... Kristina briefly opened her eyes – a good sign. He followed the ambulance ... had just arrived. No news on Kristina's condition.'

A stepladder on the roof? Had she tried changing the lights herself? Christ! She could've pitched herself off. Breathe in ... breathe out. It was going to be okay. Like a mantra, Anna kept repeating it. Say it enough times, and it'd come true. They zipped past traffic – nuns on bikes, a carload of clowns, a limousine with an inflatable pair of legs sticking out the sunroof. Was she the only one seeing this?

The car barely ground to a halt before she dived out and sprinted into the crowded waiting room. Where was he? She frantically scanned the room. C'mon, how difficult could it be to spot a six-foot-six Norse warrior god? And then saw him. He looked terrible and so vulnerable. Her heart went out to him, but then a terrifying thought … did he resemble death because that's what he'd just found—?

Daniel saw her in the same instant, and relief flooded his face. He jumped up and was across the room in three strides to give her an unexpected hug.

'I'm so happy to see you. I-I've been going crazy … sitting by myself waiting to hear some news.' His voice was hoarse with emotion as he looked behind her.

'Pip's parking the car.'

In no time, Filip came striding in and embraced his friend. The three then huddled together as Daniel recounted the story.

'I pulled up with all the timber for Kristina and saw the Back Soon sign on the door. Figured she was making space – I thought I'd seen movement on the roof – and made my way up to the studio, calling out her name … no reply … and then I s-saw it.' The little colour left in Daniel's face drained away, and she instinctively gave his hand a reassuring squeeze. He grabbed hold and didn't let go. 'A single sandal was lying on the ground. At first, I thought that was weird, but stepping forward – oh God – I saw a foot poking out from behind a raised bed. I rushed around the corner to find her lying there.' His whole body shook, eyes filled with terror. 'I thought she was dead. I frantically shouted her name – nothing. I had wits enough to check for a pulse and found a weak one … I've never been so happy about anything in my entire life. Kristina felt warm – and as I believed I'd glimpsed her on the roof, I reckon it must have just happened. I fumbled for my mobile … I'd only left it on the bloody dashboard but then remembered I'd insisted Kristina install a studio phone. With the ambulance on the way, I grabbed a nearby parasol and set it up to provide shade. But I didn't touch her; I was terrified of causing a neck injury, and then I waited – for what seemed like an eternity. As soon as I heard the siren, I tore downstairs, wrenched opened the shop door, and the paramedics followed me up to the roof.'

Filip clapped him on the back. 'You did an awesome job, mate – held it together and didn't panic.'

'I wouldn't say that,' Daniel admitted. 'The paramedics did that. They calmly talked through what they were doing and spoke to Kristina as if she was awake – which helped me. At that stage, she was still unconscious, and after checking her vital signs, they put on a neck brace and then needed to get her down the stairs on a stretcher.'

Anna's eyes widened. 'Bloody hell. It's two flights of steep stairs – how the hell did they manage?'

'With great difficulty and very slowly,' Daniel answered and took another deep breath. 'They needed to keep Kristina as still as possible. At one stage, I thought they'd never do it. However, the guys were pros. I tried to help as best I could, and the whole time they kept telling me how well I was doing and how well Kristina was doing – keeping up a steady banter as if nothing unusual was happening. I kept thanking them for doing such an amazing job, but they just laughed and said it was nothing compared to last week. It wasn't every day you climbed up a tree to render first aid to a couple of amorous teenagers.'

'Ah, the lengths some people will take for a secret rendezvous,' Filip said as he tried to find a comfortable position on the plastic moulded hospital seats.

Daniel nodded and his eyes continued to dart backwards and forwards between the couple. 'That's exactly what they said. I suspect they made the story up to make me laugh – which worked. Just as they placed Kristina in the ambulance, her eyes fluttered open, and I sobbed with relief. After that, they closed the doors and were away. I somehow remembered to switch the door sign to closed and quickly locked up.'

Anna held his shaking hands in hers and said soothingly, 'You did a brilliant job. I don't think many people would have stayed that composed, especially remembering to flip the sign.'

He gave a half-hearted chuckle. 'You wouldn't be saying that if you'd seen me when I got here. I was pretty incoherent at hospital reception – worried they wouldn't tell me anything, not being a relative. I kept babbling about past family connections and how Kristina had practically raised my mother. Bless the poor woman behind the counter.' He nodded over to the reception desk where a woman was calming down a distressed couple holding a baby. 'She was an absolute star and patted me on the hand and said it was okay. If I took a seat, I would be informed as soon as there was any news but she did say it could be some time.'

***

Anna thought the term *waiting room* was very apt. Hours on, and still no news. Daniel and herself had eventually persuaded Filip to return home – no sense in all three of them waiting – and there was a lucrative cycle tour the next day that needed prepping. At first, he refused – the hell with it, he'd cancel.

Now that a few hours had passed and the initial shock had subsided, rational Daniel was back and reasoned cancelling was a massive mistake. It wouldn't help Kristina, and she'd be mortified to think he'd done such a thing because of her. In the end, Filip was persuaded to leave after Anna promised to call with news. Daniel would drop her off.

'Mr Eckvardsson.'

Someone stirred beside her, and she felt herself gently move sideways. Anna groggily opened her eyes and realised she'd fallen asleep on Daniel and embarrassingly saw drool evidence on his T-shirt. He stood talking to a female doctor, and both looked grave. After a few minutes, he came and sat next to her.

'What's the news?' she asked nervously.

'The good news is she's regained consciousness and has miraculously escaped with only a sprained ankle and wrist. She's currently asleep, and we have permission to look in on her but must be quiet.'

'Okay, that sounds positive, but the bad news?'

'Yes, the bad news. It is impossible to determine the severity of the head trauma at this stage, and they'll be conducting more tests tomorrow morning. The doctor was cautiously optimistic from her initial investigations but didn't want to give false hope.'

'So, am I right in thinking we don't know how long Kristina will be in the hospital?'

'Correct.' He pulled her upwards. 'Come on, let's go and see her.'

Holding hands for mutual support, they were directed at the nurses' station by a forbidding Sister who gave strict instructions to only look through the glass panel in the door and not make a sound, so help them. Peeping into the softly lit room, Anna inhaled sharply before welding a hand over her mouth. Kristina looked incredibly frail and old, tucked under white sheets and hooked up to various machines. The pair tiptoed away for Anna to update Filip. He sounded shattered, and she persuaded him to head straight for bed.

Wearily climbing into the passenger seat, Anna felt something beneath her and withdrew a bundle of letters. She gave Daniel a quizzical look at the sizeable stack, neatly tied with a red ribbon.

'It was a surprise for Kristina,' Daniel sadly explained. 'I came across them clearing out the house. Kristina wrote all those to my mother in Australia, and I knew she would love to have them. She was so proud of Mama for following her dream, and that's where she met my dad.'

'And the rest is history.'

'Exactly.'

'You'll get to give Kristina the letters very soon, Daniel. She's going to be absolutely fine,' Anna declared with feigned conviction. 'After all, Kristina is like that vegetable.'

'What vegetable?'

'A tough Swede.'

He managed a slight smile at the terrible joke. And in an attempt to distract him, she asked him to recount his mother's adventures in Australia and how his parents fell in love. It worked, and as he talked about that piece of family history for the rest of the journey, he seemed to gain strength. As they drove along the beachfront road, Anna's stomach sent up a long, drawn-out howl, closely followed by Daniel's.

Anna shook her head. 'Good grief, you'd think I never got fed. I don't know about you, but I'll not be able to sleep any time soon. As neither of us has eaten in hours, why don't you come in, and I'll do us a slap-up meal of beans on toast and a cuppa? How can you refuse such a feast?'

'Yes, that sounds … just what I need.'

***

Anna bustled around the living room, switching on table lamps. 'Make yourself comfortable. I won't be a minute.'

He'd never liked this room before. It'd always felt unfriendly, too pristine, so he'd rush through to the welcoming kitchen or garden. But with Anna here, it felt safe, warm, and welcoming.

The pair tucked into their meal. Anna groaned with pleasure as she mopped up the last of her bean sauce with a sliver of toast and popped it into her mouth.

'My go-to comfort food. But it must have brown sauce,' Anna said as she cleared up.

Daniel held up his hand. 'No, you stay put. I'll clean up and make myself another cup of that fine tea. Do you want one?'

'Yes, please. And that fine tea is manufactured in good old Newcastle upon Tyne. Delivered to my mam and dad's door and then posted to me. You cannot beat it,' Anna called to the retreating figure of Daniel.

***

What the hell was he doing?

He had promised himself that maintaining a healthy distance from Anna was the only sensible course of action. And he wasn't doing that. Instead, he was revelling in being ever so helpful, sharing a meal, washing up, and making them a cup of tea. He obviously delighted in torturing himself – and for umpteen weeks, it had been just that. Torture.

He stared at the multicoloured kitchen tiles as the kettle boiled. A few months ago, he couldn't abide the woman sitting next door and had made his feelings abundantly clear. In response, Anna had become unbearably nice every time they met – he suspected she did it to annoy him.

But here was the bizarre thing. It had the reverse effect.

He grew to admire her tenacity, how she'd come out fighting, even track him down to the workshop and delight in verbally getting one over on him but always done politely and with a smile. She wouldn't back down no matter how much of an arse he kept being. He'd soon found himself working out new ways to annoy her, so she'd come to gleefully inform him how he'd failed to win – again. Soon he'd wanted her to talk to him like she did to everyone else.

His timing was terrible. The realisation of his growing feelings came at the precise moment Anna started dating Filip. He was furious at himself for not seeing it sooner. And found himself locked in a perverse battle of wills with her.

That was until those two bastards—

Daniel shuddered at how close the pair had come. Privately, he'd been with Filip – beat the living daylights out of them. And, alone at night, with no witnesses, he'd imagined cornering them and not holding back.

After that awful episode, something extraordinary happened – she changed towards him. The saccharine-sweet friendliness disappeared, and instead, they passionately discussed politics, culture, and history – he'd discovered she wasn't always cheery and nice and could rant and rave with the best of them, clambering onto her soapbox at any given opportunity. They talked about travel over cups of tea – she'd been everywhere he wanted to go and far more besides – and he found himself researching and adding those new destinations to his list. But the near-miss made her much more guarded, and no matter how hard he tried, she deflected his personal questions. In the same way, Kristina did. And in the same way, he'd found himself revealing more and more of himself. Through her infectious enthusiasm, she skilfully extracted his hopes, fears, the years of suppressed yearning to break free of Apokeri.

He filled the teapot and watched the teabags bob against and away from one another. He cherished their conversations but began to worry she'd work out his true feelings – he couldn't bear her pity. The woman was as sharp as a tack. He reckoned not much got past Anna Jenkinson. He'd hated doing it, but began to act relieved and abruptly excused himself if Alex, Filip, or Steffi interrupted them. What an utter shit.

'Are you okay in there?'

'Yes … I'm fine. I-I won't be a minute. The tea's just masting.'

That phrase came from her. The tea wouldn't brew or infuse – it'd mast from now on. So many years dreaming of escaping Apokeri, and he would be gone in a few short weeks. It'd be a relief – of sorts – to rid himself of this delightful torture.

He poured the drinks and walked into the lounge to find her sitting on a sofa surrounded by a warm pool of light, with a framed photo on her lap. Tonight, this place was a sanctuary against outside uncertainty. In here, everything felt right, soothing, and comforting.

She was deep in thought, and it allowed him to watch her.

He'd never been short of female attention, but this woman he desperately desired was beyond his reach. It was evident to everyone how much she loved Filip. Her Pip. And now they were engaged! Could it get any worse?

That was why he'd moved his flight forward and gone home after the festival to drink himself into oblivion. Of course, he tried to reason with himself, even if Filip wasn't in the picture, why did he think Anna would be interested in him? He and Filip were hardly the same type.

She looked up and gave him a tight smile. He sat down beside her and placed their drinks on the coffee table.

'I love this picture,' she murmured and traced fingers over the glass. 'It always makes me smile.'

Kristina and Anna sat in Apollo's secret garden and looked incredibly happy.

For a split second, her smile slipped, and Daniel glimpsed behind the façade and saw vulnerability. At that moment, he thought his heart would break. She had no idea how much he loved her.

'This was the night I decided to stay in Apokeri,' Anna explained, tilting the frame towards him. 'I asked Kristina if she thought I was being foolish. And she said, "everyone has one life to live, so make it count."'

He longed to brush those few stray hairs gently away from her face. 'I agree. It's why I'm going travelling before moving to Adelaide – life's too short for regrets.'

'Yes … you're right. Don't live with regret. Because you never know what's around the corner, do you?' Anna replied, and then she kissed him.

It was slow and tender, and he responded before jumping backwards as if ten thousand volts had surged through his body.

He was shaking for the umpteenth time that day. 'What the hell are you doing? You … you can't … do this.'

He watched as she stood, slipped off her dress, and closed the gap between them.

'I know you want me,' she whispered and unhooked her bra. 'I saw your reaction when Pip proposed. Is that why you've been avoiding me? Is that why you moved your flight forward?'

He was rooted to the spot and watched her slowly unbutton his shirt, push it open, and with a featherlight touch, run fingers across his chest and downwards, over his stomach until they came to rest on his belt buckle.

'I did find it amusing that you pretended to be relieved when our chats were interrupted.' In an unhurried manner, she started to loosen his belt. 'Did you never wonder why I kept coming back for more?'

The top button came undone, and she moved to the second. It took every ounce of willpower to stop her hands.

'What are you playing at? You're engaged to Filip – one of my best mates!'

Her voice was a soft caress as it stole into his heart. 'I love Pip, but … I want you. And I know you want this.'

Her eyes held his, and he couldn't look away as she unbuttoned his shorts. He must stop her – but found he couldn't. He knew it was wrong, but it didn't matter. So many nights, he'd fantasised about this. And here she was, seducing him. Never in his wildest dreams—

The final button came undone. Her fingers reached inside his waistband.

'But … Filip?'

'Let me worry about that,' she replied, and her eyes greedily devoured his naked body. 'We've only got a few weeks.'

When she kissed him the second time, he didn't pull back. Having waited so long for this, he wanted it to be right.

'Not here. Not like this … I want it to be in your bed.'

'Race you.' And she was off.

**

Their lovemaking was slow and sensual – neither wanted to rush things, not the first time. Daniel found Anna to be everything he'd longed for and more. He explored her body with his fingers, tongue, and lips. She pushed her hands into his hair, willing him on, arching upwards. And then he was inside her. Their bodies moved together – savouring every caress, every kiss. And finally, they cried out together into the silence of the moonlit house.

Afterwards, lying in each other's arms, Daniel felt Anna's breathing slow. He hated to do this and slid out from under her, extricating himself from her warm embrace, but a hand clamped hold of his wrist.

'Where do you think you're going, Mr Eckvardsson?' Anna murmured mischievously. 'I'm not finished yet.'

Daniel laughed. 'I thought you were asleep?'

'I'm garnering my strength. It's not time for you to go. It's my turn now.' She nimbly straddled him, and he ran his hands up her firm thighs. 'Lie back and relax – I promise you're going to like this.'

And with that, he surrendered himself entirely.

Chapter Twenty-One

What the—? Anna woke with a start to find she had fallen out of bed. Not entirely accurate. She had been thrown out. It was early morning, and as the light crept in, Anna realised her room was severely shaking. It was an earthquake. Think, think, think.

She was in the hospital waiting room, devouring a fellow visitor's discarded magazine only yesterday. The turgid academic publication included a study into the frequency of seismic activity in Greece – exciting stuff. It was an enormous surprise to find that the country she now lived in was ranked sixth in the world and first in Europe for damage caused by earthquakes. *Oh, joy*, had been her initial thought, but Daniel had brushed her worries away – having rarely experienced anything above a slight tremor in his twenty-eight years.

Dredging her memory, Anna recalled what to do if found indoors. Drop under heavy furniture. Cover head and torso to prevent being hit by falling objects. Hold on to the thing you are under to remain covered, and move with it until the shaking stops.

She crawled under the bed, jamming a pillow over her head – the extra protection couldn't hurt – and curled up like a dormouse, holding on tight as the shaking reverberated through her bones. Countless car alarms blared, accompanied by a low-level roaring, hopefully not a tsunami, as earthquakes often triggered them. Inside the house, small items slid and hit the floor. The vibrant pink coasters smashed on the bedroom floor, and shards harmlessly rebounded off the pillow. Coat hangers clanked inside a wardrobe still standing, but the bedside tables and a chair had already toppled. The tremors intensified, and as the old house creaked and groaned, plaster fell from the walls. Please let the carved beams above her bed stay in place.

Random earthquake facts popped into her head, and she was undecided if it was more or less comforting to know most injuries and deaths were caused by falling or flying objects than by the collapsed building itself? Perversely, she wondered if some of those falling items included the very furniture you were advised to shelter under. At least she knew not to shelter in a doorway – a mistake people made. Apart from a significant risk of being stuck, doorways of modern homes were no stronger than any other part of the house. It was a small crumb of comfort to know that the house she was cowering in was the oldest in Apokeri and had withstood everything thrown at it for over three hundred years.

Greece's seismic activity resulted from shifting tectonic plates in the eastern Mediterranean region. The Greek Bow was an earthquake zone that started close to Lefkada and curved across the sea to Rhodes, where the African lithospheric plate ground under the Eurasian one at a rate of 4.5 cm a year. The Cephalonia–Lefkada Transform Fault (CTF) was also a major tectonic structure in the Ionian area. All told, Anna had made a European earthquake hotspot her home. It was technically true, but as the article stated, severe quakes only occurred every twenty to thirty years, and in recent times the worst happened back in 1953. On 12th August, an earthquake registering 6.8 struck the southern Ionian islands. It claimed the lives of over four hundred and seventy people, levelled most of Cephalonia, crippled its economy, and forced many residents to emigrate. Its impact also caused widespread damage on Zakynthos, Ithaca, and Lefkada to a much lesser extent. A small or moderate quake lasted a few seconds whilst a large one could last several minutes, which this one was.

Clinging on for dear life, the bed started shimmying along the wall, and there was a massive crash as the wardrobe hit the floor and shattered. She sucked air through her teeth as a sliver of wood embedded itself in her calf, and warm blood trickled down her leg. The stained-glass windows exploded inwards, and flying glass showered the mattress above. When was this going to stop? Please, keep everyone safe.

But then the sound of Cassie barking from the stairwell. Had Daniel been out for an early morning walk and come to check on her? No, that was madness. But he had. She heard his voice calling out to her. If the patio doors blew out, he'd be shredded to pieces by flying glass. If outside during an earthquake, you stayed there and got to an open area away from buildings – the most dangerous place was near exterior walls. Anna had read that bit out to Daniel, so what was he thinking? She screamed at him to get out of the house and as far away from windows and walls as possible. But he was in the room now. How the hell did he sound so composed? He was even telling Cassie to sit still and behave. Slowly, Anna became aware that Daniel was calmly repeating the same phrase over and over again.

'Anna, listen to my voice. Concentrate on my voice. What you are experiencing is not real. What you are seeing is not real. You're dreaming. You're hallucinating.'

Slowly opening her eyes, Anna saw that it was indeed early morning, but her bedroom was as it should be, and she was lying in the foetal position in the middle of the floor. Less than six feet away, framed in the doorway, Daniel sat on his heels observing her. Immaculately turned out in a white running top, baggy black shorts, and trainers, the man appeared completely unfazed by the situation, and utterly gorgeous. Cassie cocked her head at the strange sight. Humans were weird.

Anna let out a groan, levered herself onto the bed and dropped her head. Brilliant. He now thought she was a complete fruit loop! Usually, Anna had plenty of time to forewarn people. All of her friends back home were aware of, and many had experienced, this often amusing and sometimes scary behaviour – it ran in the family.

As children, Anna and her big sister were entertained at breakfast by their father as he recounted their mother's frequent night-time antics. However, Anna found it less amusing when she began to have the same vivid and often terrifying night visions. It tended to happen in a new place or during particularly stressful periods. Amazingly, to her knowledge, this was the first Apokeri occurrence.

Against all hope, Anna prayed Daniel and Cassie were figments of an over-active imagination and not currently staring at her like a prized exhibit in a zoo. But no, they were real, and Daniel put a consoling arm around her shoulders.

'It's okay, Anna. I don't think you're crazy. My dad was always sleepwalking and talking.'

'Really?' Anna snapped her head upright at whiplash speed.

'Oh yeah. Mama always found him wandering around the house in the early hours, chatting away to imaginary people and would gently guide him back to bed. If he got caught having a midnight snack, my dad would pretend he was asleep.' Daniel laughed at the memory. 'I'd forgotten all about that. Mama knew but would pretend he had got one over on her. Once the illness took hold, Mama wasn't strong enough to get him to bed, and it became my job. I quickly became an extremely light sleeper as Dad left the house on night expeditions. The first time he got as far as the supermarket before I caught up with him.'

'No way. The front door is the closest I've ever got. Often living in shared houses, I never sleep in the nude – no matter how hot it gets. Imagine nipping to the loo and finding me wandering around the house in the buff.'

'Sounds good to me,' Daniel murmured and nuzzled her neck. 'What were you dreaming about anyway? You weren't making much sense. Apart from telling me to get out. I wasn't sure whether or not to be offended.'

'I was in the middle of a horrific earthquake. A direct result of that dull article I read yesterday. I was terrified you would get killed by coming to find me, so I shouted for you to get outside. Sorry, I wasn't being rude. If it makes you feel better, I was attempting to save your life. Anyway, enough of my weirdness. What are you doing here? There's hardly any light outside, so it must be early.'

'It's a little after six. I couldn't sleep and decided to go for a run, and erm, Cassie wanted to come and say hello,' he mumbled and suddenly became very interested in the duvet.

As Daniel and Anna sat on the bed, Cassie stood up, yawned, turned around and padded downstairs.

'Hmm, Cassie wanted to come and say hello, did she?' Anna smirked and traced her left forefinger down his top. 'I think that might be a fib, Mr Eckvardsson.'

Cassie had time to catch up on some sleep before Daniel descended the stairs, and the two of them slipped through the garden door and stole home through the backstreets.

***

'Thank you, it's my pleasure, and I'll pass on your best wishes. Have a safe trip home.'

Daniel waved goodbye to the middle-aged Italian couple from Foggia. It was their last day of a week-long holiday. They'd visited the gallery numerous times to view a striking seascape painting and been relieved to find the gallery open again after its unexpected closure for two days. Both were shocked by Kristina's accident, and the news spurred them into making the significant purchase. After all, you only live once.

It still amazed Daniel how lucky Kristina had been to walk away with so few injuries. He corrected himself. Walking was not something she would do soon. Returning to the hospital the next day, Daniel and Anna discovered the fears of head trauma were unfounded as Kristina had suffered only a very mild concussion. The doctor was pleased with the patient's progress but wanted to keep her under observation. Daniel profusely thanked the doctor before sitting beside a sleeping Kristina. A highly efficient ward nurse ushered them out until visiting hours resumed later that day. There was no point going back to Apokeri, so they opted for a late lunch. Anna wanted to hear all about his planned trip and pressed for all the details, and soon Daniel found himself talking excitedly. However, there was a kernel of sadness that he couldn't ignore. In a matter of weeks, he'd leave behind this intoxicating woman and was, therefore, determined to make the most of every precious moment.

On their return visit, Kristina was awake but distraught. Unchecked tears streamed down an ashen face as she apologised for being such an incredibly foolish old woman. Grabbing Daniel's arm, Kristina sounded utterly wretched, saying how it must have been terrible finding her – the shock and stress. And then she became near-hysterical. It was gone. Her gold crucifix necklace was gone. Daniel could only remember Kristina that upset once before – his mother's funeral. She was inconsolable, and Daniel felt helpless and completely lost about what to say or do.

Thank goodness for Anna, who took it in her stride. After gently prising Kristina's hand from Daniel's arm, she explained the broken chain and cross were in their safekeeping. Furthermore, diving off the top of a two-storey building was a rather extreme way of avoiding going to dinner with her. If Kristina really didn't want to share a plate of paella, all she had to do was say. It elicited a much-needed laugh, and in a soothing voice, Anna continued to calm Kristina by saying the most important thing was that she was okay. Everyone did silly things now and again, and it was just that Kristina's silly little thing was more spectacular than most. After encouraging Kristina to get some more rest and promising they'd be back to see her in the morning, the pair quietly left a sleeping Kristina. And after that, Anna continued to take charge.

Once back in Apokeri, Daniel discovered Anna had already convened a meeting with Steffi, Filip, and Alex to discuss Kristina's ongoing care. Even after a miraculous escape, the doctor explained a full recovery would take a few weeks and provided comprehensive instructions to reduce the pain and help with rehabilitation. At first, Daniel had been worried about the doctor's recommendation. Ideally, Kristina should be on the ground floor to initially avoid using stairs, but he no longer owned the house. However, the super-efficient Steffi immediately waved away any concerns. Of course, Kristina would move into the ground-floor ensuite bedroom. It was perfect with its courtyard access, and between the five of them, Kristina was in good hands. Anna was to remain in her current home to manage the gallery, with Daniel taking charge during her tour guide duties. Steffi, in turn, would step in if required to handle the cycle shop, and with her parents in the loop, Sofia organised Anna's temporary replacement in the café.

Daniel wheeled Kristina into the courtyard to a welcome home ceremony with colourful bunting in the yard, lunch courtesy of the café, and a handmade card and handpicked bouquet from Leyla. The little girl was keen to show Kristina her new bedroom and scampered ahead, holding Anna's hand.

'Anna and Leyla have been working wonders. I can't wait to see what they've done,' Daniel said as he pushed the wheelchair through the patio doors and heard Kristina inhale sharply a second after him.

'Oh my.' Kristina reached behind for Daniel's hand. 'It's … why, it's your mother's room.'

With a trembling and bruised hand, Kristina brushed the pretty floral bedspread, the embroidered cushions on the comfy armchair, and the woven blanket on the footstool. All of which Anna had discovered neatly packed in a trunk. There were also homely touches – Kristina's pictures and ornaments. Her wide-brimmed straw hat and colourful scarves hung from door hooks. 'And look at the paintings, Daniel. They're the ones I did for Lilian … which you kindly gave to me when she passed.' Kristina looked across at the chest of drawers and caught her breath for a second time. 'Is that … is that what I think it is?'

It hung suspended from the Apollo framed photo – her crucifix on a new gold chain. Kristina's hand shook so violently she couldn't grasp it.

'Let me,' Anna said and reached across. 'There you go. It's not an exact match, but I hope you like it?'

Kristina cradled the crucifix against her chest and relaxed into her wheelchair. 'My child – it's perfect. Thank you. You don't know how unbelievably precious it is to me.'

'I'm so pleased,' Anna replied and exhaled. 'In that little box next to it are the pieces of the original chain. I'm so sorry it was beyond repair.'

Daniel watched the two women hug. It'd all been Anna's idea. They'd gone to a jewellery repair shop in Lefkada town. After the accident, his brain was far too scrambled to even think about doing such a wonderfully kind thing. How did she always know to do that? And then, he heard an echo from the past. 'Many people will be with you on your journey – sometimes, and unbeknown to you, the important and inspirational ones may only pass through for a short time – remember that.'

He'd stood in that same spot as a shy and awkward sixteen-year-old – helplessly watching his mother toss and turn in a fitful sleep. She barely managed a few hours of rest when the drugs kicked in but remained immensely positive. Waking up, she'd beckoned him over. 'My beautiful son. I don't have much time left. I want you to remember … that life is a precious gift. At the moment … things seem bleak and feel utterly dreadful. But the sadness will pass. I am so proud of you and love you very much. Keep that with you when hopelessness sets in. You have so much to look forward to … so many adventures and wonderful experiences. Many people will be with you on your journey. Don't put things off, thinking there'll always be another day. Embrace every opportunity that comes your way. I know you'll grow into a confident, talented, caring, and gorgeous man with so much love to give. Look after your father for me – especially on his night-time wanderings. He'll find it hard my not being here.' A week later, she'd finally succumbed to her illness, and Daniel clung to those words in times of need to give him much-needed strength.

Standing in the same room over a decade later, Daniel believed that she would be proud of what he'd achieved, and would have given her blessing as he prepared to leave Apokeri for a new adventure.

***

Anna toggled between the various spreadsheets. Something wasn't right. Systematically, she worked through the cells and formulae. She rubbed gritty eyes. Her skin was clammy, and lank hair desperately needed washing. The yawn was so wide she almost swallowed the computer. There simply weren't enough hours in the day to do everything required, and certainly not to do them well. She was making stupid mistakes that could prove costly – like the spreadsheet. Luckily, she'd spotted it – not a good idea to double-book guests. Anna rested her head on the desk, and it felt wonderful. She could sleep like that for a week.

Ten days since Kristina's accident, and she was making fantastic progress, which was brilliant on the one hand – Anna could hand back gardening and gallery duties and not need to visit Kristina every evening. But on the other … She closed her desk drawer, and a few minutes later, there he was.

'How the hell do you ever find anything in here?' Daniel said in horror. 'It's like a bomb's gone off.'

'I'll have you know, Constable Tidy – a messy worker is a good worker.'

As she started writing on a whiteboard, he quickly began stacking untidy papers. 'Says who?'

'Me. How, man ... pack it in. I know exactly where everything is.'

'And you'll still know where everything is – but now it's in a neat pile.'

Anna put down the marker pen and pushed him against the door and pulled his t-shirt over his head. 'Don't I do a good job?' she said and turned the key.

'Yes,' he replied through a mouthful of material.

'Well ... that proves ... my point ... wouldn't you say?' Anna said as she lightly kissed his smooth chest. 'And ... there are ... definite perks ... to me working here.'

'Good grief, woman. Do you ever stop?'

The clatter and chatter of a family heading out echoed along the corridor.

'I didn't have you down as the shy type,' she remarked and slid her hand inside his shorts. 'Not after our nightly interludes in the garden. Or is that because it's dark, secret, and safe behind the walls? Okay... not so shy after all. C'mon, Daniel. The door's locked. Live a little. You don't want to be sensible all your life ... do you?'

He relaxed into the door and groaned quietly as her hand gathered momentum. 'Oh yes,' he whispered, and his hands wrenched up her denim skirt. 'But you're ... you're not wearing any underwear!'

'Are you shocked, sir?' she replied with a throaty chuckle, pressing her body against his cupped hand. 'I slipped them off ten minutes ago.'

His fingers slid between her legs and traced slow, insistent circles.

'I ... I figured ... you'd be ... heading my way,' she murmured and tilted her head back. 'See what you do to me.'

She was up against the desk and using its resistance to drive him into her. Nothing mattered except this man – the need to be with him, have him, and utterly surrender herself. She clung, clawed, and urged him on.

'How ... could ... any ... man ... say no ... to you?' he whispered.

Chapter Twenty-Two

Every week, Anna was required to give a weather report that only tortured her sun-worshipping father. Focusing on such a neutral subject meant he was far less critical, and in turn, she didn't bite back so often – reducing the need to angrily tuck hair behind her ears. The two generations could, it seemed, have a civilised conversation, and Anna gradually began looking forward to the calls.

Whilst Apokeri basked in glorious twenty-four-degree sunshine, Newcastle temperatures barely registered fourteen under overcast skies. But not everyone found late September Lefkada so pleasurable.

'Must we eat outside?' Filip grumbled. 'It's freezing. I'm Greek and not designed to operate in such low temperatures.'

'Rubbish,' Steffi retorted, delivering a well-aimed jumper at his head.

'You need to man up,' Alex said with a smirk.

It was a favourite comment of Filip's male relations – especially Vasili – if they sensed any bloke 'going soft.'

There was a tug at his arm. 'Stay here.'

Filip hugged his niece. 'Okay then … Now, sit back down.' He reluctantly pulled on the extra layer, and Leyla happily clambered back on her seat.

The conversation centred around Steffi's upcoming trip to Athens. Steffi had attended the glittering annual gala dinner for the last decade, and it was one of the premier events on the Athenian society calendar. This year, Steffi had made a generous donation and confided to Anna and Filip how it seemed apt her jewellery was to be auctioned for domestic abuse victims – when each piece had been a token apology from her ex after another beating. Steffi was both excited and nervous. It would be the first time Leyla – who was going through a particularly clingy phase – had been left overnight with her grandparents.

Kristina was also back to her engaging self, with a recovery that continued to astound everyone except the patient. The woman was chomping at the bit to get back to her own life and, as expected, continued to put up a fight about staying at Steffi's. Daniel placed his masterpiece – a giant raspberry pavlova with lashings of freshly whipped double cream – on the table as Kristina tapped a spoon against her glass.

'This is the perfect time to announce a piece of good news. I've been given a clean bill of health from my doctor today, and I can return home and resume work. I wanted everyone here tonight to thank you all in person – I know my foolishness has disrupted your lives. And thankfully, it's now time to get back to normal. Daniel, could you help me move back in tomorrow? It won't take long and will release you from gallery duties. I can also get out of Steffi's hair as she has so much to organise.' Receiving her plate, she squeezed Daniel's hand. 'And I know you only have two weeks to go. There must be plenty of people you want to see, so I don't want to take up any more of your precious time.'

'Thanks, Kristina,' he replied. 'That's not a problem about tomorrow, and don't worry, I've got my leaving do where I plan to say goodbye to most people. I still plan to help in the gallery and the garden till I go.'

'Such a good boy. I'm excited for you but will miss you terribly.'

Daniel smiled tightly. He imperceptibly paused when handing Anna her plate, and their eyes fleetingly locked. It was bittersweet news. Both were delighted for Kristina, and Anna was thankful for gaining some free time. However, it destroyed their perfect set up.

Managing the gallery provided an ideal cover for their clandestine affair. Anna continued to wrestle with her deceitful behaviour; she knew it was wrong, and that she walked an emotional tightrope that was bound to end in tears – hers most likely. But when she was with Daniel, it felt right – he gave her something Pip couldn't, and the diminishing time intensified their passion.

Conscious not to draw any attention to themselves, Daniel only once unofficially closed the gallery in the evening for a solitary hour to coincide with her finishing work before she disappeared off to visit Kristina. The other times saw the couple in various stages of undress in the kitchen or lounge as the bell above the gallery door heralded the arrival of unwanted customers. Daniel calmly called out he would be there in a minute whilst desperately fending off Anna whispering promises of what she intended to do to him. It required another course of action, which she quickly engineered by persuading Pip that Cassie, not him, could be her chaperone after visiting Kristina.

Returning home, Anna threw herself at Daniel as if an eternity had elapsed. Tearing at each other's clothes, they'd made love in the garden beneath the stars. She'd felt invigorated, truly alive, and after he left she stretched out on the grass and laughed out loud – just for the hell of it. And then there'd been those two wonderful illicit lunchtimes. One in the office and one in her bedroom – the latter after Daniel pleaded to make love in an actual bed for a change.

'That's brilliant news,' Filip exclaimed. 'I'm so pleased for you, Kristina. And Mama will be thrilled for Anna to be back behind the counter.' He pointed his spoon towards his fiancée. 'I know Papa has missed his sparring partner – prepare yourself for plenty of dinner invitations to make up for it.'

'That'll be … lovely, Pip. I can hardly wait – knowing how much your family enjoys watching Vasili trying and failing to get one over on me,' she replied, hiding the resignation from her voice. Her spare time had just evaporated.

Sitting in the courtyard with her friends, Anna urgently needed to find another way for them to be together. He was her drug of choice, her obsession – driving out thoughts of wrongdoing. She'd find a way.

Suppressing selfish feelings of regret, Anna raised a charged glass and cheered with the others.

'To Kristina. To the future.'

Chapter Twenty-Three

Due to her recent relentless schedule, Anna started later on her first day back at the café. Taking advantage of a few unexpected hours off, she decided on a clifftop run. Although weeks had passed since her narrow escape, Anna kept her promise not to run alone. She quietly opened the kitchen door, and a highly excitable Molossus of Epirus bounded forwards and enthusiastically licked her face. The routine never wavered, and Anna loved the rapturous welcome. Cassie refused to move in with Daniel and cleverly opted to remain in the main house where she was adored, pampered, and acted as Leyla's furry guardian.

There was enough light as she set off on the steep track behind the sleeping house – Cassie charged ahead to reacquaint herself with various bushes. After fifteen minutes of toiling uphill, Anna had warmed up nicely and, as the track levelled off, she drank in the view of the Ionian Sea stretching away to her left. Tharesseti looked so tranquil from here, but it was a hive of activity as Jeremy's vision of a luxury resort became a reality. Hopefully, its turbulent history was a thing of the past.

Along with the rhythmic sound of her breathing, Anna heard seabirds cry, and below her (but out of sight), the fishing fleet was galvanising itself for what would hopefully be a good day. There was something enormously satisfying about being out when most people lay tucked up in bed.

Whispers of mist swirled in the breeze as the undulating track dipped, and a figure stepped out from behind a thicket of wild olive trees. Cassie pelted ahead and leapt at the man.

'Who's a good girl.' He ruffled her fur, and she obediently sat for a treat.

'Do I get one of those?'

'You get something better,' Daniel replied and kissed her. 'C'mon.'

Anna found herself on an indistinct goat track that plunged through thick undergrowth. It was the same one to her secret cove, but instead of turning left, Cassie led the way forwards. They slipped past hawthorn bushes laden with clusters of red berries, past pine trees' outstretched branches, and under a canopy of flowering wild roses. Nature's perfume filled the air as the track descended steeply – clinging to the cliffside. Dense foliage hid two huge boulders. Turning sideways and raising their arms, they squeezed past to enter a dry, narrow gully.

Daniel produced a torch and grinned. 'Ready for an adventure?'

'Always.'

Using the walls for support, Anna picked her way over rocks until they appeared to hit a dead end, but instead, the torch highlighted a narrow chink to their right. She wriggled through and landed in a fairy grotto. Beautiful stalactites hung suspended, and dozens upon dozens of elegant stalagmites rose from the smooth floor. In many places, the two met to form intricate columns. A soft light filtered through a small gap in the ceiling and illuminated the wondrous cave. Above was a tiny patch of clear blue sky between the green fronds of gigantic ferns, where a narrow waterfall plunged into a deep pool. Tiny bubbles rose to the surface of crystal-clear water – a giant bowl of prosecco. Curiously, Anna dipped her fingers in.

'It's hot!' she cried. 'I … I didn't know Apokeri had any thermal springs.'

'It doesn't – this cave is a complete anomaly. Do you like it?'

'Do I like it? It's magical and must be thousands if not millions of years old. Who knows about it?'

'Maybe only me? I'm not sure. I've never seen signs of anyone else here. I discovered it as a boy. It's my special place, my secret place. I've wanted to bring you here for ages but could never manage it.'

'Thank you so much. It … it's one of the most beautiful places I've ever been to,' she whispered. 'It makes me want to cry.'

This time they savoured their lovemaking, knowing it might be their last. Afterwards, cocooned in blankets, Anna nestled in his arms.

'Coming here helps me. It helped me with Mama's diagnosis, after she passed away, and when Dad went back to Australia. I've been coming here a lot recently, and … and it seemed the place to ask if you would do something for me.'

'Hmm?'

'Okay … I'm not going to lie. It's a lot to ask.' His tone was serious.

Anna adjusted her position. It didn't feel right to be lounging about for whatever was coming.

'Right, I'm ready. Ask away,' she said and steeled herself.

'I need to make sure that Kristina is looked after when I leave. Both emotionally and financially. To that end, I am gifting you the apartment block, the gallery and its house. You can adapt them to your future requirements but must ensure that Kristina always has a home.'

'No. No. No. That makes no sense,' Anna forcefully replied, sitting up straighter. 'Don't be stupid. You need to gift them to Kristina, not me.'

'Yes, I would under normal circumstances. But that's not possible because, well, you see Kristina doesn't … This is difficult.' He paused and took a deep breath. 'She doesn't officially exist.'

'What? Don't be ridiculous. How can she not exist? She runs a business, for crying out loud! And she's lived in Apokeri for over sixty years.'

'The gallery and apartments are in my family's name, so Kristina's never appears anywhere. It never has because she's legally dead.'

'Hang on a minute.' She frowned, unable to comprehend what he was saying. 'How can that be right? Everyone in Apokeri knows who Kristina is. She doesn't exactly sneak around the place. I don't get it.'

'Do you know the story of how Kristina came to Apokeri?' Daniel calmly asked in the face of Anna's mounting agitation.

'Erm, no,' she admitted. 'Kristina always changes the subject, and as I could tell she doesn't want to discuss it, I haven't pushed … for once.'

'Okay, if you're sitting comfortably, I'll begin.'

And for the next thirty minutes, Anna sat spellbound as the tale unfolded.

Kristina was the youngest daughter of an extremely powerful, rich, and successful Swedish family. Lars Nilssen, a shrewd businessman, had significantly expanded the family empire and selected his bride not out of love but for financial merit. Having married two daughters off to incredibly wealthy and successful American and Swiss industrialists, his youngest was earmarked for a different union. A marriage with old Italian money to access a different class of people.

From an extremely young age, Kristina had shown herself to be the cleverest and prettiest sister and received the very best education. Only Kristina was educated in England and attended a Swiss finishing school. She accompanied her parents and sisters to glittering society events to secure the best husband – for her father and his ambitions. What Kristina wanted was of no consequence, and she was introduced to her intended during what turned out to be her final Tharesseti holiday. As far as her parents and the groom were concerned, it was a foregone conclusion. Of course, Kristina would agree. Her duty as a daughter was to further the family business and fulfil every girl's dream to marry nobility. Her parents had selected the eldest son of an Italian duke who owned Tharesseti Island, among other properties.

The eldest son was her father's age and a conceited, chauvinistic man. His second wife had died six months earlier, shortly after bearing him a second daughter. His first wife had perished after five years of marriage, without producing any children. It was no secret he had many illegitimate children – mainly sons. As a child holidaying on the island, Kristina had seen him brazenly grope and force himself on female staff. Now that she was older, he unashamedly leered at her.

Kristina refused her parents' wishes. Her first-class education had instilled self-confidence and an independent streak, unlike her two sisters. It did not matter that he was swimming in loot, well-travelled, extremely attractive, and highly educated. It was a veneer, and underneath it all he was inferior to her. She would never degrade herself and marry someone with appalling manners, behaviour, and attitude. Her parents saw marriage as an arrangement for money, business, or status and instructed their daughters to marry well from an early age. Her mother had gone further – it was a woman's responsibility to secure the best match and use any means necessary. But Kristina was not content to be married off at eighteen. She wasn't going to provide her father with lucrative business connections in exchange for a high-class lifestyle. Unlike the rest of her family, who openly had lovers, she would marry for love. She would marry Adrian Andino. He was superior to her father's choice and saw her as an equal.

And even if there were no Adrian, she would still refuse.

Her parents refused to accept the news. They would not throw away the chance to form an alliance that would create a social, political, and business powerhouse. Kristina was secretly imprisoned in the hotel with no meals until she changed her mind. However, an observant maid – who'd endured years of unwanted attention from Kristina's intended – got a message to

Adrian, and Kristina fled in the dead of night. She climbed out the window of her third-floor prison in bare feet, scrambled down an ivy-clad trellis and ran to a small rowing boat where he awaited. It meant disownment, but she didn't care and left with the clothes she wore and a single gold crucifix necklace.

'The necklace Kristina always wears,' Anna exclaimed. 'No wonder it's so precious to her.' Daniel nodded before taking up the story again.

Armed with the name of Kristina's lover, her father campaigned to get his daughter back and instructed Adrian's father and Daniel's great-grandfather to return Kristina. There was no question she would have a far better life with Italian nobility than with an inferior Greek fisherman. Well, all that did was insult Dimitri, who declared his son could marry whoever he wanted.

The next tactic was to cut off the Andino family from their source of income – mainly the hotel. The duke refused to do business with the family and would see to it that nobody else on Lefkada did. The hotel would source its seafood from another fishing family – who'd be happy to accept such a lucrative contract. But as a tight-knit community, the fishing fleet stood united, and the hotel received no seafood. With rich and powerful guests complaining, the duke had to backtrack, and Kristina's family returned empty-handed to Sweden.

'Hooray, love won out,' Anna sang before seeing Daniel's face. 'Or not?'

On the face of it, love did appear to triumph. Kristina moved in with Adrian's aunt and uncle to work on the farm, and he continued fishing. Kristina was desperate to get married as soon as possible and didn't care if her wedding dress was a sack and her ring a piece of straw, but he was proud and wanted his new bride-to-be to have the best he could afford. Kristina wanted to sell her gold necklace to get married and help with their

Australian passage, but Adrian refused. He had been saving hard and only needed one more month – and that was their undoing.

On a beautiful June evening, Adrian proposed (with a ring of straw) and promised the proper ring would be on her finger by the end of the week for everyone to see. Until then, it was their delicious secret. The following morning, Adrian set out from Apokeri harbour, never to be seen alive again.

'Oh no! What happened? Was there a storm? Did the boat sink?' Anna cried out in distress.

It was none of those. When Adrian failed to return, a search party went out. It quickly located the boat in one of his regular coves. The anchor had been dropped, there was nothing wrong with the boat, but there was a great deal of blood in the wheelhouse – evidence of a violent attack. Two days later, his body washed up on a beach south of Apokeri – bludgeoned to death. Kristina was inconsolable and was convinced her father was behind it. She received a short telegram expressing sorrow at Adrian's passing three days later. Her father expected Kristina to return; she was to forget the rather unfortunate incident and would make a far more suitable match next time. Kristina was incensed and saw it as further proof of her father's involvement.

'What did Kristina believe had happened?' Anna whispered.

Her father's and the duke's business dealings were closely entwined, so both stood to benefit. Kristina was convinced the duke (under her father's instruction) arranged Adrian's murder. The duke had never forgiven the Andino family for derailing the marriage, nor for his subsequent loss of face on retaking their seafood. What did he care if their youngest son was dead? It would serve as a lesson not to cross him. Kristina also knew that her father was not a man who changed his mind and would stop at nothing to ensure the arranged marriage took place.

Anna gripped her knees. 'What happened next?'

Kristina dictated a response to Dimitri. The letter stated Lars Nilssen was held entirely responsible for the death of Adrian by his daughter and the Andino family. They never expected any evidence to be found or charges to be brought but knew Lars Nilssen had conspired with the duke to commit the horrific crime, to make Kristina return to Sweden and enter into an arranged marriage. The letter went on to say the blood of two people was now on Lars Nilssen's hands. After the murder, and upon receiving her father's telegram, a grief-stricken Kristina went to the beach and took her own life on the exact spot Adrian's body washed up. Both families were united in grief at losing their youngest child and concluded, 'May God have mercy on your soul.'

Dimitri faithfully promised Kristina that the Andino family would love and protect her. After sending the letter, Kristina never officially used her name anywhere, and the family kept Dimitri's promise.

Anna shivered and wrapped the blanket tight. 'How … how the hell do you get over something like that? I didn't know … she never told me.'

'No, I didn't think so. She's never told me,' Daniel replied sadly. 'She's probably unaware of me knowing. The story was the last thing Dad told me before he left. And one of the final things Mama told him before she passed away. Dad made me swear to watch over Kristina and keep Dimitri's promise. To she was cared for and had a home – and I have.'

'And that's why you never left.'

'Yes, I stayed, and at first, everything was fine. But as the years passed, I longed to see the world and travel beyond the increasingly stifling confines of Apokeri. I wanted to live my life,' he wretchedly explained, and Anna heard desperation and guilt. 'I also realised that I wanted to live closer to Dad. His letters and calls weren't enough anymore. I tried to hide my growing restlessness, but Kristina knew and told me to follow my heart, be happy, and live my life. Little knowing she was the reason I couldn't go. It was awful. I kept telling her I was content in

Apokeri and not to worry, but I knew she didn't believe me. And then, a few years ago, Filip started to talk seriously about getting more involved with the business. And he's good, Anna, he's really good. I began to think perhaps it might give me an opportunity to at least go travelling for a bit, visit my family in Australia and then come back. In that way, I was still keeping my promise. It was a compromise.'

'And then I arrived.'

'Yes, and then you arrived and decided to stay. I saw you and Kristina together, kindred spirits. It was as if you were related. Kristina's long-lost granddaughter – your bond was incredibly strong. The only person I've seen her that close to was Mama. Everything started to fall into place. You moved in with Kristina and wanted to manage the apartment block.' Daniel began to fidget inside his blanket. He shuffled away from Anna now and started to fold inwards. 'For purely self-serving reasons, I wanted you to stay. If you stayed, I could perhaps escape. But ... but—'

'But what?'

His six-foot-six frame scrunched up in a protective ball – but why? Anna couldn't fathom it.

'I hated how you had no ties ... I-I hated how you'd apparently drifted through life with no responsibilities, and ... and I hated how you'd seen the world. I was so, so jealous. It ate me up. So I was nasty to you, and every time I was, I felt better. I felt smug, even when I wanted you to stay.' Anna leaned across, but Daniel curled up out of her reach and dropped his head. 'And you did stay. You effortlessly managed the apartments and all your other jobs, created a new life in Apokeri and fell in love with Filip.' Still holding himself, Daniel kept talking to the floor. 'So, I decided it was a sign. Here was my chance to strike out and create the life I wanted, and I sure as hell wasn't letting it slip through my grasp. It was time to go, and to go for good. Shit, Anna. Listen to me. I'm such a bastard. The way I've treated you. If Mama were alive, she'd be thoroughly ashamed of me. All the things Kristina went through, and here's me breaking the Andino promise for what? My selfishness.'

Still, he wouldn't look up, and rocked himself backwards and forward. Anna couldn't see his face but knew he was crying as the cave magnified his quiet sobs. She gently lifted his chin and wiped away the tears. So many secrets, so many promises, so much heartbreak.

'Sweetheart, you're not being selfish at all,' she said, pushing wavy blond hair behind his ears. 'How you first felt about me … that's all changed now. So don't worry. I'm a big girl. It'd take more than a softy like you to ruffle my feathers. Us Geordies are a tough breed.'

Daniel didn't respond.

'And more importantly than me – you and your family kept Kristina safe for more than sixty years. Do you really believe she's going to suffer any family reprisals now? Her parents are long gone. Remember what Kristina always says – you've only got one life to live, so make it count. Okay?'

Daniel nodded with a watery smile, and his shoulders relaxed.

'I solemnly swear to watch over Kristina as you have done and make sure she always has a home surrounded by the people she loves. But you don't need to pass over ownership of the house, gallery, and apartments for me to do that. I'll do it for love. Because I love Kristina. Because I love you. Why don't you retain ownership? What if you need to sell them down the line to raise funds for your new life?'

Cupping her face, he kissed her fiercely. 'You're one of the most amazing people I have ever met. No, I want you to have them. You need complete control of the properties. What if you have to raise funds and couldn't get hold of me? And besides, I've never thought of them as mine anyway. They're Kristina's, and it's not for me to profit from them. Think of it as my parting gift.'

'Bloody hell. That's one hell of a gift. But wouldn't it be a better idea to gift the property to a member of the Andino family instead? After all, there's Stelios and his three younger brothers.'

'No, and for several reasons. The main one being Dimitri only told two of his remaining three sons about the promise. He didn't tell his eldest son – Stelios' grandfather. I don't know why and my parents didn't either. So, I wouldn't divulge the secret, not after all these years. I love my cousins, but I wouldn't trust them with the property for reasons you don't need to know. Plus, you have the close connection with Kristina – not them. And I trust you, Anna. I trust you with my life.'

'Okay, if you're absolutely sure this is what you want to do, I accept.' Anna let out a massive sigh. 'I take it there never was any justice for Adrian?'

'Official justice, no. But unofficial justice – in some small way, perhaps? After his body was discovered, all food supplies immediately stopped, and all the staff quit Tharesseti. The hotel was forced to close and was soon abandoned. A short time later, the family fell from grace when the duke was declared bankrupt. He was found dead whilst apparently cleaning his gun. As for Lars Nilssen? I don't know what happened to him. But believing for the rest of his life that he had killed his daughter would be punishment enough.'

'So many lives destroyed. It is so unbelievably sad, and for what? Money and power?' Anna sighed again.

'I know. One event irreversibly altered so many people's lives – shattering their hopes and dreams. Kristina's right. You need to make the most of the time you've got.'

'That's why you're making the right decision, Daniel. And I'm incredibly proud of you.' She hoped the words would get through and remove his unnecessary guilt. 'Do you remember when I came to apologise in the workshop and thanked you for saving me?'

'Please don't remind me,' Daniel said, grimacing. 'I was an immense prick.'

'Nothing I didn't deserve,' Anna admitted. 'When I walked away, I didn't know how to repay you. I think I have.'

Daniel ran his fingers down her back and mischievously replied, 'I don't suppose you fancy adding some credit to that account?'

'Oh, I think that can be arranged.'

***

It was a fast turnaround to be on time, and like Sofia, Anna couldn't wait to be back. She loved the positive energy of the café – it fed her soul, as well as her stomach. However, there was a distinctly different atmosphere when she opened the door. Everyone seemed to be moving, talking, and serving at a slower pace.

'You're back!' Sofia, her two sisters, and the regular customers shouted.

It was as if a jolt of electricity surged through the air – Sofia dragged her behind the counter, and Adriani's mother flung off her apron and sprinted out of the place.

'That's the fastest my sister has moved since she started,' Sofia observed. 'The orderly world of accountancy is where she prefers to be … and where I wish my older sister would return to.'

Despite numerous suggestions, hints, and entreaties, Lucinda had decided it was in everyone's best interests (as well as her own) to continue there until her North American holiday of a lifetime. As Anna scurried backwards and forwards, fulfilling orders, replenishing shelves, collecting dirty dishes, cleaning tables, and serving a steady stream of tourists at the ice-cream hatch, Lucinda stood and described the six-month itinerary in detail. Anna nodded and briefly managed 'Oh yes', 'That'll be lovely' and 'You'll have a great time. I loved it there' as she flitted around

Lucinda. By mid-afternoon, Anna could recite the trip backwards. Having spent a fantastic six-week Stateside with best-mate Annalise, she knew Lucinda would love the French Quarter of New Orleans, the majestic Grand Canyon, wine tasting in the Napa Valley, and chilling in Key West.

It was some time before Anna managed to get into the kitchen, whereby Agnes promptly crushed her in a rib-cracking embrace.

'You don't know what I've endured,' Agnes cried and held fast to Anna in case she abandoned her again. 'It's my punishment for being such a bitch to you. Whereas you can talk and work, Sofia's sisters can't. It's been an absolute nightmare, and Lucinda refuses to leave! You do more singlehandedly than they do together.'

Poor Viktor, Anna thought. The only place Agnes could vent her frustrations would have been in the privacy of her home.

'There, there. Poor Head Chef,' Anna whispered. 'Everything is going to be alright now. Superstar Anna is back in the building.'

'I almost forgot your modesty,' Agnes replied and laughed. 'Get back in that café, girl. Good grief, I can still hear Lucinda waffling about her damned holiday. If she tells me once more about spending Thanksgiving in Seattle with her oldest sister, celebrating Christmas with Peter's relations in Toronto, visiting Graceland to pay homage to Elvis or driving a motorhome along Highway One, I'll scream or stick my head in the oven. I don't need to revisit America – I've already been back!'

To celebrate the return of Anna, Agnes had added a much-loved Geordie option to the menu. On her break, Anna sank her teeth into a ham and pease pudding stottie, and she hadn't been the only one to enjoy her little piece of home. Although most customers had never tasted or heard of the delicacy, it had gone down a storm. Back behind the counter, Anna reckoned there was maybe enough left for one more.

It was now time (prompted by the regulars) to restart the Geordie Phrase Phenomenon. And to that end, Anna updated the blackboard with a new saying. 'Shy bairns get nowt – quiet children do not receive anything.' Standing and admiring her handiwork, she jumped when a voice boomed out behind her.

'Aye, pet. I'd say that about sums it up. If yee divvn' ask, yee divvn' get. I'm propa clamming for some decent bait. Food on the flight owa was propa crap. Reckon I cud wolf down a scabby horse and its jockey. Here, giz uz a ham and pease pudding stottie and a cuppa to be going on with, bonny lass.'

Anna spun around, and there in the café as large as life stood Andrew, one of her nine island-hopping friends. It was all she could do not to swear out loud. Instead, she screamed, ran over, and gave him a massive hug.

'No way! What the hell are you doing back here?'

'Glad to see your old mukka then?'

'It's brilliant!'

After the initial shock, she studied her friend in his short-sleeved white polo shirt and black jeans – what a difference. His thick head of long wavy blond hair was in a new shoulder-length haircut, and his beard and handlebar moustache were neatly trimmed. The man was a picture of health.

'You look fantastic.'

'Aye, not bad, eh?' He slapped his flattened stomach. 'The beer gut is long gone. I've lost almost four stone and only have a couple more pounds to shed to hit my target weight.'

'That's amazing. Well done.'

'I'm telling you, that island-hopping holiday came at the right time – the kick up the backside I needed. Gone is the beer-swilling, pie-chomping, sofa-loving slob, replaced by a calorie-conscious, healthy-living machine. I feel ten years younger. Before joining a running club, I took your advice and started with that Couch to 5K programme. Last week, I did my first competitive 10K – never felt better.'

'I'm impressed, but that doesn't explain what you're doing here? Nobody has mentioned anything in their letters or on the group chat, and I know you'd have told them.'

'Yes, they knew, but I told them to keep quiet. We wanted it to be a surprise.'

'It certainly is. I'm gobsmacked.'

'But back to your original question. Let me present the Project Manager for Jeremy's Tharesseti hotel. That's another change. I've jacked in my job back home, rented out my house, and I start work the day after tomorrow. I reckon you've got me for at least six months.'

'That's brilliant news. How exciting! Nits, I'm working tomorrow but will be back by six if you're free?'

'Well, it's funny you should mention that. Jeremy very kindly booked me onto a coach trip tomorrow where I believe there's this awesome Geordie tour guide?'

'Are you serious?' Anna squealed.

'I certainly am. Jeremy said I had better take the chance to see Lefkada as I might not get another one.'

'Awesome.' She clapped her hands with excitement. 'You'll meet Cosimo, coach driver extraordinaire and such a gent. And at lunchtime, you get to sit down with all the other entertaining coach drivers for lunch and their tall tales. Plus, it'll be a great way to make lots of contacts. You never know when they might come in useful.'

'Thanks, Anna. That's brilliant. Anyway, I'm tied up tomorrow night. Jeremy's got us booked at some fancy restaurant to meet various suppliers, which I'm looking forward to.'

Before Andrew settled down to his much-anticipated stottie, Anna introduced Sofia and Lucinda, who'd loitered in the background for that very reason.

As soon as Andrew disappeared, Lucinda slapped her palm on the counter. 'Damn, if that isn't one fine specimen of a man. Anna, are all your male friends that hot? Please tell me he'll be popping in here more often?' Lucinda wafted herself with a menu. 'A bit of a bad boy with his mean and moody biker look, and there's nothing like a nice piece of eye candy to lust over.'

'Andrew certainly knows some interesting people, I'll say that for him. He might look intimidating but is a big teddy bear at heart and so chilled to be almost horizontal.'

Appearing from the bakery and overhearing the conversation, Vasili rolled his eyes. 'I hope your pace of work is not going to slow even further, Luci, if you're drooling and ogling over Anna's friend?'

'Never fear, darling Vasili. Although I may not have the greatest turn of speed, I excel at working whilst appraising a mighty fine member of the opposite sex – I can do that all day,' she purred.

Chapter Twenty-Four

In all the weeks Anna had been a coach tour guide, today's trip ranked as one of the best – undoubtedly because Andrew was there. He'd made her realise what it was like to be around those who'd known you for years. It was the in-jokes, the shared history, and the ability to sit in comfortable silence or simply chill out and do nothing that she missed.

In Apokeri, Anna kept in close contact with family and friends via messaging, emails, postcards, and letters – all peppered with amusing anecdotes about the residents. She was in the Post Office so often she was on first-name terms with the people who worked there. Like her trips to the supermarket, Anna often saw thirty minutes vanish and, from these chats, built up an encyclopaedic knowledge of village life. People felt compelled to open up about themselves and their neighbours. Maybe it was because she asked the right questions?

During the coach tour, Anna loved introducing Andrew to some of her new friends, along with the sights, sounds, and smells of Lefkada. As she expected, with a mutual love of motorbikes, he instantly hit it off with Cosimo and – echoing her first lunchtime – Andrew probed him for biker stories. Cosimo waxed lyrical about all the Lefkada routes he loved, and soon the other drivers were pitching in. Anna was impressed by how much conversational Greek Andrew understood, and the broad accent, not his Greek, baffled listeners. By the close of play, Cosimo and Andrew agreed to blast around Lefkada on a pair of motorbikes at the first opportunity. Anna did not envisage Cosimo's wife being too happy. Cosimo rarely climbed aboard a motorbike after a head-on collision with an inattentive car driver. Anna noticed that particular story and the subsequent long and painful road to recovery had not come up at lunch.

The day had been so enjoyable that Anna bounced along Apokeri beachfront. There was so much to tell Kristina. However, those thoughts evaporated when she entered the gallery to find a strange scene. Behind the counter, Kristina sat uneasily on her usual stool, clutching her favourite mug, her body deliberately positioned away from three individuals.

On the left was a tanned man in his mid-forties with a French air. He was about five-foot-ten and dressed in a black T-shirt and black combat-style trousers which accentuated a slim and toned physique. His black laced boots had a high shine, and based on his posture, Anna felt sure the man was – or had been – in the military. She noticed how his dark brown eyes, set in an angular face, constantly assessed his surroundings. He could no doubt accurately describe every person who had walked past the window since his arrival. There was a cup of half-drunk black coffee on the glass counter next to him alongside a fork, a plate, and an untouched slice of strawberry cheesecake.

What a complete waste, Anna thought.

The other three plates on the counter were empty, except for a few crumbs, indicating the visitors had been there some time. Kristina's demeanour suggested the two strangers were well known to Daniel, who was standing far too close, Anna thought, to a woman in her late twenties perched on the other stool. Although she had the same slim and toned build as Anna, the resemblance ended there. And instead, she had a delicately featured face which hinted at Russian heritage, and subtle make-up highlighted startling blue eyes as the woman threw back her head and laughed at something Daniel said. Good grief, the woman was a walking jewellery shop – draped in an elegant diamond necklace, matching bracelet and anklet, a thick platinum wedding band, and a diamond-encrusted engagement ring.

As soon as the party saw Anna, Kristina leapt off the chair like a gazelle. 'Anna's back. It's so good to see you. I hope it's been a wonderful day and Andrew enjoyed the trip?' And without waiting for a response, she said, 'If you'll excuse me for a moment.' She swiftly dumped crockery and cutlery on the tray and vanished.

That was one sharp exit, Anna mused, and did little to defuse the awkward atmosphere which Daniel seemed oblivious to.

'I would like to present Mr Hugo Dubois and his charming wife, Irina.'

His introduction elicited a giggle from the woman as she tenderly placed a hand on Daniel's chest. Anna was thankful that Irina turned at that exact moment.

'How formal Danny is? Always the gentleman. Do you not think so, darling?' Irina purred and shook back her long, blonde, poker-straight hair.

Anna composed herself, angry that her eyes flashed with jealousy at the intimate gesture. Luckily no one noticed, and Hugo merely nodded at his wife's comment.

Get a grip, Jenkinson, Anna silently admonished.

She had a strong compulsion to storm across the room, slap away the hand that still lingered and tell the woman to back away from her man. Of course, Anna would never do such a thing and suspected if any female tried, they wouldn't live to tell the tale. This woman was edgy. However, in the next instant, Irina slid off her stool and stalked across the room in killer four-inch stiletto heels to embrace Anna and kiss both cheeks.

'A *very good friend* of Daniel is immediately a friend of ours,' Irina said kindly and nodded to her husband, who immediately strode over, bowed to Anna, and kissed her hand.

'Enchanté, mademoiselle.'

Anna was uncomfortable in her skin. She did not like the emphasis placed on a 'very good friend', and felt naked and exposed. Her assessment of Hugo being French was correct, but she was clueless about Irina. One minute, the woman spoke fluent Greek and the next cut-glass English. Who the hell was she, how did she know Daniel, and what else did she know? Anna became aware Irina was asking a question.

'You will, of course, join us for dinner tonight? Danny has told us so much about you. With only a few days before his departure, I know you won't want to miss out on spending as much time as possible with your friend. Do you not agree?'

Anna felt the net slowly drawing in and mentally head-slapped herself. Shit, Irina knew. Anna silently telegraphed to Daniel that going to dinner would be a terrible idea.

'Excellent idea, Rini,' he responded. 'Come on, Anna, it'll be fun.'

She wanted to scream at him for being so dense, and at that moment, Kristina reappeared.

'Sadly, Kristina will be unable to join us,' Irina casually remarked and smiled sweetly at the older woman.

'Yes, unfortunately, it's true. I'm expecting a visit from an up-and-coming artist,' Kristina explained and returned an equally fake smile. 'I'm keen to showcase more Lefkada talent in the gallery. It cannot simply be all about me. I'm sorry to decline, Irina, but I'm sure you understand.'

'I understand perfectly.'

Anna listened to the exchange and realised two things. Firstly, her friend was lying. There was no budding artist. Kristina simply didn't want to go. And secondly, Irina knew Kristina was lying but also didn't want her to go – interesting.

'So, Anna, you'll be joining us?' Irina queried again.

Okay, Daniel had failed to pick up on her obvious desire to bail. He was a bloke, what did she expect? But Kristina was bound to rescue her. Alas, Anna saw that mischievous glint.

'What is this, Anna? Don't tell me that you're passing up the opportunity to dine at Nereus with such good company? I know it's your favourite Lefkada restaurant. Come now, Daniel is only with us for three more days. You wouldn't want to deprive him when he's so keen for you to become better acquainted with Hugo and Irina. Anna, I'm disappointed in you.'

That was it; she was going to kill her friend later. However, there was one last throw of the dice.

'But I'm not dressed for Nereus,' Anna pointed out, combing her fingers through her greasy hat-hair and looking down at her dust-covered clothing in sharp contrast to the couple's expensive looking attire. 'I'm a complete state. You'll miss your reservation, waiting for me. Thank you for the kind invitation, but please go without me, and I hope to see you both at Daniel's leaving do.'

'Oh Anna, you are far too well-mannered,' Irina trilled. 'Stelios is so accommodating, don't you think? He will, of course, rearrange things for us. After all, he is one of Danny's relations, and I'm such a good friend. We go way back.'

Anna knew she was beaten.

Irina smiled sweetly, and continued with a triumphant tone. 'Take your time, my dear. There's no rush. We'll wait in the bar to enjoy a drink or three, and it'll allow me to catch up with the ever-attentive Stelios.'

Irina nodded to her husband and Daniel, and the two men followed in her wake as she swept out of the building in her figure-hugging blood-red silk dress.

Kristina smirked. 'I guess you'd better get ready.'

***

It was the fastest Anna had ever showered and changed. She needed to quiz Kristina before walking into the lion's den. It was unlikely to be a relaxed evening, and she wanted to be armed with some ammunition. She clattered down the stairs, and her silent

230

prayer was answered – Kristina sat alone in an empty gallery, reinstated on her stool with a steaming mug of coffee, the picture of serenity once more. She looked up as Anna, in her rush, skidded into the gallery.

'Slow down, girl,' Kristina exclaimed. 'You look amazing. Has Filip seen you in that?'

Anna did a twirl and inwardly cheered. Take that, Irina.

'Yes, I wore it last week to Sofia and Vasili's. Pip did like it.'

Most women have a special outfit guaranteed to make them shine with confidence. And Anna was wearing *that* outfit – a simple black sleeveless dress with white embroidered flowers around the hemline that fell just below knee level. And a pair of elegantly pointed black leather kitten-heeled sandals, a black clutch bag, and understated jewellery – a silver pendant necklace, silver stud earrings, and her pretty engagement ring.

'I know you're usually very discreet, but not this time. You need to spill the beans on Irina. It's the least you can do after throwing me to the lions.'

'I'm sorry,' Kristina said. 'But I didn't want to go, and it was obvious that Irina didn't want me to go either. I, therefore, concluded a little lie was the best course of action.'

'I suppose so,' Anna conceded. 'It still doesn't excuse you for abandoning me. I couldn't believe it when you said, "I'm disappointed in you." So come on, dish the dirt.'

Kristina at least had the decency to look shamefaced.

***

Anna strode into Nereus. Knowing a bit about the enigmatic Mrs Dubois did little to steady her nerves. Irina had arrived at Apokeri first school as a scrawny nine-year-old. She was a year older than her equally skinny brother, Georg. Whereas the sister was a firecracker, Georg was shy and quiet and found himself bullied by four older boys on his first day. Daniel was equally shy but, being well-developed for his age, he'd stepped in to defend his new classmate, and the pair became inseparable. The next day, all four bullies arrived at school with blackened eyes and a host of cuts and bruises. Fiercely protective, Irina had lain in wait to dispatch each one separately, and Daniel was mesmerised. After school, at weekends, and during holidays, the three children went to Daniel's house. Georg and Irina practically lived there, which saw Daniel's mother, Lilian, feed up the malnourished pair. The trio would often find their way into the workshop to tinker away alongside Daniel's father. If he wasn't there, the friends would either help Kristina in her garden or go off exploring.

The three remained extremely close throughout their childhood and into their teenage years. Irina blossomed into a beautiful and clever young woman, but Daniel was her only friend as she deliberately kept people at arm's length. Well aware of her effect on the opposite sex, there were always rumours circulating about her involvement with married men and male teachers. However, Georg remained shy, quiet, and socially awkward. Shrugging her shoulders, Kristina conceded that Georg had not been blessed with the good looks of his sister. He remained a slight, gangly, and somewhat goofy-looking young man. However, when it came to brains, he was off the chart. Kristina and Lilian had always welcomed the siblings into their homes. Georg was a delight, but both women were disturbed at his sister's unhealthy interest in death and pain. Helping in the garden, Irina continually quizzed Kristina about plant toxicity – how much would someone have to ingest to become ill or die, and would it be an excruciating death? Kristina had always changed the subject. The girl also wanted to be on hand if a chicken needed dispatching, to find out what it felt like to break a bird's neck. Kristina ensured Irina was never present if that happened.

As a physiotherapist, Lilian was delighted when Irina showed an interest in her work. That was until she realised the teenager was working out which bones were the easiest to break, which took the longest to heal, and the swiftest way to incapacitate someone.

Kristina and Lilian had been so worried that they tried but failed to speak to Irina's parents. The father was constantly away on unknown business and the mother refused to answer the door. Instead, she spent all her time locked away in a study, undertaking what Georg said was important grown-up research. It meant the siblings were left to fend for themselves – a judging by how underweight they were.

The death of Lilian devastated Daniel and deeply affected Irina and Georg – their combined grief brought them even closer. The funeral was the first and only time Kristina met Irina and Georg's parents, who arrived for the service and afterwards stayed long enough to thank Arthur for the love and care Lilian and himself had shown their children. A year later, Irina left for university – Daniel moped about the place for weeks. Twelve months later, Georg did the same, and the parents moved away. A few months after they left, the unimaginable happened – Georg was killed. Walking home one night from his part-time job, he was the victim of a mugging gone wrong. His body was found behind bins in an unlit alleyway after an anonymous tip-off, but by the time the emergency services arrived, it was too late. Georg was already dead, having suffered a single stab wound. He was probably still alive when they dumped him. Those responsible were eventually brought to justice years later.

Instead of visiting Georg, Daniel travelled to attend his best friend's funeral, and returned with Irina. The death of Georg almost destroyed her. She moved in with Arthur and Daniel and slowly started to rally. A month later, she was gone. At that point, Daniel took Filip under his wing – probably seeing a glimpse of Georg in the youngster hanging around the garage for the last few years, helping Arthur. Under Daniel's tutelage, Filip found his niche and flourished.

Three years later, Irina turned up at Arthur's farewell party, and on the fifth anniversary of Georg's death, she landed in Apokeri again, but this time accompanied by Hugo.

Anna expressed her surprise when she heard Daniel was delighted at the couple's engagement, as he was clearly besotted.

Kristina believed Daniel would always love Irina but was happy for her all the same. That comment shook Anna. Is that why he remained single? A classic case of unrequited love? And how much did he care for his latest fling? After all, Anna initially seduced him, and she was the only one to say 'I love you'. Was Anna a bit of fun before he left? A convenient person to take care of Kristina? Doubts started to niggle, but she shook them off. No, he did care. Besides, it was a bit rich to complain, bearing in mind her own dishonest behaviour. At the end of the day, she seduced him because he was leaving. He satisfied a need, and she did the same for him – except for her, it was much more than a fling.

Kristina wrapped up by saying that Daniel had visited Hugo and Irina several times at their home in the South of France, including for their wedding. Close to both, Daniel was staying with Hugo's brother and sister-in-law in Japan. After Daniel left, Kristina did not expect Irina to revisit Apokeri. Although many years had passed, Kristina admitted the memory of Irina as a youngster clouded her judgement, but she still believed there was a great deal going on behind that beautiful face.

Whilst dwelling on Kristina's final comment, Anna smoothed her dress, took a deep breath, and entered Nereus. It was easy to spot Irina at the bar with a gin and tonic in one hand and the other resting on the arm of Stelios. The man was entranced and laughed along with Hugo and Daniel at an amusing anecdote, but Irina immediately broke off the conversation on seeing Anna approach.

'Excellent. Anna has arrived and looks stunning. Do you not agree, Danny?'

All eyes turned, Stelios let out a wolf whistle, Hugo smiled, and Daniel's eyes shone.

'You look gorgeous,' Daniel replied wistfully. 'Beautiful. Always very beautiful.'

'Come, Stelios,' Irina interrupted. 'This is a cause for celebration – a bottle of your finest champagne.'

'Of course. My eldest, will escort you to the table, and I shall bring it over.'

Walking through the crowded restaurant, Anna saw theirs was the best table – in an elevated corner, offering privacy and spectacular views across the bay. At sixteen, Stelios's daughter had inherited her father's confident, easy-going charm and ensured everything was to their satisfaction. And, like Stelios, she was captivated by Irina.

Once seated and the champagne poured, Irina proposed a toast. 'To friendship – cherishing old ones and establishing new ones. To Daniel and Anna. To whatever the future brings. To good fortune.'

After clinking glasses, Anna took a sip, and Irina asked how it compared to previous vintages. Anna laughed, and her tension dissolved. She refused to be fazed by this woman and planned to enjoy herself tonight.

'My knowledge of champagne wouldn't fill a postage stamp,' Anna remarked and took another sip. 'I once won a dodgy bottle of fizz in a nightclub for being the first person to jump on stage and snatch it out of the DJ's hand, and I drank champagne the night Pip proposed, but as I got so drunk, I only remember bubbles going up my nose. How about you? How does this one rank?'

Anna watched as Irina took a sip and pondered the question.

'I don't have a clue either – I never drink the stuff.' Irina replied, grinning.

Everyone laughed before it was down to the serious business of ordering, and Anna was delighted to discover Hugo and Irina also loved their food. For starters, the foursome opted to share a Middle Eastern mezze platter, they continued with the main course of Spanish Paella, and rounded off with all four ordering a separate dessert and putting them in the middle of the table for everyone to sample. Now that was Anna's idea of a wonderful meal. The conversation flowed easily and unsurprisingly focused on food, travel, and Daniel's upcoming trip. After Irina and Hugo insisted on paying, they opted for a stroll along the promenade to digest the delicious food. Daniel was ahead, in deep conversation with Hugo.

Walking along, Anna felt Irina slip an arm through hers. 'So, tell me, how long has Daniel been your lover?'

Anna was utterly blindsided and understood that was the intention. Although she'd never been good at lying to a direct question, she was damned if she was going to tell the truth.

'What a strange thing to ask. Why would you think such a thing?' Anna replied with what she hoped passed for a carefree laugh.

'Oh, several things. The way Danny talked about you in the gallery and when you arrived in the restaurant aroused my suspicions, and how you reacted to me placing my hand on his chest.' Irina smiled at this point. 'You thought I'd missed that, didn't you? The way you froze, and your eyes flashed. It was an instinctive territorial reaction. And the way Danny physically responds when you're anywhere near him. He lights up like a firework. I was studying your behaviour with one another during the meal. I'm sorry to say, Danny broadcasts his emotions, but if it makes you feel any better, you give nothing away.'

'We're friends. Maybe Daniel finds me mildly attractive. Who knows? Nobody else mentions it. I'm sure Kristina would've picked up on it if it was that obvious. I'd say you were reading too much into things,' Anna replied calmly, but her heart hammered away. 'Have you asked Daniel?'

'Come now.' It was Irina's turn to laugh. 'You cannot deny that Danny finds you more than mildly attractive. And as far as anyone else noticing, I find people often miss what's staring them in the face. I know people keep secrets from loved ones in Apokeri – some might be kept by yourself?'

Anna did not like the way the conversation was developing. The woman had an unnerving ability to hit the mark and strip her back to raw emotions. Was that why Irina had linked arms – to feel her tensing? She forced herself to relax and, keeping her voice steady, went on the offensive.

'You've yet to answer my question – have you asked Daniel?'

'I would counter – you have still failed to answer my first question, Anna. However, I will answer yours. No, I have not. It would be pointless. Danny is far too much of a gentleman. He'd be offended that I'd asked and would refuse to answer.'

'Why do you think that I'd tell you?' Anna asked with genuine interest.

'I didn't think for one minute you would. But I find what someone doesn't say is equally important. You've skilfully deflected my enquiries, and that speaks volumes.' The women continued to walk along in silence before Irina continued, 'I'm not here to cause trouble. That's not my intention.'

'What is your intention?'

Irina stopped and gave Anna a searching look. 'I care deeply for Danny. I want him to be happy. Since he reached adulthood, I've never seen him as happy as he is now, and I wanted to establish where this happiness stems from. Having done so, I don't need to know anything further.'

'You love him,' Anna stated. It was not a question.

'Yes, very much. He saved me. He saved me from myself. I am indebted to him for that.'

That makes two of us, Anna thought.

'I was extremely sorry to hear about your brother. I cannot begin to imagine what you must have gone through.'

'Exactly ten years ago tomorrow, his life was cut short. Not a day goes by that I don't think about Georg. He was the best brother anyone could have had – humble, unbelievably selfless, and clever. I often imagine what he would have gone on to become,' Irina said with pride and sadness.

'It must have brought some comfort that those responsible are now behind bars? Although it can never bring your brother back.'

Anna could sense Irina weighing up what to divulge as they stood at the end of the stone pier, looking over to Tharesseti.

'I was the one who found them, you know. I refused to accept the original police verdict that it was an unsolved case, and became obsessed. I spent years trying and failing to find the truth. I hired countless private investigators but to no avail, and then I met Hugo. He has certain contacts and is privy to information that enabled me to access new channels. That allowed me to find out who did it. I rang Daniel and told him my search was over and that I would dispense my own form of justice as I had no intention of seeing them go to prison. I wanted them to suffer the way Georg had suffered,' Irina explained in a cold and detached manner that sent a chill down Anna's spine.

'But you didn't go through with it. They went to prison.'

'Yes. Daniel pleaded with me not to do such a terrible thing. He tried to make me see reason – Georg would not have wanted it, and neither did Hugo or himself. Daniel calmly explained he had already lost Georg and couldn't bear to lose me as well. And I would be lost if I went down my intended route as there would be no coming back. It would change me forever as a person. It would destroy me. He said he had always loved me; he knew I was a good person and would do the right thing. I felt like I was standing on a knife-edge with so much rage inside me. Fixated on revenge for so many years, I needed to see it through to the end – regardless of what it did to me. I had to see those responsible grovel, to beg for mercy before I saw them die. They did not deserve to live.'

'What changed your mind?' Anna blurted out.

'Love,' Irina declared. 'It sounds corny, but the love I felt for Georg, Hugo, and Daniel and how much I knew they loved me. They saw through all my faults and loved me regardless. And I was exhausted from being angry and vengeful all the time. So, I agreed to hand over all the evidence to the police. I will not go into the details, but I made sure that the guilty parties confessed.'

Hugo and Daniel had been ahead the whole time, and judging by the amount of laughter, theirs was a light-hearted conversation. Arriving back at the pier, the men waited at the statue of St Peter. Reunited, Daniel suggested they stroll to Dionysus Taverna for a drink. After all, it was still reasonably early. Everyone agreed, except Anna.

'I'm sorry, but I need my bed – I can barely keep my eyes open. It's been a long day, and I've got another early start tomorrow. It's another fully-booked tour with Max, so I need my wits about me. Thank you, Irina. Thank you, Hugo. It's been lovely getting to know you both. Thank you again for the meal, and I hope we can catch up at Daniel's leaving do.'

'Are you sure?' Daniel asked. 'You do look tired.'

'Yes, I'm shattered. An early night will do me good.' Anna stifled a yawn. 'I also think it's the perfect opportunity for you all to have a proper catch-up.'

After saying farewell, she no longer felt jealous as she watched Irina link arms with Hugo and Daniel. Their laughter echoed along the promenade, and she suspected the trio would make a night of it. Turning for home, all she wanted to do was sleep.

Chapter Twenty-Five

It had been an enjoyable day and happily uneventful – apart from the weather. Anna had received a fatherly warning (delivered with great pleasure) stating there'd be storms over Lefkada all week. And her meteorological expert had been correct, as usual. For the most part, the clouds raced across the sky to deluge Karya, Egklouvi, and Vafkeri.

Today had been no exception, and luckily, the heaviest downpour broke when the tour guests were enjoying their private wine tasting. The atrocious weather provided one unforeseen benefit – an impromptu photoshoot at Cape Ducato lighthouse to capture an incredible electrical storm. Fork lightning from apocalyptic thunderclouds streaked across the sky to strike a turbulent sea. The group agreed to share their truly staggering images. Afterwards, Anna chatted to Dania while running off photocopies ahead of Friday night. Having surreptitiously collected dozens of photos of Daniel as man and boy, she intended to pin the most embarrassing ones up on the walls for his leaving do. The other ones were in a photobook – a memento of life in Apokeri.

***

Leaving Odyssey, she halted – transfixed by the approaching storm. A wall of rain obliterated the horizon with a seascape stripped back to black and white. The water was no longer inviting but menacing. Inky black, it heaved forward, thrusting the waves ever higher to crash against the shore before being dragged back and hurled forward again. Water arced over the pier, and St Peter stood alone – under siege. The screams of gulls echoed overhead, desperately battling to reach safety. The roar of the wind assaulted her ears, a wall of water engulfed Tharesseti and moved ever closer. The wind caught the cardboard tube holding the precious photocopies and threatened to rip it out from under her arm. It was enough to shake her from the hypnotic scene to turn and race ahead of Mother Nature's wrath. Telephone wires whistled as Anna felt her bare calves sandblasted. She was still ahead of the storm – just. At least the onshore wind was helping to drive her up the street. But it was catching her heels. The air pressure was dropping as the clouds streamed overhead. And now she was running, desperate to get inside, but found it exhilarating. The first blobs of rain hit the pavement in front of her, and she sprinted towards her goal, passing the rotating sign – a spinning blur of metal. She barely had time to wave as Alex pulled the van around the back before rushing ins.'Wow, that was amazing! Oh hello. I didn't expect to see you. Where's Pip?' And then he turned to face her. 'What … what's the matter?'

'Funny you should ask that.' Daniel's voice was cold and hard-edged. 'It's quite an interesting story and ties in very nicely to your first question.'

And the hatred. So much animosity caused Anna to step backwards.

He sneered. 'Oh, please don't go anywhere.' He dragged a chair, and she winced at the high-pitched metal sound against the floor tiles. 'Take a seat, Miss Jenkinson. I insist. Make yourself comfortable. Knowing how much you enjoy a good story, you're in for a real treat.'

Anna had never experienced so much open hostility, and her tear ducts filled.

Don't cry, don't cry.

She cautiously approached and gingerly perched on the stool – every sinew in her body on high alert, ready to flee at a moment's notice.

'Now that you're sitting comfortably,' Daniel mocked, his face a twisted mask of loathing. 'Then I'll begin.'

He'd been so happy last night as Irina and Hugo sang Anna's praises, and Irina had remarked that any man who could capture Anna's heart was extremely lucky. High praise indeed from a woman who does not impress easily. After a bar crawl, they headed back to his studio, drank till the early hours, and arranged to meet for a coastal walk and a picnic to commemorate Georg. Hugo left first, and Irina followed, but as the door closed, she said that, although it was none of her business, Daniel would be the greatest fool to board the plane on Saturday. It was obvious he was besotted and that the feeling was mutual. She hadn't seen him that happy since he was a kid. Yes, there would be difficulties ahead with Anna engaged to Filip, but he was clearly the wrong man for her. Irina stressed that if life had told her anything, love would find a way. Even with all the alcohol in his system, he'd laughed and said she was mistaken. Irina simply smiled, cupped his cheek, and kissed him. 'Ever the gentleman Danny. I would expect nothing less.' And with that, she'd left.

He'd stood statue-like, staring at the closed door as if struck full-force by a cricket bat, and gazed around at a spotless studio, a neatly half-filled rucksack propped against one wall and the tidy pile of remaining belongings against another. His whole life condensed right down. All he had to show for twenty-eight years. How tragic. What did he want? What was important? He did the usual – systematically listed the pros and cons – but stopped because he knew the right decision.

Hugo and Irina picked him up on a blustery day, and he felt invigorated as they strode to Georg's favourite cove. Over lunch, he'd announced his decision and felt excited and confident with their full support. Early afternoon, they dropped him off, and getting out of the car, Irina leaned out the window and wished him luck.

Throughout his monologue, Daniel refused to meet her eyes. Anna willed him to look up, but he kept them firmly fixed on the floor. She wanted to interject and shout, 'Yes, I'm the one for you!' but found her throat constricted with conflicting emotions, and no words would come out. There was unbridled joy at hearing how much she meant to him, but on the other, dread as to how the story would end.

After a pause, Daniel took a deep breath. 'I walked into the shop, hoping to find Filip alone. He was with a young couple discussing the pros and cons of road bikes versus hybrids. He smiled as I entered – the poor sod didn't have a clue what was coming. It made me so sick with guilt that I almost lost my nerve. After ten minutes, the pair left happy, and I steeled myself as I approached the counter. I'd rehearsed my speech over and over again but was too nervous, and my words jumbled up.'

He stopped and stared at her, and she blanched. No twinkling glint, no affectionate smile – instead, utter contempt as his lip curled into a loathsome grimace.

'I told Filip that I could no longer continue with the pretence. I was in love with you and had been for some time. He needed to know we were lovers, and I'd decided to stay and intended to make a new life with his fiancée. Although it would cause significant distress, he had to stand aside. I didn't pause for breath, and said that you had told me. But I didn't get to finish my sentence. He exploded. I've never seen anything like it. He picked up his chair and launched it across the room. Next, the computer would have followed if I hadn't grabbed it. Instead, he picked up his glass of half-drunk water and hurled it against the wall. It shattered on impact, showering the floor with tiny shards. His empty cup of coffee went next, thrown with such force that a broken piece ricocheted off the wall and sliced his cheek. He didn't even flinch when it started to bleed, only screaming at your betrayal, how you'd told him how much you loved and cared for him. He was out of control and continued to rant and rave about how he loved you, had never met anyone like you, had opened his heart, and in return, you plunged the knife in. You might as well have killed him. And then he stormed out.'

Her eyes instinctively strayed to the spotless floor and the back wall as the colour drained from her face, and she began to shake with fear.

Daniel studied her reaction. 'Oh yes, I tidied up the mess. I thought it was the least I could do. After all, I HAD JUST BETRAYED ONE OF MY BEST FRIENDS.' The lid on his cold, contained anger blew. He slammed his fists into the counter, bellowing out his final sentence. It was terrifying, and she braced herself as the full force of his fury hit.

'You certainly had me fooled, didn't you? I assumed – obviously wrongly – that you didn't love Filip. That you loved me. That Filip would know, deep-down, that your relationship wasn't working. But no! You told him that you loved him! How many others have there been? How many others have you done this to? With your smiles and never-ending positivity. Do you know how hard I fell for you? Do you know what it felt like to hear you say you loved me? When I had loved you from afar for months. HAVE YOU THE SLIGHTEST COMPREHENSION OF WHAT YOU HAVE DONE?' Daniel screamed as bitter tears streamed down his face, but his wrath remained. 'I must be the biggest idiot going. I cannot believe I fell for your bullshit. Did you find it funny how easily you suckered me in?'

He started giggling hysterically.

Anna didn't know which was worse, the shouting or his out-of-control laughter. He was unravelling before her eyes, and it was shockingly hypnotic.

'How many other men have fallen into the same trap? How many others have you manipulated? Am I simply the latest in a long line of conquests? John certainly had a lucky escape. I certainly envy him. And my, haven't we done well out of our time in Apokeri?' Daniel declared with sarcastic admiration. 'Why, look at you, Anna. A property owner. And not only that, you live in a beautiful home with Kristina. Do you even care about her? You're loved by half the fucking village. DO YOU GIVE A SHIT ABOUT ANY OF US? You are a self-serving bitch, and I wish I'd never met you.'

His words were a barrage of poisonous darts, repeatedly slicing, cutting, and wounding.

Fight or flight?

She'd fight – always. The iron grip on her throat ripped apart, and in a wave of anger matching his, she launched into her own tirade and held nothing back.

'YOU BASTARD. Is that what you think of me? Do you think I'm that much of a fucking actress? I have never loved anyone the way I love you,' Anna screamed as she jumped up from the chair, shaking with rage. 'How dare you. How dare you question my feelings towards Kristina and everyone else I care about in Apokeri. And let's not forget how convenient it is for you that I do care for Kristina. It enables you to fuck off to the other side of the world and start a new life. As for the property, I never bloody well wanted it in the first place, and you know that. Have it back with pleasure, you arrogant arsehole,' Anna thundered, now inches away from him. 'I'm certainly not perfect, but neither are you, Daniel.'

'What about Filip? Your precious Pip. I don't know how you can live with yourself. What a supreme con artist you are,' Daniel spat.

***

The sky overhead continued to darken as Alex parked up. It was going to be one hell of a storm. Certainly not a night to be caught outdoors. Anna had just escaped a soaking. He opened the van doors and grinned – life was good with everything slotting into place. He was joint-owner of a successful business, doing a job that he loved, and from next month the building was going to be transformed in time for next season. And to cap it all, Filip was to marry a truly remarkable woman. He was always telling Alex how unbelievable it was to have met Anna. How it must have been fate.

Exciting times lay ahead and, even better, he'd negotiated his own space. Steffi expected everyone to live under the same roof, but privacy was an issue for him – especially as Leyla kept wandering into his room at all hours. He understood the little girl was curious, but it was disconcerting to be woken up by the door opening in the early hours and find the enormous eyes of a toddler staring at you.

And then there was Cassie, who spent each night asleep in the kitchen (waiting in anticipation for Anna) or stalking the corridors. The latter usually resulted in her curled up on Leyla's bed like an enormous furry bodyguard. But Cassie's latest trick was to rise on her hind legs and, with front paws, carefully depress the handle, quietly pushing open the door and taking a flying leap to land on top of him. He'd screamed the house down the first time it happened, convinced he was under attack. Filip and Steffi charged into his room to find Cassie licking his face. It was mortifyingly embarrassing, resulting in a sheepish apology, and Cassie was ordered back to the kitchen. Brother and sister found the whole thing highly amusing. If Alex didn't watch out, he'd gain the same reputation of weirdness afforded to his father's side of the family. Locking the door didn't help. Finding her entrance barred, Cassie would sit outside the door, throw back her head, and howl. Therefore, Alex pointed out that a self-contained apartment for himself in the refurbished building would be perfect. It would restore peace to the main house and complement the new holiday accommodation. Being on hand, he could also respond quickly to any requests from the cycle tour guests.

Unloading the bikes, all Alex wanted to do was soak in a lovely warm bath after guiding an advanced group of French cyclists across Lefkada and Meganisi. They'd persuaded Alex and Filip to introduce the tour before next season. In their forties, the ten club cyclists were ultra-fit and, before booking, informed Alex they regularly tackled big mountain climbs. It saw them follow in the wheels of the Tour de France, including the iconic Alpe d'Huez ascent. Initially, the group was aloof and condescending – the Ionian island peaks were inferior – so he pushed the pace and put in huge climbs. The guests loved it, and standoffish behaviour turned into good old-fashioned banter from a highly competitive party.

After storing the final bike, he became aware of raised voices, and they were getting louder. Anna and Filip arguing? That was unusual. The pair certainly knew how to bicker – they'd win a gold medal in it. Anyone would think they'd already been married for years, the way they went on. But argue? No, that wasn't their style – they never seriously disagreed. And that was one hell of a bust-up. Intrigued, he moved to the doorway.

Wait a minute … that wasn't Filip. It was Daniel. Bizarre.

What did those two have to argue over? They only tolerated one another for Filip's sake on the rare occasion they were all together. And the odd time Alex had found Anna trying to make the effort with Daniel, the bloke never hid his enormous relief at being rescued. Even if she was just being friendly. But after Kristina's fall, she'd given up, preferring to keep her distance. During Kristina's convalescence, he'd noticed Anna only left with Cassie when Daniel closed the gallery to ensure the quickest dog handover.

Entering the shop, he walked smack-bang into a full-scale fight. His friends were crying and furious with each other. There was Daniel towering over Anna, his eyes menacing as though he

247

abhorred the very sight of her. Anna stood ramrod straight, her fingers outstretched, as if fighting every compulsion to fly at Daniel and scratch his eyes out.

'What the hell's going on?' Alex demanded. 'The way you two are behaving, they'll hear you in Nidri.'

'Back off. It's none of your business,' Daniel snapped.

'Excuse me?' Alex retorted as his temper flared.

'Don't take it out on him,' Anna implored and gently laid a hand on Daniel's chest.

Watching the affectionate gesture and the look they exchanged, Alex realised he hadn't interrupted an argument between friends but barged into a lover's tiff. Anna and Daniel? It was incomprehensible. He would never have believed it. There'd been no indication that either was remotely attracted to the other. How long had this been going on? And more importantly for him, what would be the fallout?

'Where's Filip?' Alex demanded.

'He stormed off when Daniel told him about us,' Anna answered and looked stricken. 'He thinks I've betrayed him.'

'What the hell have you done?' Alex rounded on her. 'If you've done anything to jeopardise the safety of Filip, so help me God I will not be responsible for my actions.'

***

Anna dissolved into tears and, through wracking sobs, kept saying sorry. Despite everything, Daniel seemed to be battling between love and hate. But then something spurred him into action.

Glancing up through tear-stained glasses, she was in time to see Daniel lunge at Alex, who was quick to react. The situation was spiralling out of control.

'Stop, stop right now!' She leapt between them and defiantly raised her hands. 'This is not helping matters. How long has Pip been gone?'

'About five hours,' Daniel gruffly replied.

Anna instinctively knew something was wrong. Pip would never stay away this long. He was furious, and still would be, but would have returned by now to confront her. The light was fading, and the wind had picked up, driving sheets of rain against the windows. Pip was out there and in trouble. Alex agreed. However, Daniel refused to acknowledge her, still fighting to bring his emotions under control.

Tentatively she placed a hand on his arm. 'Daniel, I know you hate me right now because of my deceitful behaviour, and if I were in your shoes, so would I. But Pip is in trouble. Alex and I need you. Will you help us?'

'I'll help,' Daniel slowly replied as he removed Anna's hand and let it drop. 'But let me make one thing crystal clear. I'm not doing this for you, Anna. I'm doing it for Filip.'

'I understand,' she sorrowfully replied, but her inner resolve reasserted itself. 'Okay. Daniel, can you go and find Cassie? We need her help. She'll be hiding under a bed – you know she hates raised voices. And whilst you're there, please check the house. I'd love to be proved wrong, and maybe Pip is fuming over a cup of coffee in the kitchen. But he won't be.'

He hurried out the door, and Anna turned to Alex. 'Come with me. We're going to need supplies.'

Anna and Alex returned to the shop, each with a compact rucksack strapped to their backs. Daniel stood with Cassie and shook his head. As expected, Pip was not there. It was one of those rare occasions when she took no pleasure in being right.

'Are you going to tell us where we're going?' Daniel asked as he tightened his head torch. 'I don't know about Alex, but I haven't a clue where you're leading us.'

'We're going to Pip's favourite place. We're going to the clifftop lookout.'

Chapter Twenty-Six

Anna did not expect the revelation to go down well. Alex begged her to say she was mistaken. Daniel remained silent, but his worried face spoke volumes. Cassie was the only happy one, wagging her tail and excited for the adventure ahead.

Bending down, Anna scratched Cassie under the chin. 'I need you to find Pip, okay? Can you do that for me?' The dog let out a woof and licked her face. 'Good girl. Okay, guys. Let's go.'

The party headed out from the dry, warm, and brightly lit interior to be immediately hit by the wind, rain, and cold. They made their way across the deserted road to be swallowed up by the trees. Cassie bounded ahead, her bulky white form glowing faintly in the gloom, and Anna was close behind. Years of running were paying dividends, but instead of blasting off, she kept a steady pace. They needed to reach their destination with plenty of energy to spare. After all, there would be the return leg, perhaps with an injured Pip.

Whilst packing their supplies, Anna tried to explain her behaviour to Alex, resulting in an apology of sorts. However, she was acutely aware that ultimately, her actions had resulted in Pip storming off. At the moment, Pip and Daniel hated her, and Alex wasn't that enamoured either. But none of that mattered. What mattered was finding Pip and making sure he was safe.

Focusing on the track ahead helped keep a tight rein on her fears. She had walked this route many times with Pip, usually in the evening once the shop was closed, but she'd only run to the viewpoint a couple of times. Although Cassie enjoyed it, Anna found the unstable terrain intensely annoying and preferred to run along the northern clifftops.

The going underfoot was as frustrating as she remembered – crumbly in the dry, slippery in the wet. While walking boots were not ideal, they gave more purchase than trainers. The stinging words of Daniel whirled around her head, building into a destructive cyclone of shame. The realisation Pip was in danger because of her incredibly selfish, stupid, and deceitful behaviour was unbearable. She prayed it would not end in tragedy. To keep positive, she sang tunes from her favourite childhood films, but the lyrics from *The Jungle Book*, *Sleeping Beauty*, *The Slipper and the Rose* and *Grease* soon vanished, snatched away by the ongoing storm.

***

Alex trailed immediately behind Anna. Cycling kept him fit, but his legs were protesting after two days in the saddle, and especially after today's gruelling circuit around Meganisi. He was now wishing he hadn't agreed to his clients' request. At least his guests had agreed it was one of the best trips and would spread the word about Round the Bend Cycle Tours. A fantastic result, but did little to ease the intense discomfort in his legs. To focus on something other than the pain, he glanced around. The trees afforded a modicum of protection, and his trusty waterproof jacket was doing its job. But what about Filip? He'd been outdoors for more than five hours now, and there was no chance he would even have a jumper on, let alone a coat. Inside the bike shop, Filip always wore his Round the Bend uniform of a short-sleeved polo-neck T-shirt with combat pants and he would have stormed off wearing only those. Knowing this, Alex tried to keep his fear under control – every second hoping for Filip to materialise. A bedraggled figure, fuming, and hobbling down the increasingly unpredictable slope on a twisted ankle. But so far, nothing – only the figures of Anna and Cassie up ahead.

The pace slowed as the gradient increased. Anna slipped numerous times, but the woman was a machine and kept going. No matter what he thought about her at this precise moment, he conceded Daniel and himself had known Filip for years, but only she knew where he'd gone. He recalled Filip mentioning something about a favourite place now and again but never paid much attention, too keen to get out on the bikes or go rock climbing. Well, he was going to see Filip's favourite spot soon enough.

***

Bringing up the rear was Daniel, and he was struggling the most. Periodically, Cassie stopped to sniff the air, trying to catch Filip's scent and, once found, she'd set off again. It allowed Daniel to narrow the gap between Alex and himself before it stretched out again. Daniel cursed himself for letting his fitness dramatically drop over the last few months. He had rarely been out on his bike and found no pleasure in running, preferring to catch up with friends once he'd decided to leave Apokeri. There had been an occasional swim in the bay, but his exercise consisted of walking Cassie and raising his heartbeat with Anna.

He quickly cast aside those images. The confrontation with Filip, Anna, and Alex left him reeling, further sapping his strength. He'd known Filip from a self-conscious kid, hanging around the workshop, desperate to be noticed. With pride, he'd seen him mature into a witty, intelligent, and self-assured man. Therefore, it had been frightening to see Filip explode into an uncontrollable rage, but what did Daniel expect? He'd betrayed his best mate by happily jumping into bed with the man's fiancée. Daniel would have responded the same – no, much worse – if it was the other way around. And he was doubly ashamed.

Consumed with guilt towards Filip, he had turned the emotion into fury at Anna – as if the affair was entirely her doing. There'd been plenty of opportunities for him to call the whole thing off. Hell, he could have stopped it before it even started. But no, by thinking only of himself, he was now paying the price.

Spitefulness – plain and simple – had made him say he was only helping for Filip's sake. He laughed bitterly. He thought the cruel barb would make him feel better but it made him feel far worse. He had lost one of his best mates and the woman he loved in one fell swoop. Alex was wrong. Anna was not at fault if anything happened to Filip – the blame lay firmly at his feet. It was fear that drove Daniel forwards. Fear of being too late.

***

She burst out of the undergrowth and onto the sodden grass of the lookout. The light was rapidly fading as ragged clouds passed swiftly overhead. Thankfully the rain had stopped, but the wind continued to howl. Sweeping her head from side to side, she inhaled sharply as the headtorch illuminated recently disturbed soil. It was right at the edge, as if something or someone had slipped over the cliff.

Her voice was hoarse from constantly shouting Pip's name into the gathering gloom. Finally, a muffled response. Dropping to the ground, she combat-crawled with Cassie to stare over the precipice and suppressed a sob. Thirty feet below was Pip. Miraculously, the thinnest of ledges had broken his fall. He was soaking wet from the rain and water streaming down the cliff face. Outstretched arms desperately clung to exposed tree roots at the colossal effort it must be taking to hang on. The onshore wind helped pin him against the rockface, but the soaring cliffs created vortexes that groped finger-like to find a gap and rip him off.

The torchlight picked up two sets of eyes. The first belonged to Pip and reflected terror, exhaustion, and relief. The second was from a tiny brown bird. It was sitting above his right shoulder, utterly unfazed by the sudden appearance of Anna and Cassie. Indeed, it was chirruping away, and for all the world it looked like a guardian angel, protecting Pip from harm and telling him everything would be okay.

'Oh, hello there,' Filip shouted. 'Would you be a love and throw down a rope? I'm nearly spent.'

'I certainly can,' Anna replied, forcing her voice to remain calm. 'Alex and Daniel are with me. We'll have you out of there in a jiffy.'

She slithered back to Alex, who was already harnessed up and securing the second set of ropes to a pair of rather ancient-looking pine trees. Explaining the situation, they quickly agreed on a plan. Daniel was out of earshot and, with a fear of heights, he stood rooted to the spot, staring horror-stricken at the cliff edge. In a matter of minutes, Anna was secure in her harness and, after last-minute checks, she nodded to Alex. Now came the straightforward task – informing Daniel what would happen and the part he needed to play. Unexpectedly, the plan did not go down well.

'What! No way. If you think for one moment I'm going to stand by and let Anna hurl herself into the abyss on a bit of string attached to flimsy twigs sticking out of the ground, you're sadly mistaken. Are you both mad?' Daniel ranted.

'We're highly experienced rock climbers. Neither of us takes unnecessary risks. Those trees are incredibly strong and will barely feel the weight of Pip or me,' Anna patiently explained, even though Alex and herself were not entirely convinced.

'Okay, but why does it have to be you that scales down the cliff? Why not Alex?' Daniel stubbornly replied.

'For two excellent reasons,' Anna pointed out. 'One, I'm the lightest, and weighing less than nine stone I'll create the least disturbance to the unstable cliffs, which is much safer for Pip. And secondly, Alex is far stronger than me, so it makes more sense for him to lower me down and bring me back up than the other way around. It's the best way to rescue Pip.'

'Alright, but I'm not happy about it.' Daniel pouted. 'Please be careful.'

'It'll be a walk in the park. My job's easy. I don't need to pull anyone up. You'll need all your significant strength. Pip won't be much use – it's taking every ounce of effort to remain on that ledge.'

She headed towards the edge, and a hand grabbed her arm.

'I'm so sorry,' Daniel uttered. 'I didn't mean all those nasty things I said. You're the most fantastic person I know, and I … I couldn't cope if something happened. I should've said this much earlier – I love you.'

'It's nice to hear you say it,' Anna replied and kissed him. 'I love you too. Don't worry; I'll be back soon to bask in your adoration.'

Her cheeky grin produced the hint of a smile, and the last thing she saw before being lowered over the edge was Daniel's undisguised fear and a troubled Alex. Even the usual buoyant Cassie sat solemnly. And then they were gone. In a flash of black humour, Anna thought at least if she plummeted to her death, Daniel would be comforted to know she'd forgiven him.

Mercifully, the wind had lessened, and it enabled her to serenade Pip with 'I Have Confidence' from *The Sound of Music* whilst lightly placing her feet one below the other on the chalky cliff. She continued to walk backwards, with legs at right angles to her body. It was like traversing loose scree as the earth continued to break off and harmlessly tumble three hundred feet to the violent sea below. The stench of guano was unbelievable, and the resident sea birds also made it known how unhappy they were at being disturbed. Luckily, they only felt the need to flap their wings and squawk instead of taking flight and dive bombing her. Harnessed above, Alex stood on the edge and gradually let out the rope till she was eventually level with Pip.

Now came the hard part.

'Almost there. You're doing a terrific job,' Anna called over to Pip, who was watching her progress with his guardian angel. 'I will track across now and step one leg over before securely tying you off. Once done, Daniel will haul you up.'

'Excellent. Are you going to stop singing now? I don't mind it, but my new friend Sapphi the sparrow says you've yet to hit a right note.'

'Charming. I'll happily accept pointers once this is over.'

The wind was picking up again, and the gusts kept buffeting her sideways like a ragdoll – away from Pip or perilously close – and there was a real risk of knocking him off. Taking deep breaths to steady frayed nerves, she bent her knees and found it helped. The wind had less of an effect, and – like a squat toad – she continued. Pushing against the cliff with her left leg, she swung her right over Pip to nestle him between clenched thighs.

'I like your technique – let's try it the next time we go rock climbing,' Filip commented. 'Good grief, woman, that's some strength you've got. Do you mind easing up a bit? Otherwise, my eyes will pop out.'

'Cheeky sod. Right, I've secured you. After I give the signal, Daniel will pull you up. But before I do that, you need to take hold of the rope, okay?'

'I can't l-let go. My fingers are l-locked. I can't feel them … they aren't r-responding.'

His fear-laced words held no hope. He was fading fast.

'That's understandable. Okay, here's what we're going to do. I'll push my feet against the rockface, straighten my legs, and pull myself up on the rope to reach your hands. I'll work to ease open your fingers, and you take hold of the rope.'

Please let this work. Hand over fist, she proceeded up the rope. Mercifully, Alex cottoned on and shortened it. Yes, she could reach. That was the first obstacle cleared. Next, she massaged the vice-like grip on Pip's left hand. Each finger slowly responded and he grabbed the rope. The right hand took longer and resulted in a flurry of swearing with the returning blood flow and undoubtably excruciating pins and needles. Anna returned to her original position and flashed the headtorch three times. At the signal, Daniel hauled on the rope. Inch by inch, Pip began to rise. He desperately tried to help by pushing against the vertical wall with his legs, but his strength kept failing. In the end, it was all he could do to keep hold. That approach worked better for Anna as it stopped debris raining down on her, but made it harder for Daniel.

***

Filip was a dead weight, and Daniel battled in the elements to make any headway. His feet were sliding out from under him; the harness dug in, and every sinew in his body was on fire as he fought against gravity. He needed to make things right – he had to save Filip. But it wasn't working, and his strength was failing. Come on! He kept hauling, swearing, and skidding forwards. A stricken Alex shouted encouragement – the only thing he could do.

***

Anna dangled below and wanted to throw up. Pip wasn't going upwards anymore but hanging lifelessly. She screamed into the howling wind for a response – nothing. Oh God, what had she done? Her ragged breathing increased as she started to hyperventilate. This wasn't helping. Get hold of yourself, Jenkinson. Beside her, Sapphi sang a lullaby as she got her breathing under control.

And then, beyond all hope, Pip began moving upwards again. It was barely noticeable at first, then built up momentum. Her world centred on the sight of his feet slowly moving skywards and eventually disappearing.

***

As Anna fought her demons below, Daniel fought against the laws of nature and could make no headway. The harness was the only thing holding him and Filip in place. He leaned into it, focused on the trampled earth, summoned up his little remaining strength for a final effort, and then felt the rope slacken.

The distressing sight of her master in dire need spurred Cassie into action. Clamping the rope between powerful jaws, she dug her claws into the mud and pulled for all her worth. Daniel joined in and marvelled at the sight of his beloved companion heaving, snarling, and fighting to winch Filip to safety, spurred on by praise and the knowledge that he was running on empty.

As soon as Filip flopped onto the grass, Cassie raced over and frantically licked and pawed him until, with a weak gesture, he patted her head and whispered, 'It's okay, girl. I'm alive.'

Daniel collapsed to his knees, and as Cassie bounded back, he buried his face into her fur and sobbed.

***

Anna was touched that Sapphi decided to stay and keep her company. After they watched Pip reach safety, the plucky sparrow cocked its head and began insistently chirruping.

'Yes, I know I've got a terrible singing voice,' Anna remarked, dangling in mid-air. 'You're not the first to mention it.'

The bird continued twittering.

'Lessons? Am I not a lost cause?'

Another tuneful burst.

'Everyone can sing? Interesting. Okay, I'll think about it.'

After a few minutes, Alex flashed his head torch three times. It was her turn. She shot up the cliff face and desperately scrambled for a foothold. Not content with one rescue, Cassie and an exhausted Daniel pitched in. She thudded onto the mud and, after thanking Sapphi (who rose up and, with a final trill, vanished), sprang up and rushed to Pip. Anxiously she felt along his arms, legs, torso, neck, and head.

'Nothing's broken. Apart from complete exhaustion and being soaked to the bone, I'm fine,' Filip said quietly as he took hold of her hands.

'You need to get out of those wet clothes. The last thing we want is you getting hypothermia,' Anna instructed as she pulled out a change of clothes, a towel, and a silver foil emergency blanket.

Only when Filip was in warm and dry Round the Bend merchandise would she dish out energy drinks and trail bars. And then the adrenaline evaporated.

She burst into floods of tears. 'This is all my fault. We thought we'd lost you, with your last moments hating me and believing I'd betrayed you.'

'Don't be so stupid. I don't hate you. I stormed up here, so it's not your fault.' Filip gently stroked her cheek and slowly turned to Daniel. 'Thank you for saving my life. And it's time we talked.'

'It's the least I could do after my behaviour.' He breathed heavily. The rescue mission had left him emotionally and physically wiped out. 'We do need to talk but not until everyone is safely back home, in warm clothes, and with decent food inside us. I don't know about everyone else, but I've never liked energy drinks or cereal bars.'

The return journey took far longer. Filip and Daniel needed frequent recovery stops. Everyone sighed with relief when Round the Bend came into view almost two hours later. Once Filip was settled in the kitchen, the others went their separate ways for a shower and change of clothes. Anna was the last to return as Alex served up.

'Perfect timing as always,' Filip joked as she took her seat.

'Tuck in,' Alex instructed.

No one spoke until all the plates were empty.

Filip collapsed back in his chair. 'That was awesome. Scrambled eggs and beans on toast, just what I needed.'

'Don't forget the tea,' Anna said. 'You cannot beat a proper brew.'

'I've never understood the British obsession with tea,' Alex observed. 'For me, it's something to drink when you're ill. And even then, it would be herbal.'

'I'm with Anna,' Daniel added. 'Dad loves the stuff, so I guzzled it from an early age.'

'In the café, Mama says if customers order a hot drink, Irish and Brits go for tea. Every other nation opts for coffee,' Filip remarked.

'I never realised that, but Sofia's right,' Anna said and piled the plates up. She made ready to stand but Filip shook his head.

'Well, enough about tea and who drinks it,' Filip stated and took a deep breath. 'I said we needed to talk, Daniel, but what I meant was, I would like you to listen.'

As a young child, Filip suspected he was different and, after hitting puberty, he knew. Growing up in a masculine society, Filip kept his feelings quiet, and National Service did nothing to alleviate his concerns. The way his fellow recruits talked and behaved confirmed he must guard his secret well. He played his part, and no one suspected a thing. His mother often asked when would he find a nice girl and settle down, but he always trotted out the same well-worn explanation of being too busy with work, helping Daniel develop the business and turn their grand plans into reality. There would be plenty of time for marriage and kids later. Once Steffi married, the pressure was off, and with the arrival of Leyla, his mother seemed content to let the matter drop.

During National Service, Filip met Alex, and the pair became firm friends. However, returning home, the friendship drifted until a letter arrived almost a year later. Alex was planning a holiday to the Parnitha Mountains, close to Athens, and would Filip like to join him? As it was one of the premier rock-climbing areas in Greece, Filip jumped at the chance, and it was as if they'd never been apart, making him realise how much he'd missed the friendship.

On the last night, they'd got roaring drunk, and Alex admitted his feelings – terrified of doing so earlier. Filip was gobsmacked; he'd had no idea and confessed to feeling the same way. Both were elated and became a couple but agreed their relationship must remain a secret. Alex suspected his parents knew about his sexuality (although neither side ever broached the subject) and took comfort that his parents were tolerant – in sharp contrast to Filip's relations. If the topic of conversation cropped up, usually in response to a character in a film or from a customer in the café, Filip's male relations would launch into a scathing attack. Words including 'unnatural', 'disgusting', 'vile', 'against God', and 'shameful' were bandied about, and had been for as long as Filip could remember, filling him with sadness, shame, and despair. Coupled with his father's stance that any child of his who turned out to be 'that way inclined' would be immediately disowned, he knew to keep his mouth firmly shut.

Filip had enormous respect for Anna, who never let any homophobic comment or, for that matter, any other discriminatory remark go unchallenged. She continually stood up to Vasili and any number of relations. His family liked her, and he sensed a slight softening of attitudes but thought it was more likely his father failed to raise the subject because it was an unwinnable argument. He had no idea if opinions would change if they knew the truth. The stakes were too high, and he did not want to drive a wedge down the centre of his family.

His clandestine relationship with Alex had continued undetected for a couple of years, but its long-distance nature was challenging. The couple desperately wanted to spend more time together but knew they needed to be very careful when Alex took the plunge to quit his job and move to Apokeri. Then the answer to their prayers arrived from an unlikely source – Anna. She came to Apokeri and immediately hit it off with them and, by some sixth sense, perceived what no one else had. Fear turned to disbelief when she proposed a fictitious romance.

Filip thought he'd hit the jackpot. It was the perfect solution, especially as he knew his mother was already trying to set him up with Anna. However, Alex was stunned and saw only problems ahead. He could not comprehend why she would enter into such a thing? Ever the optimist, Filip could not understand why he was so worried. It took a whole afternoon, on a rock-climbing expedition, for Anna to persuade Alex that she knew what she was doing. Her focus was on establishing a new life in Apokeri and coming out of another intense relationship; love was the last thing on her mind. Knowing the heartache friends had gone through with their own families, she wanted to help. The trio set ground rules. If Anna met someone, her relationship must be conducted in secret. Believing there was no chance of that happening, she agreed. In turn, she had one stipulation of her own – Filip was not tied to the romance in any way. If he wanted to call it off, that was fine.

'I wanted Pip to know he was not straight-jacketed by the charade,' Anna interrupted. 'The last thing he needed was to feel trapped, so if expectations from his parents about our romance became too intense, Pip needed to know he could walk away.'

She fell silent again, and Filip continued. Far from being constrained, the agreement allowed Filip and Alex a degree of freedom. Especially when the three of them were together. This emboldened Filip, and with Alex's blessing, he proposed. Everything slotted into place, and with Steffi owning the house, everyone was under the same roof. However, it soon became apparent that this was going to be problematic. Still, with the help of Filip and Anna, Alex persuaded Steffi that he would be better off in his separate studio flat, which would allow Filip and Alex their own private space, and Steffi would be none the wiser.

'So, you see, Anna never did betray me,' Filip explained and watched for a reaction. The last few hours had severely affected his friend. Shame, guilt, and suffering were etched on his face

'Bloody hell, mate. I couldn't give a shit what your sexuality is,' Daniel replied. 'I never suspected a thing, Filip. Keeping it secret all those years must have been incredibly difficult. I'm unbelievably proud of the man you've become and so happy you've found Alex.' Daniel levered himself up and hugged them. 'Your secret's safe with me.'

'I wanted to tell you so many times,' Filip tearfully replied. 'A few years ago, I decided to – before Alex and I got together.'

'So, what stopped you?' Daniel asked.

'You were away in France, staying with Irina and Hugo, and I waited until you returned. But then you told me something that put paid to that.'

'I told you about Georg, didn't I?' Daniel said and sat back, crushed. 'I'm so sorry, Filip. I completely understand why you kept quiet.'

Judging by the reaction in the room, Anna was the only one out of the loop. 'I don't understand. What has Georg got to do with this?'

'Irina told me the reason behind Georg's stabbing, and I, in turn, told Filip.'

It was then Daniel's turn to recount what had happened that fateful night ten years ago, and the subsequent events. It was a routine mugging, and Georg quickly handed his wallet over. It was four against one, and being smart, he didn't put up a fight. The three instigators let him go, and Georg walked away, undoubtedly relieved his ordeal was over. But then the fourth and newest gang member, standing quietly in the shadows, shouted, 'He's nothing but a fucking queer', ran up behind Georg, and plunged a knife into his back. The other three were horrified and wanted to get help. But being threatened with the knife, they helped drag Georg further into the alleyway and fled. One of the three ignored the threats and rang emergency services. For years the man, now in his late twenties, had been expecting someone to turn up and exact their revenge. Instead, he complied with Irina's request to turn himself in, give up the names of those involved, provide a full confession, and testify against them. All four men had been teenagers when they committed the terrible crime and were now married fathers. Their wives and families knew nothing until the arrests. Irina sat through the whole court case but, instead of being happy at the verdict, she left incredibly dejected. She had closure but, for the first time, understood how one crime had destroyed the lives of multiple families.

'After Daniel told me the story, I was terrified. Somebody killed Georg because they believed he was gay. What might happen to me? Someone who was gay?' Filip said sorrowfully.

Daniel was happy for Filip and Alex, but the truth did nothing to lessen his guilt. Anna hadn't been disloyal, but he had. It didn't matter that Filip wasn't even angry. He had gone behind his friend's back.

'Anna, you truly are amazing,' he said. 'Most people's natural inclination is to explain their actions and put themselves in the best possible light, but you never did that. You—'

'Kept up the deception, so you thought you were betraying your friend. I'm incredibly sorry, Daniel.' Her voice faltered, and Cassie placed her head on Anna's lap. She stroked the soft fur and swallowed hard. 'I was selfish. I never stopped to think how my actions might affect you – I was too busy thinking about myself.'

'Don't you dare apologise. Regardless of the circumstances, I'm in control of my actions and must be held accountable.'

'When it comes down to it, I don't think any of us have covered ourselves in glory,' Alex observed.

Silence descended around the table until Anna voiced the unspoken question, 'So, what happens now?'

Filip placed Daniel's left hand in Anna's right. 'Whatever happened has happened, and it's time to draw a line under it and move on. I do know that the two of you should be together. That much is clear.'

'Are you sure?' Daniel hesitantly responded.

'Yes, I'm positive. If hanging off a cliff has told me one thing, it's that I need to let my two best mates be happy.'

'Thank you,' they said together as smiles started to play across their faces.

Joy bubbled up inside Daniel as Anna squeezed his hand and beamed with happiness. There would be a shitstorm when everyone found out about him and Anna, but perhaps it might not be too bad? After all, they would have the backing of Filip. If Filip and Anna told Sofia, Vasili, and Steffi the news together, would everything be okay? Anna loved Apokeri and didn't want to leave. And he didn't blame her. Not when she'd worked so hard to make a life, to make her mark.

'But … but what about you?' Anna stammered. 'Pip, Alex, I'm so sorry. I never meant this to happen. I've let you both down and made a right mess of everything. What will you do?'

Alex and Filip exchanged glances, and it was impossible to tell what either was thinking.

'You haven't let us down,' Alex said. 'We'll always be eternally grateful for what you've done for us, but perhaps we were a bit naïve in believing it could be that easy. In respect of what we're going to do? I think Filip and myself need to sit down together and work that out.'

It was then that the telephone in the hallway began to ring.

Chapter Twenty-Seven

According to the kitchen clock, it was almost midnight.

'It'll be Steffi,' Filip advised. 'I'll get it; otherwise, she'll ring all night. I bet she's tipsy after one too many drinks at her posh do and wants to tell me what her auction lots raised. Bless, she was so excited about it.' But the guess was wrong. 'It's your scatty aunt,' Filip said to Daniel. 'She didn't realise the time.'

'I might have known,' Daniel said and rolled his eyes. 'The woman has only been ringing here for three decades and still can't grasp the time difference. I wouldn't be surprised if she's forgotten I'm going to Japan. Memory like a sieve. It'll be a quick chat as I'm done in. I need a good night's sleep before breaking the news to Dad and my aunt that I won't be moving. I've something far better right here.'

Daniel kissed Anna and left the table. She grinned like the cat that had got the proverbial cream and was happy to see Filip and Alex smile. As usual, Daniel couldn't get a word in edgeways with his talkative aunt, and after twenty minutes reappeared – his expression spoke volumes.

'What's wrong?' Anna cried and was up and out of her chair.

Daniel stood stock-still in the doorway with a ghastly white complexion. It was as if his entire world had ended. She gently steered him back to the table. Once seated, he looked at Alex, Filip, and lastly, Anna, who read heartbreak, fear, regret, and despair in his eyes.

'It's my dad. He's got terminal cancer. They've given him nine months at best. Can you believe he wasn't going to tell me until I arrived in Adelaide?' Daniel explained in disbelief. 'The man actually intended to keep quiet, not to upset my travel plans! How unbelievably stupid! He and my aunt had a massive argument. She told him he was being ridiculous. What if I changed my plans mid-trip and didn't arrive back for six months or more? My dad can be such an idiot sometimes. I'd happily wring his neck if I wasn't so petrified at losing him. He forbid his sister from telling me, which she rightly ignored. I can't even speak to him at the moment. The stupid sod has gone out with my cousins to round up sheep!'

In that instant, everything changed, and Anna's heart cleaved in two – no happy-ever-after ending, again. But of course. Her love life was an unmitigated disaster area of epic proportions. And she immediately felt ashamed. How could she possibly feel sorry for herself when Daniel was losing his father. There was only one thing for it.

'You need to go.'

'I know.'

***

Sixteen hours later and operating on little sleep, reorganised flights still saw him departing Preveza in two days. The new two-stop journey was to take two days via London and Kuala Lumpur. Daniel had found his father in good spirits on the phone. The man was a battler, determined to prove the doctors wrong and would be waiting in Adelaide Arrivals to welcome his son home. The fight with his sister was forgotten.

Once the flights were in place, Daniel agreed to go ahead with his leaving party the following evening. It would give him a chance to say his final farewells, but whether he would mention his father's illness was currently undecided. However, there were three people Daniel was determined to tell. He first visited Kristina and then Irina and Hugo. The time spent in their

267

company helped enormously, and he returned to the bike shop feeling less fraught.

During Daniel's absence, Filip, Alex, and Anna reached a decision. Regardless of what had happened, all three agreed to continue with the deception. She first mooted the idea, but only after Filip and Alex told her their decision. Fortuitously, with Steffi still away, Anna worked in the bike shop all day. With a strong cup of coffee to keep her awake, she sat at the counter, making small amends to the cycle tour website, when a nervous Alex and Filip approached. The pair had spent much of the night discussing what they intended to do, and the conversation continued as they serviced bikes in the workshop. The couple had decided not to disclose their sexuality and their relationship. There would be no 'coming out'.

'I know you must think us complete cowards,' Filip said, fiddling with the counter bell. 'But we cannot do it. The risks are too great. I can't bear to put my parents through more heartache, especially not after our recent family fallout. And they've had enough to deal with in their lives. I know they've got their faults, but I love them too much. And Anna, this is one area where you cannot change my mind, so please don't think about hatching any plans. Do you promise?'

'Yes, I promise by all I hold dear. I will not meddle this time. I will leave well alone.' And she meant it.

'However, we both agreed that the engagement no longer binds you. It's not fair.'

'Well, as you've brought it up, I've also been thinking. Daniel is leaving and never coming back, so we continue as before.'

'What are you saying? So, I'm clear on this?' Filip said, and his leg began to jiggle.

'The engagement and the wedding continue to cover your relationship.'

Alex frowned. 'I don't know. After everything … it's probably a bad idea – what do you think, Filip?'

'I'm not sure. Half of me says no … the other half yes.'

'Howay, lads. Don't you see, me falling in love with Daniel and it going tits up proves once and for all that I should avoid love at all costs. You know my history and must admit I'm like Tharesseti – cursed. Perhaps I'm the biggest coward here. I'm only twenty-six, but I'm sick and tired of putting my heart on the line to get stomped on.'

Before their original agreement, Anna had given a no-holds-barred account of her tumultuous love life. Doing so persuaded Filip and Alex to agree, and it helped them understand something about her mindset. Their friend had no luck in matters of the heart. Despite this, it took all afternoon and frequent visits from the workshop before Filip and Alex finally agreed. And when the trio announced their decision to Daniel over dinner, he questioned each one long and hard until he determined that this time all three were entering into the decision with their eyes open. He wished them luck.

'I think we will all need it.' Anna raised her glass. 'To luck.'

'To luck,' came the heartfelt response.

***

Daniel was smiling and laughing. The party was doing him good, and it kept his mind occupied. The shop was almost unrecognisable. Instead of bikes and associated paraphernalia, tables and chairs surrounded a packed dance floor. Balloons, streamers, and banners decked the walls, and a few of the former were part of an impromptu volleyball game. Parents occasionally berated their offspring when one landed on the buffet table or knocked over a drink, but the game continued as their hearts were not really in it.

Behind the counter, a former school friend of Daniel's provided the tunes and, being easy on the eye, found himself surrounded by a gaggle of teenage girls. Even an hour after the buffet opened, there was barely a dent in the glorious spread and the intoxicating smell of Greek, Indian, Italian, and Middle Eastern cuisines intermingled with perfume, aftershave, and alcohol. There was plenty of the latter. In addition to a free bar, most people turned up with contributions, and empty or half-consumed bottles of wine, beer, Greek brandy, and ouzo littered every spare surface. However, the soumada was long gone. Everyone drank the traditional almond-based 'drink of happiness' (that was traditionally served at weddings) for toasting after emotional speeches from Kristina, Filip, and Daniel.

The drinks flowed; people ate their fill, catching up with friends while wishing Daniel good luck for the umpteenth time. Everyone was having a great time. The door stood open to let in some much-needed fresh air, and with glasses and plates in hand, people spilled outside with warm jumpers, jackets, shawls, and coats hiding smart outfits. A mixture of Europop, American rock and traditional Greek music floated away on the early October air, and only Anna braved the elements with bare arms. Filip announced to anyone listening that his fiancée was a crazy Geordie, a strange breed that shunned outer garments even in the depths of winter. There was a constant stream of people arriving. It seemed that all the village was there and many more besides. Daniel had decided, if asked, to say he was going to visit his family first before travelling. In the end, everyone was too caught up in the party to question his change of plan.

During a spare minute, Daniel picked up his photobook. He loved it and could see Anna's care and attention as he flicked through the pages. It was like watching his life on fast-forward. Some photos were wholly new to him, like the one in the workshop with his father showing Irina, Georg, and himself how to change a back tyre. Everyone looked so young; he must have only been eleven. Daniel felt a lump in his throat and fought back the tears. Georg was gone, and his dad's life was slipping away. It might be more than nine months, but it could be less. He would have to make the best of it, having already spent seven years apart from his remaining parent.

***

Anna watched Daniel reminisce over the pages of his photobook before finally getting to thank Inspector Jace Marinos in person for his help all those weeks ago. The skinny man with bags under his eyes, a furrowed brow, and a slightly grey complexion looked far older than twenty-eight. She suspected Inspector Marinos survived on takeaways rather than good homecooked meals. He was pleased to hear of no lasting effects from her close call. There was no news from his UK counterparts, but he believed it was only a matter of time before justice caught up with the pair.

After checking everything was running smoothly (whilst clearing empties), Anna fell into her natural habit of people-watching. It was fascinating. She loved inventing stories, and her eyes lingered on the various married couples around the room – Sofia and Vasili, Lucinda and Peter, Agnes and Viktor, and Dania and Max. Everywhere she looked everyone seemed to be paired up.

'Anything interesting?' A voice beside her asked. She turned to find Irina looking stunning in a knee-length raspberry dress with charcoal grey stilettos. Her signature diamonds sparkled.

'I was watching people in love.' Anna failed to hide the melancholy in her voice.

'It will get better.' Irina consoled her new friend with a side hug. 'Come, let's go outside. I believe the fresh air will do you good. Tonight isn't for sadness. It's a celebration.'

'You're right, and I could do with a breather. It's so hot and stuffy in here, even with the door open. But won't you be cold?'

'Hugo has my wool coat. You'll also be glad to hear he has plates of food and warm drinks awaiting us.'

'Well, why didn't you say? Lead on.'

Although Anna spent a large part of the evening chatting with guests, she gravitated towards Irina and Hugo. It made her feel better because they knew about her relationship with Daniel, and people kept their distance from Mr and Mrs Dubois. With everyone so engrossed in their own enjoyment the trio was essentially left alone. That suited her perfectly as she could enjoy their company and be ignored. It was after one when Irina and Hugo finally made a move. They would be driving Daniel to the airport in less than twelve hours but would say goodbye to Anna now.

After embracing her, Irina handed her a small, black embossed card. 'Anything you ever need, contact us. Whatever passes between us will be strictly confidential. By that, I mean it goes no further than Hugo and myself. I think you might need our assistance in the future.'

With a nod to her husband, Irina turned and the pair vanished from sight. Anna heard the hire car blast up the twisting road a minute later. The last remark had been so strange that Anna stood lost in thought and failed to notice someone approaching.

'Hello, stranger.'

'Andrew,' she cried and hugged her friend.

'Sorry, it's taken so long to catch up with you tonight. That Cosimo has got some amazing stories, and his family are brilliant. I lost track of time.'

'Don't be silly; there's no need to apologise. It's a sign of a good party.'

'You're right, and I love that photobook. Daniel has been showing everyone and that reminds me – we found a whole load of old snapshots ripping out Jeremy's place. Charles was right. In its heyday, the place was amazing. The likes of you and me … we'd never have been able to afford anything like that in a million years.'

'Brilliant. I love stuff like that.'

'Each room was perfect – like a stage set. They had Scandinavian inspired snugs with chunky wooden furniture, candles, and throws. Moroccan-themed bathrooms. And the bedrooms were incredible. The most opulent one was—'

'French Renaissance?'

'Yes … how on earth did you know that?'

'Oh, just a wild guess.'

'I'll show you the photos next time. They capture—'

'Moments frozen in time.'

'Exactly. Another time, another place. All those posh people living the high life. They'll be pushing up the daisies now.'

Anna glanced past him and into the packed party. It was easy to spot the brightly coloured headscarf. Kristina stood chatting with Sofia and Vasili. Her friend was so full of youthful energy. Was that because she kept one foot firmly in the past?

'I can imagine there'd not be many left alive after such a long time,' Anna replied. 'Just think if walls could talk?'

'Especially in that place. Luckily, I've not bumped into any ghosts. Anyway—'

'You want to tell me something.'

'I swear you're psychic.'

'If only. No, you … well, you look preoccupied.'

'You know I care about you.'

'Yes, of course.'

'And you know I wouldn't want to see anything happen.'

'Yeeeessss,' Anna replied slowly. Despite his psychic comment she had no idea where the conversation was going.

'I say it like it is – so don't be offended by what comes next.'

'As if! I've known you long enough.'

'Good. Anyway, that couple who just left – the one you've spent most of the night with.'

She brightened. 'Oh yes. Irina and Hugo – they're good friends of Daniel.'

'Be that as it may. I want you to watch yourself there. I know many types of people, and I'm being serious when I say those two operate in a different world from the one you do. And it's not a world you want to get mixed up in.'

'What?' Anna almost laughed if it hadn't been for the fact Andrew was so sombre. Instead, she gently lay a hand on his sizeable forearm. 'There's really nothing to worry about. I know they come across as a bit intense, but once you get to know them, they're dead canny.'

Andrew smiled indulgently. 'You always see the best in everyone. It's one of your finest qualities. I'm happy they're nice to you. But I wouldn't be a mate if I didn't say anything. Okay?'

Anna gave him another hug. 'Thanks. I might see the best in everyone, but you're always straight down the line and that's just as important.'

***

Daniel had covertly been keeping tabs on Anna all night, watching as she glided around the room, making sure everyone was happy and automatically tidying with an understated style all her own. She mentioned people often mistook her for being French, and he could see why. Tonight, she wore a chocolate brown sleeveless top that complemented her skin tone, sand-coloured linen trousers that skimmed the floor and red sandals peeking out as she walked. Anna easily outshone all the other women with their flamboyant outfits, make-up, and jewellery. They looked great, but none came close to his Anna, unaware of the other men watching her. She looked radiant even though his decision to leave was tearing her apart, and he felt the same.

He was secretly pleased that Anna, Filip, and Alex continued their charade and hadn't tried too hard to dissuade them. It meant men would keep away – the thought of another man with her was unbearable. It was utterly selfish, but he couldn't help it. When

Jace had talked with Anna, he felt the green-eyed monster stir, only relaxing when his friend moved off to chat with Steffi. However, Daniel gained pleasure seeing her in the company of Irina and Hugo. The couple were fiercely loyal and, from his own experience, he knew they'd go through a brick wall to defend their friends. Watching the three of them together, Daniel noticed the marked resemblance between Hugo and Anna – they could easily pass for siblings. When Daniel finally drifted off to sleep for the last time on Greek soil, it was comforting to know that Anna had a good support network. She was going to be okay.

Chapter Twenty-Eight

Daniel entered the bike shop, and it was as if the party had never been. Filip and Alex laboured away in the workshop, and Anna stood behind the counter.

'Hello there. Decided to join us in the land of the living?'

'It's only just turned nine,' Daniel responded with mock affront.

'Really? It feels later than that. I've been up since six.'

'You look remarkably well, considering you've had four hours sleep.'

'I wanted to make sure everything was tidy for opening, but to be honest, there wasn't much to do with so many people pitching in last night.'

'Well, I think you deserve a break then,' Daniel said and disappeared for a few minutes. 'Okay, grab your coat. Alex will mind the shop.'

Irina and Hugo would arrive in a few short hours, so they struck out on the well-worn track. Cassie joined them for the last time and led the way. Turning their collars up and shoving hands into pockets, the pair angled into the wind and trudged along the northern clifftop path, past Kristina's bench, past the thicket of wild olive trees, and past the long stretch of brambles that caught at their jeans. The main track was muddy and desolate under a threatening sky. Even the gulls were silent. On the goat track, the wet undergrowth fought back. The spiky hawthorn bushes scratched, pine branches caught in their hair, rain-soaked rose petals stuck to their boots, and they slipped and slithered along the narrow boulder-strewn gully.

Daniel steered her to a flat rock. 'Stand there with Cassie and close your eyes.' She listened to him moving about. 'Okay, open them.'

Dozens of tealights bathed the cave in a warm glow, banishing the oppressive darkness.

There was a lump in her throat as she whispered, 'It's beautiful.'

The sun broke through the clouds and sent a shaft of light into the cave. It bounced off the waterfall and lit up the pool. She smiled, despite herself.

'That's better'. He laced his fingers in hers. 'I hate to see you looking so sad.'

'I'm sorry, but I … I didn't think it would hurt this much. If I had, I might not have been so quick to seduce you.'

'You don't mean that?'

'No, I don't.' She slowly shook her head and kissed him before moving away to trail her fingers through the warm pool. 'Even though I want to crawl under a rock and die … I'm immensely grateful for the last few weeks together. You've made me incredibly happy. Even for a short time.'

Daniel joined Anna and pulled her close. 'Same here. And some people never get that. Can you imagine – never finding love?'

'No … I can't.'

They sat side by side, dabbling their toes in the bubbling water.

'Did you ever think that very first time we met at Nereus – and you were only interested in Cassie – that we'd end up together?'

She started laughing, and the uplifting sound bounced off the walls. 'Not a chance. And how about you? I bet you never expected to end up with Little Miss Bloody Sunshine?' His shocked face made her laugh even more. 'Yes, I heard you in the garden ... it's amazing how far your voice carries.'

'Flipping heck, I'll never know why you ever wanted to seduce me.'

Her sadness welled up again. 'Glutton for punishment, I suppose.'

'Come here and give me a hug, you crazy Geordie.'

They remained like that for some time before Daniel stirred. 'There's time for one more thing.' He scrolled through his phone, and gentle music filled the space. 'May I have this dance?'

For the first and last time, they waltzed around in the flickering light to a song Anna always hummed – 'He/She Danced with Me' from *The Slipper and the Rose*. And in those few precious moments, he was her Prince Charming, and she was Cinderella.

'I didn't want you to think you were the only one who could pull off a surprise,' he whispered. 'I even watched the musical and found myself singing along.'

The music stopped, and she hugged him tightly. She'd never forget this. Never forget the feeling of him keeping her safe. 'Thank you.'

'It's time.'

'I know.'

Daniel prised open her fingers. 'You need to let me go.'

Reluctantly, she released him. After a final kiss, he clambered towards the narrow chink in the rocks, and she watched him go.

'I love you, Anna. With all my heart.'

'I love you, Daniel. More than you'll ever know.' Before he reached the narrow fissure, she called out. 'Good luck.'

'Same to you.' He blew one last kiss and vanished.

The candles fizzled out as damp leached into her bones, and the thermal spring spluttered and fell silent. She drew her knees up to her chest and curled into a ball. In the gloom, the cave became a troll's lair – its stalactites, stalagmites, and columns now prison bars. Next to her, Cassie whimpered.

He was gone and was never coming back. Another love – lost. Another hope of happiness – dashed. Her father was right. That's all she did: drift through life long enough to attach herself to someone, come untethered, and drift off again. A meaningless existence. It didn't matter if she moved to a new country and started a new life. The problem was inside. She'd just keep repeating the same pattern over and over again. Not so smart, not so clever after all, and hot tears splashed down her legs.

***

Daniel stumbled over the rocks and headed towards the light, blinded by tears. She was right; he hadn't realised it would hurt this much. Two days to wallow in abject misery was all he could allow himself before presenting a happy face to the world. His dad was already upset about disrupting his son's long-held travel dreams and didn't need another guilt trip. And to remain strong for what lay ahead, he must never mention Anna's name again – it was the only way.

Chapter Twenty-Nine

Ever since Daniel had left, two personalities fought for control – she felt like a passenger in her own body. Public Anna remained cheerful and ever so helpful. Nothing was too much trouble for Public Anna. Laughing in the right places, asking the illuminating questions, entertainingly debating, working extra hours, and always there for everyone to offer unwavering assistance with a smile – no matter what. And Private Anna, who closed the bedroom door on the world and sank into inconsolable grief, pain, and loss that threatened to overwhelm herIf not for Cassie – and a little help from Mother Nature – she might still be in the cave. Her faithful pooch had pawed, whined, and nuzzled until she responded. And when a shaft of sunlight shone down through the damp, limp fern fronds and the thermal spring bubbled back into life, it had been enough.

Even Public Anna, with carefully applied make-up, couldn't hide black bags, bloodshot eyes, a waxy complexion, and a pinched look. The realistic dreams were back with a vengeance – her loved ones were in mortal danger, and only she could save them – and the tangled sweat-soaked sheets needed changing each day. Private Anna was on a roll and went sleepwalking as the week progressed. The first time, Kristina found her on the landing, shouting and warding off unseen assailants, preventing them from hurting Leyla. The second she was halted whilst climbing the stairs, desperate to hide Cassie from evil dognappers. Kristina now locked the rooftop door and kept its key hidden.

Severe sleep deprivation lent an agitated edge to Anna's behaviour, which hadn't gone unnoticed. And the biggest indicator something was amiss – no appetite. She picked at food or, more accurately, listlessly moved it around the plate. Agnes, Sofia, Lucinda, Kristina, Steffi, Max, and Cosimo commented on the change. The time-of-the-month lie fooled everyone – apart from Filip and Alex.

The pair issued a dinner instruction to make her consume something more substantial than a cup of tea and a slice of toast. Anna was persuaded to stop over, and Kristina was assured a decent night's sleep. It was nice they were concerned, and Anna managed to finish a small portion of vegetable lasagne before Cassie's evening walk. Alex first broached the subject of Daniel. With her appetite returning, was she feeling more like herself? Yes.

After a pause, she explained although she longed for him, missed him, and would always love him, his leaving was for the best. A howl of protests – how could she say such a thing? Anna patiently explained that after a great deal of thought (and tears), she'd realised the relationship was doomed never to work. Not because they didn't love each other – there was no denying that – but because they wanted very different things.

Daniel still had a burning desire to travel, see the world, and escape his oppressive Apokeri cage. In contrast, she'd finally found her forever home and wouldn't give it up. Could they have stayed and been happy? Anna didn't think so. Sofia and Vasili would have changed towards her – even with Filip's blessing. And even if they'd stayed, Daniel would have resented it – resented her – and he'd answer the worldwide adventure call before long. It was a foregone conclusion that Daniel would travel in time, and although it hurt like hell at the moment, it was for the best in the long run. Each person must be true to themselves.

***

281

Perhaps it was eating a decent meal or the confession about her ill-fated relationship with Daniel – either way, Anna enjoyed a peaceful night, and felt reinvigorated when she woke up in the downstairs bedroom. It was still dark outside, and the illuminated clock read five fifty-nine. There was something intensely satisfying about leaning over and knocking off the alarm with a minute to spare. She was about to throw back the covers when she heard a gentle knock.

'Come in. I'm awake.' She quickly sat up when Steffi entered. 'What's wrong?'

'Everything's fine, but I wanted to catch you first thing.' Steffi passed over a paper bag.

Looking inside, Anna let out a short, sharp bark of laughter. 'No way. Not a chance.'

Steffi crossed her arms across her chest and gave her an enigmatic look. 'Okay. I'm going to hazard a guess here. Despite spinning a story about period pains, you are over a week late. And have convinced yourself it's fine because your cycle is erratic, unlike some women. Five days late is typical, so what's a few more. Am I right?'

'Yes,' she mumbled with downcast eyes and fiddled with the quilt. 'It's ten days now.'

'I would also be willing to bet that you've never been that late. Am I again, correct?'

'Yes, you are,' Anna whispered and averted her eyes like a naughty child.

'So, the sensible course of action would be to take the bag and put your mind at rest. Would you agree with that?'

'Bloody hell, man. You're good. Did you ever lose a case?'

'Not if I approached it the right way.'

'As much as I would love to continue this chat, my bladder is about to burst.'

'Excellent. First thing is the best time to take the test. Off you toddle.'

She had to hand it to Steffi for skilfully and effortlessly outmanoeuvring her. 'Alright, Mam – you win. But I'm stating for the record you're completely wrong. Furthermore, as compensation, you'll buy me an ice cream for having such an idiotic notion.'

'If … I'm proved wrong,' Steffi answered with a tone that suggested she wasn't going to be, 'I'll happily buy you the largest ice cream Aphrodite sells. But if I'm right, you will buy me and Leyla one. Do we have a deal?'

They shook hands, and Steffi went to leave.

Anna threw up her hands. 'Hold your horses, missy. Don't be scuttling off like some smug crustacean. You're not going anywhere until I come out with a negative result and I hear you admit to being wrong.'

Steffi parked herself on the bed with a withering glance at Anna as she flounced into the ensuite. The minutes ticked by until the door finally opened. However, it was not a triumphant Anna that faced Steffi but someone with an ashen complexion who handed over a stick and collapsed onto the bed. She was half-conscious of Steffi talking ten to the dozen – jabbering away about being an aunt, her brother being a father, Leyla having a cousin, and her parents being ecstatic about a second grandchild. Would the wedding be moved forward? And without waiting for a response, Steffi was off again. Had she not said the house was big enough for kids? Never in her wildest dreams did she think it would happen this quickly. It was so exciting.

Anna sat staring at the blue line on the other two strips – having done all three tests – and willed them to change. She'd surpassed herself this time, going above and beyond all her other fuck-ups – and there'd been plenty. How the hell could this happen? Okay, she obviously knew how it had happened, but she'd been so careful.

A horrible realisation replaced the initial shock. What was she going to do? However, one thing was certain – she was not telling

Daniel. She was probably damning herself in the eyes of some who would be appalled at such a decision. But ring him up and say, 'Oh, hello there. How's it going? I know you feel like shit at the moment, what with your dad having terminal cancer, but I thought I'd add to that by saying I'm expecting our child!' Not a chance. Daniel had enough on his plate. If she told him, he'd come back out of a sense of duty and hate her for trapping him with an unwanted kid. Hadn't he always got on his soapbox and said the world was crowded enough, so it was a good job he never wanted them. He had no desire to be around children and had always given Leyla a wide berth. Anna tried and failed to recall any time when she'd seen Daniel happily interact with a child and couldn't think of a single instance. He had never understood why she volunteered to babysit. Why spend time with kids if you didn't need to? He had provided children's cycling lessons, but he'd admitted to having an ulterior motive – it was good for business. And then there was Pip. What was he going to think? What was he going to say? What was he going to do? It was one thing to fake a marriage, but implications her frazzled brain couldn't yet comprehend.

She remembered asking Pip if he ever wanted children – after getting off her soapbox about never wanting them. He'd shrugged his shoulders and accepted he would never be a father, so was thrilled to be part of Leyla's upbringing. That suited Anna down to the ground as she'd forcefully declared to friends, family, work colleagues, and anyone else on planet Earth that she'd never be wanting kids. Oh no, she was going to have to tell her parents. That'd be a fun conversation. She slowly became aware of being asked something.

'Anna, are you okay?' Steffi tentatively asked.

'No.'

'I'm so sorry. I got completely carried away. How are you feeling?'

'I don't know.' She put her head between her knees and took deep breaths before raising her head. 'How the hell did you know I was pregnant when I didn't?'

'I just do. From the three to four-week mark, I can sense when a woman is pregnant. I always knew at work long before any official announcement. It's a horrible talent and not something I broadcast.'

'I bet. How weird.'

'I know. But enough about my peculiarity. What would you like me to do?'

'Could you please go and get Pip. I'm so j-jittery … I don't trust my legs.'

'Certainly. I'll go rouse Sleeping Beauty. I do find it hysterical that the pair of you insist on sleeping apart in my home.'

She continued deep breathing and had no idea how long it took for Pip to burst through the door, closely followed by Steffi.

He hurried to the bed and knelt with concern etched on his face. 'What's wrong? Steffi said it was urgent.'

She passed him two sticks. 'I'm so sorry, Pip.'

Filip silently stood up with an inscrutable expression. She had no idea what was going on behind those soulful eyes.

He held up the two tests. 'I like to see you made sure.'

'There's another one on the drawers. All show the same thing. What a bloody mess.'

A grin formed and grew until his whole face beamed. He grabbed Anna and swung her around, letting out an almighty cheer.

'Are you okay?'

'Okay! It's the most fantastic news I've ever heard. I'm going to be a father – me – Filip Makris. It's amazing. You know I always thought I'd make a pretty cool dad.'

'What a swell head,' Steffi cried as she playfully punched her brother on the arm.

'Well, sis, I'll give you one guess what Papa will say.'

'What?'

'Like father, like son, of course,' Filip replied with a wink at Anna.

***

Even with three positive tests, Anna refused to accept the inevitable until her doctor confirmed it. It also gave her time to intensively quiz Filip to ensure he accepted the commitment. This was a lifetime decision. Once made, there was no going back. The child would believe Filip was the father, and even if, for whatever reason, they separated, he would have that bond with his child forever. If he was going to walk away, he should do it now, and she would bring the child up on her own. Yes, he knew what it meant and would love and protect his son or daughter – regardless of what happened between them.

Unbeknown to her, Filip and Alex had been angry and disappointed at Daniel when he left. Their friend claimed to love Anna so much but had never promised to return. Why not? They concluded Daniel could not bear to be shackled by any commitment to Anna and, as such, he went down in their estimation. This conviction conveniently absolved Filip of any guilt when he declared Daniel was not part of the equation. As he had no intention of returning (regardless of the circumstances), and as far as Filip was concerned, Daniel had therefore given up any rights to his unborn child. Anna wanted to make sure Alex was on board with the decision as a child would irreversibly change the couple's lives. Filip's reaction drove home how seriously her fiancé saw his impending responsibilities. The decision went beyond his relationship, and if it did not sit well with Alex, his lover would have to act in whatever way best suited him. She never asked how Alex received the news, but he was signed up for the long haul, judging by his excitement at being an uncle (of sorts). So far, so good. Next up came Sofia and Vasili.

Filip announced the news over dinner, and after the initial shocked silence, there were hugs, kisses, and congratulations for the young couple. Vasili did indeed slap his son on the back, told him history was repeating itself and warned the pair they didn't know what was in store. However, having children was the best thing Sofi and him had ever done.

Sofia had previously been focused on the Apokeri Flower and Food Festival, but that paled in comparison to her single-mindedness for the forthcoming nuptials, and she decided to organise it all. Secretly, Anna was relieved. Greek weddings to her were a baffling array of seemingly endless traditions.

Speed was of the essence. It made life much easier if the wedding came first. Before the house was ripped apart, the business refurbished, the next holiday season started, and the baby arrived. However, Anna's reason surprised everyone as it was based on vanity. She wanted to look the best she could and had heard it was virtually impossible to get your pre-baby figure back. And Sofia threw a final superstitious belief into the mix. It was supposedly bad luck to get married within forty days of Christmas. Why? The reason was never clearly explained to Anna. It just was.

To that end, Sofia moved heaven and earth to secure a suitable date, and the whole wedding plan was sewn up within seven days. Anna realised the enormous benefit of growing up in the same village and knowing everyone. The Makris family was immensely well-respected in the community, as was Anna if she'd known, so when word went out that a wedding needed organising, the villagers responded. As part of this, Agnes became Anna's adviser on all the intricacies of Greek weddings. During one of these conversations, the role of the Koumbari, consisting of a Koumbara and a Koumbaros, was explained. It was a great honour to be asked, as the positions involved a crucial role in the wedding ceremony and the couple's future life. The Koumbara, which Anna understood to be something akin to a Maid of

Honour, and the Koumbaros, similar to a Best Man, would be godparents to the newlywed's children.

Traditionally, the Koumbaros was the godfather of the groom or bride. However, Filip and Anna broke with tradition. They needed Alex involved, and when asked, he cried. Alex was the epitome of Greek masculinity with rippling muscles, a washboard stomach, and a no-nonsense approach to life, so seeing him shed tears always surprised Anna. It was a given Steffi would be the Koumbara and she likewise broke down.

Marrying in November meant none of Anna's family or non-Greek friends, except Andrew, could attend. The ceremony was out of season, and even if there had been flights available, none of her friends could have afforded it with such short notice. And the lack of relations and friends resulted in another break with tradition. With Anna's father absent, Vasili would walk her to the church. The usually gruff Greek had also shed a tear on being asked. Anna brought so much joy to his family he would be immensely proud to step in. That was another Greek tradition, she discovered. The bride and groom walked into the church together. After the bride and her father went to the church, he presented his daughter's hand to the groom at the church entrance. Sofia and Vasili grumbled at the erosion of tradition, which saw many fathers walk their daughters down the aisle. The very thought of it! Anna couldn't see the big deal herself but wisely kept quiet.

*****

The relationship with her parents had improved since she'd moved hundreds of miles away from them. Therefore, it was upsetting to inform them they'd be missing their youngest daughter's wedding again. Her mother was very understanding regarding the house renovations, but her father got straight to the point in his typically blunt style.

'For God's sake, Alice. She's only gotten herself knocked up. I'm right, aren't I? That's why it's a rush job. There's absolutely no other explanation for excluding us from your wedding for a second time.'

'Yes, Dad, I'm with child, as you so eloquently surmised.'

'Good grief, girl. You don't do things by half, do you? Last night, your mam and I said that it'd been a bit quiet from Lefkiona recently. No bombshells. Making up for it now, aren't you? So let me get this right, in less than five months, you left university, went on an island-hopping adventure, and we saw the demise of yet another boyfriend—'

'For crying out loud, Dad – for the umpteenth time, it's Lefkada. Why can't you remember where I live? And I'll have you know I do not rattle through relationships. And even if I did—'

'Okay, okay. There's no need to get your knickers in a twist. You're very hormonal already. When Julia was pregnant, she was the epitome of serenity.'

Anna clamped her mouth shut. The man was insufferable.

Her dad continued with his monologue. 'So, as I was saying, you graduated with a First. At the same time, you're living in Greece to juggle heaven knows how many jobs, became engaged, got yourself pregnant, and will shortly be married. What's next? World domination?'

'Erm, well, I thought I might stick to moving house and having a baby for now.'

'Moving house?'

'Obviously, Dad. I'm not going to live with Kristina after I'm married.'

'Oh. I assumed you were already living with Pip.'

'No. When I ring, haven't you noticed that it's always from the same place? My bedroom at Kristina's.'

'Why on earth would I notice the background?'

Because you're too busy criticising me, she almost blurted out.

'And let's face it, it's never stopped you before. All those other times you couldn't wait—'

'Bloody hell, Dad. You make it sound like I've shacked up with every bloke going. Twice before. The first, we were a couple for two years before I moved in – which you know fine well – and we all know how that ended, so for once, let's not go there. And the second, we became a couple after I moved in – which again, you know – or have you conveniently forgotten?'

The calming voice of her mother broke the silence.

'How you doing, pet? It must have been a right shock to find out you were pregnant.'

'Hi, Mam. I'm doing okay now. I'm sorry you can't come to the wedding, but we wanted to get married as soon as possible.'

'That's alright. I understand. Have you told Julia yet? Or do you want us to?'

'Can you? I never seem to be able to get through. and this isn't something I want to message her with—'

'Anyway, what have Pip's parents said about this little accident?' Her dad butted in, unable to contain himself for more than thirty seconds. 'I cannot imagine they're very—'

'Robert Jenkinson. For once in your life, will you just shut up and give us a minute's peace. Are you deliberately trying to destroy the relationship with our daughter for a second time? It has taken us years to get back on an even keel after everything you did, which I went along with for some reason. But not this time. I will not repeat the same mistake. Not when Anna's so far away. I will never forgive you if she stops talking to us. Have I made myself crystal clear?'

'Flipping heck, Mam. I've never heard you talk like that.'

'I'm sorry, Anna, but your father can sometimes be a right pain in the arse.'

It was so unexpected, so out of character, that she started laughing and couldn't stop. Then her mam was giggling, and her dad began chuckling. It was years since she'd shared a joke with her parents. A proper joke. Not a polite titter but a bellyache, tears streaming down your aching face type of joke. It nudged open the door to happy family memories – camping holidays, helping her dad in the allotment, walking the dog, getting trounced at badminton, and Sunday afternoons spent vegging out in front of the telly, watching old romcom films. There had been plenty of great times. Maybe, just maybe, this was the start of something that might last?

The remainder of the conversation went much better. It involved a quick family round-up (Julia was doing so well at work) and a promise to visit next summer. They needed to meet everyone, especially their son-in-law and grandchild. Then she argued with her father after point-blank refusing money for the wedding. It was wrong to expect them to pay anything when they couldn't attend. Anna had some savings she was going to use. Eventually, her parents relented but promised to make up for it when they visited, and Anna agreed to end the conversation.

Her mother's last comment concerned Anna's next call. 'I take it you'll be ringing Annalise? I bet that'll be entertaining.'

**

Anna and Annalise had grown up in the same unremarkable suburban street and were forever in each other's houses, so their parents regarded them as part of the furniture. The pair had many misadventures together and shared many secrets. Although they now lived on different continents it didn't stop them talking every week and Annalise had been privy to all of her friend's video call rants about the obnoxious Daniel and Agnes during Anna's first few months in Apokeri. However, for the first time in her life Anna had held back telling Annalise about her affair with Daniel and the truth about her and Pip.

Anna waited for the inevitable reaction to her speedily arranged wedding. Annalise immediately guessed the reason and burst out laughing. After considerable time, she gained enough control to bombard her with questions. Did it feel weird having another life inside her? Not yet. Did she have any cravings? Lemon & ginger tea. Was she throwing up? It was supposedly too early. Was she hoping to get bigger boobs? Yes! It was a standing joke – Annalise had Anna's allocation. But she was also concerned about her friend's emotional state. How was she doing? Okay now. Did she have a good support network in Apokeri? Most definitely. Did she feel ready for motherhood? Certainly not. Annalise then begged permission to tell her parents.

'Please, please, please. You know my mam and dad still think you're such a bloody goody two shoes. Which is hilarious considering all the things you've got up to over the years. Growing up, I was only ever allowed to do things if you did because you were the quiet, intellectual, and sensible one. If I tell them about your amazing cock-up—'

'Nice choice of words.'

'Oh yes, I see what you mean.' Annalise sniggered. 'Anyway, don't you see that anything I do can't be any worse?'

'Charming. You want me to be your get-out-of-jail-free card,' Anna replied in a bemused tone.

'Exactly. I've kept quiet tons of times before, much to your dad's annoyance. Go on. You'd be doing me a massive favour.'

Anna was waiting to hit the three-month mark before making the news common knowledge. Only her and Pip's immediate family, plus Alex, Kristina, and now Annalise, knew. She extracted a promise whereby Annalise would wait before gleefully announcing Anna's spectacular fall from her pedestal. What are friends for? Anna thought when she hung up.

***

Steffi watched as Anna chased her giggling daughter around the courtyard. To think by next summer, Anna would have a child of her own. Life never stopped. After twenty minutes, Anna flopped into a chair, and Leyla busied herself with toy trucks in her sandpit.

'I've developed quite a taste for this stuff, thanks to you,' Steffi acknowledged as she supped her tea.

Anna puffed out her rosy cheeks and took a gulp. 'My job here is done.'

'You're looking very pleased with yourself.'

Steffi listened as Anna delighted in telling her how she'd won an argument with her father to pay for her wedding.

'Back up there.' Steffi put down her empty cup. 'Did I hear correctly? You're paying for your wedding?'

Anna nodded. 'That's right.'

'No, no, no, no!'

'Erm – yes, yes, yes, yes!'

'It's not the done thing, Anna.'

'Since when has that ever stopped anyone doing anything?'

'I won't allow it.' Steffi thumped her fist down on the table.

Anna threw back her head and laughed. 'How on earth do you think you'll stop me?'

'I'm your Koumbara, and it's my responsibility to pay.'

'No, it's not. The Koumbari split the cost of the wedding crowns, candles, gratitude to the priest, and favours for the wedding guests. I know that's right because Agnes told me and she's the wedding expert. Traditionally, the bride's parents and the groom split the other costs. The bride's parents pay for the bridal gown, the photography, the bridesmaid dresses and the reception, including the cake. The groom covered the church fees, the honeymoon, buttonholes, and his bride's flowers.'

Steffi's eyes narrowed. 'I think I preferred it when Agnes hated you. Now that you're bosom buddies, she's far too helpful.'

'I know, it's brilliant.' Anna stretched before relaxing into her chair. 'I knew I'd wear her down. All it took was for Pip to propose.'

'Seems a rather extreme way to solve a problem,' Steffi remarked, repeatedly slapping a teaspoon into her palm.

'Yes, I'd have to agree with you there. But as you can see, my soon-to-be-sister-in-law, I know the facts. Under the rules of the Koumbara, you aren't allowed to pay for anything else. I'm covering the bride's parents' costs, and Pip's sorting the rest out with his dad.' Polishing fingernails against her jumper, she smirked. 'You've got to be up pretty early to get one over on Anna Jenkinson.'

However, Steffi had no intention of backing down, and they were so engrossed in outwitting each other that neither noticed Filip and his parents arrive, expecting a civilised homecooked supper.

'Enough, the pair of you. Sofi and I are paying. We weren't permitted to contribute anything to our own daughter's wedding. That scum paid for everything.' Vasili spat out the last sentence. Steffi began to say something, but a forbidding fatherly look stopped her, and he pointed at Anna. 'You are already like a daughter to us. We are already deeply in your debt for healing our family breach, which I firmly believe nobody else could have done. And as I'm fulfilling your father's role by walking with you to the church, I'm technically the bride's parent. Therefore, we get to pay. It is not open for discussion. Do I make myself clear?'

Anna and Steffi gawped with mouths open, like goldfish gasping for air. Vasili and Sofia defiantly stood with hands on their hips, daring them to argue back. Neither woman did.

'Papa, that is the first time I've ever seen those two speechless. Well done. You've achieved the impossible.' Filip clapped his father on the back. 'Come on, let's eat. I've made us lamb kleftiko, and I'm sure Anna's starving.'

Chapter Thirty

Her Koumbara was making up for losing the wedding argument by pulling out all the stops for the hen do and whisking Anna to a hilltop five-star resort in southwest Lefkada. With uninterrupted views of the Ionian Sea, Kristina, Sofia, Agnes and Lucinda joined her and Steffi for an afternoon's pampering with treatments and full use of the spa.

'Thank you so much for organising this, Steffi,' Anna said dreamily from her sun lounger. 'My facial was so relaxing I started snoring.'

'It's my pleasure and gave me the perfect excuse to come here. I'm looking forward to slipping into that infinity pool. Look at the view – amazing.'

'Not before this,' Lucinda interrupted and handed them a card entitled 'How Well Do You Know the Bride', which Anna also completed. Nobody gained full marks, but Kristina came close with one incorrect answer. Although some of the answers were wrong, Anna awarded points for entertainment value and read the best ones out.

Favourite food? **Everything**

How many wedding dresses did the bride try on? **Probably not many. She knows what she wants and would have flicked through the rails, disregarding most.** (Agnes gained half a point for her accurate observation).

How long have the couple been together? **Not long.**

It was sobering when she calculated the short time they'd been a couple. Most answers were probably in years or many months – not a few weeks.

'That's the end of the quiz, ladies, and it's high time we took advantage of that fantastic pool,' Lucinda proclaimed and slipped off her robe. 'We can wallow like sexy hippos whilst Anna torpedoes through the water like—'

'An Emperor Penguin,' Anna spluttered after surfacing. 'Coolest animal on the planet.'

'I suppose they would be, coming from Antarctica,' Agnes observed and sank beneath the water.

As the six women relaxed into heated bliss, Lucinda caught the eye of their waiter and blew him a kiss. Barely out of his teens, he blushed furiously before scuttling away.

'You're shocking,' Sofia scolded.

'I know. And we've still got tonight.' Lucinda cackled as she floated away.

***

Dressed to kill, the six ladies swept across Apokeri village square to Apollo's entrance, where Steffi had hired the secret garden for the night. A temporary bar stood in one corner, and a dance floor took centre stage, hemmed in by chairs and tables. Anna was pleased to see a buffet table. Although empty, its generous length spoke of things to come. Her party was the first to arrive, except for six men standing to attention.

'Oh my,' she said. 'I take it this is your doing, Lucinda?'

'Of course. What's a hen do without eye candy?'

Lined up by the bar were their waiters for the night. Each wore highly polished black shoes, black socks, extremely short and tight black denim shorts, a white shirt collar with a black bow tie and nothing else. In their early twenties, each gorgeous man had a washboard stomach, six-pack, well-defined pecs, muscular arms and legs, and not an inch of fat between them. They could have stepped off a catwalk with their chiselled good looks. Anna walked along the line, and each kissed her hand and gave assurances to supply whatever she desired. From the corridor behind came laughter and the clatter of high heels. The next instant, a throng of women burst into the courtyard, and at the front was a very appreciative Nereus Head Chef.

'Well, hello there. Come to Mama,' she purred.

Poor lads. Anna thought they were going to be eaten alive.

The party hit full throttle immediately. Every female made each second count. The music blasted, drinks flowed, and the dance floor was packed. The waiters served only a handful of drinks all night, spending their time on the dance floor with a gaggle of women or acting as pieces of furniture for females to drape themselves across. As the night progressed and the consumption of alcohol increased, the men became props to stop raucous women from toppling over. A constant flow of women – decked out in their finest – joined the party, and everywhere Anna saw women she knew having fun. And it suddenly hit home – she was part of this fantastic community.

There was proud mother hen Helena from the supermarket with her two daughters chatting with their regular customers, Adriani – back from filming – regaled Dania and Steffi with acting stories, and bakery apprentice Nikki danced and guzzled cocktails with Agnes and two waiters. Stelios's severe-looking wife was for once relaxed with her sister-in-law Sarah, who was unsurprisingly talking ten to the dozen. Despite being in their mid-seventies, Anna's two cleaning ladies had snagged a waiter. The couples tried to outdo one another and everybody else on the dance floor. The girls from the Post Office steadily demolished the delicious buffet food. Adriani's studious younger sister was having an in-depth conversation with the fifth waiter about the wonders of the universe. The fearsome-yet-fair headteacher Irene was talking to the mothers of her young charges and undoubtedly putting the fear of God into them. Sofia, her sisters, and Kristina (trading village gossip) sat in the corner, holding court with the unofficial Aphrodite knitting club (these older ladies met daily in the café), and all appeared miraculously unaffected by their countless ouzo toasts.

Squeezing through the crowds of the café's regular customers and a multitude of Sofia and Vasili's relations, Cosimo's wife, planted a drunken kiss on Anna's cheek and declared she was having the best time. With a food-laden plate and drink, she wobbled precariously across to where her eldest daughter plied the final waiter with drinks while her youngest unashamedly fed him grapes. Lucinda had chosen the waiters well; they were having a ball.

Anna hadn't known every guest (some being friends of Sofia who lived further afield), but after hugs, kisses, and plenty of sound marital advice, they were no longer strangers when everyone staggered home. With Steffi, Kristina, and Sofia working as a team to mask her abstinence from alcohol, she was one of the very few who woke up the next day with a clear head.

***

Yesterday afternoon had seen the centuries-old Krevati or Bed Making Ceremony, designed to bless the marital bed and the couple's fertility. An assortment of friends and family descended on Anna and Filip's soon-to-be marital home and watched as the women made the bed with white linen. Rose petals, rice, and money were then thrown on the covers for good luck. Leyla got in on the act by jumping and rolling around in the middle of the bed. Supposedly, it foretold that the first child would be a girl.

Anna had fought a strong compulsion to cradle her stomach. Would the prediction prove to be accurate? The night after the wedding, the husband's job was to strip the bed three times for all the couple's dreams to come true. Afterwards, an amused Filip told her their dreams were likely to revolve around keeping their secret and not getting caught. The comment simply fed Anna's mounting anxiety.

On the one hand, she was excited about the wedding, and it was lovely to see their friends and Filip's family so happy. On the other was rising unease which began her night wanderings again. Kristina had taken to double locking, bolting, and chaining the front and back doors after finding Anna walking barefoot in the flowerbeds at three o'clock in the morning. It was the first time Anna had ever made it outside, and it scared the life out of her.

It was three days after Filip's stag do, and for the first time, he'd felt able to join her and Cassie for an evening stroll. The day spent cycling and drinking across Meganisi with his more active friends and family, followed by a wild night in Nidri with the rest of them had left him a pathetic, barely functioning shell. Anna felt so sorry for him that she didn't even make fun of his pitiable state. She was simply grateful to Alex for returning him (there'd been one plot to put him on a ferry) in one piece (shaved bald, tarred, and feathered was another).

She patted her coat pocket – it was still there – and, preoccupied, she barely registered her surroundings.

'Are you okay?' Filip asked. 'You're very quiet.'

'I'm fine.'

They were striding along the northern clifftop track into a chilly breeze.

Filip zipped up his fleece. 'Out with it. I know "I'm fine" is code for something's up.'

'Am I that obvious?' Anna stopped and looked out across the bay to Tharesseti. The weather was changing, becoming blustery. They came to Kristina's bench and sat down. From her jacket, she handed him two sheets of folded paper. 'My dad sent me these. And … well … I'll let you read them.'

Dear Anna,

It was so good to talk to you the other day. We haven't laughed together for such a long time, and your mam's right – I can be a pain in the arse sometimes. Please believe me when I say my family is the most important thing to me. I've always had your best interests at heart, but I know that often it doesn't come out that way.

Every conversation since you turned sixteen is full of tension and aggravation – it makes me sad. If I could turn back the clock, I would, but I can't. So, the next best thing is to draw a line under what has gone before. I'll try my hardest to do this. Bear with me as I try to change my stubborn ways.

I hope you will do me a favour? I've written a Father of the Bride speech (it's not a secret, so please feel free to read it before the ceremony). Could you ask Vasili to read it at the Wedding Breakfast?

I am immensely proud of you.

Lots of love
Dad

PS Hi Pip – if I know my daughter, she'll have given you this to read. Thank you for continuing to make my daughter smile and laugh. I'm deeply in your debt.

Father of the Bride speech

Dear Anna and Filip's family and friends,

Today is a celebration. Congratulations to Anna and Pip. I hope you will do me the honour of listening for a few minutes.

Anna has probably told lots of you that I try her patience, and she's right – but I hope this speech will undo some of those wrongs. Ever since she was little, Anna has either had her nose in a book, desperately learning new facts, or off having an adventure – even if that was digging for worms in the back garden or helping others (sometimes when they said they didn't need it!).

My daughter has always had the drive to better herself – night classes, online classes and most recently, as a mature student in Ancient History – luckily, she gets the brains from her mam. And she had a desire to see the world and experience different cultures.

Everyone who knows and loves Anna will agree – she sees the best in people. She'll be the one to stand up against injustices and try to right a wrong, solve a problem or offer help in her unique way. Many of you will have experienced the 'Jenkinson Stubborn Gene' – apologies, that's from me – but you'll agree that this dogged determination combined with a cheery "hello, how are you?" wins people around.

Anna is far braver than me – unafraid of giving it a go. Where others see failure and throw in the towel, Anna views it as a learning experience – a minor setback on the path to success. It's a wonderful outlook, and I'm trying to do this myself – she'll be thrilled to hear! I have not said this in the past, and it was wrong – Anna, I love you very much. You bring so much joy into our lives. I'm blessed and proud to have you as my daughter.

Thank you for welcoming our daughter to Apokeri and into your hearts. You have made Anna extremely happy, and we cannot thank you enough. Please

charge your glasses and toast my beautiful, talented,
and kind daughter. To Anna.

Filip finished reading and handed the printouts back. 'Yes, I can
see why they would make you think about things.'

'My dad has never told me he loves me or he's proud of me.
It's all I've ever wanted.'

'Same here. It wasn't until we were up on Kristina's rooftop
that Papa told me he loved me and was proud of who I am.'

The sun sank, and she watched Cassie sniff along the cliff
edge. 'Pip, are we doing the right thing? Am I condemning your
immortal soul to hell with a fake church wedding?'

'That's rather dramatic – even for you. If it makes you feel any
better, some believe a practising gay man is going to hell anyway.'
Filip looked up as Anna gasped. 'It's a joke. Don't look so
horrified or worry about my immortal soul – it'll be fine.'

Anna was lost for words.

'Do you love me?' he asked.

'Yes.'

'Do you think I love you?'

'Yes. I know you do.'

'Are you planning on seducing anyone soon and falling in love
with them?'

She pulled apart strands of grass and watched them tumble to
the ground. 'No. I'm done. I'll leave love to you and Alex.'

'Well, there's your answer. We're entering our marriage with
complete honesty – more than many other couples.'

'You're right. I guess … it just feels odd because … well …
it's my second time around – and I remember how the first one
ended.'

Filip grasped her hands. 'But this is completely different.'

Cassie bounded over, jumped between them, and flipped onto
her back with legs spread.

Anna obliged with a tummy tickle. 'What a tart.'

'It's going to be alright. You'll see – I promise.'

'Okay … yes, you're right.'

Before them, nature put on her best show as the whole sky lit up in fiery reds and pinks.

She pulled Pip up as Cassie leapt down to join them. 'Come on. Let's get back before it's dark.'

Chapter Thirty-One

The wedding day dawned. Anna threw open the balcony doors to be greeted with – threatening black skies.

'I don't believe it! Get married in Greece, it'll be gorgeous. Not likely.'

Her father was right about the weather – per usual.

'Why the serious face?' Kristina asked from the doorway.

She tightened her dressing gown. 'Oh, nothing … just hoping … everything goes according to plan.'

'Everything will be fine. Time to get you ready.'

Kristina gave the signal, and the quiet was shattered with chattering, giggling, and, it had to be said, slightly merry women. Sofia entered last wearing a gorgeous fitted silver-grey knee-length dress and matching swing coat with beautiful beadwork around the hem and collar that flattered her fuller figure.

'You look amazing,' Anna said and ran over to kiss her.

'Thank you … and here you go – provisions to keep us going.'

'You're a lifesaver.' She gave Sofia another kiss and gratefully accepted a heavy plate stacked with her favourite sweet pastries. 'I'm famished.'

Everyone tucked in and supped on champagne from Steffi – Anna enjoyed a lemon and ginger tea. Over the next two hours, torrential rain obliterated the outside world, and powerful gusts rattled the patio doors as she underwent her transformation. Unruly shoulder-length hair was tamed in an elaborate knot with flowers specifically selected by Kristina from her garden. Her hair and make-up were in the expert hands of Cosimo's youngest and she secured the hairstyle with that much hairspray and pins, not even the storm outside would shift it.

In the practice session, Anna had repeatedly wailed, 'I look like a circus clown', as her make-up was toned down to such an extent that an exasperated Steffi snapped, 'For crying out loud, the woman's a professional. Let her get on with it.' Anna relented – a little.

Studying herself in the mirror, she beamed. 'Thank you – it's perfect.'

'Phew. Make sure to tell Papa that. He said he'd flay me alive if you weren't happy.'

'We all know you've ticked off something old, new, borrowed, and blue,' said Kristina. 'But I need to throw a spanner in the works. Close your eyes – this is to replace something old and borrowed.' Kristina fastened something around her neck. 'Open your eyes.'

And there on Anna's bare skin – Kristina's gold crucifix necklace.

A golf ball lump formed in her throat. 'I-I-I don't know what to say.'

'Don't you dare cry,' Steffi warned as she refilled her glass. 'Not until you get inside that church anyway.'

'No … no … I won't,' she replied, dabbing her eyes with a hanky. Deep breaths, deep breaths. 'I know how much this means to you.'

Kristina squeezed Anna's shoulders and smiled in the mirror. 'So do you … that's why I want you to wear it. And to mark this momentous day, I've decided it's time for a change.' She cast off her scarf with a wrist flick to reveal a beautiful triple strand of pearls and beads. 'It seems silly not to showcase what I sell, don't you think?'

'Finally!' Sofia said, swigging back her champagne and signalling for more. 'I've been telling you that for years.'

The storm continued to rage on as Anna stepped into her dress – an elegant white A-line gown with a plain satin bateau neckline, delicate lace bodice, and half-length lace sleeves. Below the empire sash waistband was a simple satin skirt with a chapel train. She'd immediately known it was the one – it showed off one of her best features (collarbones) and gave her a slight cleavage. The A-line style hid an expanding waistline, and the train length minimised the risk of breaking her neck. She'd spun around for Sofia and Steffi in the shop, and both women agreed it was perfect – an understated classic, like Anna.

The dress tried to shine out in the darkened room as she did a twirl. 'I scrub up pretty well, don't you think?'

Steffi cocked her head and mused. 'Pre-pregnancy, was your stomach concaved?'

'Cheeky sod,' she retorted, passing over an almost empty bottle of champagne. 'Here, finish this off.'

Steffi had happily agreed to wear any chosen bridesmaid dress selected and looked gorgeous in her dusky blue floor-length chiffon dress with a lace bodice and a matching pashmina. But in a nod to her Geordie heritage, Anna declined to wear a pashmina having banked on it being a balmy nineteen degrees. But looking out the patio doors, the sun was nowhere to be seen – although the rain had stopped. Just as well, as it was now time for the Shoe Fitting tradition.

Alex and the four groomsmen arrived, looking mighty fine in dark blue two-piece fitted suits, matching ties, and crisp white shirts.

She cornered Alex. 'How's Pip doing?'

'He's … fine-ish.'

'Hey, Sofi, I've never seen Filip so nervous,' Vasili shouted across the room. 'All those delicious pastries I made – he hasn't touched a single one. And all he's drunk is water!'

'Everything'll be okay,' Alex whispered. 'C'mon, I need to get you into those shoes.'

'Do they fit?' everyone chorused.

'No!' Anna cried.

Alex carefully took off the shoes, filled them with money, and repeated until she declared them a perfect fit. It was supposed to be fun, but Alex and Vasili's comments had made Anna jittery, and her foot kept missing the ballet pump, or she'd knock it, and the money spilt onto the floor. It was finally time to leave for the church. The out-of-season beachfront was empty, and all the businesses were closed for the wedding.

***

Vasili proudly escorted Anna along the road. His son was one lucky boy. This young English woman had landed in Apokeri only a few months ago, but it felt like she'd lived there forever. Anna was perfect for Filip – hardworking, clever, charming yet feisty. Those traits would keep his son in line. He was hardworking but sometimes needed a kick up the backside. Making a joke of everything and lapsing into a happy-with-his-lot mentality was infuriating. But after Anna sowed the cycle tour business idea, his son rose to the challenge.

And, of course, her determination and refusal to give up. He'd forever be grateful for what she'd done. Family meant everything, and soon he would be a grandfather again. His grandchild would be gorgeous with a beautiful mother and his son's handsome looks, and they'd make fantastic parents. Life didn't get much better than this – all those sacrifices had been worth it. Approaching the village square, he squeezed Anna's arm.

***

The sun broke through tattered clouds and reflected in the puddles Anna sought to avoid on an eerily quiet street. Sand blew along the deserted beach – its tourists and sun loungers long gone. Murky water shifted restlessly, undecided on which way to go. Shopfront awnings slapped in the wind, arguing with the struts that held them in place, desperately trying to break free. Anna wished she hadn't eaten so many pastries – they sat in her stomach like lead weights.

Vasili squeezed her arm as their little procession entered the village square, and she reciprocated. She needed that. All those declarations of being non-religious and unfazed by a church wedding stood for nothing. She was a bag of nerves. Pip shifted from foot to foot on the church steps. He clutched her bridal bouquet and beside him stood Alex – undoubtedly giving final words of encouragement and support. On catching sight of Anna, Pip visibly relaxed, but it did nothing to relieve her mounting panic.

She fought to regain control of her mind. Was she doing the right thing? Probably … maybe. Were her actions going to have unforeseen repercussions down the line? Definitely. Did she want to stay in Apokeri? Yes. Did she want to let anyone down? No. Could she rationalise what she was doing? Yes – she was the queen of rationalisation.

The facts: she was about to marry a gay man who she loved like a brother to keep his sexuality and lover a secret because he feared family disownment and wider reprisals from a society that could demonstrate pathological homophobic behaviour.

Additionally, she was carrying the unborn child of another man who didn't want to be a father or live in Apokeri. And her fiancé desperately wanted to be a father and raise the child as theirs. And finally, she wanted to marry Pip and let him be the dad. She wanted to be part of his wonderfully charracterful family, part of this parcel of Greek life. And everyone was so pleased for them – including her dad. Was she asking too much? Was it so wrong to want to be happy? Her life was a soap opera because of an assortment of choices and decisions made with the best intentions. They had all led up to this moment. And here she was – terrified.

Filip stood on the stone steps. He never got nervous – not really. But since this morning, he'd felt sick. His groomsmen put it down to pre-wedding jitters, but their jokes failed to help.

Thank God she'd arrived – and he realised part of him thought maybe she wouldn't. His father and mother, Steffi, and Kristina looked so happy. Anna was stunning. Any man—

Of course, how stupid of him. Another man would capture her heart. How could they not? Anna had dismissed his concerns, and he'd believed that she was done with love and that providing a solid family unit to raise their child was her focus. But had he believed her? No, not really. He'd let himself believe because he wanted to – he wanted to be a father so badly and at the same time keep his relationship secret and be safe. Alex had been right to call off the engagement, but, in the end, he'd agreed to the plan so as not to lose Filip. And this time, when Anna fell in love, she'd be a married woman with a child in a small Greek village surrounded by Filip's family. They'd hate her for it and drive her out with her child – not his. Was he being unbelievably selfish in letting her enter into a marriage to satisfy a desperate need to have a child and keep his true identity a secret? But then there was the baby to consider, and he so wanted to be a father, and Anna said she wanted him to be the dad. Plus, Daniel hadn't been bothered about Anna in the end. There was no easy solution. And time was running out. She was so close – he could smell her light floral perfume.

Vasili kissed Anna on the cheek and placed her hand on his son's arm. Nodding to the couple and with a tear in his eye, Vasili followed Alex, Kristina, and Steffi into the church, hand in hand with the love of his life.

Left on the deserted village square steps, Filip handed Anna her bouquet. 'You look stunning.'

'So do you.'

The sky darkened – another storm was on the way – but for now, a double rainbow soared above them.

'Let's do this,' they said in perfect unison.

ABOUT THE AUTHOR

Jackie Watson was born in Newcastle-upon-Tyne and graduated from Northumbria University with an undergraduate degree in Marketing. After a twenty-year career in her chosen specialism, it was time for a change. The Apokeri trilogy was born out of a recurring dream that demanded to be written. She lives with her partner and their adored pooch not too far from Newcastle and close to the banks of the Tyne.

If you enjoyed Apokeri Bay, please consider leaving a review:

- www.amazon.co.uk
- www.amazon.com
- www.goodreads.com

Connect with Jackie Watson online:

- www.facebook.com/jackiewatsonwrites
- www.jackiewatsonwrites.com

Sign up to the Apokeri newsletter at the website to receive updates on the next instalment in the trilogy, character backstories and much more.

AUTHOR'S NOTE

Although this novel is a work of fiction, the island of Lefkada is real. This beautiful gem in the Ionian chain of islands is so close to the Greek mainland that it can be accessed by a road bridge. The island is a popular destination with its charming mountainous villages, beautiful beaches and a warm welcome from locals. However, it is safe to say Lefkada is probably not as well known or visited by British tourists as other Ionian islands such as Corfu, Kefalonia and Zakynthos.

Apokeri village and Tharesseti island are fictitious, and I have used touches of artistic licence in describing Lefkada's geology, geography, flora, and fauna. The artistic brush has also been used when painting a picture of Lefkada's towns and villages and the neighbouring island of Meganisi. All the characters are born out of my imagination and any resemblance to real persons, living or dead, is purely coincidental.

The cover image is a nod to the dramatic white cliffs found in Lefkada. In the novel they surround Apokeri and weave in and out of the story.

ACKNOWLEDGEMENTS

Did I know how long it would take to write Apokeri Bay when I first sat down to draft out the story? A most definite no. Did I enjoy bringing my ideas to life? A most definite yes. The process of reigning in my overactive imagination transported me beyond the confines of a desk in the spare room.

Throughout it all, I am deeply grateful to my family and friends for their unwavering support. A massive thank you to my mam and dad for everything they have done and continue to do for me. To my sister, Leigh, for her rational thinking when I needed it. To my editor Manda Waller for her eagle-eyed professionalism and to Debs Southwood and her team at Wigwam Studios, who captured my imagination and transformed it into the front cover. To my amazing partner, Graeme, who unfailingly believes in me. And finally, a special thank you to Jacqueline. My fantastic friend who has always been there to laugh, cry and rant with as we both continue to chase our dreams.

Printed in Great Britain
by Amazon

43044485R00182